THE HUGO WINNERS

Volume 3, Book 2

Fawcett Books by Isaac Asimov:

THE BEST OF ISAAC ASIMOV   23653-6 $1.95
THE BICENTENNIAL MAN
   AND OTHER STORIES   23573-4 $1.75
BUY JUPITER   23828-8 $1.75
THE CAVES OF STEEL   23782-6 $1.75
THE CURRENTS OF SPACE   23829-6 $1.75
THE EARLY ASIMOV, *Book One*   23873-3 $1.95
THE EARLY ASIMOV, *Book Two*   23700-1 $1.95
EARTH IS ROOM ENOUGH   23383-9 $1.75
THE END OF ETERNITY   23704-4 $1.75
THE GODS THEMSELVES   23756-7 $1.95
I, ROBOT   23949-7 $1.95
NIGHTFALL AND OTHER STORIES   23672-2 $1.95

And these anthologies by Isaac Asimov:

THE HUGO WINNERS, *Volume I*   23190-9 $1.75
STORIES FROM THE HUGO WINNERS,
   Volume II   23791-5 $1.95
MORE STORIES FROM THE HUGO WINNERS,
   Volume II   23883-0 $1.95
THE HUGO WINNERS, *Volume III*,
   Book I   23841-5 $1.95
THE HUGO WINNERS, *Volume III*,
   Book II   24045-2 $1.95
BEFORE THE GOLDEN AGE, *Book 1*   22913-0 $1.95
BEFORE THE GOLDEN AGE, *Book 2*   Q2452 $1.50
BEFORE THE GOLDEN AGE, *Book 3*   23593-9 $1.95

THE HUGO WINNERS

WINNERS

Volume 3, Book 2

edited by
ISAAC ASIMOV

FAWCETT CREST • NEW YORK

THE HUGO WINNERS: Volume 3, Book 2

This book, published by Fawcett Crest Books, a unit of CBS Publications, the Consumer Publishing Division of CBS Inc., comprises the second half of *THE HUGO WINNERS: Volume 3* and is reprinted by arrangement with Doubleday and Company, Inc.

ISBN: 0-449-24045-2

Selection of the Science Fiction Book Club

Printed in the United States of America

10 9 8 7 6 5 4 3 2 1

CONTENTS

INTRODUCTION

Good Lord, it's happened again!

Some years ago, when the delightful people at Fawcett decided to put my anthology, *THE HUGO WINNERS, Volume 2*, into soft covers, they found they had to put it out in two parts. My well-written introduction to the volume as a whole they used to introduce the first part, but they didn't want to repeat it in the second part—lest some casual browser be prevented from buying it by thinking it was an old book he had already read.

What they did was to get me to spin another skillful web of words for the second part.

Well, then, you can easily imagine that all those verbose people who write Hugo-winning stories continue to produce bulk as well as quality and when it came time to do *Volume 3* of my Hugo Winner anthologies, it turned out to be every bit as ponderous and weighty as *Volume 2*.

"But we can't produce a paperback that is three inches thick," said all the Fawcett people to each other. "We'll have to do it in two parts again."

"Right," they all replied to each other, "and that will leave us with no introduction for the second part. Whatever shall we do?"

They thought about it for a while and then one of them said, "What did we do in the case of *Volume 2?*"

"What we did then," came the answer rapidly, "was to get Asimov to write a second introduction."

Again there was deep thought and then one of them shouted, "I've got it. I've got it. —Let's stick Asimov with the job *again*."

You can't possibly imagine the enthusiasm that burst out all over at this terrific notion. They were on the phone at once and now here I am to give you the necessary reassurance.

This is a *new* paperback. It is the *second* part of *THE HUGO WINNERS, Volume 3*. What you have read before was the first part. If you have just bought this book and suddenly realize you've never read the first part, then buy the first part also—instantly. Scour the town's bookstores, if necessary. If you do so, it will please me and make the nice people at Fawcett simply ecstatic.

1973

31st CONVENTION
TORONTO

The thirty-first convention was held in Toronto in 1973 and it was by far the most remarkable of the world conventions for reasons I'll get to later. (I have three more cracks at this one.)

For now, I'll just say that I attended the thirty-first convention with Janet, who was soon to become my wife. That in itself was a vast improvement on the twenty-ninth convention, which I attended alone.

You might think that attending a convention *alone* would insure the height of vice and revelry and perhaps you're right. I myself don't know about such things. Nor was I to be given a chance to find out. Lester del Rey and his new bride, Judy-Lynn, were in attendance too. They made sure that they had the room right next to me; they supervised my every breakfast and continually dogged my footsteps. All I was allowed to do was to wave at girls from a distance.

They said they were trying to save me from myself and to this day I don't know what they meant. I wasn't planning to do anything by myself. Anyway, by 1973, Janet was along and she was intent on saving me from myself too.

But to business. Here we have a Hugo-winning story that is written by a woman. As you all know (if you are old enough) there was once a time when science fiction was as masculine as testosterone. There were women writers and women readers but somehow they were ignored. Now things are different.

In Volume One, there were nine Hugo winners in the less-than-novel categories and not one, *not one*, was written by a woman. In Volume Two, there were fourteen stories and *one* was written by a woman, "Weyr Search" by the silver-throated Anne McCaffrey. Now, in Volume Three, we have fifteen stories of which two, count them, *two*, are written by women. At this rate, when *The Hugo Winners, Volume Fifteen* comes out in 2051 (with myself as editor, of course; who else?) we will have all the stories by women.

To be sure, there's the small complication that both stories by women in this volume were written by Ursula. If we continue to extrapolate, then, in sober scientific fashion, considering the undeniable fact that so far each volume has one more story by a woman than the volume before, but that each time a woman is represented, only *one* woman is (are you confused?), then all fifteen stories in *The Hugo Winners, Volume Fifteen* will have been written by the same woman.

You can't beat logic.

I've never met Ursula, by the way. I'm not sure I ought to. In the last few years, she has become just about the most highly regarded writer in science fiction and if I should, by sheer force of habit, greet her with the suavity which is usual to me in my approach to young women, she might be offended at the *lèse majesté* and slosh me one.

THE WORD FOR WORLD IS FOREST

I

Two pieces of yesterday were in Captain Davidson's mind when he woke, and he lay looking at them in the darkness for a while. One up: the new shipload of women had arrived. Believe it or not. They were here, in Centralville, twenty-seven lightyears from Earth by NAFAL and four hours from Smith Camp by hopper, the second batch of breeding females for the New Tahiti Colony, all sound and clean, 212 head of prime human stock. Or prime enough, anyhow. One down: the report from Dump Island of crop failures, massive erosion, a wipe-out. The line of 212 buxom beddable breasty little figures faded from Davidson's mind as he saw rain pouring down onto ploughed dirt, churning it to mud, thinning the mud to a red broth that ran down rocks into the rainbeaten sea. The erosion had begun before he left Dump Island to run Smith Camp, and being gifted with an exceptional visual memory, the kind they called eidetic, he could recall it now all too clearly. It looked like that bigdome Kees was right and you had to leave a lot of trees standing where you planned to put farms. But he still couldn't see why

11

a soybean farm needed to waste a lot of space on trees if the land was managed really scientifically. It wasn't like that in Ohio; if you wanted corn you grew corn, and no space wasted on trees and stuff. But then Earth was a tamed planet and New Tahiti wasn't. That's what he was here for: to tame it. If Dump Island was just rocks and gullies now, then scratch it; start over on a new island and do better. Can't keep us down, we're Men. You'll learn what that means pretty soon, you godforsaken damn planet, Davidson thought, and he grinned a little in the darkness of the hut, for he liked challenges. Thinking Men, he thought Women, and again the line of little figures began to sway through his mind, smiling, jiggling.

"Ben!" he roared, sitting up and swinging his bare feet onto the bare floor. "Hot water get-ready, hurry-up-quick!" The roar woke him satisfyingly. He stretched and scratched his chest and pulled on his shorts and strode out of the hut into the sunlit clearing all in one easy series of motions. A big, hard-muscled man, he enjoyed using his well-trained body. Ben, his creechie, had the water ready and steaming over the fire, as usual, and was squatting staring at nothing, as usual. Creechies never slept, they just sat and stared. "Breakfast. Hurry-up-quick!" Davidson said, picking up his razor from the rough board table where the creechie had laid it out ready with a towel and a propped-up mirror.

There was a lot to be done today, since he'd decided, that last minute before getting up, to fly down to Central and see the new women for himself. They wouldn't last long, 212 among over two thousand men, and like the first batch probably most of them were Colony Brides, and only twenty or thirty had come as Recreation Staff; but those babies were real good greedy girls and he intended to be first in line with at least one of them this time. He grinned on the left, the right cheek remaining stiff to the whining razor.

The old creechie was moseying round taking an hour to bring his breakfast from the cookhouse. "Hurry-up-quick!" Davidson yelled, and Ben pushed his boneless saunter into a walk. Ben was about a meter high and his back fur was more white than green; he was old, and dumb even for a creechie, but Davidson knew how to handle him. A lot of men couldn't handle creechies worth a damn, but Davidson had never had trouble with them; he could tame any of them, if it was worth the effort. It wasn't, though. Get enough humans here, build machines and robots, make farms and cities, and

12

nobody would need the creechies any more. And a good thing too. For this world, New Tahiti, was literally made for men. Cleaned up and cleaned out, the dark forests cut down for open fields of grain, the primeval murk and savagery and ignorance wiped out, it would be a paradise, a real Eden. A better world than worn-out Earth. And it would be his world. For that's what Don Davidson was, way down deep inside him: a world-tamer. He wasn't a boastful man, but he knew his own size. It just happened to be the way he was made. He knew what he wanted, and how to get it. And he always got it.

Breakfast landed warm in his belly. His good mood wasn't spoiled even by the sight of Kees Van Sten coming towards him, fat, white, and worried, his eyes sticking out like blue golf-balls.

"Don," Kees said without greeting, "the loggers have been hunting red deer in the Strips again. There are eighteen pair of antlers in the back room of the Lounge."

"Nobody ever stopped poachers from poaching, Kees."

"You can stop them. That's why we live under martial law, that's why the Army runs this colony. To keep the laws."

A frontal attack from Fatty Bigdome! It was almost funny. "All right," Davidson said reasonably, "I could stop 'em. But look, it's the men I'm looking after; that's my job, like you said. And it's the men that count. Not the animals. If a little extra-legal hunting helps the men get through this godforsaken life, then I intend to blink. They've got to have some recreation."

"They have games, sports, hobbies, films, teletapes of every major sporting event of the past century, liquor, marijuana, hallies, and a fresh batch of women at Central. For those unsatisfied by the Army's rather unimaginative arrangements for hygienic homosexuality. They are spoiled rotten, your frontier heroes, and they don't need to exterminate a rare native species 'for recreation.' If you don't act, I must record a major infraction of Ecological Protocols in my report to Captain Gosse."

"You can do that if you see fit, Kees," said Davidson, who never lost his temper. It was sort of pathetic the way a euro like Kees got all red in the face when he lost control of his emotions. "That's your job, after all. I won't hold it against you; they can do the arguing at Central and decide who's right. See, you want to keep this place just like it is, actually, Kees. Like one big National Forest. To look at, to study. Great, you're a spesh. But see we're just ordinary joes getting

13

the work done. Earth needs wood, needs it bad. We find wood on New Tahiti. So—we're loggers. See, where we differ is that with you Earth doesn't come first, actually. With me it does."

Kees looked at him sideways out of those blue golf-ball eyes. "Does it? You want to make this world into Earth's image, eh? A desert of cement?"

"When I say Earth, Kees, I mean people. Men. You worry about deer and trees and fibreweed, fine, that's your thing. But I like to see things in perspective, from the top down, and the top, so far, is humans. We're here, now; and so this world's going to go our way. Like it or not, it's a fact you have to face; it happens to be the way things are. Listen, Kees, I'm going to hop down to Central and take a look at the new colonists. Want to come along?"

"No thanks, Captain Davidson," the spesh said, going on towards the Lab Hut. He was really mad. All upset about those damn deer. They were great animals, all right. Davidson's vivid memory recalled the first one he had seen, here on Smith Land, a big red shadow, two meters at the shoulder, a crown of narrow golden antlers, a fleet, brave beast, the finest game-animal imaginable. Back on Earth they were using ro-bodeer even in the High Rockies and Himalaya Parks now, the real ones were about gone. These things were a hunter's dream. So they'd be hunted. Hell, even the wild creechies hunted them, with their lousy little bows. The deer would be hunted because that's what they were there for. But poor old bleeding-heart Kees couldn't see it. He was actually a smart fellow, but not realistic, not tough-minded enough. He didn't see that you've got to play on the winning side or else you lose. And it's Man that wins, every time. The old Conquistador.

Davidson strode on through the settlement, morning sunlight in his eyes, the smell of sawn wood and woodsmoke sweet on the warm air. Things looked pretty neat, for a logging camp. The two hundred men here had tamed a fair patch of wilderness in just three E-months. Smith Camp: a couple of big corruplast geodesics, forty timber huts built by creechie-labor, the sawmill, the burner trailing a blue plume over acres of logs and cut lumber; uphill, the airfield and the big prefab hanger for helicopters and heavy machinery. That was all. But when they came here there had been nothing. Trees. A dark huddle and jumble and tangle of trees, endless, meaningless. A sluggish river overhung and choked by trees, a few creechie-warrens hidden among the trees, some red deer, hairy monkeys, birds. And trees. Roots, boles, branches, twigs, leaves, leaves overhead and underfoot and in your face and in your eyes, endless leaves on endless trees.

New Tahiti was mostly water, warm shallow seas broken here and there by reefs, islets, archipelagoes, and the five big Lands that lay in a 2,500-kilo arc across the Northwest Quartersphere. And all those flecks and blobs of land were covered with trees. Ocean: forest. That was your choice on New Tahiti. Water and sunlight, or darkness and leaves.

But men were here now to end the darkness, and turn the tree-jumble into clean sawn planks, more prized on Earth than gold. Literally, because gold could be got from seawater and from under the Antarctic ice, but wood could not; wood came only from trees. And it was a really necessary luxury on Earth. So the alien forests became wood. Two hundred men with robosaws and haulers had already cut eight mile-wide Strips on Smith Land, in three months. The stumps of the Strip nearest camp were already white and punky; chemically treated, they would have fallen into fertile ash by the time the permanent colonists, the farmers, came to settle Smith Land. All the farmers would have to do was plant seeds and let 'em sprout.

It had been done once before. That was a queer thing, and the proof, actually, that New Tahiti was intended for humans to take over. All the stuff here had come from Earth, about a million years ago, and the evolution had followed so close a path that you recognized things at once: pine, oak, walnut, chestnut, fir, holly, apple, ash; deer, bird, mouse, cat, squirrel, monkey. The humanoids on Hain-Davenant of course claimed they'd done it at the same time as they colonised Earth, but if you listened to those ETs you'd find they claimed to have settled every planet in the Galaxy and invented everything from sex to thumbtacks. The theories about Atlantis were a lot more realistic, and this might well be a lost Atlantean colony. But the humans had died out. And the nearest thing that had developed from the monkey line to replace them was the creechie—a meter tall and covered with green fur. As ETs they were about standard, but as men they were a bust, they just hadn't made it. Give 'em another million years, maybe. But the Conquistadors had arrived first. Evolution moved now at the pace of a random mutation once a millennium, but with the speed of the starships of the Terran Fleet.

"Hey Captain!"

Davidson turned, only a microsecond late in his reaction, but that was late enough to annoy him. There was something about this damn planet, its gold sunlight and hazy sky, its mild winds smelling of leafmould and pollen, something that made you day-dream. You mooched along thinking about conquistadors and destiny and stuff, till you were acting as thick and slow as a creechie. "Morning, Ok!" he said crisply to the logging foreman.

Black and tough as wire rope, Oknanawi Nabo was Kee's physical opposite, but he had the same worried look. "You got half a minute?"

"Sure. What's eating you, Ok?"

"The little bastards."

They leaned their backsides on a split rail fence. Davidson lit his first reefer of the day. Sunlight, smoke-blued, slanted warm across the air. The forest behind camp, a quarter-mile-wide uncut Strip, was full of the faint, ceaseless, cracking, chuckling, stirring, whirring, silvery noises that woods in the morning are full of. It might have been Idaho in 1950, this clearing. Or Kentucky in 1830. Or Gaul in 50 B.C. "Te-whet," said a distant bird.

"I'd like to get rid of 'em, Captain."

"The creechies? How d'you mean, Ok?"

"Just let 'em go. I can't get enough work out of 'em in the mill to make up for their keep. Or for their being such a damn headache. They just don't work."

"They do if you know how to make 'em. They built the camp."

Oknanawi's obsidian face was dour. "Well, you got the touch with 'em, I guess. I don't." He paused. "In that Applied History course I took in training for Far-out, it said that slavery never worked. It was uneconomical."

"Right, but this isn't slavery, Ok baby. Slaves are humans. When you raise cows, you call that slavery? No. And it works."

Impassive, the foreman nodded; but he said, "They're too little. I tried starving the sulky ones. They just sit and starve."

"They're little, all right, but don't let 'em fool you, Ok. They're tough; they've got terrific endurance; and they don't feel pain like humans. That's the part you forget, Ok. You think hitting one is like hitting a kid, sort of. Believe me, it's more like hitting a robot for all they feel it. Look, you've laid some of the females, you know how they don't seem to feel anything, no pleasure, no pain, they just lay there like

16

mattresses no matter what you do. They're all like that. Probably they've got more primitive nerves than humans do. Like fish. I'll tell you a weird one about that. When I was in Central, before I came up here, one of the tame males jumped me once. I know they'll tell you they never fight, but this one went spla, right off his nut, and lucky he wasn't armed or he'd have killed me. I had to damn near kill him before he'd even let go. And he kept coming back. It was incredible the beating he took and never even felt it. Like some beetle you have to keep stepping on because it doesn't know it's been squashed already. Look at this." Davidson bent down his close-cropped head to show a gnarled lump behind one ear. "That was damn near a concussion. And he did it after I'd broken his arm and pounded his face into cranberry sauce. He just kept coming back and coming back. The thing is, Ok, the creechies are lazy, they're dumb, they're treacherous, and they don't feel pain. You've got to be tough with 'em and stay tough with 'em."

"They aren't worth the trouble, Captain. Damn sulky little green bastards, they won't fight, won't work, won't nothing. Except give me the pip." There was a geniality in Oknanawi's grumbling which did not conceal the stubbornness beneath. He wouldn't beat up creechies because they were so much smaller; that was clear in his mind, and clear now to Davidson, who at once accepted it. He knew how to handle his men. "Look, Ok. Try this. Pick out the ringleaders and tell 'em you're going to give them a shot of hallucinogen. Mesc, lice, any one, they don't know one from the other. But they're scared of them. Don't overwork it, and it'll work. I can guarantee."

"Why are they scared of hallies?" the foreman asked curiously.

"How do I know? Why are women scared of rats? Don't look for good sense from women or creechies, Ok! Speaking of which I'm on the way to Central this morning, shall I put the finger on a Collie Girl for you?"

"Just keep the finger off a few till I get my leave," Ok said grinning. A group of creechies passed, carrying a long 12×12 beam for the Rec Room being built down by the river. Slow, shambling little figures, they worried the big beam along like a lot of ants with a dead caterpillar, sullen and inept. Oknanawi watched them and said, "Fact is, Captain, they give me the creeps."

That was queer, coming from a tough, quiet guy like Ok.

"Well, I agree with you, actually, Ok, that they're not worth the trouble, or the risk. If that fart Lyubov wasn't around and the Colonel wasn't so stuck on following the Code, I think we might just clean out the areas we settle, instead of this Voluntary Labor routine. They're going to get rubbed out sooner or later, and it might as well be sooner. It's just how things happen to be. Primitive races always have to give way to civilised ones. Or be assimilated. But we sure as hell can't assimilate a lot of green monkeys. And like you say, they're just bright enough that they'll never be quite trustworthy. Like those big monkeys used to live in Africa, what were they called."

"Gorillas?"

"Right. We'll get on better without creechies here, just like we get on better without gorillas in Africa. They're in our way . . . But Daddy Ding-Dong he say use creechie-labor, so we use creechie-labor. For a while. Right? See you tonight, Ok."

"Right, Captain."

Davidson checked out the hopper from Smith Camp HQ: a pine-plank 4-meter cube, two desks, a watercooler, Lt. Birno repairing a walkytalky. "Don't let the camp burn down, Birno."

"Bring me back a Collie, Cap. Blonde. 34-22-36."

"Christ, is that all?"

"I like 'em neat, not floppy, see?" Birno expressively outlined his preference in the air. Grinning, Davidson went on up to the hangar. As he brought the helicopter back over camp he looked down at it: kid's blocks, sketch-lines of paths, long stump-stubbled clearings, all shrinking as the machine rose and he saw the green of the uncut forests of the great island, and beyond that dark green the pale green of the sea going on and on. Now Smith Camp looked like a yellow spot, a fleck on a vast green tapestry.

He crossed Smith Straits and the wooded, deep-folded ranges of north Central Island, and came down by noon in Centralville. It looked like a city, at least after three months in the woods; there were real streets, real buildings, it had been there since the Colony began four years ago. You didn't see what a flimsy little frontier-town it really was, until you looked south of it a halfmile and saw glittering above the stumplands and the concrete pads a single golden tower, taller than anything in Centralville. The ship wasn't a big one but it looked so big, here. And it was only a launch, a lander, a ship's boat; the NAFAL ship of the line, *Shackleton*, was

18

half a million kilos up, in orbit. The launch was just a hint, just a fingertip of the hugeness, the power, the golden precision and grandeur of the star-bridging technology of Earth.

That was why tears came to Davidson's eyes for a second at the sight of the ship from home. He wasn't ashamed of it. He was a patriotic man, it just happened to be the way he was made.

Soon enough, walking down those frontier-town streets with their wide vistas of nothing much at each end, he began to smile. For the women were there, all right, and you could tell they were fresh one's. They mostly had long tight skirts and big shoes like galoshes, red or purple or gold, and gold or silvery frilly shirts. No more nipplepeeps. Fashions had changed; too bad. They all wore their hair piled up high, it must be sprayed with that glue stuff they used. Ugly as hell, but it was the sort of thing only women would do to their hair, and so it was provocative. Davidson grinned at a chesty little euraf with more hair than head; he got no smile, but a wag of the retreating hips that said plainly, Follow follow follow me. But he didn't. Not yet. He went to Central HQ: quickstone and plastiplate Standard Issue, 40 offices 10 watercoolers and a basement arsenal, and checked in with New Tahiti Central Colonial Administration Command. He met a couple of the launch-crew, put in a request for a new semirobo bark-stripper at Forestry, and got his old pal Juju Sereng to meet him at the Luau Bar at fourteen hundred.

He got to the bar an hour early to stock up on a little food befor the drinking began. Lyubov was there, sitting with a couple of guys in Fleet uniform, some kind of speshes that had come down on the *Shackleton*'s launch. Davidson didn't have a high regard for the Navy, a lot of fancy sunhoppers who left the dirty, muddy, dangerous on-planet work to the Army; but brass was brass, and anyhow it was funny to see Lyubov acting chummy with anybody in uniform. He was talking, waving his hands around the way he did. Just in passing Davidson tapped his shoulder and said, "Hi, Raj old pal, how's tricks?" He went on without waiting for the scowl, though he hated to miss it. It was really funny the way Lyubov hated him. Probably the guy was effeminate like a lot of intellectuals, and resented Davidson's virility. Anyhow Davidson wasn't going to waste any time hating Lyubov, he wasn't worth the trouble.

The Luau served a first-rate venison steak. What would they say on old Earth if they saw one man eating a kilogram

19

of meat at one meal? Poor damn soybeansuckers! Then Juju arrived with—as Davidson had confidently expected—the pick of the new Collie Girls: two fruity beauties, not Brides, but Recreation Staff. Oh the old Colonial Administration sometimes came through! It was a long, hot afternoon.

Flying back to camp he crossed Smith Straits level with the sun that lay on top of a great gold bed of haze over the sea. He sang as he lolled in the pilot's seat. Smith Land came in sight hazy, and there was smoke over the camp, a dark smudge as if oil had got into the waste-burner. He couldn't even make out the buildings through it. It was only as he dropped down to the landing-field that he saw the charred jet, the wrecked hoppers, the burned-out hangar.

He pulled the hopper up again and flew back over the camp, so low that he might have hit the high cone of the burner, the only thing left sticking up. The rest was gone, mill, furnace, lumberyards, HQ, huts, barracks, creechie compound, everything. Black hulks and wrecks, still smoking. But it hadn't been a forest fire. The forest stood there, green, next to the ruins. Davidson swung back round to the field, set down and lit out looking for the motorbike, but it too was a black wreck along with the stinking, smouldering ruins of the hangar and the machinery. He loped down the path to camp. As he passed what had been the radio hut, his mind snapped back into gear. Without hesitating for even a stride he changed course, off the path, behind the gutted shack. There he stopped. He listened.

There was nobody. It was all silent. The fires had been out a long time; only the great lumber-piles still smouldered, showing a hot red under the ash and char. Worth more than gold, those oblong ash-heaps had been. But no smoke rose from the black skeletons of the barracks and huts; and there were bones among the ashes.

Davidson's brain was super-clear and active, now, as he crouched behind the radio shack. There were two possibilities. One: an attack from another camp. Some officer on King or New Java had gone spla and was trying a coup de planète. Two: an attack from off-planet. He saw the golden tower on the space-dock at Central. But if the *Shackleton* had gone privateer why would she start by rubbing out a small camp, instead of taking over Centralville? No, it must be invasion, aliens. Some unknown race, or maybe the Cetians or the Hainish had decided to move in on Earth's colonies. He'd never trusted those damned smart humanoids. This must have been done with a heatbomb. The invading force, with jets, air-cars, nukes, could easily be hidden on an island or reef anywhere in the SW Quartersphere. He must get back to his hopper and send out the alarm, then try a look around, reconnoiter, so he could tell HQ his assessment of the actual situation. He was just straightening up when he heard the voices.

Not human voices. High, soft, gabble-gobble. Aliens.

Ducking on hands and knees behind the shack's plastic roof, which lay on the ground deformed by heat into a bat-wing shape, he held still and listened.

Four creechies walked by a few yards from him, on the path. They were wild creechies, naked except for loose leather belts on which knives and pouches hung. None wore the shorts and leather collar supplied to tame creechies. The Volunteers in the compound must have been incinerated along with the humans.

They stopped a little way past his hiding-place, talking their slow gabble-gobble, and Davidson held his breath. He didn't want them to spot him. What the devil were creechies doing here? They could only be serving as spies and scouts for the invaders.

One pointed south as it talked, and turned, so that Davidson saw its face. And he recognised it. Creechies all looked alike, but this one was different. He had written his own signature all over that face, less than a year ago. It was the one that had gone spla and attacked him down in Central, the homicidal one, Lyubov's pet. What in the blue hell was it doing here?

Davidson's mind raced, clicked; reactions fast as always, he stood up, sudden, tall, easy, gun in hand. "You creechies. Stop. Stay-put. No moving!"

His voice cracked out like a whiplash. The four little green creatures did not move. The one with the smashed-in face looked at him across the black rubble with huge, blank eyes that had no light in them.

"Answer now. This fire, who start it?"

No answer.

"Answer now: hurry-up-quick! No answer, then I burn-up first one, then one, then one, see? This fire, who start it?"

"We burned the camp, Captain Davidson," said the one from Central, in a queer soft voice that reminded Davidson of some human. "The humans are all dead."

"You burned it, what do you mean?"

He could not recall Scarface's name for some reason.

"There were two hundred humans here. Ninety slaves of my people. Nine hundred of my people came out of the forest. First we killed the humans in the place in the forest where they were cutting trees, then we killed those in this place, while the houses were burning. I had thought you were killed. I am glad to see you, Captain Davidson."

It was all crazy, and of course a lie. They couldn't have killed all of them, Ok, Birno, Van Sten, all the rest, two hundred men, some of them would have got out. All the creechies had was bows and arrows. Anyway the creechies couldn't have done this. Creechies didn't fight, didn't kill, didn't have wars. They were intraspecies non-aggressive, that meant sitting ducks. They didn't fight back. They sure as hell didn't massacre two hundred men at a swipe. It was crazy. The silence, the faint stink of burning in the long, warm evening light, the pale-green faces with unmoving eyes that watched him, it all added up to nothing, to a crazy bad dream, a nightmare.

"Who did this for you?"

"Nine hundred of my people," Scarface said in that damned fake-human voice.

"No, not that. Who else? Who were you acting for? Who told you what to do?"

"My wife did."

Davidson saw then the telltale version of the creature's stance, yet it sprang at him so lithe and oblique that his shot missed, burning an arm or shoulder instead of smack between the eyes. And the creechie was on him, half his size and weight yet knocking him right off balance by its onslaught, for he had been relying on the gun and not expecting attack. The thing's arms were thin, tough, coarse-furred in his grip, and as he struggled with it, it sang.

He was down on his back, pinned down, disarmed. Four green muzzles looked down at him. The scarfaced one was still singing, a breathless gabble, but with a tune to it. The other three listened, their white teeth showing in grins. He had never seen a creechie smile. He had never looked up into a creechies face from below. Always down, from above. From on top. He tried not to struggle, for at the moment it was wasted effort. Little as they were, they outnumbered him, and Scarface had his gun. He must wait. But there was a sickness in him, a nausea that made his body twitch and strain against his will. The small hands held him down effort-lessly, the small green faces bobbed over him grinning.

22

Scarface ended his song. He knelt on Davidson's chest, a knife in one hand, Davidson's gun in the other.

"You can't sing, Captain Davidson, is that right? Well, then, you may run to your hopper, and fly away, and tell the Colonel in Central that this place is burned and the humans are killed."

Blood, the same startling red as human blood, clotted the fur of the creechie's right arm, and the knife shook in the green paw. The sharp, scarred face looked down into Davidson's from very close, and he could see now the queer light that burned way down in the charcoal-dark eyes. The voice was still soft and quiet.

They let him go.

He got up cautiously, still dizzy from the fall Scarface had given him. The creechies stood well away from him now, knowing his reach was twice theirs; but Scarface wasn't the only one armed, there was a second gun pointing at his guts. That was Ben holding the gun. His own creechie Ben, the little grey mangy bastard, looking stupid as always but holding a gun.

It's hard to turn your back on two pointing guns, but Davidson did it and started walking towards the field.

A voice behind him said some creechie word, shrill and loud. Another said, "Hurry-up-quick!" and there was a queer noise like birds twittering that must be creechie laughter. A shot clapped and whined on the road right by him. Christ, it wasn't fair, they had the guns and he wasn't armed. He began to run. He could outrun any creechie. They didn't know how to shoot a gun.

"Run," said the quiet voice far behind him. That was Scarface—Selver, that was his name. Sam, they'd called him, till Lyubov stopped Davidson from giving him what he deserved and made a pet out of him, then they'd called him Selver. Christ, what was all this, it was a nightmare. He ran. The blood thundered in his ears. He ran through the golden, smoky evening. There was a body by the path, he hadn't even noticed it coming. It wasn't burned, it looked like a white balloon with the air gone out. It had staring blue eyes. They didn't dare kill him, Davidson. They hadn't shot at him again. It was impossible. They couldn't kill him. There was the hopper, safe and shining, and he lunged into the seat and had her up before the creechies could try anything. His hands shook, but not much, just shock. They couldn't kill him. He circled the hill and then came back fast and low, looking for the four creechies. But nothing moved in the streaky rubble of the camp.

There had been a camp there this morning. Two hundred men. There had been four creechies there just now. He hadn't dreamed all this. They couldn't just disappear. They were there, hiding. He opened up the machinegun in the hopper's nose and raked the burned ground, shot holes in the green leaves of the forest, strafed the burned bones and cold bodies of his men and the wrecked machinery and the rotting white stumps, returning again and again until the ammo was gone and the gun's spasms stopped short.

Davidson's hands were steady now, his body felt appeased, and he knew he wasn't caught in any dream. He headed back over the Straits, to take the news to Centralville. As he flew he could feel his face relax into its usual calm lines. They couldn't blame the disaster on him, for he hadn't even been there. Maybe they'd see that it was significant that the creechies had struck while he was gone, knowing they'd fail if he was there to organise the defense. And there was one good thing would come out of this. They'd do like they should have done to start with, and clean up the planet for human occupation. Not even Lyubov could stop them from rubbing out the creechies now, not when they heard it was Lyubov's pet creechie who'd led the massacre! They'd go in for rat-extermination for a while, now; and maybe, just maybe, they'd hand that little job over to him. At that thought he could have smiled. But he kept his face calm.

The sea under him was greyish with twilight, and ahead of him lay the island hills, the deep-folded, many-streamed, many-leaved forests in the dusk.

II

All the colors of rust and sunset, brown-reds and pale greens, changed ceaselessly in the long leaves as the wind blew. The roots of the copper willows, thick and ridged, were moss-green down by the running water, which like the wind moved slowly with many soft eddies and seeming pauses, held back by rocks, roots, hanging and fallen leaves. No way was clear, no light unbroken, in the forest. Into wind, water, sunlight, starlight, there always entered leaf and branch, bole and root, the shadowy, the complex. Little paths ran under the branches, around the boles, over the roots; they did not go straight, but yielded to every obstacle, devious as nerves. The ground was not dry and solid but damp and rather springy, product of the collaboration of living things with the long, elaborate death of leaves and trees; and from that rich graveyard grew ninety-foot trees, and tiny mushrooms that sprouted in circles half an inch across. The smell of the air was subtle, various, and sweet. The view was never long, unless looking up through the branches you caught sight of the stars. Nothing was pure, dry, arid, plain. Revelation was lacking. There was no seeing everything at once: no certainty. The colors of rust and sunset kept changing in the hanging leaves of the copper willows, and you could not say even whether the leaves of the willows were brownish-red, or reddish-green, or green.

Selver came up a path beside the water, going slowly and often stumbling on the willow roots. He saw an old man dreaming, and stopped. The old man looked at him through the long willow-leaves and saw him in his dreams.

"May I come to your Lodge, My Lord Dreamer? I've come a long way."

The old man sat still. Presently Selver squatted down on his heels just off the path, beside the stream. His head drooped down, for he was worn out and had to sleep. He had been walking five days.

"Are you of the dream-time or of the world-time?" the old man asked at last.

"Of the world-time."

"Come along with me then." The old man got up promptly and led Selver up the wandering path out of the willow grove into dryer, darker regions of oak and thorn. "I took you for a god," he said, going a pace ahead. "And it seemed to me I had seen you before, perhaps in a dream."

"Not in the world-time. I come from Sornol, I have never been here before."

"This town is Cadast. I am Coro Mena. Of the Whitethorn."

"Selver is my name. Of the Ash."

"There are Ash people among us, both men and women. Also your marriage-clans, Birch and Holly; we have no women of the Apple. But you don't come looking for a wife, do you?"

"My wife is dead," Selver said.

They came to the Men's Lodge, on high ground in a stand of young oaks. They stooped and crawled through the tunnel-entrance. Inside, in the firelight, the old man stood up,

25

but Selver stayed crouching on hands and knees, unable to rise. Now that help and comfort was at hand his body, which he had forced too far, would not go farther. It lay down and the eyes closed; and Selver slipped, with relief and gratitude, into the great darkness.

The men of the Lodge of Cadast looked after him, and their healer came to tend the wound in his right arm. In the night Coro Mena and the healer Torber sat by the fire. Most of the other men were with their wives that night; there were only a couple of young prentice-dreamers over on the benches, and they had both gone fast asleep. "I don't know what would give a man such scars as he has on his face," said the healer, "and much less, such a wound as that in his arm. A very queer wound."

"It's a queer engine he wore on his belt," said Coro Mena.

"I saw it and didn't see it."

"I put it under his bench. It looked like polished iron, but not like the handiwork of men."

"He comes from Sornol, he said to you."

They were both silent a while. Coro Mena felt unreasoning fear press upon him, and slipped into dream to find the reason for the fear; for he was an old man, and long adept. In the dream the giants walked, heavy and dire. Their dry scaly limbs were swathed in cloths; their eyes were little and light, like tin beads. Behind them crawled huge moving things made of polished iron. The trees fell down in front of them.

Out from among the falling trees a man ran, crying aloud, with blood on his mouth. The path he ran on was the door-path of the Lodge of Cadast.

"Well, there's little doubt of it," Coro Mena said, sliding out of the dream. "He came oversea straight from Sornol, or else came afoot from the coast of Kelme Deva on our own land. The giants are in both those places, travellers say."

"Will they follow him," said Torber; neither answered the question, which was no question but a statement of possibility.

"You saw the giants once, Coro?"

"Once," the old man said.

He dreamed; sometimes, being very old and not so strong as he had been, he slipped off to sleep for a while. Day broke, noon passed. Outside the Lodge a hunting-party went out, children chirped, women talked in voices like running water. A dryer voice called Coro Mena from the door. He crawled out into the evening sunlight. His sister stood outside, sniffing the aromatic wind with pleasure, but looking stern all the same. "Has the stranger waked up, Coro?"

"Not yet. Torber's looking after him."

"We must hear his story."

"No doubt he'll wake soon."

Ebor Dendep frowned. Headwoman of Cadast, she was anxious for her people; but she did not want to ask that a hurt man be disturbed, nor to offend the Dreamers by insisting on her right to enter their Lodge. "Can't you wake him, Coro?" she asked at last. "What if he is . . . being pursued?"

He could not run his sister's emotions on the same rein with his own, yet he felt them; her anxiety bit him. "If Torber permits, I will," he said.

"Try to learn his news, quickly. I wish he was a woman and would talk sense . . ."

The stranger had roused himself, and lay feverish in the half-dark of the Lodge. The unreined dreams of illness moved in his eyes. He sat up, however, and spoke with control. As he listened Coro Mena's bones seemed to shrink within him trying to hide from this terrible story, this new thing.

"I was Selver Thele, when I lived in Eshreth in Sornol. My city was destroyed by the yumens when they cut down the trees in that region. I was one of those made to serve them, with my wife Thele. She was raped by one of them and died. I attacked the yumen that killed her. He would have killed me then, but another of them saved me and set me free. I left Sornol, where no town is safe from the yumens now, and came here to the North Isle, and lived on the coast of Kelme Deva in the Red Groves. There presently the yumens came and began to cut down the world. They destroyed a city there, Penle. They caught a hundred of the men and women and made them serve them, and live in the pen. I was not caught. I lived with others who had escaped from Penle, in the bogland north of Kelme Deva. Sometimes at night I went among the people in the yumen's pens. They told me that that one was there. That one whom I had tried to kill. I thought at first to try again; or else to set the people in the pen free. But all the time I watched the trees fall and saw the world cut open and left to rot. The men might have escaped, but the women were locked in more safely and could not, and they were beginning to die. I talked with the people hiding in the boglands. We were all very frightened and very angry, and had no way to let our fear and anger free. So at last after

27

long talking, and long dreaming, and the making of a plan, we went in daylight, and killed the yumens of Kelme Deva with arrows and hunting-lances, and burned their city and their engines. We left nothing. But that one had gone away. He came back alone. I sang over him, and let him go."

Selver fell silent.

"Then," Coro Mena whispered.

"Then a flying ship came from Sornol, and hunted us in the forest, but found nobody. So they set fire to the forest; but it rained, and they did little harm. Most of the people freed from the pens and the others have gone farther north and east, towards the Holle Hills, for we were afraid many yumens might come hunting us. I went alone. The yumens know me, you see, they know my face; and this frightens me, and those I stay with."

"What is your wound?" Torber asked.

"That one, he shot me with their kind of weapon; but I sang him down and let him go."

"Alone you downed a giant?" said Torber with a fierce grin, wishing to believe.

"Not alone. With three hunters, and with his weapon in my hand—this."

Torber drew back from the thing.

None of them spoke for a while. At last Coro Mena said, "What you tell us is very black, and the road goes down. Are you a Dreamer of your Lodge?"

"I was. There's no Lodge of Eshreth any more."

"That's all one; we speak the Old Tongue together. Among the willows of Asta you first spoke to me calling me Lord Dreamer. So I am. Do you dream, Selver?"

"Seldom now," Selver answered, obedient to the catechism, his scarred, feverish face bowed.

"Awake?"

"Awake."

"Do you dream well, Selver?"

"Not well."

"Do you hold the dream in your hands?"

"Yes."

"Do you weave and shape, direct and follow, start and cease at will?"

"Sometimes, not always."

"Can you walk the road your dream goes?"

"Sometimes. Sometimes I am afraid to."

"Who is not? It is not altogether bad with you, Selver."

"No, it is altogether bad," Selver said, "there's nothing good left," and he began to shake.

Torber gave him the willow-draught to drink and made him lie down. Coro Mena still had the headwoman's question to ask; reluctantly he did so, kneeling by the sick man. "Will the giants, the yumens you call them, will they follow your trail, Selver?"

"I left no trail. No one has seen me between Kelme Deva and this place, six days. That's not the danger." He struggled to sit up again. "Listen, listen. You don't see the danger. How can you see it? You haven't done what I did, you have never dreamed of it, making two hundred people die. They will not follow me, but they may follow us all. Hunt us, as hunters drive coneys. That is the danger. They may try to kill us. To kill us all, all men."

"Lie down—"

"No, I'm not raving, this is true fact and dream. There were two hundred yumens at Kelme Deva and they are dead. We killed them. We killed them as if they were not men. So will they not turn and do the same? They have killed us by ones, now they will kill us as they kill the trees, by hundreds, and hundreds, and hundreds."

"Be still," Torber said. "Such things happen in the fever-dream, Selver. They do not happen in the world."

"The world is always new," said Coro Mena, "however old its roots. Selver, how is it with these creatures, then? They look like men and talk like men, are they not men?"

"I don't know. Do men kill men, except in madness? Does any beast kill its own kind? Only the insects. These yumens kill us as lightly as we kill snakes. The one who taught me said that they kill one another, in quarrels, and also in groups, like ants fighting. I haven't seen that. But I know they don't spare one who asks life. They will strike a bowed neck, I have seen it! There is a wish to kill in them, and therefore I saw fit to put them to death."

"And all men's dreams," said Coro Mena, cross-legged in shadow, "will be changed. They will never be the same again. I shall never walk again that path I came with you yesterday, the way up from the willow grove that I've walked on all my life. It is changed. You have walked on it and it is utterly changed. Before this day the thing we had to do was the right thing to do; the way we had to go was the right way and led us home. Where is our home now? For you've done what you had to do, and it was not right. You have killed men. I saw

29

them, five years ago, in the Lemgan Valley, where they came in a flying ship; I hid and watched the giants, six of them, and saw them speak, and look at rocks and plants, and cook food. They are men. But you have lived among them, tell me, Selver: do they dream?"

"As children do, in sleep."

"They have no training?"

"No. Sometimes they talk of their dreams, the healers try to use them in healing, but none of them are trained, or have any skill in dreaming. Lyubov, who taught me, understood me when I showed him how to dream, and yet even so he called the world-time 'real' and the dream-time 'unreal,' as if that were the difference between them."

"You have done what you had to do," Coro Mena repeated after a silence. His eyes met Selver's, across shadows. The desperate tension lessened in Selver's face; his scarred mouth relaxed, and he lay back without saying more. In a little while he was asleep.

"He's a god," Coro Mena said.

Torber nodded, accepting the old man's judgment almost with relief.

"But not like the others. Not like the Pursuer, nor the Friend who has no face, nor the Aspen-leaf Woman who walks in the forest of dreams. He is not the Gatekeeper, nor the Snake. Nor the Lyre-player nor the Carver nor the Hunter, though he comes in the world-time like them. We may have dreamed of Selver these last few years, but we shall no longer; he has left the dream-time. In the forest, through the forest he comes, where leaves fall, where trees fall, a god that knows death, a god that kills and is not himself reborn."

The headwoman listened to Coro Mena's reports and prophecies, and acted. She put the town of Cadast on alert, making sure that each family was ready to move out, with some food packed, and litters ready for the old and ill. She sent young women scouting south and east for news of the yumens. She kept one armed hunting-group always around town, though the others went out as usual every night. And when Selver grew stronger she insisted that he come out of the Lodge and tell his story: how the yumens killed and enslaved people in Sornol, and cut down the forests; how the people of Kelme Deva had killed the yumens. She forced women and undreaming men who did not understand these things to listen again, until they understood, and were frightened. For Ebor Dendep was a practical woman. When a Great Dreamer, her brother, told her that Selver was a god, a changer, a bridge between realities, she believed and acted. It was the Dreamer's responsibility to be careful, to be certain that his judgment was true. Her responsibility was then to take that judgment and act upon it. He saw what must be done; she saw that it was done.

"All the cities of the forest must hear," Coro Mena said. So the headwoman sent out her young runners, and head-women in other towns listened, and sent out their runners. The killing at Kelme Deva and the name of Selver went over North Island and oversea to the other lands, from voice to voice, or in writing; not very fast, for the Forest People had no quicker messengers than footrunners; yet fast enough.

They were not all one people on the Forty Lands of the world. There were more languages than lands, and each with a different dialect for every town that spoke it; there were infinite ramifications of manners, morals, customs, crafts; physical types differed on each of the five Great Lands. The people of Sornol were tall, and pale, and great traders; the people of Rieshwel were short, and many had black fur, and they ate monkeys; and so on and on. But the climate varied little, and the forest little, and the sea not at all. Curiosity, regular trade-routes, and the necessity of finding a husband or wife of the proper Tree, kept up an easy movement of people among the towns and between the lands, and so there were certain likenesses among all but the remotest extremes, the half-rumored barbarian isles of the Far East and South. In all the Forty Lands, women ran the cities and towns, and almost every town had a Men's Lodge. Within the Lodges the Dreamers spoke an old tongue, and this varied little from land to land. It was rarely learned by women or by men who remained hunters, fishers, weavers, builders, those who dreamed only small dreams outside the Lodge. As most writing was in this Lodge-tongue, when headwomen sent fleet girls carrying messages, the letters went from Lodge to Lodge, and so were interpreted by the Dreamers to the Old Women, as were other documents, rumors, problems, myths, and dreams. But it was always the Old Women's choice whether to believe it or not.

Selver was in a small room at Eshsen. The door was not locked, but he knew if he opened it something bad would come in. So long as he kept it shut everything would be all right. The trouble was that there were young trees, a sapling orchard, planted out in front of the house; not fruit or nut trees but some other kind, he could not remember what kind. He went out to see what kind of trees they were. They all lay broken and uprooted. He picked up the silvery branch of one and a little blood ran out of the broken end. No, not here, not again, Thele, he said: O Thele, come to me before your death! But she did not come. Only her death was there, the broken birchtree, the opened door. Selver turned and went quickly back into the house, discovering that it was all built above ground like a yumen house, very tall and full of light. Outside the other door, across the tall room, was the long street of the yumen city Central. Selver had the gun in his belt. If Davidson came, he could shoot him. He waited, just inside the open door, looking out into the sunlight. Davidson came, huge, running so fast that Selver could not keep him in the sights of the gun as he doubled crazily back and forth across the wide street, very fast, always closer. The gun was heavy. Selver fired it but no fire came out of it, and in rage and terror he threw the gun and the dream away.

Disgusted and depressed, he spat, and sighed.

"A bad dream?" Ebor Dendep inquired.

"They're all bad, and all the same," he said, but the deep unease and misery lessened a little as he answered. Cool morning sunlight fell flecked and shafted through the fine leaves and branches of the birch grove of Cadast. There the headwoman sat weaving a basket of blackstem fern, for she liked to keep her fingers busy, while Selver lay beside her in half-dream and dream. He had been fifteen days at Cadast, and his wound was healing well. He still slept much, but for the first time in many months he had begun to dream waking again, regularly, not once or twice in a day and night but in the true pulse and rhythm of dreaming which should rise and fall ten to fourteen times in the diurnal cycle. Bad as his dreams were, all terror and shame, yet he welcomed them. He had feared that he was cut off from his roots, that he had gone too far into the dead land of action ever to find his way back to the springs of reality. Now, though the water was very bitter, he drank again.

Briefly he had Davidson down again among the ashes of the burned camp, and instead of singing over him this time he hit him in the mouth with a rock. Davidson's teeth broke, and blood ran between the white splinters.

The dream was useful, a straight wish-fulfillment, but he stopped it there, having dreamed it many times, before he met Davidson in the ashes of Kelme Deva, and since. There was nothing to that dream but relief. A sip of bland water. It was the bitter he needed. He must go clear back, not to Kelme Deva but to the long dreadful street in the alien city called Central, where he had attacked Death, and had been defeated.

Ebor Dendep hummed as she worked. Her thin hands, their silky green down silvered with age, worked black fern-stems in and out, fast and neat. She sang a song about gathering ferns, a girl's song: I'm picking ferns, I wonder if he'll come back . . . Her faint old voice trilled like a cricket's. Sun trembled in birch leaves. Selver put his head down on his arms.

The birch grove was more or less in the center of the town of Cadast. Eight paths led away from it, winding narrowly off among trees. There was a whiff of woodsmoke in the air; where the branches were thin at the south edge of the grove you could see smoke rise from a house-chimney, like a bit of blue yarn unravelling among the leaves. If you looked closely among the live-oaks and other trees you would find houseroofs sticking up a couple of feet above ground, between a hundred and two hundred of them, it was very hard to count. The timber houses were three-quarters sunk, fitted in among tree-roots like badgers' setts. The beam roofs were mounded over with a thatch of small branches, pinestraw, reeds, earthmould. They were insulating, waterproof, almost invisible. The forest and the community of eight hundred people went about their business all around the birch grove where Ebor Dendep sat making a basket of fern. A bird among the branches over her head said, "Te-whet," sweetly. There was more people-noise than usual, for fifty or sixty strangers, young men and women mostly, had come drifting in these last few days, drawn by Selver's presence. Some were from other cities of the North, some were those who had done the killing at Kelme Deva with him; they had followed rumor here to follow him. Yet the voices calling here and there and the babble of women bathing or children playing down by the stream, were not so loud as the morning bird-song and insect-drone and under-noise of the living forest of which the town was one element.

A girl came quickly, a young huntress the color of the pale birch leaves. "Word of mouth from the southern coast, mother," she said. "The runner's at the Women's Lodge."

"Send her here when she's eaten," the headwoman said softly. "Sh, Tolbar, can't you see he's asleep?"

The girl stooped to pick a large leaf of wild tobacco, and laid it lightly over Selver's eyes, on which a shaft of the steepening, bright sunlight had fallen. He lay with his hands half open and his scarred, damaged face turned upward, vulnerable and foolish, a Great Dreamer gone to sleep like a child. But it was the girl's face that Ebor Dendep watched. It shone, in that uneasy shade, with pity and terror, with adoration.

Tolbar darted away. Presently two of the Old Women came with the messenger, moving silent in single file along the sun-flecked path. Ebor Dendep raised her hand, enjoining silence. The messenger promptly lay down flat, and rested; her brown-dappled green fur was dusty and sweaty, she had run far and fast. The Old Women sat down in patches of sun, and became still. Like two old grey-green stones they sat there, with bright living eyes.

Selver, struggling with a sleep-dream beyond his control, cried out as if in great fear, and woke.

He went to drink from the stream; when he came back he was followed by six or seven of those who always followed him. The headwoman put down her half-finished work and said, "Now be welcome, runner, and speak."

The runner stood up, bowed her head to Ebor Dendep, and spoke her message: "I come from Trethat. My words come from Sorbron Deva, before that from sailors of the Strait, before that from Broter in Sornol. They are for the hearing of all Cadast but they are to be spoken to the man called Selver who was born of the Ash in Eshreth. Here are the words: There are new giants in the great city of the giants in Sornol, and many of these new ones are females. The yellow ship of fire goes up and down at the place that was called Peha. It is known in Sornol that Selver of Eshreth burned the city of the giants at Kelme Deva. The Great Dreamers of the Exiles in Broter have dreamed giants more numerous than the trees of the Forty Lands. These are all the words of the message I bear."

After the singsong recitation they were all silent. The bird, a little farther off, said, "Whet-whet?" experimentally.

"This is a very bad world-time," said one of the Old Women, rubbing a rheumatic knee.

A grey bird flew from a huge oak that marked the north

edge of town, and went up in circles, riding the morning up-draft on lazy wings. There was always a roosting-tree of these grey kites near a town; they were the garbage service.

A small, fat boy ran through the birch grove, pursued by a slightly larger sister, both shrieking in tiny voices like bats. The boy fell down and cried, the girl stood him up and scrubbed his tears off with a large leaf. They scuttled off into the forest hand in hand.

"There was one called Lyubov," Selver said to the head-woman. "I have spoken of him to Coro Mena, but not to you. When that one was killing me, it was Lyubov who saved me. It was Lyubov who healed me, and set me free. He wanted to know about us; so I would tell him what he asked, and he too would tell me what I asked. Once I asked how his race could survive, having so few women. He said that in the place where they come from, half the race is women; but the men would not bring women to the Forty Lands until they had made a place ready for them."

"Until the men made a fit place for the women? Well! they may have quite a wait," said Ebor Dendep. "They're like the people in the Elm Dream who come at you rump-first, with their heads put on front to back. They make the forest into a dry beach"—her language had no word for 'desert'—"and call that making things ready for the women? They should have sent the women first. Maybe with them the women do the Great Dreaming, who knows? They are backwards, Selver. They are insane."

"A people can't be insane."

"But they only dream in sleep, you said; if they want to dream waking they take poisons so that the dreams go out of control, you said! How can people be any madder? They don't know the dream-time from the world-time, any more than a baby does. Maybe when they kill a tree they think it will come alive again!"

Selver shook his head. He still spoke to the headwoman as if he and she were alone in the birch grove, in a quiet hesi-tant voice, almost drowsily. "No, they understand death very well . . . Certainly they don't see as we do, but they know more and understand more about certain things than we do. Lyubov mostly understood what I told him. Much of what he told me, I couldn't understand. It wasn't the language that kept me from understanding; I know his tongue, and he learned ours; we made a writing of the two languages to-gether. Yet there were things he said I could never under-

35

stand. He said the yumens are from outside the forest. That's quite clear. He said they want the forest: the trees for wood, the land to plant grass on." Selver's voice, though still soft, had taken on resonance; the people among the silver trees listened. "That too is clear, to those of us who've seen them cutting down the world. He said the yumens are men like us, that we're indeed related, as close kin maybe as the Red Deer to the Grey-buck. He said that they come from another place which is not the forest; the trees there are all cut down; it has a sun, not our sun, which is a star. All this, as you see, wasn't clear to me. I say his words but don't know what they mean. It does not matter much. It is clear that they want our forest for themselves. They are twice our stature, they have weapons that outshoot ours by far, and fire-throwers, and flying ships. Now they have brought more women, and will have children. There are maybe two thousand, maybe three thousand of them here now, mostly in Sornol. But if we wait a lifetime or two they will breed; their number will double and redouble. They kill men and women; they do not spare those who ask life. They cannot sing in contest. They have left their roots behind them, perhaps, in this other forest from which they came, this forest with no trees. So they take poison to let loose the dreams in them, but it only makes them drunk or sick. No one can say certainly whether they're men or not men, whether they're sane or insane, but that does not matter. They must be made to leave the forest, because they are dangerous. If they will not go they must be burned out of the Lands, as nests of stinging-ants must be burned out of the groves of cities. If we wait, it is we that will be smoked out and burned. They can step on us as we step on stinging-ants. Once I saw a woman, it was when they burned my city Eshreth, she lay down in the path before a yumen to ask him for life, and he stepped on her back and broke the spine, and then kicked her aside as if she was a dead snake. I saw that. If the yumens are men they are men unfit or untaught to dream and to act as men. Therefore they go about in torment killing and destroying, driven by the gods within, whom they will not set free but try to uproot and deny. If they are men they are evil men, having denied their own gods, afraid to see their own faces in the dark. Headwoman of Cadast, hear me." Selver stood up, tall and abrupt among the seated women. "It's time, I think, that I go back to my own land, to Sornol, to those that are in exile and those that are enslaved. Tell any people who dream of a city

36

burning to come after me to Broter." He bowed to Ebor Dendep and left the birch grove, still walking lame, his arm bandaged; yet there was a quickness to his walk, a poise to his head, that made him seem more whole than other men. The young people followed quietly after him.

"Who is he?" asked the runner from Trethat, her eyes following him.

"The man to whom your message came, Selver of Eshreth, a god among us. Have you ever seen a god before, daughter?"

"When I was ten the Lyre-Player came to our town."

"Old Ertel, yes. He was of my Tree, and from the North Vales like me. Well, now you've seen a second god, and a greater. Tell your people in Trethat of him."

"Which god is he, mother?"

"A new one," Ebor Dendep said in her dry old voice. "The son of forest-fire, the brother of the murdered. He is the one who is not reborn. Now go on, all of you, go on to the Lodge. See who'll be going with Selver, see about food for them to carry. Let me be a while. I'm as full of forebodings as a stupid old man, I must dream . . ."

Coro Mena went with Selver that night as far as the place where they first met, under the copper willows by the stream. Many people were following Selver south, some sixty in all, as great a troop as most people had ever seen on the move at once. They would cause great stir and thus gather many more to them, on their way to the sea-crossing to Sornol. Selver had claimed his Dreamer's privilege of solitude for this one night. He was setting off alone. His followers would catch him up in the morning; and thenceforth, implicated in crowd and act, he would have little time for the slow and deep running of the great dreams.

"Here we met," the old man said, stopping among the bowing branches, the veils of dropping leaves, "and here part. This will be called Selver's Grove, no doubt, by the people who walk our paths hereafter."

Selver said nothing for a while, standing still as a tree, the restless leaves about him darkening from silver as clouds thickened over the stars. "You are surer of me than I am," he said at last, a voice in darkness.

"Yes, I'm sure, Selver . . . I was well taught in dreaming, and then I'm old. I dream very little for myself any more. Why should I? Little is new to me. And what I wanted from my life, I have had, and more. I have had my whole life.

37

Days like the leaves of the forest. I'm an old hollow tree, only the roots live. And so I dream only what all men dream. I have no visions and no wishes. I see what is. I see the fruit ripening on the branch. Four years it has been ripening, that fruit of the deep-planted tree. We have all been afraid for four years, even we who live far from the yumens' cities, and have only glimpsed them from hiding, or seen their ships fly over, or looked at the dead places where they cut down the world, or heard mere tales of these things. We are all afraid. Children wake from sleep crying of giants; women will not go far on their trading-journeys; men in the Lodges cannot sing. The fruit of fear is ripening. And I see you gather it. You are the harvester. All that we fear to know, you have seen, you have known: exile, shame, pain, the roof and walls of the world fallen, the mother dead in misery, the children untaught, uncherished . . . This is a new time for the world: a bad time. And you have suffered it all. You have gone farthest. And at the farthest, at the end of the black path, there grows the Tree; there the fruit ripens; now you reach up, Selver, now you gather it. And the world changes wholly, when a man holds in his hand the fruit of that tree, whose roots are deeper than the forest. Men will know it. They will know you, as we did. It doesn't take an old man or a Great Dreamer to recognise a god! Where you go, fire burns; only the blind cannot see it. But listen, Selver, this is what I see that perhaps others do not, this is why I have loved you: I dreamed of you before we met here. You were walking on a path, and behind you the young trees grew up, oak and birch, willow and holly, fir and pine, alder, elm, white-flowering ash, all the roof and walls of the world, forever renewed. Now farewell, dear god and son, go safely."

The night darkened as Selver went, until even his night-seeing eyes saw nothing but masses and planes of black. It began to rain. He had gone only a few miles from Cadast when he must either light a torch, or halt. He chose to halt, and groping found a place among the roots of a great chestnut tree. There he sat, his back against the broad, twisting bole that seemed to hold a little sun-warmth in it still. The fine rain, falling unseen in darkness, pattered on the leaves overhead, on his arms and neck and head protected by their thick silk-fine hair, on the earth and ferns and undergrowth nearby, on all the leaves of the forest, near and far. Selver sat as quiet as the grey owl on a branch above him, unsleeping, his eyes wide open in the rainy dark.

III

Captain Raj Lyubov had a headache. It began softly in the muscles of his right shoulder, and mounted crescendo to a smashing drumbeat over his right ear. The speech centers are in the left cerebral cortex, he thought, but he couldn't have said it; couldn't speak, or read, or sleep, or think. Cortex, vortex. Migraine headache, margarine breadache, ow, ow, ow. Of course he had been cured of migraine once at college and again during his obligatory Army Prophylactic Psychotherapy Sessions, but he had brought along some ergotamine pills when he left Earth, just in case. He had taken two, and a superhyperduper-analgesic, and a tranquillizer, and a digestive pill to counteract the caffein which counteracted the ergotamine, but the awl still bored out from within, just over his right ear, to the beat of the big bass drum. Awl, drill, ill, pill, oh God. Lord deliver us. Liver sausage. What would the Athsheans do for a migraine? They wouldn't have one, they would have daydreamed the tensions away a week before they got them. Try it, try daydreaming. Begin as Selver taught you. Although knowing nothing of electricity he could not really grasp the principle of the EEG, as soon as he heard about alpha waves and when they appear he had said, "Oh yes, you mean this," and there appeared the unmistakable alpha-squiggles on the graph recording what went on inside his small green head; and he had taught Lyubov how to turn on and off the alpha-rhythms in one half-hour lesson. There really was nothing to it. But not now, the world is too much with us, ow, ow, ow above the right ear I always hear Time's winged chariot hurrying near, for the Athsheans had burned Smith Camp day before yesterday and killed two hundred men. To hundred and seven to be precise. Every man alive except the Captain. No wonder pills couldn't get at the center of his migraine, for it was on an island two hundred miles away two days ago. Over the hills and far away. Ashes, ashes, all fall down. And amongst the ashes, all his knowledge of the High Intelligence Life Forms of World 41. Dust, rubbish, a mess of false data and fake hypotheses. Nearly five E-years here, and he had believed the Athsheans to be incapable of killing men, his kind or their kind. He had written long papers to explain how and why they couldn't kill men. All wrong. Dead wrong.

What had he failed to see?

It was nearly time to be going over to the meeting at HQ. Cautiously Lyubov stood up, moving all in one piece so that the right side of his head would not fall off; he approached his desk with the gait of a man underwater, poured out a shot of General Issue vodka, and drank it. It turned him inside out: it extraverted him: it normalized him. He felt better. He went out, and unable to stand the jouncing of his motorbike, started to walk down the long, dusty main street of Centralville to HQ. Passing the Luau he thought with greed of another vodka; but Captain Davidson was just going in the door, and Lyubov went on.

The people from the *Shackleton* were already in the conference room. Commander Yung, whom he had met before, had brought some new faces down from orbit this time. They were not in Navy uniform; after a moment Lyubov recognised them, with a slight shock, as non-Terran humans. He sought an introduction at once. One, Mr. Or, was a Hairy Cetian, dark grey, stocky, and dour; the other, Mr. Lepennon, was tall, white, and comely: a Hainishman. They greeted Lyubov with interest, and Lepennon said, "I've just been reading your report on the conscious control of paradoxical sleep among the Athsheans, Dr. Lyubov," which was pleasant, and it was pleasant also to be called by his own, earned title of doctor. Their conversation indicated that they had spent some years on Earth, and that they might be hilfers, or something like it; but the Commander, introducing them, had not mentioned their status or position.

The room was filling up. Gosse, the colony ecologist, came in; so did all the high brass; so did Captain Susun, head of Planet Development—logging operations—whose captaincy like Lyubov's was an invention necessary to the peace of the military mind. Captain Davidson came in alone, straight-backed and handsome, his lean, rugged face calm and rather stern. Guards stood at all the doors. The Army necks were all stiff as crowbars. The conference was plainly an Investigation. *Whose fault?* My fault, Lyubov thought despairingly; but out of his despair he looked across the table at Captain Don Davidson with detestation and contempt.

Commander Yung had a very quiet voice. "As you know, gentlemen, my ship stopped here at World 41 to drop you off a new load of colonists, and nothing more; *Shackleton*'s mission is to World 88, Prestno, one of the Hainish Group. However, this attack on your outpost camp, since it chanced to occur during our week here, can't be simply ignored; particularly in the light of certain developments which you would have been informed of a little later, in the normal course of events. The fact is that the status of World 41 as an Earth Colony is now subject to revision, and the massacre at your camp may precipitate the Administration's decisions on it. Certainly the decisions *we* can make must be made quickly, for I can't keep my ship here long. Now first, we wish to make sure that the relevant facts are all in the possession of those present. Captain Davidson's report on the events at Smith Camp was taped and heard by all of us on ship; by all of you here also? Good. Now if there are questions any of you wish to ask Captain Davidson, go ahead. I have one myself. You returned to the site of the camp the following day, Captain Davidson, in a large hopper with eight soldiers; had you the permission of a senior officer here at Central for that flight?"

Davidson stood up. "I did, sir."

"Were you authorised to land and to set fires in the forest near the campsite?"

"No, sir."

"You did, however, set fires?"

"I did, sir. I was trying to smoke out the creechies that killed my men."

"Very well. Mr. Lepennon?"

The tall Hainishman cleared his throat. "Captain Davidson," he said, "do you think that the people under your command at Smith Camp were mostly content?"

"Yes, I do."

Davidson's manner was firm and forthright; he seemed indifferent to the fact that he was in trouble. Of course these Navy officers and foreigners had no authority over him; it was to his own Colonel that he must answer for losing two hundred men and making unauthorized reprisals. But his Colonel was right there, listening.

"They were well fed, well housed, not overworked, then, as well as can be managed in a frontier camp?"

"Yes."

"Was the discipline maintained very harsh?"

"No, it was not."

"What, then, do you think motivated the revolt?"

"I don't understand."

"If none of them were discontented, why did some of them massacre the rest and destroy the camp?"

There was a worried silence.

41

"May I put in a word," Lyubov said. "It was the native hilfs, the Athsheans employed in the camp, who joined with an attack by the forest people against the Terran humans. In his report Captain Davidson referred to the Athsheans as 'creechies.'"

Lepennon looked embarrassed and anxious. "Thank you, Dr. Lyubov. I misunderstood entirely. Actually I took the word 'creechie' to stand for a Terran caste that did rather menial work in the logging camps. Believing, as we all did, that the Athsheans were intraspecies non-aggressive, I never thought they might be the group meant. In fact I didn't realise that they cooperated with you in your camps.—However, I am more at a loss than ever to understand what provoked the attack and mutiny."

"I don't know, sir."

"When he said the people under his command were content, did the Captain include native people?" said the Cetian, Or, in a dry mumble. The Hainishman picked it up at once, and asked Davidson, in his concerned, courteous voice, "Were the Athsheans living at the camp content, do you think?"

"So far as I know."

"There was nothing unusual in their position there, or the work they had to do?"

Lyubov felt the heightening of tension, one turn of the screw, in Colonel Dongh and his staff, and also in the starship commander. Davidson remained calm and easy. "Nothing unusual."

Lyubov knew now that only his scientific studies had been sent up to the *Shackleton*; his protests, even his annual assessments of 'Native Adjustment to Colonial Presence' required by the Administration, had been kept in some desk drawer deep in HQ. These two N.-T.H.'s knew nothing about the exploitation of the Athsheans. Commander Yung did, of course; he had been down before today and had probably seen the creechie-pens. In any case a Navy commander on Colony runs wouldn't have much to learn about Terran-hilf relations. Whether or not he approved of how the Colonial Administration ran its business, not much would come as a shock to him. But a Cetian and a Hainishman, how much would they know about Terran colonies, unless chance brought them to one on the way to somewhere else? Lepennon and Or had not intended to come on-planet here at all. Or possibly they had not been intended to come on-planet, but, hearing of trouble,

42

had insisted. Why had the commander brought them down: his will, or theirs? Whoever they were they had about them a hint of authority, a whiff of the dry, intoxicating odor of power. Lyubov's headache had gone, he felt alert and excited, his face was rather hot. "Captain Davidson," he said, "I have a couple of questions, concerning your confrontation with the four natives, day before yesterday. You're certain that one of them was Sam, or Selver Thele?"

"I believe so."

"You're aware that he has a personal grudge against you."

"I don't know."

"You don't? Since his wife died in your quarters immediately subsequent to sexual intercourse with you, he holds you responsible for her death; you didn't know that? He attacked you once before, here in Centralville; you had forgotten that? Well, the point is, that Selver's personal hatred for Captain Davidson may serve as a partial explanation or motivation for this unprecedented assault. The Athsheans aren't incapable of personal violence, that's never been asserted in any of my studies of them. Adolescents who haven't mastered controlled dreaming or competitive singing do a lot of wrestling and fist-fighting, not all of it good-tempered. But Selver is an adult and an adept; and his first, personal attack on Captain Davidson, which I happened to witness part of, was pretty certainly an attempt to kill. As was the Captain's retaliation, incidentally. At the time, I thought that attack an isolated psychotic incident, resulting from grief and stress, not likely to be repeated. I was wrong.—Captain, when the four Athsheans jumped you from ambush, as you describe in your report, did you end up prone on the ground?"

"Yes."

"In what position?"

Davidson's calm face tensed and stiffened, and Lyubov felt a pang of compunction. He wanted to corner Davidson in his lies, to force him into speaking truth once, but not to humiliate him before others. Accusations of rape and murder supported Davidson's image of himself as the totally virile man, but now that image was endangered: Lyubov had called up a picture of him, the soldier, the fighter, the cool tough man, being knocked down by enemies the size of six-year-olds . . . What did it cost Davidson, then, to recall that moment when he had lain looking up at the little green men, for once, not down at them?

"I was on my back."

"Was your head thrown back, or turned aside?"

"I don't know."

"I'm trying to establish a fact here, Captain, one that might help explain why Selver didn't kill you, although he had a grudge against you and had helped kill two hundred men a few hours earlier. I wondered if you might by chance have been in one of the positions which, when assumed by an Athshean, prevent his opponent from further physical aggression."

"I don't know."

Lyubov glanced round the conference table; all the faces showed curiosity and some tension. "These aggression-halting gestures and positions may have some innate basis, may rise from a surviving trigger-response, but they are socially developed and expanded, and of course learned. The strongest and completest of them is a prone position, on the back, eyes shut, head turned so the throat is fully exposed. I think an Athshean of the local cultures might find it impossible to hurt an enemy who took that position. He would have to do something else to release his anger or aggressive drive.—When they had all got you down, Captain, did Selver by any chance sing?"

"Did he what?"

"Sing."

"I don't know."

Block. No go. Lyubov was about to shrug and give it up when the Cetian said, "Why, Mr. Lyubov?" The most winning characteristic of the rather harsh Cetian temperament was curiosity, inopportune and inexhaustible curiosity; Cetians died eagerly, curious as to what came next.

"You see," Lyubov said, "the Athsheans use a kind of ritualised singing to replace physical combat. Again it's a universal social phenomenon that might have a physiological foundation, though it's very hard to establish anything as 'innate' in human beings. However the higher primates here all go in for vocal competing between two males, a lot of howling and whistling; the dominant male may finally give the other a cuff, but usually they just spend an hour or so trying to outbellow each other. The Athsheans themselves see the similarity to their singing-matches, which are also only between males; but as they observe, theirs are not only aggression-releases, but an art-form. The better artist wins. I wondered if Selver sang over Captain Davidson, and if so, whether he did because he could not kill, or because he pre-

44

ferred the bloodless victory. These questions have suddenly become rather urgent."

"Dr. Lyubov," said Lepennon, "how effective are these aggression-channelling devices? Are they universal?"

"Among adults, yes. So my informants state, and all my observation supported them, until day before yesterday. Rape, violent assault, and murder virtually don't exist among them. There are accidents, of course. And there are psychotics. Not many of the latter."

"What do they do with dangerous psychotics?"

"Isolate them. Literally. On small islands."

"The Athsheans are carnivorous, they hunt animals?"

"Yes, meat is a staple."

"Wonderful," Lepennon said, and his white skin paled further with pure excitement. "A human society with an effective war-barrier! What's the cost, Dr. Lyubov?"

"I'm not sure, Mr. Lepennon. Perhaps change. They're a static, stable, uniform society. They have no history. Perfectly integrated, and wholly unprogressive. You might say that like the forest they live in, they've attained a climax state. But I don't mean to imply that they're incapable of adaptation."

"Gentlemen, this is very interesting but in a somewhat specialist frame of reference, and it may be somewhat out of the context which we're attempting to clarify here—"

"No, excuse me, Colonel Dongh, this may be the point. Yes, Dr. Lyubov?"

"Well, I wonder if they're not proving their adaptability, now. By adapting their behavior to us. To the Earth Colony. For four years they've behaved to us as they do to one another. Despite the physical differences, they recognised us as members of their species, as men. However, we have not responded as members of their species should respond. We have ignored the responses, the rights and obligations of non-violence. We have killed, raped, dispersed, and enslaved the native humans, destroyed their communities, and cut down their forests. It wouldn't be surprising if they'd decided that we are not human."

"And therefore can be killed, like animals, yes yes," said the Cetian, enjoying logic; but Lepennon's face now was stiff as white stone. "Enslaved?" he said.

"Captain Lyubov is expressing his personal opinions and theories," said Colonel Dongh, "which I should state I consider possibly to be erroneous, and he and I have discussed

45

this type of thing previously, although the present context is unsuitable. We do not employ slaves, sir. Some of the natives serve a useful role in our community. The Voluntary Autochthonous Labor Corps is a part of all but the temporary camps here. We have very limited personnel to accomplish our tasks here and we need workers and use all we can get, but on any kind of basis that could be called a slavery basis, certainly not."

Lepennon was about to speak, but deferred to the Cetian, who said only, "How many of each race?"

Gosse replied: "2641 Terrans, now. Lyubov and I estimate the native hilf population very roughly at 3 million."

"You should have considered these statistics, gentlemen, before you altered the native traditions!" said Or, with a disagreeable but perfectly genuine laugh.

"We are adequately armed and equipped to resist any type of aggression these natives could offer," said the Colonel. "However there was a general consensus by both the first Exploratory Missions and our own research staff of specialists here headed by Captain Lyubov, giving us to understand that the New Tahitians are a primitive, harmless, peace-loving species. Now this information was obviously erroneous—"

Or interrupted the Colonel. "Obviously! You consider the human species to be primitive, harmless, and peace-loving, Colonel? No. But you knew that the hilfs of this planet are human? As human as you or I or Lepennon—since we all came from the same, original, Hainish stock?"

"That is the scientific theory, I am aware—"

"Colonel, it is the historic fact."

"I am not forced to accept it as a fact," the old Colonel said, getting hot, "and I don't like opinions stuffed into my own mouth. The fact is that these creechies are a meter tall, they're covered with green fur, they don't sleep, and they're not human beings in my frame of reference!"

"Captain Davidson," said the Cetian, "do you consider the native hilfs human, or not?"

"I don't know."

"But you had sexual intercourse with one—this Selver's wife. Would you have sexual intercourse with a female animal? What about the rest of you?" He looked about at the purple colonel, the glowering majors, the livid captains, the cringing specialists. Contempt came into his face. "You have not thought things through," he said. By his standards it was a brutal insult.

46

The Commander of the *Shackleton* at last salvaged words from the gulf of embarrassed silence. "Well, gentlemen, the tragedy at Smith Camp clearly is involved with the entire colony-native relationship, and is not by any means an insignificant or isolated episode. That's what we had to establish. And this being the case, we can make a certain contribution towards easing your problems here. The main purpose of our journey was not to drop off a couple of hundred girls here, though I know you've been waiting for 'em, but to get to Prestno, which has been having some difficulties, and give the government there an ansible. That is, an ICD transmitter."

"What?" said Sereng, an engineer. Stares became fixed, all round the table.

"The one we have aboard is an early model, and it cost a planetary annual revenue, roughly. That, of course, was twenty-seven years ago planetary time, when we left Earth. Nowadays they're making them relatively cheaply; they're SI on Navy ships; and in the normal course of things a robo or manned ship would be coming out here to give your colony one. As a matter of fact it's a manned Administration ship, and is on the way, due here in 9.4 E-years if I recall the figure."

"How do you know that?" somebody said, setting it up for Commander Yung, who replied smiling, "By the ansible: the one we have aboard. Mr. Or, your people invented the device, perhaps you'd explain it to those here who are unfamiliar with the terms?"

The Cetian did not unbend. "I shall not attempt to explain the principles of ansible operation to those present," he said. "It's effect can be stated simply: the instantaneous transmission of a message over any distance. One element must be on a large-mass body, the other can be anywhere in the cosmos. Since arrival in orbit the *Shackleton* has been in daily communication with Terra, now twenty-seven lightyears distant. The message does not take fifty-four years for delivery and response, as it does on an electromagnetic device. It takes no time. There is no more time-gap between worlds."

"As soon as we came out of NAFAL time-dilatation into planetary space-time, here, we rang up home, as you might say," the soft-voiced Commander went on. "And were told what had happened during the twenty-seven years we were travelling. The time-gap for bodies remains, but the information lag does not. As you can see, this is as important to us as an interstellar species, as speech itself was to us earlier in our

47

evolution. It'll have the same effect: to make a society possible."

"Mr. Or and I left the Earth, twenty-seven years ago, as Legates for our respective governments, Tau II and Hain," said Lepennon. His voice was still gentle and civil, but the warmth had gone out of it. "When we left, people were talking about the possibility of forming some kind of league among the civilised worlds, now that communication was possible. The League of Worlds now exists. It has existed for eighteen years. Mr. Or and I are now Emissaries of the Council of the League, and so have certain powers and responsibilities we did not have when we left Earth."

The three of them from the ship kept saying these things: an instantaneous communicator exists, an interstellar super-government exists . . . Believe it or not. They were in league, and lying. This thought went through Lyubov's mind; he considered it, decided it was a reasonable but unwarranted suspicion, a defense-mechanism, and discarded it. Some of the military staff, however, trained to compartmentalize their thinking, specialists in self-defense, would accept it as unhesitatingly as he discarded it. They must believe that anyone claiming a sudden new authority was a liar or conspirator. They were no more constrained than Lyubov, who had been trained to keep his mind open whether he wanted to or not.

"Are we to take all—all this simply on your word, sir?" said Colonel Dongh, with dignity and some pathos; for he, too muddleheaded to compartmentalize neatly, knew that he shouldn't believe Lepennon and Or and Yung, but did believe them, and was frightened.

"No," said the Cetian. "That's done with. A colony like this had to believe what passing ships and outdated radio-messages told them. Now you don't. You can verify. We are going to give you the ansible destined for Prestno. We have League authority to do so. Received, of course, by ansible. Your colony here is in a bad way. Worse than I thought from your reports. Your reports are very incomplete; censorship or stupidity have been at work. Now, however, you'll have the ansible, and can talk with your Terran Administration; you can ask for orders, so you'll know how to proceed. Given the profound changes that have been occurring in the organisation of the Terran Government since we left there, I should recommend that you do so at once. There is no longer any excuse for acting on outdated orders; for ignorance; for irresponsible autonomy."

48

Sour a Cetian and, like milk, he stayed sour. Mr. Or was being overbearing, and Commander Yung should shut him up. But could he? How did an "Emissary of the Council of the League of Worlds" rank? Who's in charge here, thought Lyubov, and he too felt a qualm of fear. His headache had returned as a sense of constriction, a sort of tight headband over the temples.

He looked across the table at Lepennon's white, long-fingered hands, lying left over right, quiet, on the bare polished wood of the table. The white skin was a defect to Lyubov's Earth-formed aesthetic taste, but the serenity and strength of those hands pleased him very much. To the Hainish, he thought, civilisation came naturally. They had been at it so long. They lived the social-intellectual life with the grace of a cat hunting in a garden, the certainty of a swallow following summer over the sea. They were experts. They never had to pose, to fake. They were what they were. Nobody seemed to fit the human skin so well. Except, perhaps, the little green men? the deviant, dwarfed, over-adapted, stagnated creechies, who were as absolutely, as honestly, as serenely what they were . . .

An officer, Benton, was asking Lepennon if he and Or were on this planet as observers for the (he hesitated) League of Worlds, or if they claimed any authority to . . . Lepennon took him up politely: "We are observers here, not empowered to command, only to report. You are still answerable only to your own government on Earth."

Colonel Dongh said with relief, "Then nothing has essentially changed—"

"You forget the ansible," Or interrupted. "I'll instruct you in its operation, Colonel, as soon as this discussion is over. You can then consult with your Colonial Administration."

"Since your problem here is rather urgent, and since Earth is now a League member and may have changed the Colonial Code somewhat during recent years, Mr. Or's advice is both proper and timely. We should be very grateful to Mr. Or and Mr. Lepennon for their decision to give this Terran colony the ansible destined for Prestno. It was their decision; I can only applaud it. Now, one more decision remains to be made, and this one I have to make, using your judgment as my guide. If you feel the colony is in imminent peril of further and more massive attacks from the natives, I can keep my ship here for a week or two, as a defense arsenal; I can also evacuate the women. No children yet, right?"

"No, sir," said Gosse. "482 women now."

"Well, I have space for 380 passengers; we might crowd a hundred more in; the extra mass would add a year or so to the trip home, but it could be done. Unfortunately that's all I can do. We must proceed to Prestno; your nearest neighbor, as you know, 1.8 lightyears distant. We'll stop here on the way home to Terra, but that's going to be three and a half more E-years at least. Can you stick it out?"

"Yes," said the Colonel, and others echoed him. "We've had warning now and we won't be caught napping again."

"Equally," said the Cetian, "can the native inhabitants stick it out for three and a half Earth-years more?"

"Yes," said the Colonel. "No," said Lyubov. He had been watching Davidson's face, and a kind of panic had taken hold of him.

"Colonel?" said Lepennon, politely.

"We've been here four years now and the natives are flourishing. There's room enough and to spare for all of us, as you can see the planet's heavily underpopulated and the Administration wouldn't have cleared it for colonisation purposes if that hadn't been as it is. As for if this entered anyone's head, they won't catch us off guard again, we were erroneously briefed concerning the nature of these natives, but we're fully armed and able to defend ourselves, but we aren't planning any reprisals. That is expressly forbidden in the Colonial Code, though I don't know what new rules this new government may have added on, but we'll just stick to our own as we have been doing and they definitely negative mass reprisals or genocide. We won't be sending any messages for help out, after all a colony twenty-seven lightyears from home has come out expecting to be on its own and to in fact be completely self-sufficient, and I don't see that the ICD really changes that, due to ship and men and material still have to travel at near lightspeed. We'll just keep on shipping the lumber home, and look out for ourselves. The women are in no danger."

"Mr. Lyubov?" said Lepennon.

"We've been here four years. I don't know if the native human culture will survive four more. As for the total land ecology, I think Gosse will back me if I say that we've irrecoverably wrecked the native life-systems on one large island, have done great damage on this subcontinent Sornol, and if we go on logging at the present rate, may reduce the major habitable lands to desert within ten years. This isn't the fault

50

of the colony's HQ or Forestry Bureau; they've simply been following a Development Plan drawn up on Earth without sufficient knowledge of the planet to be exploited, its life-systems, or its native human inhabitants."

"Mr. Gosse?" said the polite voice.

"Well, Raj, you're stretching things a bit. There's no denying that Dump Island, which was overlogged in direct contravention to my recommendations, is a dead loss. If more than a certain percentage of the forest is cut over a certain area, then the fibreweed doesn't reseed, you see, gentlemen, and the fibreweed root-system is the main soil-binder on clear land; without it the soil goes dusty and drifts off very fast under wind-erosion and the heavy rainfall. But I can't agree that our basic directives are at fault, so long as they're scrupulously followed. They were based on careful study of the planet. We've succeeded, here on Central, by following the Plan: erosion is minimal, and the cleared soil is highly arable. To log off a forest doesn't, after all, mean to make a desert—except perhaps from the point of view of a squirrel. We can't forecast precisely how the native forest life-systems will adapt to the new woodland-prairie-plowland ambiance foreseen in the Development Plan, but we know the chances are good for a large percentage of adaptation and survival."

"That's what the Bureau of Land Management said about Alaska during the First Famine," said Lyubov. His throat had tightened so that his voice came out high and husky. He had counted on Gosse for support. "How many Sitka spruce have you seen in your lifetime, Gosse? Or snowy owl? or wolf? or Eskimo? The survival percentage of native Alaskan species in habitat, after fifteen years of the Development Program, was .3 percent. It's now zero.—A forest ecology is a delicate one. If the forest perishes, its fauna may go with it. The Athshean word for *world* is also the word for *forest*. I submit, Commander Yung, that though the colony may not be in imminent danger, the planet is—"

"Captain Lyubov," said the old Colonel, "such submissions are not properly submitted by staff specialist officers to officers of other branches of the service but should rest on the judgment of the senior officers of the Colony, and I cannot tolerate any further such attempts as this to give advice without previous clearance."

Caught off guard by his own outburst, Lyubov apologised and tried to look calm. If only he didn't lose his temper, if his voice didn't go weak and husky, if he had poise . . .

The Colonel went on. "It appears to us that you made some serious erroneous judgments concerning the peacefulness and non-aggressiveness of the natives here, and because we counted on this specialist description of them as non-aggressive is why we left ourselves open to this terrible tragedy at Smith Camp, Captain Lyubov. So I think we have to wait until some other specialists in hilfs have had time to study them, because evidently your theories were basically erroneous to some extent."

Lyubov sat and took it. Let the men from the ship see them all passing the blame around like a hot brick: all the better. The more dissension they showed, the likelier were these Emissaries to have them checked and watched over. And he was to blame; he had been wrong. To hell with my self-respect so long as the forest people get a chance, Lyubov thought, and so strong a sense of his own humiliation and self-sacrifice came over him that tears rose to his eyes.

He was aware that Davidson was watching him.

He sat up stiff, the blood hot in his face, his temples drumming. He would not be sneered at by that bastard Davidson. Couldn't Or and Lepennon see what kind of man Davidson was, and how much power he had here, while Lyubov's powers, called "advisory," were simply derisory? If the colonists were left to go on with no check on them but a super-radio, the Smith Camp massacre would almost certainly become the excuse for systematic aggression against the natives. Bacteriological extermination, most likely. The *Shackleton* would come back in three and a half or four years to "New Tahiti," and find a thriving Terran colony, and no more Creechie Problem. None at all. Pity about the plague, we took all precautions required by the Code, but it must have been some kind of mutation, they had no natural resistance, but we did manage to save a group of them by transporting them to the New Falkland Isles in the southern hemisphere and they're doing fine there, all sixty-two of them . . .

The conference did not last much longer. When it ended he stood up and leaned across the table to Lepennon. "You must tell the League to do something to save the forests, the forest people," he said almost inaudibly, his throat constricted, "you must, please, you must."

The Hainishman met his eyes; his gaze was reserved, kindly, and deep as a well. He said nothing.

52

IV

It was unbelievable. They'd all gone insane. This damned alien world had sent them all right round the bend, into bye-bye dreamland, along with the creechies. He still wouldn't believe what he'd seen at that "conference" and the briefing after it, if he saw it all over again on film. A Starfleet ship's commander bootlicking two humanoids. Engineers and techs cooing and ooing over a fancy radio presented to them by a Hairy Cetian with a lot of sneering and boasting, as if ICD's hadn't been predicted by Terran science years ago! The humanoids had stolen the idea, implemented it, and called it an "ansible" so nobody would realise it was just an ICD. But the worst part of it had been the conference, with that psycho Lyubov raving and crying, and Colonel Dongh letting him do it, letting him insult Davidson and HQ staff and the whole Colony; and all the time the two aliens sitting and grinning, the little grey ape and the big white fairy, sneering at humans.

It had been pretty bad. It hadn't got any better since the *Shackleton* left. He didn't mind being sent down to New Java Camp under Major Muhamed. The Colonel had to discipline him; old Ding Dong might actually be very happy about that fire-raid he'd pulled in reprisal on Smith Island, but the raid had been a breach of discipline and he had to reprimand Davidson. All right, rules of the game. But what wasn't in the rules was this stuff coming over that overgrown TV set they called the ansible—their new little tin god at HQ.

Orders from the Bureau of Colonial Administration in Karachi: *Restrict Terran-Athshean contact to occasions arranged by Athsheans*. In other words you couldn't go into a creechie warren and round up a work-force any more. *Employment of volunteer labor is not advised; employment of forced labor is forbidden*. More of same. How the hell were they supposed to get the work done? Did Earth want this wood or didn't it? They were still sending the robot cargo ships to New Tahiti, weren't they, four a year, each carrying about thirty million new-dollars worth of prime lumber back to Mother Earth. Sure the Development people wanted those millions. They were businessmen. These messages weren't coming from them, any fool could see that.

The colonial status of World 41—why didn't they call it New Tahiti any more?—*is under consideration. Until deci-*

53

sion is reached colonists should observe extreme caution in all dealings with native inhabitants . . . The use of weapons of any kind except small side-arms carried in self-defense is absolutely forbidden—just as on Earth, except that there a man couldn't even carry side-arms any more. But what the hell was the use coming twenty-seven lightyears to a frontier world and then get told No guns, no firejelly, no bugbombs, no no, just sit like nice little boys and let the creechies come spit in your faces and sing songs at you and then stick a knife in your guts and burn down your camp, but don't you hurt the cute little green fellers, no sir!

A policy of avoidance is strongly advised; a policy of aggression or retaliation is strictly forbidden.

That was the gist of all the messages actually, and any fool could tell that that wasn't the Colonial Administration talking. They couldn't have changed that much in thirty years. They were practical, realistic men who knew what life was like on frontier planets. It was clear, to anybody who hadn't gone spla from geoshock, that the "ansible" messages were phoneys. They might be planted right in the machine, a whole set of answers to high-probability questions, computer run. The engineers said they could have spotted that; maybe so. In that case the thing did communicate instantaneously with another world. But that world wasn't Earth. Not by a long long shot! There weren't any men typing the answers onto the other end of that little trick: they were aliens, humanoids. Probably Cetians, for the machine was Cetian-made, and they were a smart bunch of devils. They were the kind that might make a real bid for interstellar supremacy. The Hainish would be in the conspiracy with them, of course; all that bleeding-heart stuff in the so-called directives had a Hainish sound to it. What the long-term objective of the aliens was, was hard to guess from here; it probably involved weakening the Terran Government by tying it up in this "league of worlds" business, until the aliens were strong enough to make an armed takeover. But their plan for New Tahiti was easy to see. They'd let the creechies wipe out the humans for them. Just tie the humans' hands with a lot of fake "ansible" directives and let the slaughter begin. Humanoids help humanoids: rats help rats.

And Colonel Dongh had swallowed it. He intended to obey orders. He had actually said that to Davidson. "I intend to obey my orders from Terra-HQ, and by God, Don, you'll obey my orders the same way, and in New Java you'll obey

Major Muhamed's orders there." He was stupid, old Ding Dong, but he liked Davidson, and Davidson liked him. If it meant betraying the human race to an alien conspiracy then he couldn't obey his orders, but he still felt sorry for the old soldier. A fool, but a loyal and brave one. Not a born traitor like that whining, tattling prig Lyubov. If there was one man he hoped the creechies did get, it was bigdome Raj Lyubov, the alien-lover.

Some men, especially the asiatiforms and hindi types, are actually born traitors. Not all, but some. Certain other men are born saviors. It just happened to be the way they were made, like being of euraf descent, or like having a good physique; it wasn't anything he claimed credit for. If he could save the men and women of New Tahiti, he would; if he couldn't, he'd make a damn good try; and that was all there was to it, actually.

The women, now, that rankled. They'd pulled out the ten Collies who'd been in New Java and none of the new ones were being sent out from Centralville. "Not safe yet," HQ bleated. Pretty rough on the three outpost camps. What did they expect the outposters to do when it was hands off the she-creechies, and all the she-humans were for the lucky bastards at Central? It was going to cause terrific resentment. But it couldn't last long, the whole situation was too crazy to be stable. If they didn't start easing back to normal now the *Shackleton* was gone, then Captain D. Davidson would just have to do a little extra work to get things headed back towards normalcy.

The morning of the day he left Central, they had let loose the whole creechie work-force. Made a big noble speech in pidgin, opened the compound gates, and let out every single tame creechie, carriers, diggers, cooks, dustmen, houseboys, maids, the lot. Not one had stayed. Some of them had been with their masters ever since the start of the colony, four E-years ago. But they had no loyalty. A dog, a chimp would have hung around. These things weren't even that highly developed, they were just about like snakes or rats, just smart enough to turn around and bite you as soon as you let 'em out of the cage. Ding Dong was spla, letting all those creechies loose right in the vicinity. Dumping them on Dump Island and letting them starve would have been actually the best final solution. But Dongh was still panicked by that pair of humanoids and their talky-box. So if the wild creechies on

55

Central were planning to imitate the Smith Camp atrocity, they now had lots of real handy new recruits, who knew the layout of the whole town, the routines, where the arsenal was, where guards were posted, and the rest. If Centralville got burned down, HQ could thank themselves. It would be what they deserved, actually. For letting traitors dupe them, for listening to humanoids and ignoring the advice of men who really knew what the creechies were like.

None of those guys at HQ had come back to camp and found ashes and wreckage and burned bodies, like he had. And Ok's body, out where they'd slaughtered the logging crew, it had had an arrow sticking out of each eye like some sort of weird insect with antennae sticking out feeling the air, Christ, he kept seeing that.

One thing anyhow, whatever the phoney "directives" said, the boys at Central wouldn't be stuck with trying to use "small side-arms" for self-defense. They had fire-throwers and machine guns; the 16 little hoppers had machine guns and were useful for dropping firejelly cans from; the five big hoppers had full armament. But they wouldn't need the big stuff. Just take up a hopper over one of the deforested areas and catch a mess of creechies there, with their damned bows and arrows, and start dropping firejelly cans and watch them run around and burn. It would be all right. It made his belly churn a little to imagine it, just like when he thought about making a woman, or whenever he remembered about when that Sam creechie had attacked him and he had smashed in his whole face with four blows one right after the other. It was eidetic memory plus a more vivid imagination than most men had, no credit due, just happened to be the way he was made.

The fact is, the only time a man is really and entirely a man is when he's just had a woman or just killed another man. That wasn't original, he'd read it in some old books; but it was true. That was why he liked to imagine scenes like that. Even if the creechies weren't actually men.

New Java was the southernmost of the five big lands, just north of the equator, and so was hotter than Central or Smith which were just about perfect climate-wise. Hotter and a lot wetter. It rained all the time in the wet seasons anywhere on New Tahiti, but in the northern lands it was a kind of quiet fine rain that went on and on and never really got you wet or cold. Down here it came in buckets, and there was a monsoon-type storm that you couldn't even walk in, let alone work in. Only a solid roof kept that rain off you, or else the forest. The damn forest was so thick it kept out the storms. You'd get wet from all the drippings off the leaves, of course, but if you were really inside the forest during one of those monsoons you'd hardly notice the wind was blowing; then you came out in the open and wham! got knocked off your feet by the wind and slobbered all over with the red liquid mud that the rain turned the cleared ground into, and you couldn't duck back into the forest quick enough; and inside the forest it was dark, and hot, and easy to get lost.

Then the C.O., Major Muhamed, was a sticky bastard. Everything at N.J. was done by the book: the logging all in kilo-strips, the fibreweed crap planted in the logged strips, leave to Central granted in strict non-preferential rotation, hallucinogens rationed and their use on duty punished, and so on and so on. However, one good thing about Muhamed was he wasn't always radioing Central. New Java was his camp, and he ran it his way. He didn't like orders from HQ. He obeyed them all right, he'd let the creechies go, and locked up all the guns except little popgun pistols, as soon as the orders came. But he didn't go looking for orders, or for advice. Not from Central or anybody else. He was a self-righteous type: knew he was right. That was his big fault.

When he was on Dongh's staff at HQ Davidson had had occasion sometimes to see the officers' records. His unusual memory held on to such things, and he could recall for instance that Muhamed's IQ was 107. Whereas his own happened to be 118. There was a difference of 11 points; but of course he couldn't say that to old Moo, and Moo couldn't see it, and so there was no way to get him to listen. He thought he knew better than Davidson, and that was that.

They were all a bit sticky at first, actually. None of the men at N. J. knew anything about the Smith Camp atrocity, except that the camp C.O. had left for Central an hour before it happened, and so was the only human that escaped alive. Put like that, it did sound bad. You could see why at first they looked at him like a kind of Jonah, or worse, a kind of Judas even. But when they got to know him they'd know better. They'd begin to see that, far from being a deserter or traitor, he was dedicated to preventing the colony of New Tahiti from betrayal. And they'd realise that getting rid of the creechies was going to be the only way to make this world safe for the Terran way of life.

It wasn't too hard to start getting that message across to the loggers. They'd never liked the little green rats, having to drive them to work all day and guard them all night; but now they began to understand that the creechies were not only re- plusive but dangerous. When Davidson told them what he'd found at Smith; when he explained how the two humanoids on the Fleet ship had brainwashed HQ; when he showed them that wiping out the Terrans on New Tahiti was just a small part of the whole alien conspiracy against Earth; when he reminded them of the cold hard figures, twenty-five *hundred* humans to three *million* creechies—then they began to really get behind him.

Even the Ecological Control Officer here was with him. Not like poor old Kees, mad because men shot Red Deer and then getting shot in the guts himself by the sneaking creechies. This fellow, Atranda, was a creechie-hater. Actu- ally he was kind of spla about them, he had geoshock or something; he was so afraid the creechies were going to at- tack the camp that he acted like some woman afraid of get- ting raped. But it was useful to have the local spesh on his side anyhow.

No use trying to line up the C.O.; a good judge of men, Davidson had seen it was no use almost at once. Muhamed was rigid-minded. Also he had a prejudice against Davidson which he wouldn't drop; it had something to do with the Smith Camp affair. He as much as told Davidson he didn't consider him a trustworthy officer.

He was a self-righteous bastard, but his running N. J. camp on such rigid lines was an advantage. A tight organiza- tion, used to obeying orders, was easier to take over than a loose one full of independent characters, and easier to keep together as a unit for defensive and offensive military oper- ations, once he was in command. He would have to take command. Moo was a good logging-camp boss, but no soldier.

Davidson kept busy getting some of the best loggers and junior officers really firmly with him. He didn't hurry. When he had enough of them he could really trust, a squad of ten lifted a few items from old Moo's locked-up room in the Rec House basement full of war toys, and then went off one Sun- day into the woods to play.

Davidson had located the creechie town some weeks ago, and had saved up the treat for his men. He could have done it single-handed, but it was better this way. You got the sense of comradeship, of a real bond among men. They just walked into the place in broad open daylight, and coated all the creechies caught above-ground with firejelly and burned them, then poured kerosene over the warren-roofs and roasted the rest. Those that tried to get out got jellied; that was the artistic part, waiting at the rat-holes for the little rats to come out; letting them think they'd made it, and then just frying them from the feet up so they made torches. That green fur sizzled like crazy.

It actually wasn't much more exciting than hunting real rats, which were about the only wild animals left on Mother Earth, but there was more thrill to it; the creechies were a lot bigger than rats, and you knew they could fight back, though this time they didn't. In fact some of them even lay down instead of running away, just lay there on their backs with their eyes shut. It was sickening. The other fellows thought so too, and one of them actually got sick and vomited after he'd burned up one of the lying-down ones.

Hard up as the men were, they didn't leave even one of the females alive to rape. They had all agreed with Davidson beforehand that it was too damn near perversity. Homosexuality was with other humans, it was normal. These things might be built like human women but they weren't human, and it was better to get your kicks from killing them, and stay *clean*. That had made good sense to all of them, and they stuck to it.

Every one of them kept his trap shut back at camp, no boasting even to their buddies. They were sound men. Not a word of the expedition got to Muhamed's ears. So far as old Moo knew, all his men were good little boys just sawing up logs and keeping away from creechies, yes sir; and he could go on believing that until D-Day came.

For the creechies would attack. Somewhere. Here, or one of the camps on King Island, or Central. Davidson knew that. He was the only officer in the entire colony that did know it. No credit due, he just happened to know he was right. Nobody else had believed him, except these men here whom he'd had time to convince. But the others would all see, sooner or later, that he was right.

And he was right.

V

It had been a shock, meeting Selver face to face. As he flew back to Central from the foothill village, Lyubov tried to

59

decide why it had been a shock, to analyse out the nerve that had jumped. For after all one isn't usually terrified by a chance meeting with a good friend.

It hadn't been easy to get the headwoman to invite him. Tuntar had been his main locus of study all summer; he had several excellent informants there and was on good terms with the Lodge and with the headwoman, who had let him observe and participate in the community freely. Wangling an actual invitation out of her, via some of the ex-serfs still in the area, had taken a long time, but at last she had complied, giving him, according to the new directives, a genuine "occasion arranged by the Athsheans." His own conscience, rather than the Colonel, had insisted on this. Dongh wanted him to go. He was worried about the Creechie Threat. He told Lyubov to size them up, to "see how they're reacting now that we're leaving them strictly alone." He hoped for reassurance. Lyubov couldn't decide whether the report he'd be turning in would reassure Colonel Dongh, or not.

For ten miles out of Central, the plain had been logged and the stumps had all rotted away; it was now a great dull flat of fibreweed, hairy grey in the rain. Under those hirsute leaves the seedling shrubs got their first growth, the sumacs, dwarf aspens, and salviforms which, grown, would in turn protect the seedling trees. Left alone, in this even, rainy climate, this area might reforest itself within thirty years and reattain the full climax forest within a hundred. Left alone.

Suddenly the forest began again, in space not time: under the helicopter the infinitely various green of leaves covered the slow swells and foldings of the hills of North Sornol.

Like most Terrans on Terra, Lyubov had never walked among wild trees at all, never seen a wood larger than a city block. At first on Athshe he had felt oppressed and uneasy in the forest, stifled by its endless crowd and incoherence of trunks, branches, leaves in the perpetual greenish or brownish twilight. The mass and jumble of various competitive lives all pushing and swelling outwards and upwards towards light, the silence made up of many little meaningless noises, the total vegetable indifference to the presence of mind, all this had troubled him, and like the others he had kept to clearings and to the beach. But little by little he had begun to like it. Gosse teased him, calling him Mr. Gibbon; in fact Lyubov looked rather like a gibbon, with a round, dark face, long arms, and hair greying early; but gibbons were extinct. Like it or not, as a hilfer he had to go into the forests to find the hilfs; and now after four years of it he was completely at home under the trees, more so perhaps than anywhere else.

He had also come to like the Athsheans' names for their own lands and places, sonorous two-syllabled words: Sornol, Tuntar, Eshreth, Eshsen—that was now Centralville—Endtor, Abtan, and above all Athshe, which meant the Forest, and the World. So earth, terra, tellus mean both the soil and the planet, two meanings and one. But to the Athsheans soil, ground, earth, was not that to which the dead return and by which the living live: the substance of their world was not earth, but forest. Terran man was clay, red dust. Athshean man was branch and root. They did not carve figures of themselves in stone, only in wood.

He brought the hopper down in a small glade north of the town, and walked in past the Women's Lodge. The smell of an Athshean settlement hung pungent in the air, woodsmoke, dead fish, aromatic herbs, alien sweat. The atmosphere of an underground house, if a Terran could fit himself in at all, was a rare compound of CO_2 and stinks. Lyubov had spent many intellectually stimulating hours doubled up and suffocating in the reeking gloom of the Men's Lodge in Tuntar. But it didn't look as if he would be invited in this time.

Of course the townsfolk knew of the Smith Camp massacre, now six weeks ago. They would have known of it soon, for word got around fast among the islands, though not so fast as to constitute a "mysterious power of telepathy" as the loggers liked to believe. The townsfolk also knew that the twelve hundred slaves at Centralville had been freed soon after the Smith Camp massacre, and Lyubov agreed with the Colonel that the natives might take the second event to be a result of the first. That gave what Colonel Dongh would call "an erroneous impression," but it probably wasn't important. What was important was that the slaves had been freed. Wrongs done could not be righted, but at least they were not still being done. They could start over: the natives without that painful, unanswerable wonder as to why the "yumens" treated men like animals; and he without the burden of explanation and the gnawing of irremediable guilt.

Knowing how they valued candor and direct speech concerning frightening or troublous matters, he expected that people in Tuntar would talk about these things with him, in triumph, or apology, or rejoicing, or puzzlement. No one did. No one said much of anything to him.

He had come in late afternoon, which was like arriving in

a Terran city just after dawn. Athsheans did sleep—the colonists' opinion, as often, ignored observable fact—but their physiological low was between noon and 4 P.M., whereas with Terrans it is usually between 2 and 5 A.M.; and they had a double-peak cycle of high temperature and high activity, coming in the two twilights, dawn and evening. Most adults slept five or six hours in twenty-four, in several catnaps; and adept men slept as little as two hours in twenty-four; so, if one discounted both their naps and their dreaming-states as "laziness," one might say they never slept. It was much easier to say that than to understand what they actually did do.—At this point, in Tuntar, things were just beginning to stir again after the late-day slump.

Lyubov noticed a good many strangers. They looked at him, but none approached; they were mere presences passing on other paths in the dusk of the great oaks. At last someone he knew came along his path, the headwoman's cousin Sherrar, an old woman of small importance and small understanding. She greeted him civilly, but did not or would not respond to his inquiries about the headwoman and his two best informants, Egath the orchard-keeper and Tubab the Dreamer. Oh, the headwoman was very busy, and who was Egath, did he mean Geban, and Tubab might be here or perhaps he was there, or not. She stuck to Lyubov, and nobody else spoke to him. He worked his way, accompanied by the hobbling, complaining, tiny, green crone, across the groves and glades to Tuntar to the Men's Lodge. "They're busy in there," said Sherrar.

"Dreaming?"

"However should I know? Come along now, Lyubov, come see . . ." She knew he always wanted to see things, but she couldn't think what to show him to draw him away. "Come see the fishing-nets," she said feebly.

A girl passing by, one of the Young Hunters, looked up at him: a black look, a stare of animosity such as he had never received from any Athshean, unless perhaps from a little child frightened into scowling by his height and his hairless face. But this girl was not frightened.

"All right," he said to Sherrar, feeling that his only course was docility. If the Athsheans had indeed developed—at last, and abruptly—the sense of group enmity, then he must accept this, and simply try to show them that he remained a reliable, unchanging friend.

But how could their way of feeling and thinking have

changed so fast, after so long? And why? At Smith Camp, provocation had been immediate and intolerable: Davidson's cruelty would drive even Athsheans to violence. But this town, Tuntar, had never been attacked by the Terrans, had suffered no slave-raids, had not seen the local forest logged or burned. He, Lyubov himself, had been there—the anthropologist cannot always leave his own shadow out of the picture he draws—but not for over two months now. They had got the news from Smith, and there were among them now refugees, ex-slaves, who had suffered at the Terrans' hands and would talk about it. But would news and hearsay change the hearers, change them radically?—when their unaggressiveness ran so deep in them, right through their culture and society and on down into their subconscious, their "dream time," and perhaps into their very physiology? That an Athshean could be provoked, by atrocious cruelty, to attempt murder, he knew: he had seen it happen—once. That a disrupted community might be similarly provoked by similarly intolerable injuries, he had to believe: it had happened at Smith Camp. But that talk and hearsay, no matter how frightening and outrageous, could enrage a settled community of these people to the point where they acted against their customs and reason, broke entirely out of their whole style of living, this he couldn't believe. It was psychologically improbable. Some element was missing.

Old Tubab came out of the Lodge, just as Lyubov passed in front of it. Behind the old man came Selver.

Selver crawled out of the tunnel-door, stood upright, blinked at the rain-greyed, foliage-dimmed brightness of daylight. His dark eyes met Lyubov's, looking up. Neither spoke. Lyubov was badly frightened.

Flying home in the hopper, analysing out the shocked nerve, he thought, why fear? Why was I afraid of Selver? Unprovable intuition or mere false analogy? Irrational in any case.

Nothing between Selver and Lyubov had changed. What Selver had done at Smith Camp could be justified, even if it couldn't be justified, it made no difference. The friendship between them was too deep to be touched by moral doubt. They had worked very hard together; they had taught each other, in rather more than the literal sense, their languages. They had spoken without reserve. And Lyubov's love for his friend was deepened by that gratitude the savior feels towards the one whose life he has been privileged to save.

Indeed he had scarcely realised until that moment how

deep his liking and loyalty to Selver were. Had his fear in fact been the personal fear that Selver might, having learned racial hatred, reject him, despise his loyalty, and treat him not as "you," but as "one of them"?

After that long first gaze Selver came forward slowly and greeted Lyubov, holding out his hands.

Touch was a main channel of communication among the forest people. Among Terrans touch is always likely to imply threat, aggression, and so for them there is often nothing between the formal handshake and the sexual caress. All that blank was filled by the Athsheans with varied customs of touch. Caress as signal and reassurance was as essential to them as it is to mother and child or to lover and lover; but its significance was social, not only maternal and sexual. It was part of their language. It was therefore patterned, codified, yet infinitely modifiable. "They're always pawing each other," some of the colonists sneered, unable to see in these touch-exchanges anything but their own eroticism which, forced to concentrate itself exclusively on sex and then repressed and frustrated, invades and poisons every sensual pleasure, every humane response: the victory of a blinded, furtive Cupid over the great brooding mother of all the seas and stars, all the leaves of trees, all the gestures of men, Venus Genetrix . . .

So Selver came forward with his hands held out, shook Lyubov's hand Terran fashion, and then took both his arms with a stroking motion just above the elbow. He was not much more than half Lyubov's height, which made all gestures difficult and ungainly for both of them, but there was nothing uncertain or childlike in the touch of his small, thin boned green-furred hand on Lyubov's arms. It was reassurance. Lyubov was very glad to get it.

"Selver, what luck to meet you here. I want very much to talk with you—"

"I can't, now, Lyubov."

He spoke gently, but when he spoke Lyubov's hope of an unaltered friendship vanished. Selver had changed. He was changed, radically: from the root.

"Can I come back," Lyubov said urgently, "another day, and talk with you, Selver? It is important to me—"

"I leave here today," Selver said even more gently, but letting go Lyubov's arms, and also looking away. He thus put himself literally out of touch. Civility required that Lyubov do the same, and let the conversation end. But then there would be no one to talk to. Old Tubab had not even looked at him; the town had turned its back on him. And this was Selver, who had been his friend.

"Selver, this killing at Kelme Deva, maybe you think that lies between us. But it does not. Maybe it brings us closer together. And your people in the slave-pens, they've all been set free, so that wrong no longer lies between us. And even if it does—it always did—all the same I . . . I am the same man I was, Selver."

At first the Athshean made no response. His strange face, the large deepset eyes, the strong features misshapen by scars and blurred by the short silken fur that followed and yet obscured all contours, this face turned from Lyubov, shut, obstinate. Then suddenly he looked round as if against his own intent. "Lyubov, you shouldn't have come here. You should leave Central two nights from now. I don't know what you are. It would be better if I had never known you."

And with that he was off, a light walk like a long-legged cat, a green flicker among the dark oaks of Tuntar, gone. Tubab followed slowly after him, still without a glance at Lyubov. A fine rain fell without sound on the oak-leaves and on the narrow pathways to the Lodge and the river. Only if you listened intently could you hear the rain, too multitudinous a music for one mind to grasp, a single endless chord played on the entire forest.

"Selver is a god," said old Sherrar. "Come and see the fishing-nets now."

Lyubov declined. It would be impolite and impolitic to stay; anyway he had no heart to.

He tried to tell himself that Selver had not been rejecting him, Lyubov, but him as a Terran. It made no difference. It never does.

He was always disagreeably surprised to find how vulnerable his feelings were, how much it hurt him to be hurt. This sort of adolescent sensitivity was shameful, he should have a tougher hide by now.

The little crone, her green fur all dusted and besilvered with raindrops, sighed with relief when he said goodbye. As he started the hopper he had to grin at the sight of her, hop-hobbling off into the trees as fast as she could go, like a little toad that has escaped a snake.

Quality is an important matter, but so is quantity: relative size. The normal adult reaction to a very much smaller person may be arrogant, or protective, or patronising, or affec-

65

tionate, or bullying, but whatever it is it's liable to be better fitted to a child than to an adult. Then, when the child-sized person was furry, a further response got called upon, which Lyubov had labelled the Teddybear Reaction. Since the Athsheans used caress so much, its manifestation was not inappropriate, but its motivation remained suspect. And finally there was the inevitable Freak Reaction, the flinching away from what is human but does not quite look so.

But quite outside all that was the fact that the Athsheans, like Terrans, were simply funny-looking at times. Some of them did look like little toads, owls, caterpillars. Sherrar was not the first little old lady who had struck Lyubov as looking funny from behind . . .

And that's one trouble with the colony, he thought as he lifted the hopper and Tuntar vanished beneath the oaks and the leafless orchards. We haven't got any old women. No old men either, except Dongh and he's only about sixty. But old women are different from everybody else, they say what they think. The Athsheans are governed, in so far as they have government, by old women. Intellect to the men, politics to the women, and ethics to the interaction of both: that's their arrangement. It has charm, and it works—for them. I wish the Administration had sent out a couple of grannies along with all those nubile fertile high-breasted young women. Now that girl I had over the other night, she's really very nice, and nice in bed, she has a kind heart, but my God it'll be forty years before she'll say anything to a man . . .

But all the time, beneath his thoughts concerning old women and young ones, the shock persisted, the intuition or recognition that would not let itself be recognised.

He must think this out before he reported to HQ.

Selver: what about Selver, than?

Selver was certainly a key figure to Lyubov. Why? Because he knew him well, or because of some actual power in his personality, which Lyubov had never consciously appreciated?

But he had appreciated it; he had picked Selver out very soon as an extraordinary person. "Sam," he had been then, bodyservant for three officers sharing a prefab. Lyubov remembered Benson boasting what a good creechie they'd got, they'd broke him in right.

Many Athsheans, especially Dreamers from the Lodges, could not change their polycyclic sleep-pattern to fit the Terran one. If they caught up with their normal sleep at night,

66

that prevented them from catching up with the REM or para-doxical sleep, whose 120-minute cycle ruled their life both day and night, and could not be fitted in to the Terran work-day. Once you have learned to do your dreaming wide awake, to balance your sanity not on the razor's edge of rea-son but on the double support, the fine balance, of reason and dream, once you have learned that, you cannot unlearn it any more than you can unlearn to think. So many of the men became groggy, confused, withdrawn, even catatonic. Women, bewildered and abased, behaved with the sullen list-lessness of the newly enslaved. Male non-adepts and some of the younger Dreamers did best; they adapted, working hard in the logging camps or becoming clever servants. Sam had been one of these, an efficient, characterless bodyservant, cook, laundry-boy, butler, backsoaper and scapegoat for his three masters. He had learned how to be invisible. Lyubov borrowed him as an ethnological informant, and had, by some affinity of mind and nature, won Sam's trust at once. He found Sam the ideal informant, trained in his people's customs, perceptive of their significances, and quick to trans-late them, to make them intelligible to Lyubov, bridging the gap between two languages, two cultures, two species of the genus Man.

For two years Lyubov had been travelling, studying, inter-viewing, observing, and had failed to get at the key that would let him into the Athshean mind. He didn't even know where the lock was. He had studied the Athsheans' sleeping-habits and found that they apparently had no sleeping-habits. He had wired countless electrodes onto countless furry green skulls, and failed to make any sense at all out of the familiar patterns, the spindles and jags, the alphas and deltas and thetas, that appeared on the graph. It was Selver who had made him understand, at last, the Athshean significance of the word "dream," which was also the word for "root," and so hand him the key of the kingdom of the forest people. It was with Selver as EEG subject that he had first seen with comprehension the extraordinary impulse-patterns of a brain entering a dream-state neither sleeping nor awake: a condi-tion which related to Terran dreaming-sleep as the Parthenon to a mud hut: the same thing basically, but with the addition of complexity, quality, and control.

What then, what more?

Selver might have escaped. He stayed, first as a valet, then (through one of Lyubov's few useful perquisites as a Spesh)

67

as Scientific Aide, still locked up nightly with all other creechies in the pen (the Voluntary Autochthonous Labor Personnel Quarters). "I'll fly you up to Tuntar and work with you there," Lyubov had said, about the third time he talked with Selver, "for God's sake why stay here?"—"My wife Thele is in the pen," Selver had said. Lyubov had tried to get her released, but she was in the HQ kitchen, and the sergeants who managed the kitchen-gang resented any interference from "brass" and "speshes." Lyubov had to be very careful, lest they take out their resentment on the woman. She and Selver had both seemed willing to wait patiently until both could escape or be freed. Male and female creechies were strictly segregated in the pens—why, no one seemed to know —and husband and wife rarely saw each other. Lyubov managed to arrange meetings for them in his hut, which he had to himself at the north end of town. It was when Thele was returning to HQ from one such meeting that Davidson had seen her and apparently been struck by her frail, frightened grace. He had had her brought to his quarters that night, and had raped her.

He had killed her in the act, perhaps; this had happened before, a result of the physical disparity; or else she had stopped living. Like some Terrans the Athsheans had the knack of the authentic death-wish, and could cease to live. In either case it was Davidson who had killed her. Such murders had occurred before. What had not occurred before was what Selver did, the second day after her death.

Lyubov had got there only at the end. He could recall the sounds; himself running down Main Street in hot sunlight; the dust, the knot of men. The whole thing could have lasted only five minutes, a long time for a homicidal fight. When Lyubov got there Selver was blinded with blood, a sort of toy for Davidson to play with, and yet he had picked himself up and was coming back, not with berserk rage but with intelligent despair. He kept coming back. It was Davidson who was scared into rage at last by that terrible persistence; knocking Selver down with a side-blow he had moved forward lifting his booted foot to stamp on the skull. Even as he moved, Lyubov had broken into the circle. He stopped the fight (for whatever blood-thirst the ten or twelve men watching had had, was more than appeased, and they backed Lyubov when he told Davidson hands off); and thenceforth he hated Davidson, and was hated by him, having come between the killer and his death.

For if it's all the rest of us who are killed by the suicide, it's himself whom the murderer kills; only he has to do it over, and over, and over.

Lyubov had picked up Selver, a light weight in his arms. The mutilated face had pressed against his shirt so that the blood soaked through against his own skin. He had taken Selver to his own bungalow, splinted his broken wrist, done what he could for his face, kept him in his own bed, night after night tried to talk to him, to reach him in the desolation of his grief and shame. It was, of course, against regulations.

Nobody mentioned the regulations to him. They did not have to. He knew he was forfeiting most of what favor he had ever had with the officers of the colony.

He had been careful to keep on the right side of HQ, objecting only to extreme cases of brutality against the natives, using persuasion not defiance, and conserving what shred of power and influence he had. He could not prevent the exploitation of the Athsheans. It was much worse than his training had led him to expect, but he could do little about it here and now. His reports to the Administration and to the Committee on Rights might—after the roundtrip of fifty-four years—have some effect; Terra might even decide that the Open Colony policy for Athshe was a bad mistake. Better fifty-four years late than never. If he lost the tolerance of his superiors here they would censor or invalidate his reports, and there would be no hope at all.

But he was too angry now to keep up his strategy. To hell with the others, if they insisted on seeing his care of a friend as an insult to Mother Earth and a betrayal of the colony. If they labelled him "creechie-lover" his usefulness to the Athsheans would be impaired; but he could not set a possible, general good above Selver's imperative need. You can't save a people by selling your friend. Davidson, curiously infuriated by the minor injuries Selver had done him and by Lyubov's interference, had gone around saying he intended to finish off that rebel creechie; he certainly would do so if he got the chance. Lyubov stayed with Selver night and day for two weeks, and then flew him out of Central and put him down in a west coast town, Broter, where he had relatives.

There was no penalty for aiding slaves to escape, since the Athsheans were not slaves at all except in fact: they were Voluntary Autochthonous Labor Personnel. Lyubov was not even reprimanded. But the regular officers distrusted him totally, instead of partially, from then on; and even his colleagues in the Special Services, the exobiologist, the ag and forestry coordinators, the ecologists, variously let him know that he had been irrational, quixotic, or stupid. "Did you think you were coming on a picnic?" Gosse had demanded.

"No. I didn't think it would be any bloody picnic," Lyubov answered, morose.

"I can't see why any hilfer voluntarily ties himself up to an Open Colony. You know the people you're studying are going to get plowed under, and probably wiped out. It's the way things are. It's human nature, and you must know you can't change that. Then why come and watch the process? Masochism?"

"I don't know what 'human nature' is. Maybe leaving descriptions of what we wipe out is part of human nature.—Is it much pleasanter for an ecologist, really?"

Gosse ignored this. "All right then, write up your descriptions. But keep out of the carnage. A biologist studying a rat colony doesn't start reaching in and rescuing pet rats of his that get attacked, you know."

At this Lyubov had blown loose. He had taken too much. "No, of course not," he said. "A rat can be a pet, but not a friend. Selver is my friend. In fact he's the only man on this world whom I consider to be a friend." That had hurt poor old Gosse, who wanted to be a father-figure to Lyubov, and it had done nobody any good. Yet it had been true. And the truth shall make you free . . . I like Selver, respect him; saved him; suffered with him; fear him. Selver is my friend.

Selver is a god.

So the little green crone had said as if everybody knew it, as flatly as she might have said So-and-so is a hunter. "Selver sha'ab." What did *sha'ab* mean, though? Many words of the Women's Tongue, the everyday speech of the Athsheans, came from the Men's Tongue that was the same in all communities, and these words often were not only two-syllabled but two-sided. They were coins, obverse and reverse. *Sha'ab* meant god, or numinous entity, or powerful being; it also meant something quite different, but Lyubov could not remember what. By this stage in his thinking, he was home in his bungalow, and had only to look it up in the dictionary which he and Selver had compiled in four months of exhausting but harmonious work. Of course: *sha'ab*, translator.

It was almost too pat, too apposite.

Were the two meanings connected? Often they were, yet not so often as to constitute a rule. If a god was a translator,

70

what did he translate? Selver was indeed a gifted interpreter, but that gift had found expression only through the fortuity of a truly foreign language having been brought into his world. Was a *sha'ab* one who translated the language of dream and philosophy, the Men's Tongue, into the everyday speech? But all Dreamers could do that. Might he then be one who could translate into waking life the central experience of vision: one serving as a link between the two realities, considered by the Athsheans as equal, the dream-time and the world-time, whose connections, though vital, are obscure. A link: one who could speak aloud the perceptions of the subconscious. To "speak" that tongue is to act. To do a new thing. To change or to be changed, radically, from the root. For the root is the dream.

And the translator is the god. Selver had brought a new word into the language of his people. He had done a new deed. The word, the deed, murder. Only a god could lead so great a newcomer as Death across the bridge between the worlds.

But had he learned to kill his fellowmen among his own dreams of outrage and bereavement, or from the undreamed-of actions of the strangers? Was he speaking his own language, or was he speaking Captain Davidson's? That which seemed to rise from the root of his own suffering and express his own changed being, might in fact be an infection, a foreign plague, which would not make a new people of his race, but would destroy them.

It was not in Raj Lyubov's nature to think, "What can I do?" Character and training disposed him not to interfere in other men's business. His job was to find out what they did, and his inclination was to let them go on doing it. He preferred to be enlightened, rather than to enlighten; to seek facts rather than the Truth. But even the most unmissionary soul, unless he pretend he has no emotions, is sometimes faced with a choice between commission and omission. "What are they doing?" abruptly becomes, "What are we doing?" and then, "What must I do?"

That he had reached such a point of choice now, he knew, and yet did not know clearly why, nor what alternatives were offered him.

He could do no more to improve the Athsheans' chance of survival at the moment; Lepennon, Or, and the ansible had done more than he had hoped to see done in his lifetime. The

Administration on Terra was explicit in every ansible communication, and Colonel Dongh, though under pressure from some of his staff and the logging bosses to ignore the directives, was carrying out orders. He was a loyal officer; and besides, the *Shackleton* would be coming back to observe and report on how orders were being carried out. Reports home meant something, now that this ansible, this *machina ex machina*, functioned to prevent all the comfortable old colonial autonomy, and make you answerable within your own lifetime for what you did. There was no more fifty-four-year margin for error. Policy was no longer static. A decision by the League of Worlds might now lead overnight to the colony's being limited to one Land, or forbidden to cut trees, or encouraged to kill natives—no telling. How the League worked and what sort of policies it was developing could not yet be guessed from the flat directives of the Administration. Dongh was worried by these multiple-choice futures, but Lyubov enjoyed them. In diversity is life and where there's life there's hope, was the general sum of his creed, a modest one to be sure.

The colonists were letting the Athsheans alone and they were letting the colonists alone. A healthy situation, and one not to be disturbed unnecessarily. The only thing likely to disturb it was fear.

At the moment the Athsheans might be expected to be suspicious and still resentful, but not particularly afraid. As for the panic felt in Centralville at news of the Smith Camp massacre, nothing had happened to revive it. No Athshean anywhere had shown any violence since; and with the slaves gone, the creechies all vanished back into their forests, there was no more constant irritation of xenophobia. The colonists were at last beginning to relax.

If Lyubov reported that he had seen Selver at Tuntar, Dongh and the others would be alarmed. They might insist on trying to capture Selver and bring him in for trial. The Colonial Code forbade prosecution of a member of one planetary society under the laws of another, but the Court Martial over-rode such distinctions. They could try, convict, and shoot Selver. With Davidson brought back from New Java to give evidence. Oh no, Lyubov thought, shoving the dictionary onto an overcrowded shelf. Oh no, he thought, and thought no more about it. So he made his choice without even knowing he had made one.

He turned in a brief report next day. It said that Tuntar

was going about its business as usual, and that he had not been turned away or threatened. It was a soothing report, and the most inaccurate one Lyubov ever wrote. It omitted everything of significance: the headwoman's non-appearance, Tubab's refusal to greet Lyubov, the large number of strangers in town, the young huntress' expression, Selver's presence . . . Of course that last was an intentional omission, but otherwise the report was quite factual, he thought; he had merely omitted subjective impressions, as a scientist should. He had a severe migraine whilst writing the report, and a worse one after submitting it.

He dreamed a lot that night, but could not remember his dreams in the morning. Late in the second night after his visit to Tuntar he woke, and in the hysterical whooping of the alarm-siren and the thudding of explosions he faced, at last, what he had refused. He was the only man in Centralville not taken by surprise. In that moment he knew what he was: a traitor.

And yet even now it was not clear in his mind that this was an Athshean raid. It was the terror in the night.

His own hut had been ignored, standing in its yard away from other houses; perhaps the trees around it protected it, he thought as he hurried out. The center of town was all on fire. Even the stone cube of HQ burned from within like a broken kiln. The ansible was in there: the precious link. There were fires also in the direction of the helicopter port and the Field. Where had they got explosives? How had the fires got going all at once? All the buildings along both sides of Main Street, built of wood, were burning; the sound of the burning was terrible. Lyubov ran towards the fires. Water flooded the way; he thought at first it was from a fire-hose, then realised the main from the river Menend was flooding uselessly over the ground while the houses burned with that hideous sucking roar. How had they done this? There were guards, there were always guards in jeeps at the Field . . . Shots: volleys, the yatter of a machinegun. All around Lyubov were small running figures, but he ran among them without giving them much thought. He was abreast of the Hostel now, and saw a girl standing in the doorway, fire flickering at her back and a clear escape before her. She did not move. He shouted at her, then ran across the yard to her and wrested her hands free of the doorjambs which she clung to in panic, pulling her away by force, saying gently, "Come on, honey, come on." She came then, but not quite soon enough.

73

As they crossed the yard the front of the upper storey, blazing from within, fell slowly forward, pushed by the timbers of the collapsing roof. Shingles and beams shot out like shell-fragments; a blazing beam-end struck Lyubov and knocked him sprawling. He lay face down in the firelit lake of mud. He did not see a little green-furred huntress leap at the girl, drag her down backwards, and cut her throat. He did not see anything.

VI

No songs were sung that night. There was only shouting and silence. When the flying ships burned Selver exulted, and tears came into his eyes, but no words into his mouth. He turned away in silence, the fire thrower heavy in his arms, to lead his group back into the city.

Each group of people from the West and North was led by an ex-sláve like himself, one who had served the yumens in Central and knew the buildings and ways of the city.

Most of the people who came to the attack that night had never seen the yumen city; many of them had never seen a yumen. They had come because they followed Selver, because they were driven by the evil dream and only Selver could teach them how to master it. There were hundreds and hundreds of them, men and women; they had waited in utter silence in the rainy darkness all around the edges of the city, while the ex-slaves, two or three at a time, did those things which they judged must be done first: break the water-pipe, cut the wires that carried light from Generator House, break into and rob the Arsenal. The first deaths, those of guards, had been silent, accomplished with hunting weapons, noose, knife, arrow, very quickly, in the dark. The dynamite, stolen earlier in the night from the logging camp ten miles south, was prepared in the Arsenal, the basement of HQ Building, while fires were set in other places; and then the alarm went off and the fires blazed and both night and silence fled. Most of the thunderclap and tree-fall crashing of gunfire came from the yumens defending themselves, for only ex-slaves had taken weapons from the Arsenal and used them; all the rest kept to their own lances, knives, and bows. But it was the dynamite, placed and ignited by Reswan and others who had worked in the loggers' slave-pen, that made the noise that conquered all other noises, and blew out the walls of the HQ Building and destroyed the hangars and the ships.

74

There were about seventeen hundred yumens in the city that night, about five hundred of them female; all the yumen females were said to be there now, that was why Selver and the others had decided to act, though not all the people who wished to come had yet gathered. Between four and five thousand men and women had come through the forests to the Meeting at Endtor, and from there to this place, to this night.

The fires burned huge, and the smell of burning and of butchering was foul.

Selver's mouth was dry and his throat sore, so that he could not speak, and longed for water to drink. As he led his group down the middle path of the city, a yumen came running towards him, looming huge in the black and dazzle of the smoky air. Selver lifted the fire-thrower and pulled back on the tongue of it, even as the yumen slipped in mud and fell scrambling to its knees. No hissing jet of flame sprang from the machine, it had all been spent on burning the airships that had not been in the hangar. Selver dropped the heavy machine. The yumen was not armed, and was male. Selver tried to say, "Let him run away," but his voice was weak, and two men, hunters of the Abtam Glades, had leapt past him even as he spoke, holding their long knives up. The big, naked hands clutched at air, and dropped limp. The big corpse lay in a heap on the path. There were many others lying dead, there in what had been the center of the city. There was not much noise anymore except the noise of the fires.

Selver parted his lips and hoarsely sent up the home-call that ends the hunt; those with him took it up more clearly and loudly, in carrying falsetto; other voices answered it, near and far off in the mist and reek and flame-shot darkness of the night. Instead of leading his group at once from the city, he signalled them to go on, and himself went aside, onto the muddy ground between the path and a building which had burned and fallen. He stepped across a dead female yumen and bent over one that lay pinned down under a great, charred beam of wood. He could not see the features obliterated by mud and shadow.

It was not just; it was not necessary; he need not have looked at that one among so many dead. He need not have known him in the dark. He started to go after his group. Then he turned back; straining, lifted the beam off Lyubov's back; knelt down, slipping one hand under the heavy head so that Lyubov seemed to lie easier, his face clear of the earth; and so knelt there, motionless.

He had not slept for four days and had not been still to dream for longer than that—he did not know how long. He had acted, spoken, travelled, planned, night and day, ever since he left Broter with his followers from Cadast. He had gone from city to city speaking to the people of the forest, telling them the new thing, waking them from the dream into the world, arranging the thing done this night, talking, always talking and hearing others talk, never in silence and never alone. .They had listened, they had heard and had come to follow him, to follow the new path. They had taken up the fire they feared into their own hands: taken up the mastery over the evil dream: and loosed the death they feared upon their enemy. All had been done as he said it should be done. All had gone as he said it would go. The lodges and many dwellings of the yumens were burnt, their airships burnt or broken, their weapons stolen or destroyed: and their females were dead. The fires were burning out, the night growing very dark, fouled with smoke. Selver could scarcely see; he looked up to the east, wondering if it were nearing dawn. Kneeling there in the mud among the dead he thought, This is the dream now, the evil dream. I thought to drive it, but it drives me.

In the dream, Lyubov's lips moved a little against the palm of his own hand; Selver looked down and saw the dead man's eyes open. The glare of dying fires shone on the surface of them. After a while he spoke Selver's name.

"Lyubov, why did you stay here? I told you to be out of the city this night." So Selver spoke in dream, harshly, as if he were angry at Lyubov.

"Are you the prisoner?" Lyubov said, faintly and not lifting his head, but in so commonplace a voice that Selver knew for a moment that this was not the dream-time but the world-time, the forest's night. "Or am I?"

"Neither, both, how do I know? All the engines and machines are burned. All the women are dead. We let the men run away if they would. I told them not to set fire to your house, the books will be all right. Lyubov, why aren't you like the others?"

"I am like them. A man. Like them. Like you."

"No. You are different—"

"I am like them. And so are you. Listen, Selver. Don't go on. You must not go on killing other men. You must go back . . . to your own . . . to your roots."

76

"When your people are gone, then the evil dream will stop."

"*Now*," Lyubov said, trying to lift his head, but his back was broken. He looked up at Selver and opened his mouth to speak. His gaze dropped away and looked into the other time, and his lips remained parted, unspeaking. His breath whistled a little in his throat.

They were calling Selver's name, many voices far away, calling over and over. "I can't stay with you, Lyubov!" Selver said in tears, and when there was no answer stood up and tried to run away. But in the dream-darkness he could go only very slowly, like one wading through deep water. The Ash Spirit walked in front of him, taller than Lyubov or any yumen, tall as a tree, not turning its white mask to him. As Selver went he spoke to Lyubov: "We'll go back," he said. "I will go back. Now. We will go back, now, I promise you, Lyubov!"

But his friend the gentle one, who had saved his life and betrayed his dream, Lyubov did not reply. He walked somewhere in the night near Selver, unseen, and quiet as death.

A group of the people of Tuntar came on Selver wandering in the dark, weeping and speaking, overmastered by dream; they took him with them in their swift return to Endtor.

In the makeshift Lodge there, a tent on the river-bank, he lay helpless and insane for two days and nights, while the Old Men tended him. All that time people kept coming in to Endtor and going out again, returning to the Place of Eshsen which had been called Central, burying their dead there and the alien dead: of theirs more than three hundred, of the others more than seven hundred. There were about five hundred yumens locked into the compound, the creechie-pens, which, standing empty and apart, had not been burnt. As many more had escaped, some of whom had got to the logging camps farther south, which had not been attacked; those who were still hiding and wandering in the forest or the Cut Lands were hunted down. Some were killed, for many of the younger hunters and huntresses still heard only Selver's voice saying *Kill them*. Others had left the night of killing behind them as if it had been a nightmare, the evil dream that must be understood lest it be repeated; and these, faced with a thirsty, exhausted yumen cowering in a thicket, could not kill him. So maybe he killed them. There were groups of ten and twenty yumens, armed with logger's axes and hand-guns, though few had ammunition left; these groups were tracked until sufficient numbers were hidden in the forest about them, then overpowered, bound, and led back to Eshsen. They were all captured within two or three days, for all that part of Sornol was swarming with the people of the forest, there had never in the knowledge of any man been half or a tenth so great a gathering of people in one place; some still coming in from distant towns and other Lands, others already going home again. The captured yumens were put in among the others in the compound, though it was overcrowded and the huts were too small for yumens. They were watered, fed twice daily, and guarded by a couple of hundred armed hunters at all times.

In the afternoon following the Night of Eshsen an airship came rattling out of the east and flew low as if to land, then shot upward like a bird of prey that misses its kill, and circled the wrecked landing-place, the smouldering city, and the Cut Lands. Reswan had seen to it that the radios were destroyed, and perhaps it was the silence of the radios that had brought the airship from Kushil or Rieshwel, where there were three small towns of yumens. The prisoners in the compound rushed out of the barracks and yelled at the machine whenever it came rattling overhead, and once it dropped an object on a small parachute into the compound: at last it rattled off into the sky.

There were four such winged ships left on Athshe now, three on Kushil and one on Rieshwel, all of the small kind that carried four men; they also carried machineguns and flamethrowers, and they weighed much on the minds of Reswan and the others, while Selver lay lost to them, walking the cryptic ways of the other time.

He woke into the world-time on the third day, thin, dazed, hungry, silent. After he had bathed in the river and had eaten, he listened to Reswan and the headwoman of Berre and the others chosen as leaders. They told him how the world had gone while he dreamed. When he had heard them all, he looked about at them and they saw the god in him. In the sickness of disgust and fear that followed the Night of Eshsen, some of them had come to doubt. Their dreams were uneasy and full of blood and fire; they were surrounded all day by strangers, people come from all over the forests, hundreds of them, thousands, all gathered here like kites to carrion, none knowing another: and it seemed to them as if the end of things had come and nothing would ever be the same, or be right, again. But in Selver's presence they remembered purpose; their distress was quietened, and they waited for him to speak.

"The killing is all done," he said. "Make sure that everyone knows that." He looked round at them. "I have to talk with the ones in the compound. Who is leading them in there?"

"Turkey, Flapfeet, Weteyes," said Reswan, the ex-slave.

"Turkey's alive? Good. Help me get up, Greda, I have eels for bones . . ."

When he had been afoot a while he was stronger, and within the hour he set off for Eshsen, two hours' walk from Endtor.

When they came Reswan mounted a ladder set against the compound wall and bawled in the pidgin-English taught the slaves, "Dong-a come to gate hurry-up-quick!"

Down in the alleys between the squat cement barracks, some of the yumens yelled and threw clods of dirt at him. He ducked, and waited.

The old Colonel did not come out, but Gosse, whom they called Weteyes, came limping out of a hut and called up to Reswan, "Colonel Dongh is ill, he cannot come out."

"Ill what kind?"

"Bowels, water-illness. What you want?"

"Talk-talk.—My lord god," Reswan said in his own language, looking down at Selver, "the Turkey's hiding, do you want to talk with Weteyes?"

"All right."

"Watch the gate there, you bowmen!—To gate, Mis-ter Goss-a, hurry-up-quick!"

The gate was opened just wide enough and long enough for Gosse to squeeze out. He stood in front of it alone, facing the group led by Selver. He favored one leg, injured on the night of Eshsen. He was wearing torn pajamas, mud-stained and rain-sodden. His greying hair hung in lank festoons around his ears and over his forehead. Twice the height of his captors, he held himself very stiff, and stared at them in courageous, angry misery. "What you want?"

"We must talk, Mr. Gosse," said Selver, who had learned plain English from Lyubov. "I'm Selver of the Ash Tree of Eshreth. I'm Lyubov's friend."

"Yes, I know you. What have you to say?"

"I have to say that the killing is over, if that be made a promise kept by your people and my people. You may all go free, if you will gather in your people from the logging camps in South Sornol, Kushil, and Rieshwel, and make them all stay together here. You may live here where the forest is dead, where you grow your seed-grasses. There must not be any more cutting of trees."

Gosse's face had grown eager: "The camps weren't attacked?"

"No."

Gosse said nothing.

Selver watched his face, and presently spoke again: "There are less than two thousand of your people left living in the world, I think. Your women are all dead. In the other camps there are still weapons; you could kill many of us. But we have some of your weapons. And there are more of us than you could kill. I suppose you know that, and that's why you have not tried to have the flying ships bring you fire-throwers, and kill the guards, and escape. It would be not good; there really are so many of us. If you make the promise with us it will be much the best, and then you can wait without harm until one of your Great Ships comes, and you can leave the world. That will be in three years, I think."

"Yes, three local years—How do you know that?"

"Well, slaves have ears, Mr. Gosse."

Gosse looked straight at him at last. He looked away, fidgeted, tried to ease his leg. He looked back at Selver, and away again. "We had already 'promised' not to hurt any of your people. It's why the workers were sent home. It did no good, you didn't listen—"

"It was not a promise made to us."

"How can we make any sort of agreement or treaty with a people who have no government, no central authority?"

"I don't know. I'm not sure you know what a promise is. This one was soon broken."

"What do you mean? By whom, how?"

"In Rieshwel, New Java. Fourteen days ago. A town was burned and its people killed by yumens of the Camp in Rieshwel."

"What are you talking about?"

"About news brought us by messengers from Rieshwel."

"It's a lie. We were in radio contact with New Java right along, until the massacre. Nobody was killing natives there or anywhere else."

"You're speaking the truth you know," Selver said, "I the truth I know. I accept your ignorance of the killings on
80

Rieshwel; but you must accept my telling you that they were done. This remains: the promise must be made to us and with us, and it must be kept. You'll wish to talk about these matters with Colonel Dongh and the others."

Gosse moved as if to re-enter the gate, then turned back and said in his deep hoarse voice, "Who are you, Selver? Did you—was it you that organised the attack? Did you lead them?"

"Yes, I did."

"Then all this blood is on your head," Gosse said, and with sudden savagery, "Lyubov's too, you know. He's dead—your 'friend Lyubov.'"

Selver did not understand the idiom. He had learned murder, but of guilt he knew little beyond the name. As his gaze locked for a moment with Gosse's pale, resentful stare, he felt afraid. A sickness rose up in him, a mortal chill. He tried to put it away from him, shutting his eyes a moment. At last he said, "Lyubov is my friend, and so not dead."

"You're children," Gosse said with hatred. "Children, savages. You have no conception of reality. This is no dream, this is real! You killed Lyubov. He's dead. You killed the women—the *women*—you burned them alive, slaughtered them like animals!"

"Should we have let them live?" said Selver with vehemence equal to Gosse's, but softly, his voice singing a little. "To breed like insects in the carcass of the World? To overrun us? We killed them to sterilise you. I know what a realist is, Mr. Gosse. Lyubov and I have talked about these words. A realist is a man who knows both the world and his own dreams. You're not sane: there's not one man in a thousand of you who knows how to dream. Not even Lyubov and he was the best among you. You sleep, you wake and forget your dreams, you sleep again and wake again, and so you spend your whole lives, and you think that is being, life, reality! You are not children, you are grown men, but insane. And that's why we had to kill you, before you drove us mad. Now go back and talk about reality with the other insane men. Talk long, and well!"

The guards opened the gate, threatening the crowding yumens inside with their spears; Gosse re-entered the compound, his big shoulders hunched as if against the rain.

Selver was very tired. The headwoman of Berre and another woman came to him and walked with him, his arms over their shoulders so that if he stumbled he should not fall.

The young hunter Greda, a cousin of his Tree, joked with him, and Selver answered light-headedly, laughing. The walk back to Endtor seemed to go on for days.

He was too weary to eat. He drank a little hot broth and lay down by the Men's Fire. Endtor was no town but a mere camp by the great river, a favorite fishing place for all the cities that had once been in the forest round about, before the yumens came. There was no Lodge. Two fire-rings of black stone and a long grassy bank over the river where tents of hide and plaited rush could be set up, that was Endtor. The river Menend, the master river of Sornol, spoke ceaselessly in the world and in the dream at Endtor.

There were many old men at the fire, some whom he knew from Broter and Tuntar and his own destroyed city Eshreth, some whom he did not know; he could see in their eyes and gestures, and hear in their voices, that they were Great Dreamers; more dreamers than had ever been gathered in one place before, perhaps. Lying stretched out full length, his head raised on his hands, gazing at the fire, he said, "I have called the yumens mad. Am I mad myself?"

"You don't know one time from the other," said old Tubab, laying a pine-knot on the fire, "because you did not dream either sleeping or waking for far too long. The price for that takes long to pay."

"The poisons the yumens take do much the same as does the lack of sleep and dream," said Heben, who had been a slave both at Central and Smith Camp. "The yumens poison themselves in order to dream. I saw the dreamer's look in them after they took the poisons. But they couldn't call the dreams, nor control them, nor weave nor shape nor cease to dream; they were driven, overpowered. They did not know what was within them at all. So it is with a man who hasn't dreamed for many days. Though he be the wisest of his Lodge, still he'll be mad, now and then, here and there, for a long time after. He'll be driven, enslaved. He will not understand himself."

A very old man with the accent of South Sornol laid his hand on Selver's shoulder, caressing him, and said, "My dear young god, you need to sing, that would do you good."

"I can't. Sing for me."

The old man sang; others joined in, their voices high and reedy, almost tuneless, like the wind blowing in the water-reeds of Endtor. They sang one of the songs of the ash-tree, about the delicate parted leaves that turn yellow in autumn

82

when the berries turn red, and one night the first frost silvers them.

While Selver was listening to the song of the Ash, Lyubov lay down beside him. Lying down he did not seem so monstrously tall and large-limbed. Behind him was the half-collapsed, fire-gutted building, black against the stars. "I am like you," he said, not looking at Selver, in that dream-voice which tries to reveal its own untruth. Selver's heart was heavy with sorrow for his friend. "I've got a headache," Lyubov said in his own voice, rubbing the back of his neck as he always did, and at that Selver reached out to touch him, to console him. But he was shadow and firelight in the world-time, and the old men were singing the song of the Ash, about the small white flowers on the black branches in spring among the parted leaves.

The next day the yumens imprisoned in the compound sent for Selver. He came to Eshsen in the afternoon, and met with them outside the compound, under the branches of an oak-tree, for all Selver's people felt a little uneasy under the bare open sky. Eshsen had been an oak grove; this tree was the largest of the few the colonists had left standing. It was on the long slope behind Lyubov's bungalow, one of the six or eight houses that had come through the night of the burning undamaged. With Selver under the oak were Reswan, the headwoman of Berre, Greda of Cadast, and others who wished to be in on the parley, a dozen or so in all. Many bowmen kept guard, fearing the yumens might have hidden weapons, but they sat behind bushes or bits of wreckage left from the burning, so as not to dominate the scene with the hint of threat. With Gosse and Colonel Dongh were three of the yumens called officers and two from the logging camp, at the sight of one of whom, Benton, the ex-slaves drew in their breaths. Benton had used to punish "lazy creechies" by castrating them in public.

The Colonel looked thin, his normally yellow-brown skin a muddy yellow-grey; his illness had been no sham. "Now the first thing is," he said when they were all settled, the yumens standing, Selver's people squatting or sitting on the damp, soft oak-leafmould, "the first thing is that I want first to have a working definition of just precisely what these terms of yours mean and what they mean in terms of guaranteed safety of my personnel under my command here."

There was a silence.

"You understand English, don't you, some of you?"

"Yes. I don't understand your question, Mr. Dongh."

"Colonel Dongh, if you please!"

"Then you'll call me Colonel Selver, if you please." A singing note came into Selver's voice; he stood up, ready for the contest, tunes running in his mind like rivers.

But the old yumen just stood there, huge and heavy, angry yet not meeting the challenge. "I did not come here to be insulted by you little humanoids," he said. But his lips trembled as he said it. He was old, and bewildered, and humiliated. All anticipation of triumph went out of Selver. There was no triumph in the world any more, only death. He sat down again. "I didn't intend insult, Colonel Dongh," he said resignedly. "Will you repeat your question, please?"

"I want to hear your terms, and then you'll hear ours, that's all there is to it."

Selver repeated what he had said to Gosse.

Dongh listened with apparent impatience. "All right. Now you don't realise that we've had a functioning radio in the prison compound for three days now." Selver did know this, as Reswan had at once checked on the object dropped by the helicopter, lest it be a weapon; the guards reported it was a radio, and he let the yumens keep it. Selver merely nodded. "So we've been in contact with the three outlying camps, the two on King Land and one on New Java, right along, and if we had decided to make a break for it and escape from that prison compound then it would have been very simple for us to do that, with the helicopters to drop us weapons and covering our movements with their mounted weapons, one flamethrower could have got us out of the compound and in case of need they also have the bombs that can blow up an entire area. You haven't seen those in action of course."

"If you'd left the compound, where would you have gone?"

"The point is, without introducing into this any beside the point or erroneous factors, now we are certainly greatly outnumbered by your forces, but we have the four helicopters at the camps, which there's no use you trying to disable as they are under fully armed guard at all times now, and also all the serious fire-power, so that the cold reality of the situation is we can pretty much call it a draw and speak in positions of mutual equality. This of course is a temporary situation. If necessary we are enabled to maintain a defensive police action to prevent all-out war. Moreover we have behind us the entire fire-power of the Terran Interstellar Fleet, which could blow your entire planet right out of the sky. But these ideas are pretty intangible to you, so let's just put it as plainly and simply as I can, that we're prepared to negotiate with you, for the present time, in terms of an equal frame of reference."

Selver's patience was short; he knew his ill-temper was a symptom of his deteriorated mental state, but he could no longer control it. "Go on, then!"

"Well, first I want it clearly understood that as soon as we got the radio we told the men at the other camps not to bring us weapons and not to try any airlift or rescue attempts, and reprisals were strictly out of order—"

"That was prudent. What next?"

Colonel Dongh began an angry retort, then stopped; he turned very pale. "Isn't there anything to sit down on," he said.

Selver went around the yumen group, up the slope, into the empty two-room bungalow, and took the folding desk-chair. Before he left the silent room he leaned down and laid his cheek on the scarred, raw wood of the desk, where Lyubov had always sat when he worked with Selver or alone; some of his papers were lying there now; Selver touched them lightly. He carried the chair out and set it in the rainwet dirt for Dongh. The old man sat down, biting his lips, his almond-shaped eyes narrow with pain.

"Mr. Gosse, perhaps you can speak for the Colonel," Selver said. "He isn't well."

"I'll do the talking," Benton said, stepping forward, but Dongh shook his head and muttered, "Gosse."

With the Colonel as auditor rather than speaker it went more easily. The yumens were accepting Selver's terms. With a mutual promise of peace, they would withdraw all their outposts and live in one area, the region they had forested in Middle Sornol: about seventeen hundred square miles of rolling land, well watered. They undertook not to enter the forest; the forest people undertook not to trespass on the Cut Lands.

The four remaining airships were the cause of some argument. The yumens insisted they needed them to bring their people from the other islands to Sornol. Since the machines carried only four men and would take several hours for each trip, it appeared to Selver that the yumens could get to Eshsen rather sooner by walking, and he offered them ferry service across the straits; but it appeared that yumens never walked far. Very well, they could keep the hoppers for what

85

they called the "Airlift Operation." After that, they were to destroy them.—Refusal. Anger. They were more protective of their machines than of their bodies. Selver gave in, saying they could keep the hoppers if they flew them only over the Cut Lands and if the weapons in them were destroyed. Over this they argued, but with one another, while Selver waited, occasionally repeating the terms of his demand, for he was not giving in on this point.

"What's the difference, Benton," the old Colonel said at last, furious and shaky, "can't you see that we can't use the damned weapons? There's three million of these aliens all scattered out all over every damned island, all covered with trees and undergrowth, no cities, no vital network, no centralised control. You can't disable a guerrilla type structure with bombs, it's been proved, in fact my own part of the world where I was born proved it for about thirty years fighting off major super-powers one after the other in the twentieth century. And we're not in a position until a ship comes to prove our superiority. Let the big stuff go, if we can hold on to the side-arms for hunting and self-defense!"

He was their Old Man, and his opinion prevailed in the end, as it might have done in a Men's Lodge. Benton sulked. Gosse started to talk about what would happen if the truce was broken, but Selver stopped him. "These are possibilities, we aren't yet done with certainties. Your Great Ship is to return in three years, that is three and a half years of your count. Until that time you are free here. It will not be very hard for you. Nothing more will be taken away from Centralville, except some of Lyubov's work that I wish to keep. You still have most of your tools of tree-cutting and ground-moving; if you need more tools, the iron-mines of Peldel are in your territory. I think all this is clear. What remains to be known is this: When that ship comes, what will they seek to do with you, and with us?"

"We don't know," Gosse said. Dongh amplified: "If you hadn't destroyed the ansible communicator first thing off, we might be receiving some current information on these matters, and our reports would of course influence the decisions that may be made concerning a finalised decision on the status of this planet, which we might then expect to begin to implement before the ship returns from Prestno. But due to wanton destruction due to your ignorance of your own interests, we haven't even got a radio left that will transmit over a few hundred miles."

"What is the ansible?" The word had come up before in this talk; it was a new one to Selver.

"ICD," the Colonel said, morose.

"A kind of radio," Gosse said, arrogant. "It put us in instant touch with our home-world."

"Without the twenty-seven-year waiting?"

Gosse stared down at Selver. "Right. Quite right. You learned a great deal from Lyubov, didn't you?"

"Didn't he just," said Benton. "He was Lyubov's little green buddyboy. He picked up everything worth knowing and a bit more besides. Like all the vital points to sabotage, and where the guards would be posted, and how to get into the weapon stock-pile. They must have been in touch right up to the moment the massacre started."

Gosse looked uneasy. "Raj is dead. All that's irrelevant now, Benton. We've got to establish—"

"Are you trying to infer in some way that Captain Lyubov was involved in some activity that could be called treachery to the Colony, Benton?" said Dongh, glaring and pressing his hands against his belly. "There were no spies or treachers on my staff, it was absolutely handpicked before we ever left Terra and I know the kind of men I have to deal with."

"I'm not inferring anything, Colonel. I'm saying straight out that it was Lyubov stirred up the creechies, and if orders hadn't been changed on us after that Fleet ship was here, it never would have happened."

Gosse and Dongh both started to speak at once. "You are all very ill," Selver observed, getting up and dusting himself off, for the damp brown oak-leaves clung to his short body-fur as to silk. "I'm sorry we've had to hold you in the creechie-pen, it is not a good place for the mind. Please send for your men from the camps. When all are here and the large weapons have been destroyed, and the promise has been spoken by all of us, then we shall leave you alone. The gates of the compound will be opened when I leave here today. Is there more to be said?"

None of them said anything. They looked down at him. Seven big men, with tan or brown hairless skin, cloth-covered, dark-eyed, grim-faced; twelve small men, green or brownish-green, fur-covered, with the large eyes of the semi-nocturnal creature, with dreamy faces; between the two groups, Selver, the translator, frail, disfigured, holding all their destinies in his empty hands. Rain fell softly on the brown earth about them.

"Farewell then," Selver said, and led his people away.

"They're not so stupid," said the headwoman of Berre as she accompanied Selver back to Endtor. "I thought such giants must be stupid, but they saw that you're a god, I saw it in their faces at the end of the talking. How well you talk that goggle-gubble. Ugly they are, do you think even their children are hairless?"

"That we shall never know, I hope."

"Ugh, think of nursing a child that wasn't furry. Like trying to suckle a fish."

"They are all insane," said old Tubab, looking deeply distressed. "Lyubov wasn't like that, when he used to come to Tuntar. He was ignorant, but sensible. But these ones, they argue, and sneer at the old man, and hate each other, like this," and he contorted his grey-furred face to imitate the expressions of the Terrans, whose words of course he had not been able to follow. "Was that what you said to them, Selver, that they're mad?"

"I told them that they were ill. But then, they've been defeated, and hurt, and locked in that stone cage. After that anyone might be ill and need healing."

"Who's to heal them," said the headwoman of Berre, "their women are all dead. Too bad for them. Poor ugly things—great naked spiders they are, ugh!"

"They are men, men, like us, men," Selver said, his voice shrill and edged like a knife.

"Oh, my dear lord god, I know it, I only meant they *look* like spiders," said the old woman, caressing his cheek. "Look here, you people, Selver is worn out with this going back and forth between Endtor and Eshsen, let's sit down and rest a bit."

"Not here," Selver said. They were still in the Cut Lands, among stumps and grassy slopes, under the bare sky. "When we come under the trees . . ." He stumbled, and those who were not gods helped him to walk along the road.

VII

Davidson found a good use for Major Muhamed's tape recorder. Somebody had to make a record of events on New Tahiti, a history of the crucifixion of the Terran Colony. So that when the ships came from Mother Earth they could learn the truth. So that future generations could learn how much treachery and cowardice and folly humans were capa-

88

ble of, and how much courage against all odds. During his free moments—not much more than moments since he had assumed command—he recorded the whole story of the Smith Camp Massacre, and brought the record up to date for New Java, and for King and Central also, as well as he could with the garbled hysterical stuff that was all he got by way of news from Central HQ.

Exactly what had happened there nobody would ever know, except the creechies, for the humans were trying to cover up their own betrayals and mistakes. The outlines were clear, though. An organised bunch of creechies, led by Selver, had been let into the Arsenal and the Hangars, and turned loose with dynamite, grenades, guns, and flamethrowers to totally destruct the city and slaughter the humans. It was an inside job, the fact that HQ was the first place blown up proved that. Lyubov of course had been in on it, and his little green buddies had proved just as grateful as you might expect, and cut his throat like the others. At least, Gosse and Benton claimed to have seen him dead the morning after the massacre. But could you believe any of them, actually? You could assume that any human left alive in Central after that night was more or less of a traitor. A traitor to his race.

The women were all dead, they claimed. That was bad enough, but what was worse, there was no reason to believe it. It was easy for the creechies to take prisoners in the woods, and nothing would be easier to catch than a terrified girl running out of a burning town. And wouldn't the little green devils like to get hold of a human girl and try experiments on her? God knows how many of the women were still alive in the creechie warrens, tied down underground in one of those stinking holes, being touched and felt and crawled over and defiled by the filthy, hairy little monkeymen. It was unthinkable. But by God sometimes you have to be able to think about the unthinkable.

A hopper from King had dropped the prisoners at Central a receiver-transmitter the day after the massacre, and Muhamed had taped all his exchanges with Central starting that day. The most incredible one was a conversation between him and Colonel Dongh. The first time he played it Davidson had torn the thing right off the reel and burned it. Now he wished he had kept it, for the records, as a perfect proof of the total incompetence of the C.O.'s at both Central and New Java. He had given in to his own hotbloodedness, destroying it. But how could he sit there and listen to the recording of the Colonel and the Major discussing total surrender to the creechies, agreeing not to try retaliation, not to defend themselves, to give up all their big weapons, to all squeeze together onto a bit of land picked out for them by the creechies, a reservation conceded to them by their generous conquerors, the little green beasts. It was incredible. Literally incredible.

Probably old Ding Dong and Moo were not actually traitors by intent. They had just gone spla, lost their nerve. It was this damned planet that did it to them. It took a very strong personality to withstand it. There was something in the air, maybe pollens from all those trees, acting as some kind of drug maybe, that made ordinary humans begin to get as stupid and out of touch with reality as the creechies were. Then, being so outnumbered, they were pushovers for the creechies to wipe out.

It was too bad Muhamed had had to be put out of the way, but he would never have agreed to accept Davidson's plans, that was clear; he'd been too far gone. Anyone who'd heard that incredible tape would agree. So it was better he got shot before he really knew what was going on, and now no shame would attach to his name, as it would to Dongh's and all the other officers left alive at Central.

Dongh hadn't come on the radio lately. Usually it was Juju Sereng, in Engineering. Davidson had used to pal around a lot with Juju and had thought of him as a friend, but now you couldn't trust anybody any more. And Juju was another asiatiform. It was really queer how many of them had survived the Centralville Massacre; of those he'd talked to, the only non-asio was Gosse. Here in Java the fifty-five loyal men remaining after the reorganization were mostly eurafs like himself, some afros and afrasians, not one pure asio. Blood tells, after all. You couldn't be fully human without some blood in your veins from the Cradle of Man. But that wouldn't stop him from saving those poor yellow bastards at Central, it just helped explain their moral collapse under stress.

"Can't you realise what kind of trouble you're making for us, Don?" Juju Sereng had demanded in his flat voice. "We've made a formal truce with the creechies. And we're under direct orders from Earth not to interfere with the hilfs and not to retaliate. Anyhow how the hell can we retaliate? Now all the fellows from King Land and South Central are here with us we're still less than two thousand, and what have you got there on Java, about sixty-five men isn't it? Do you really think two thousand men can take on three million intelligent enemies, Don?"

"Juju, fifty men can do it. It's a matter of will, skill, and weaponry."

"Batshit! But the point is, Don, a truce has been made. And if it's broken, we've had it. It's all that keeps us afloat, now. Maybe when the ship gets back from Prestno and sees what happened, they'll decide to wipe out the creechies. We don't know. But it does look like the creechies intend to keep the truce, after all it was their idea, and we have got to. They can wipe us out by sheer numbers, any time, the way they did Centralville. There were thousands of them. Can't you understand that, Don?"

"Listen, Juju, sure I understand. If you're scared to use the three hoppers you've still got there, you could send 'em over here, with a few fellows who see things like we do here. If I'm going to liberate you fellows singlehanded, I sure could use some more hoppers for the job."

"You aren't going to liberate us, you're going to incinerate us, you damned fool. Get that last hopper over here to Central now: that's the Colonel's personal order to you as Acting C.O. Use it to fly your men here; twelve trips, you won't need more than four local dayperiods. Now act on those orders, and get to it." Ponk, off the air—afraid to argue with him any more.

At first he worried that they might send their three hoppers over and actually bomb or strafe New Java Camp; for he was, technically, disobeying orders, and old Dongh wasn't tolerant of independent elements. Look how he'd taken it out on Davidson already, for that tiny reprisal-raid on Smith. Initiative got punished. What Ding Dong liked was submission, like most officers. The danger with that is that it can make the officer get submissive himself. Davidson finally realized, with a real shock, that the hoppers were no threat to him, because Dongh, Sereng, Gosse, even Benton were *afraid* to send them. The creechies had ordered them to keep the hoppers inside the Human Reservation: and they were obeying orders.

Christ, it made him sick. It was time to act. They'd been waiting around nearly two weeks now. He had his camp well defended; they had strengthened the stockade fence and built it up so that no little green monkeymen could possibly get over it, and that clever kid Aabi had made lots of neat home-made land mines and sown 'em all around the stockade in a hundred-meter belt. Now it was time to show the creechies that they might push around those sheep on Central but on New Java it was men they had to deal with. He took the hopper up and with it guided an infantry squad of fifteen to a creechie-warren south of camp. He'd learned how to spot the things from the air; the giveaway was the orchards, concentrations of certain kinds of tree, though not planted in rows like humans would. It was incredible how many warrens there were once you learned to spot them. The forest was crawling with the things. The raiding party burned up that warren by hand, and then flying back with a couple of his boys he spotted another, less than four kilos from camp. On that one, just to write his signature real clear and plain for everybody to read, he dropped a bomb. Just a firebomb, not a big one, but baby did it make the green fur fly. It left a big hole in the forest, and the edges of the hole were burning.

Of course that was his real weapon when it actually came to setting up massive retaliation. Forest fire. He could set one of these whole islands on fire, with bombs and firejelly dropped from the hopper. Have to wait a month or two, till the rainy season was over. Should he burn King or Smith or Central? King first, maybe, as a little warning, since there were no humans left there. Then Central, if they didn't get in line.

"What are you trying to do?" said the voice on the radio, and it made him grin, it was so agonised, like some old woman being held up. "Do you know what you're doing, Davidson?"

"Yep."

"Do you think you're going to subdue the creechies?" It wasn't Juju this time, it might be that bigdome Gosse, or any of them; no difference; they all bleated baa.

"Yes, that's right," he said with ironic mildness.

"You think if you keep burning up villages they'll come to you and surrender—three million of them. Right?"

"Maybe."

"Look, Davidson," the radio said after a while, whining and buzzing; they were using some kind of emergency rig, having lost the big transmitter, along with that phoney ansible which was no loss. "Look, is there somebody else standing by there we can talk to?"

"No; they're all pretty busy. Say, we're doing great here, but we're out of dessert stuff, you know, fruit cocktail, peaches, crap like that. Some of the fellows really miss it. And we were due for a load of maryjanes when you fellows got blown up. If I sent the hopper over, could you spare us a few crates of sweet stuff and grass?"

A pause. "Yes, send it on over."

"Great. Have the stuff in a net, and the boys can hook it without landing." He grinned.

There was some fussing around at the Central end, and all of a sudden old Dongh was on, the first time he'd talked to Davidson. He sounded feeble and out of breath on the whining shortwave. "Listen, Captain, I want to know if you fully realize what form of action your actions on New Java are going to be forcing me into taking. If you continue to disobey your orders. I am trying to reason with you as a reasonable and loyal soldier. In order to ensure the safety of my personnel here at Central I'm going to be put into the position of being forced to tell the natives here that we can't assume any responsibility at all for your actions."

"That's correct, sir."

"What I'm trying to make clear to you is that means that we are going to be put into the position of having to tell them that we can't stop you from breaking the truce there on Java. Your personnel there is sixty-six men, is that correct, well I want those men safe and sound here at Central with us to wait for the *Shackleton* and keep the Colony together. You're on a suicide course and I'm responsible for those men you have there with you."

"No, you're not, sir. I am. You just relax. Only when you see the jungle burning, pick up and get out into the middle of a Strip, because we don't want to roast you folks along with the creechies."

"Now listen, Davidson, I order you to hand your command over to Lt. Temba at once and report to me here," said the distant whining voice, and Davidson suddenly cut off the radio, sickened. They were all spla, playing at still being soldiers, in full retreat from reality. There were actually very few men who could face reality when the going got tough.

As he expected, the local creechies did absolutely nothing about his raids on the warrens. The only way to handle them, as he'd known from the start, was to terrorise them and never let up on them. If you did that, they knew who was boss, and knuckled under. A lot of the villages within a thirty-kilo radius seemed to be deserted now before he got to them, but he kept his men going out to burn them up every few days.

The fellows were getting rather jumpy. He had kept them logging, since that's what forty-eight of the fifty-five loyal survivors were, loggers. But they knew that the robo-freighters from Earth wouldn't be called down to load up the lumber, but would just keep coming in and circling in orbit waiting for the signal that didn't come. No use cutting trees just for the hell of it; it was hard work. Might as well burn them. He exercised the men in teams, developing fire-setting techniques. It was still too rainy for them to do much, but it kept their minds busy. If only he had the other three hoppers, he'd really be able to hit and run. He considered a raid on Central to liberate the hoppers, but did not yet mention this idea even to Aabi and Temba, his best men. Some of the boys would get cold feet at the idea of an armed raid on their own HQ. They kept talking about "when we get back with the others." They didn't know those others had abandoned them, betrayed them, sold their skins to the creechies. He didn't tell them that, they couldn't take it.

One day he and Aabi and Temba and another good sound man would just take the hopper over, then three of them jump out with machineguns, take a hopper apiece, and so home again, home again, jiggety jog. With four nice egg-beaters to beat eggs with. Can't make an omelet without beating eggs. Davidson laughed aloud, in the darkness of his bungalow. He kept that plan hidden just a little longer, because it tickled him so much to think about it.

After two more weeks they had pretty well closed out the creechie-warrens within walking distance, and the forest was neat and tidy. No vermin. No smoke-puffs over the trees. Nobody hopping out of bushes and flopping down on the ground with their eyes shut, waiting for you to stomp them. No little green men. Just a mess of trees and some burned places. The boys were getting really edgy and mean; it was time to make the hopper-raid. He told his plan one night to Aabi, Temba, and Post.

None of them said anything for a minute, then Aabi said, "What about fuel, Captain?"

"We got enough fuel."

"Not for four hoppers; wouldn't last a week."

"You mean there's only a month's supply left for this one?"

Aabi nodded.

"Well then, we pick up a little fuel too, looks like."

"How?"

"Put your minds to it."

They all sat there looking stupid. It annoyed him. They

looked to him for everything. He was a natural leader, but he liked men who thought for themselves too. "Figure it out, it's your line of work, Aabi," he said, and went out for a smoke, sick of the way everybody acted, like they'd lost their nerve. They just couldn't face the cold hard facts.

They were low on maryjanes now and he hadn't had one for a couple of days. It didn't do anything for him. The night was overcast and black, damp, warm, smelling like spring. Ngenene went by walking like an ice-skater, or almost like a robot on treads; he turned slowly through a gliding step and gazed at Davidson, who stood on the bungalow porch in the dim light from the doorway. He was a power-saw operator, a huge man. "The source of my energy is connected to the Great Generator I cannot be switched off," he said in a level tone, gazing at Davidson.

"Get to your barracks and sleep it off!" Davidson said in the whipcrack voice that nobody ever disobeyed, and after a moment Ngenene skated carefully on, ponderous and graceful. Too many of the men were using hallies more and more heavily. There was plenty, but the stuff was for loggers relaxing on Sundays, not for soldiers of a tiny outpost marooned on a hostile world. They had no time for getting high, for dreaming. He'd have to lock the stuff up. Then some of the boys might crack. Well, let 'em crack. Can't make an omelet without cracking eggs. Maybe he could send them back to Central in exchange for some fuel. You give me two, three tanks of gas and I'll give you two, three warm bodies, loyal soldiers, good loggers, just your type, a little far gone in bye-bye dreamland . . .

He grinned, and was going back inside to try this one out on Temba and the others, when the guard posted up on the lumberyard smoke stack yelled. "They're coming!" he screeched out in a high voice, like a kid playing Blacks and Rhodesians. Somebody else over on the west side of the stockade began yelling too. A gun went off.

And they came. Christ, they came. It was incredible. There were thousands of them, thousands. No sound, no noise at all, until that screech from the guard; then one gunshot; then an explosion—a land mine going up—and another, one after another, and hundreds and hundreds of torches flaring up lit one from another and being thrown and soaring through the black wet air like rockets, and the walls of the stockade coming alive with creechies, pouring in, pouring over, pushing, swarming, thousands of them. It was like an army of rats

95

Davidson had seen once when he was a little kid, in the last Famine, in the streets of Cleveland, Ohio, where he grew up. Something had driven the rats out of their holes and they had come up in daylight, seething up over the wall, a pulsing blanket of fur and eyes and little hands and teeth, and he had yelled for his mom and run like crazy, or was that only a dream he'd had when he was a kid? It was important to keep cool. The hopper was parked in the creechie-pen; it was still dark over on that side and he got there at once. The gate was locked, he always kept it locked in case one of the weak sisters got a notion of flying off to Papa Ding Dong some dark night. It seemed to take a long time to get the key out and fit it in the lock and turn it right, but it was just a matter of keeping cool, and then it took a long time to sprint to the hopper and unlock it. Post and Aabi were with him now. At last came the huge rattle of the rotors, beating eggs, covering up all the weird noises, the high voices yelling and screeching and singing. Up they went, and hell dropped away below them: a pen full of rats, burning.

"It takes a cool head to size up an emergency situation quickly," Davidson said. "You men thought fast and acted fast. Good work. Where's Temba?"

"Got a spear in his belly," Post said.

Aabi, the pilot, seemed to want to fly the hopper, so Davidson let him. He clambered into one of the rear seats and sat back, letting his muscles relax. The forest flowed beneath them, black under black.

"Where you heading, Aabi?"

"Central."

"No. We don't want to go to Central."

"Where do we want to go to?" Aabi said with a kind of womanish giggle. "New York? Peking?"

"Just keep her up a while, Aabi, and circle camp. Big circles. Out of earshot."

"Captain, there isn't any Java Camp any more by now," said Post, a logging-crew foreman, a stocky, steady man.

"When the creechies are through burning the camp, we'll come in and burn the creechies. There must be four thousand of them all in one place there. There's six flamethrowers in the back of this helicopter. Let's give 'em about twenty minutes. Start with the jelly bombs and then catch the ones that run with the flamethrowers."

"Christ," Aabi said violently, "some of our guys might be there, the creechies might take them prisoners, we don't

96

know. I'm not going back there and burn up humans, maybe." He had not turned the hopper.

Davidson put the nose of his revolver against the back of Aabi's skull and said, "Yes, we're going back; so pull yourself together, baby, and don't give me a lot of trouble."

"There's enough fuel in the tank to get us to Central, Captain," the pilot said. He kept trying to duck his head away from the touch of the gun, like it was a fly bothering him. "But that's all. That's all we got."

"Then we'll get a lot of mileage out of it. Turn her, Aabi."

"I think we better go on to Central, Captain," Post said in his stolid voice, and this ganging up against him enraged Davidson so much that reversing the gun in his hand he struck out fast as a snake and clipped Post over the ear with the gun-butt. The logger just folded over like a Christmas card, and sat there in the front seat with his head between his knees and his hands hanging to the floor. "Turn her, Aabi," Davidson said, the whiplash in his voice. The helicopter swung around in a wide arc. "Hell, where's camp, I never had this hopper up at night without any signal to follow," Aabi said, sounding dull and snuffly like he had a cold.

"Go east and look for the fire," Davidson said, cold and quiet. None of them had any real stamina, not even Temba. None of them had stood by him when the going got really tough. Sooner or later they all joined up against him, because they just couldn't take it the way he could. The weak conspire against the strong, the strong man has to stand alone and look out for himself. It just happened to be the way things are. Where was the camp?

They should have been able to see the burning buildings for miles in this blank dark, even in the rain. Nothing showed. Grey-black sky, black ground. The fires must have gone out. Been put out. Could the humans have driven off the creechies? After he'd escaped? The thought went like a spray of icewater through his mind. No, of course not, not fifty against thousands. But by God there must be a lot of pieces of blown-up creechie lying around on the minefields, anyway. It was just that they'd come so damned thick. Nothing could have stopped them. He couldn't have planned for that. Where had they come from? There hadn't been any creechies in the forest anywhere around for days and days. They must have poured in from somewhere, from all directions, sneaking along in the woods, coming up out of their holes like rats. There wasn't any way to stop thousands and thousands of them like that. Where the hell was camp? Aabi was tricking, faking course. "Find the camp, Aabi," he said softly.

"For Christ's sake I'm trying to," the boy said.

Post never moved, folded over there by the pilot.

"It couldn't just disappear, could it, Aabi? You got seven minutes to find it."

"Find it yourself," Aabi said, shrill and sullen.

"Not till you and Post get in line, baby. Take her down lower."

After a minute Aabi said, "That looks like the river."

There was a river, and a big clearing; but where was Java Camp? It didn't show up as they flew north over the clearing. "This must be it, there isn't any other big clearing in there," Aabi said, coming back over the treeless area. Their landing-lights glared but you couldn't see anything outside the tunnels of the lights; it would be better to have them off. Davidson reached over the pilot's shoulder and switched the lights off. Blank wet dark was like black towels slapped on their eyes. "For Christ's sake!" Aabi screamed, and flipping the lights back on slewed the hopper left and up, but not fast enough. Trees leaned hugely out of the night and caught the machine.

The vanes screamed, hurling leaves and twigs in a cyclone through the bright lanes of the lights, but the boles of the trees were very old and strong. The little winged machine plunged, seemed to lurch and tear itself free, and went down sideways into the trees. The lights went out. The noise stopped.

"I don't feel so good," Davidson said. He said it again. Then he stopped saying it, for there was nobody to say it to. Then he realised he hadn't said it anyway. He felt groggy. Must have hit his head. Aabi wasn't there. Where was he? This was the hopper. It was all slewed around, but he was still in his seat. It was so dark, like being blind. He felt around, and so found Post, inert, still doubled up, crammed in between the front seat and the control panel. The hopper trembled whenever Davidson moved, and he figured out at last that it wasn't on the ground but wedged in between trees, stuck like a kite. His head was feeling better, and he wanted more and more to get out of the black, tilted-over cabin. He squirmed over into the pilot's seat and got his legs out, hung by his hands, and could not feel ground, only branches scraping his dangling legs. Finally he let go, not knowing how far he'd fall, but he had to get out of that cabin. It was only a few feet down. It jolted his head, but he felt better standing up. If only it wasn't so dark, so black. He had a torch in his belt, he always carried one at night around camp. But it wasn't there. That was funny. It must have fallen out. He'd better get back into the hopper and get it. Maybe Aabi had taken it. Aabi had intentionally crashed the hopper, taken Davidson's torch, and made a break for it. The slimy little bastard, he was like all the rest of them. The air was black and full of moisture, and you couldn't tell where to put your feet, it was all roots and bushes and tangles. There were noises all around, water dripping, rustling, tiny noises, little things sneaking around in the darkness. He'd better get back up into the hopper, get his torch. But he couldn't see how to climb back up. The bottom edge of the doorway was just out of reach of his fingers.

There was a light, a faint gleam seen and gone away off in the trees. Aabi had taken the torch and gone off to reconnoiter, get orientated, smart boy. "Aabi!" he called in a piercing whisper. He stepped on something queer while he was trying to see the light among the trees again. He kicked at it with his boots, then put a hand down on it, cautiously, for it wasn't wise to go feeling things you couldn't see. A lot of wet stuff, slick, like a dead rat. He withdrew his hand quickly. He felt in another place after a while; it was a boot under his hand, he could feel the crossings of the laces. It must be Aabi lying there right under his feet. He'd got thrown out of the hopper when it came down. Well, he'd deserved it with his Judas trick, trying to run off to Central. Davidson did not like the wet feel of the unseen clothes and hair. He straightened up. There was the light again, black-barred by near and distant tree-trunks, a distant glow that moved.

Davidson put his hand to his holster. The revolver was not in it.

He'd had it in his hand, in case Post or Aabi acted up. It was not in his hand. It must be up in the helicopter with his torch.

He stood crouching, immobile; then abruptly began to run. He could not see where he was going. Tree-trunks jolted him from side to side as he knocked into them, and roots tripped up his feet. He fell full length, crashing down among bushes. Getting to hands and knees he tried to hide. Bare, wet twigs dragged and scraped over his face. He squirmed farther into the bushes. His brain was entirely occupied by the complex smells of rot and growth, dead leaves, decay, new shoots,

99

fronds, flowers, the smells of night and spring and rain. The light shone full on him. He saw the creechies.

He remembered what they did when cornered, and what Lyubov had said about it. He turned over on his back and lay with his head tipped back, his eyes shut. His heart stuttered in his chest.

Nothing happened.

It was hard to open his eyes, but finally he managed it. They just stood there: a lot of them, ten or twenty. They carried those spears they had for hunting, little toy-looking things but the iron blades were sharp, they could cut right through your guts. He shut his eyes and just kept lying there.

And nothing happened.

His heart quieted down, and it seemed like he could think better. Something stirred down inside him, something almost like laughter. By God they couldn't get him down! If his own men betrayed him, and human intelligence couldn't do any more for him, then he used their own trick against them— played dead like this, and triggered this instinct reflex that kept them from killing anybody who took that position. They just stood around him, muttering at each other. *They couldn't hurt him.* It was as if he was a god.

"Davidson."

He had to open his eyes. Again. The resin-flare carried by one of the creechies still burned, but it had grown pale, and the forest was dim grey now, not pitch-black. How had that happened? Only five or ten minutes had gone by. It was still hard to see but it wasn't night any more. He could see the leaves and branches, the forest. He could see the face looking down at him. It had no color in this toneless twilight of dawn. The scarred features looked like a man's. The eyes were like dark holes.

"Let me get up," Davidson said suddenly in a loud, hoarse voice. He was shaking with cold from lying on the wet ground. He could not lie there with Selver looking down at him.

Selver was emptyhanded, but a lot of the little devils around him had not only spears but revolvers. Stolen from his stockpile at camp. He struggled to his feet. His clothes clung icy to his shoulders and the backs of his legs, and he could not stop shaking.

"Get it over with," he said. "Hurry-up-quick!"

Selver just looked at him. At least now he had to look up, way up, to meet Davidson's eyes.

"Do you wish me to kill you now?" he inquired. He had learned that way of talking from Lyubov, of course; even his voice, it could have been Lyubov talking. It was uncanny.

"It's my choice, is it?"

"Well, you have lain all night in the way that means you wished us to let you live; now do you want to die?"

The pain in his head and stomach, and his hatred for this horrible little freak that talked like Lyubov and that had got him at its mercy, the pain and the hatred combined and set his belly churning, so he retched and was nearly sick. He shook with cold and nausea. He tried to hold on to courage. He suddenly stepped forward a pace and spat in Selver's face.

There was a little pause, and then Selver, with a kind of dancing movement, spat back. And laughed. And made no move to kill Davidson. Davidson wiped the cold spittle off his lips.

"Look, Captain Davidson," the creechie said in that quiet little voice that made Davidson go dizzy and sick, "we're both gods, you and I. You're an insane one, and I'm not sure whether I'm sane or not. But we are gods. There will never be another meeting in the forest like this meeting now between us. We bring each other such gifts as gods bring. You gave me a gift, the killing of one's kind, murder. Now, as well as I can, I give you my people's gift, which is not killing. I think we each find each other's gift heavy to carry. However, you must carry it alone. Your people at Eshsen tell me that if I bring you there, they have to make a judgment on you and kill you, it's their law to do so. So, wishing to give you life, I can't take you with the other prisoners to Eshsen; and I can't leave you to wander in the forest, for you do too much harm. So you'll be treated like one of us when we go mad. You'll be taken to Rendlep where nobody lives any more, and left there."

Davidson stared at the creechie, could not take his eyes off it. It was as if it had some hypnotic power over him. He couldn't stand this. Nobody had any power over him. Nobody could hurt him. "I should have broken your neck right away, that day you tried to jump me," he said, his voice still hoarse and thick.

"It might have been best," Selver answered. "But Lyubov prevented you. As he now prevents me from killing you.—All the killing is done now. And the cutting of trees. There aren't trees to cut on Rendlep. That's the place you call Dump Island. Your people left no trees there, so you can't make a boat and sail from it. Nothing much grows there any more, so we shall have to bring you food and wood to burn. There's nothing to kill on Rendlep. No trees, no people. There were trees and people, but now there are only the dreams of them. It seems to me a fitting place for you to live, since you must live. You might learn how to dream there, but more likely you will follow your madness through to its proper end, at last."

"Kill me now and quit your damned gloating."

"Kill you?" Selver said, and his eyes looking up at Davidson seemed to shine, very clear and terrible, in the twilight of the forest. "I can't kill you, Davidson. You're a god. You must do it yourself."

He turned and walked away, light and quick, vanishing among the grey trees within a few steps.

A noose slipped over Davidson's head and tightened a little on his throat. Small spears approached his back and sides. They did not try to hurt him. He could run away, make a break for it, they didn't dare kill him. The blades were polished, leaf-shaped, sharp as razors. The noose tugged gently at his neck. He followed where they led him.

VIII

Selver had not seen Lyubov for a long time. That dream had gone with him to Rieshwel. It had been with him when he spoke the last time to Davidson. Then it had gone, and perhaps it slept now in the grave of Lyubov's death at Eshsen, for it never came to Selver in the town of Broter where he now lived.

But when the great ship returned, and he went to Eshsen, Lyubov met him there. He was silent and tenuous, very sad, so that the old carking grief awoke in Selver.

Lyubov stayed with him, a shadow in the mind, even when he met the yumens from the ship. These were people of power; they were very different from all yumens he had known, except his friend, but they were much stronger men than Lyubov had been.

His yumen speech had gone rusty, and at first he mostly let them talk. When he was fairly certain what kind of people they were, he brought forward the heavy box he had carried from Broter. "Inside this there is Lyubov's work," he said, groping for the words. "He knew more about us than the others do. He learned my language and the Men's Tongue; we wrote all that down. He understood somewhat how we live and dream. The others do not. I'll give you the work, if you'll take it to the place he wished."

The tall, white-skinned one, Lepennon, looked happy, and thanked Selver, telling him that the papers would indeed be taken where Lyubov wished, and would be highly valued. That pleased Selver. But it had been painful to him to speak his friend's name aloud, for Lyubov's face was still bitterly sad when he turned to it in his mind. He withdrew a little from the yumens, and watched them. Dongh and Gosse and others of Eshsen were there along with the five from the ship. The new ones looked clean and polished as new iron. The old ones had let the hair grow on their faces, so that they looked a little like huge, black-furred Athsheans. They still wore clothes, but the clothes were old and not kept clean. They were not thin, except for the Old Man, who had been ill ever since the Night of Eshsen; but they all looked a little like men who are lost or mad.

This meeting was at the edge of the forest, in that zone where by tacit agreement neither the forest people nor the yumens had built dwellings or camped for these past years. Selver and his companions settled down in the shade of a big ash-tree that stood out away from the forest eaves. Its berries were only small green knots against the twigs as yet, its leaves were long and soft, labile, summer-green. The light beneath the great tree was soft, complex with shadows.

The yumens consulted and came and went, and at last one came over to the ash-tree. It was the hard one from the ship, the Commander. He squatted down on his heels near Selver, not asking permission but not with any evident intention of rudeness. He said, "Can we talk a little?"

"Certainly."

"You know that we'll be taking all the Terrans away with us. We brought a second ship with us to carry them. Your world will no longer be used as a colony."

"This was the message I heard at Broter, when you came three days ago."

"I wanted to be sure that you understand that this is a permanent arrangement. We're not coming back. Your world has been placed under the League Ban. What that means in your terms is this: I can promise you that no one will come here to cut the trees or take your lands, so long as the League lasts."

103

"None of you will ever come back," Selver said, statement or question.

"Not for five generations. None. Then perhaps a few men, ten or twenty, no more than twenty, might come to talk to your people, and study your world, as some of the men here were doing."

"The scientists, the Speshes," Selver said. He brooded. "You decide matters all at once, your people," he said, again between statement and question.

"How do you mean?" The Commander looked wary.

"Well, you say that none of you shall cut the trees of Athshe: and all of you stop. And yet you live in many places. Now if a headwoman in Karach gave an order, it would not be obeyed by the people of the next village, and surely not by all the people in the world at once . . ."

"No, because you haven't one government over all. But we do—now—and I assure you its orders are obeyed. By all of us at once. But, as a matter of fact, it seems to me from the story we've been told by the colonists here, that when *you* gave an order, Selver, it was obeyed by everybody on every island here at once. How did you manage that?"

"At that time I was a god," Selver said, expressionless.

After the Commander had left him, the long white one came sauntering over and asked if he might sit down in the shade of the tree. He had tact, this one, and was extremely clever. Selver was uneasy with him. Like Lyubov, this one would be gentle; he would understand, and yet would himself be utterly beyond understanding. For the kindest of them was as far out of touch, as unreachable, as the cruellest. That was why the presence of Lyubov in his mind remained painful to him, while the dreams in which he saw and touched his dead wife Thele were precious and full of peace.

"When I was here before," Lepennon said, "I met this man, Raj Lyubov. I had very little chance to speak with him, but I remember what he said; and I've had time to read some of his studies of your people, since. His work, as you say. It's largely because of that work of his that Athshe is now free of the Terran Colony. This freedom had become the direction of Lyubov's life, I think. You, being his friend, will see that his death did not stop him from arriving at his goal, from finishing his journey."

Selver sat still. Uneasiness turned to fear in his mind. This one spoke like a Great Dreamer.

He made no response at all.

"Will you tell me one thing, Selver? If the question doesn't offend you. There will be no more questions after it . . . There were the killings: at Smith Camp, then at this place, Eshsen, then finally at New Java Camp where Davidson led the rebel group. That was all. No more since then . . . Is that true? Have there been no more killings?"

"I did not kill Davidson."

"That does not matter," Lepennon said, misunderstanding; Selver meant that Davidson was not dead, but Lepennon took him to mean that someone else had killed Davidson. Relieved to see that the yumen could err, Selver did not correct him.

"There has been no more killing, then?"

"None. They will tell you," Selver said, nodding towards the Colonel and Gosse.

"Among your own people, I mean. Athsheans killing Athsheans."

Selver was silent.

He looked up at Lepennon, at the strange face, white as the mask of the Ash Spirit, that changed as it met his gaze.

"Sometimes a god comes," Selver said. "He brings a new way to do a thing, or a new thing to be done. A new kind of singing, or a new kind of death. He brings this across the bridge between the dream-time and the world-time. When he has done this, it is done. You cannot take things that exist in the world and try to drive them back into the dream, to hold them inside the dream with walls and pretenses. That is insanity. What is, is. There is no use pretending, now, that we do not know how to kill one another."

Lepennon laid his long hand on Selver's hand, so quickly and gently that Selver accepted the touch as if the hand were not a stranger's. The green-gold shadows of the ash leaves flickered over them.

"But you must not pretend to have reasons to kill one another. Murder has no reason," Lepennon said, his face as anxious and sad as Lyubov's face. "We shall go. Within two days we shall be gone. All of us. Forever. Then the forests of Athshe will be as they were before."

Lyubov came out of the shadows of Selver's mind and said, "I shall be here."

"Lyubov will be here," Selver said. "And Davidson will be here. Both of them. Maybe after I die people will be as they were before I was born, and before you came. But I do not think they will."

Here's Poul again. Poul happens to be the only writer represented in all three *Hugo Winners* volumes. Here is the list of his stories:

VOLUME ONE   *"The Longest Voyage"*
VOLUME TWO   *"No Truce with Kings"*
                     "The Sharing of Flesh"
VOLUME THREE *"The Queen of Air and Darkness"*
                     "Goat Song"

You see, he has five stories included altogether, which ties him with Harlan Ellison, whose five are to be found in Volumes Two and Three only.

Well, I have always believed in returning good for evil, so Poul's vicious behavior in this regard (for which, I am sure, he will be punished in the other world) shall elicit from me only a saintly smile and I will tell you another one of the jokes that I heard from him. (For heaven's sake, if you don't like these jokes, send nasty letters to Poul. If you *do* like them, on the other hand, you may write to me. I'm willing to share *part* of the burden.)

The scene is set in a nasty, cruel dictatorship—just about anywhere. A long line of people, four abreast, stretches out for many blocks in the queue for the daily ration of inferior hamburger meat.

Our hero, whom we shall call Smith, in order to make it impossible to guess to which nation we are referring, is working his way through a slow burn, and finally bubbles over. Turning to his companion, who is standing to his right, he says:

"I can endure this no longer. Since that scoundrel who rules us took over the government by his coup, he and his cronies live in the lap of luxury while we, the people, are slowly starving to death. My friend, I am dashing home for the rifle which I hid when they took away our arms. I will make my way to the Presidential Palace and, though it cost me my life, I shall assassinate that vicious criminal who lords it over us."

And he left at a run.

An hour later, the line had inched forward a block and a half, and our hero returned, silent and glum. He took his old place in the line and said nothing. His friend whispered to him out of the corner of his mouth, "Well?"

Our hero shook his head and said, with infinite bitterness, "You call *this* a line?"

GOAT SONG

Three women: one is dead; one is alive; One is both and neither, and will never live and never die, being immortal in SUM.

On a hill above that valley through which runs the highroad, I await Her passage. Frost came early this year, and the grasses have paled. Otherwise the slope is begrown and blackberry bushes that have been harvested by men and birds, leaving only briars, and with certain apple trees. They are very old, those trees, survivors of an orchard raised by generations which none but SUM now remembers (I can see a few fragments of wall thrusting above the brambles)—scattered crazily over the hillside and as crazily gnarled. A little fruit remains on them. Chill across my skin, a gust shakes loose an apple. I hear it knock on the earth, another stroke of some eternal clock. The shrubs whisper to the wind.

Elsewhere the ridges around me are wooded, afire with scarlets and brasses and bronzes. The sky is huge, the westering sun wan-bright. The valley is filling with a deeper blue, a haze whose slight smokiness touches my nostrils. This is Indian summer, the funeral pyre of the year.

There have been other seasons. There have been other lifetimes, before mine and hers; and in those days they had words to sing with. We still allow ourselves music, though, and I have spent much time planting melodies around my rediscovered words. *"In the greenest growth of the Maytime——"* I unsling the harp on my back, and tune it afresh, and sing to her, straight into autumn and the waning day.

> "——You came, and the sun came after,
> And the green grew golden above;
> And the flag-flowers lightened with laughter,
> And the meadowsweet shook with love."

A footfall stirs the grasses, quite gently, and the woman says, trying to chuckle, "Why, thank you."

Once, so soon after my one's death that I was still dazed by it, I stood in the home that had been ours. This was on the hundred and first floor of a most desirable building. After dark the city flamed for us, blinked, glittered, flung immense sheets of radiance forth like banners. Nothing but SUM could have controlled the firefly dance of a million aircars among the towers, or, for that matter, have maintained the entire city, from nuclear powerplants through automated factories, physical and economic distribution networks, sanitation, repair, services, education, culture, order, everything as one immune immortal organism. We had gloried in belonging to this as well as to each other.

But that night I told the kitchen to throw the dinner it had made for me down the waste chute, and ground under my heel the chemical consolations which the medicine cabinet extended to me, and kicked the cleaner as it picked up the mess, and ordered the lights not to go on, anywhere in our suite. I stood by the vieWall, looking out across megalopolis, and it was tawdry. In my hands I had a little clay figure she had fashioned herself. I turned it over and over and over.

But I had forgotten to forbid the door to admit visitors. It recognized this woman and opened for her. She had come with the kindly intention of teasing me out of a mood that seemed to her unnatural. I heard her enter, and looked around through the gloom. She had almost the same height as my girl did, and her hair chanced to be bound in a way that my girl often favored, and the figurine dropped from my grasp and shattered, because for an instant I thought she was my girl. Since then I have been hard put not to hate Thrakia.

This evening, even without so much sundown light, I would not make that mistake. Nothing but the silvery bracelet about her left wrist bespeaks the past we share. She is in wildcountry garb: boots, kilt of true fur and belt of true leather, knife at hip and rifle slung on shoulder. Her locks are matted and snarled, her skin brown from weeks of weather; scratches and smudges show beneath the fantastic zigzags she has painted in many colors on herself. She wears a necklace of bird skulls.

Now that one who is dead was, in her own way, more a child of trees and horizons than Thrakia's followers. She was so much at home in the open that she had no need to put off clothes or cleanliness, reason or gentleness, when we sickened of the cities and went forth beyond them. From this trait I got many of the names I bestowed on her, such as Wood's Colt or Fallow Hind or, from my prowlings among ancient books, Dryad and Elven. (She liked me to choose her names, and this pleasure had no end, because she was inexhaustible.)

I let my harpstring ring into silence. Turning about, I say to Thrakia, "I wasn't singing for you. Not for anyone. Leave me alone."

She draws a breath. The wind ruffles her hair and brings me an odor of her: not female sweetness, but fear. She clenches her fists and says, "You're crazy."

"Wherever did you find a meaningful word like that?" I gibe; for my own pain and—to be truthful—my own fear must strike out at something, and here she stands. "Aren't you content any longer with 'untranquil' or 'disequilibrated'?"

"I got it from you," she says defiantly, "you and your damned archaic songs. There's another word, 'damned.' And how it suits you! When are you going to stop this morbidity?"

"And commit myself to a clinic and have my brain laundered nice and sanitary? Not soon, darling." I use *that* last word aforethought, but she cannot know what scorn and sadness are in it for me, who know that once it could also have been a name for my girl. The official grammar and pronunciation of language is as frozen as every other aspect of our civilization, thanks to electronic recording and neuronic teaching; but meanings shift and glide about like subtle serpents. (O adder that stung my Foalfoot!)

I shrug and say in my driest, most city-technological voice, "Actually, I'm the practical, non-morbid one. Instead of running away from my emotions—via drugs, or neuroadjustment, or playing at savagery like you, for that matter—I'm about to implement a concrete plan for getting back the person who made me happy."

"By disturbing Her on Her way home?"

"Anyone has the right to petition the Dark Queen while She's abroad on earth."

"But this is past the proper time—"

"No law's involved, just custom. People are afraid to meet Her outside a crowd, a town, bright flat lights. They won't admit it, but they are. So I came here precisely not to be a part of a queue. I don't want to speak into a recorder for subsequent computer analysis of my words. How could I be sure She was listening? I want to meet Her as myself, a unique being, and look in Her eyes while I make my prayer."

Thrakia chokes a little. "She'll be angry."

"Is She able to be angry, any more?"

"I . . . I don't know. What you mean to ask for is so impossible, though. So absurd. That SUM should give you back your girl. You know It never makes exceptions."

"Isn't She Herself an exception?"

"That's different. You're being silly. SUM has to have a, well, a direct human liaison. Emotional and cultural feedback, as well as statistics. How else can It govern rationally? And She must have been chosen out of the whole world. Your girl, what was she? Nobody!"

"To me, she was everybody."

"You—" Thrakia catches her lip in her teeth. One hand reaches out and closes on my bare forearm, a hard hot touch, the grimy fingernails biting. When I make no response, she lets go and stares at the ground. A V of outbound geese passes overhead. Their cries come shrill through the wind, which is loudening in the forest.

"Well," she says, "you are special. You always were. You went to space and came back, with the Great Captain. You're maybe the only man alive who understands about the ancients. And your singing, yes, you don't really entertain, your songs trouble people and can't be forgotten. So maybe She will listen to you. But SUM won't. It can't give special resurrections. Once that was done, a single time, wouldn't it have to be done for everybody? The dead would overrun the living."

"Not necessarily," I say. "In any event, I mean to try."

"Why can't you wait for the promised time? Surely, then, SUM will re-create you two in the same generation."

"I'd have to live out this life, at least, without her," I say, looking away also, down to the highroad which shines through shadow like death's snake, the length of the valley. "Besides, how do you know there ever will be any resurrections? We have only a promise. No, less than that. An announced policy."

110

She gasps, steps back, raises her hands as if to fend me off. Her soul bracelet casts light into my eyes. I recognize an embryo exorcism. She lacks ritual; every "superstition" was patiently scrubbed out of our metal-and-energy world, long ago. But if she has no word for it, no concept, nevertheless she recoils from blasphemy.

So I say, wearily, not wanting an argument, wanting to wait here alone: "Never mind. There could be some natural catastrophe, like a giant asteroid striking, that wiped out the system before conditions had become right for resurrections to commence."

"That's impossible," she says, almost frantic. "The homeostats, the repair functions—"

"All right, call it a vanishingly unlikely theoretical contingency. Let's declare that I'm so selfish I want Swallow Wing back now, in this life of mine, and don't give a curse whether that'll be fair to the rest of you."

You won't care either, anyway, I think. None of you. You don't grieve. It is your own precious private consciousnesses that you wish to preserve; no one else is close enough to you to matter very much. Would you believe me if I told you I am quite prepared to offer SUM my own death in exchange for It releasing Blossom-in-the-Sun?

I don't speak that thought, which would be cruel, nor repeat what is crueller: my fear that SUM lies, that the dead never will be disgorged. For (I am not the All-Controller, I think not with vacuum and negative energy levels but with ordinary earth-begotten molecules; yet I can reason somewhat dispassionately, being disillusioned) consider—

The object of the game is to maintain a society stable, just, and sane. This requires satisfaction not only of somatic, but of symbolic and instinctual needs. Thus children must be allowed to come into being. The minimum number per generation is equal to the maximum: that number which will maintain a constant population.

It is also desirable to remove the fear of death from men. Hence the promise: At such time as it is socially feasible, SUM will begin to refashion us, with our complete memories but in the pride of our youth. This can be done over and over, life after life across the millennia. So death is, indeed, a sleep.

—*in that sleep of death, what dreams may come*— No. I myself dare not dwell on this. I ask merely, privately: Just when and how does SUM expect conditions (in a stabilized society, mind you) to have become so different from today's that the reborn can, in their millions, safely be welcomed back?

I see no reason why SUM should not lie to us. We, too, are objects in the world that It manipulates.

"We've quarreled about this before, Thrakia," I sigh. "Often. Why do you bother?"

"I wish I knew," she answers low. Half to herself, she goes on: "Of course I want to copulate with you. You must be good, the way that girl used to follow you about with her eyes, and smile when she touched your hand, and—But you can't be better than everyone else. That's unreasonable. There are only so many possible ways. So why do I care if you wrap yourself up in silence and go off alone? Is it that that makes you a challenge?"

"You think too much," I say. "Even here. You're a pretend primitive. You visit wildcountry to 'slake inborn atavistic impulses' . . . but you can't dismantle that computer inside yourself and simply feel, simply be."

She bristles. I touched a nerve there. Looking past her, along the ridge of fiery maple and sumac, brassy elm and great dun oak, I see others emerge from beneath the trees. Women exclusively, her followers, as unkempt as she; one has a brace of ducks lashed to her waist, and their blood has trickled down her thigh and dried black. For this movement, this unadmitted mystique has become Thrakia's by now: that not only men should forsake the easy routine and the easy pleasure of the cities, and become again, for a few weeks each year, the carnivores who begot our species; women too should seek out starkness, the better to appreciate civilization when they return.

I feel a moment's unease. We are in no park, with laid-out trails and campground services. We are in wildcountry. Not many men come here, ever, and still fewer women; for the region is, literally, beyond the law. No deed done here is punishable. We are told that this helps consolidate society, as the most violent among us may thus vent their passions. But I have spent much time in wildcountry since my Morning Star went out—myself in quest of nothing but solitude—and I have watched what happens through eyes that have also read anthropology and history. Institutions are developing; ceremonies, tribalisms, acts of blood and cruelty and acts elsewhere called unnatural are becoming more elaborate and more expected every year. Then the practitioners go home to their

112

cities and honestly believe they have been enjoying fresh air, exercise, and good tension-releasing fun.

Let her get angry enough and Thrakia can call knives to her aid.

Wherefore I make myself lay both hands on her shoulders, and meet the tormented gaze, and say most gently, "I'm sorry. I know you mean well. You're afraid She will be annoyed and bring misfortune on your people."

Thrakia gulps. "No," she whispers. "That wouldn't be logical. But I'm afraid of what might happen to you. And then—" Suddenly she throws herself against me. I feel arms, breasts, belly press through my tunic, and smell meadows in her hair and musk in her mouth. "You'd be gone!" she wails. "Then who'd sing to us?"

"Why, the planet's crawling with entertainers," I stammer.

"You're more than that," she says. "So much more. I don't like what you sing, not really—and what you've sung since that stupid girl died, oh, meaningless, horrible!—but, I don't know why, I *want* you to trouble me."

Awkward, I pat her back. The sun now stands very little above the treetops. Its rays slant interminably through the booming, frosting air. I shiver in my tunic and buskins and wonder what to do.

A sound rescues me. It comes from one end of the valley below us, where further view is blocked off by two cliffs; it thunders deep in our ears and rolls through the earth into our bones. We have heard that sound in the cities, and been glad to have walls and lights and multitudes around us. Now we are alone with it, the noise of Her chariot.

The women shriek, I hear them faintly across wind and rumble and my own pulse, and they vanish into the woods. They will seek their camp, dress warmly, build enormous fires; presently they will eat their ecstatics, and rumors are uneasy about what they do after that.

Thrakia seizes my left wrist, above the soul bracelet, and hauls. "Harper, come with me!" she pleads. I break loose from her and stride down the hill toward the road. A scream follows me for a moment.

Light still dwells in the sky and on the ridges, but as I descend into that narrow valley I enter dusk, and it thickens. Indistinct bramblebushes whicker where I brush them, and claw back at me. I feel the occasional scratch on my legs, the tug as my garment is snagged, the chill that I breathe, but dimly. My perceived-outer-reality is overpowered by the rushing of Her chariot and my blood. My inner-universe is fear, yes, but exaltation, too, a drunkenness which sharpens instead of dulling the senses, a psychedelia which opens the reasoning mind as well as the emotions; I have gone beyond myself, I am embodied purpose. Not out of need for comfort, but to voice what Is, I return to words whose speaker rests centuries dust, and lend them my own music. I sing:

> "—Gold is my heart, and the world's golden,
> And one peak tipped with light;
> And the air lies still about the hill
> With the first fear of night;
>
> Till mystery down the soundless valley
> Thunders, and dark is here;
> And the wind blows, and the light goes,
> And the night is full of fear.
>
> And I know one night, on some far height,
> In the tongue I never knew.
> I yet shall hear the tidings clear
> From them that were friends of you.
>
> They'll call the news from hill to hill,
> Dark and uncomforted,
> Earth and sky and the winds; and I
> Shall know that you are dead.—"

But I have reached the valley floor, and She has come in sight.

Her chariot is unlit, for radar eyes and inertial guides need no lamps, nor sun nor stars. Wheelless, the steel tear rides on its own roar and thrust of air. The pace is not great, far less than any of our mortals' vehicles are wont to take. Men say the Dark Queen rides thus slowly in order that She may perceive with Her own senses and so be the better prepared to counsel SUM. But now Her annual round is finished; She is homeward bound; until spring She will dwell with It Which is our lord. Why does She not hasten tonight?

Because Death has never a need of haste? I wonder. And as I step into the middle of the road, certain lines from the yet more ancient past rise tremendous within me, and I strike my harp and chant them louder than the approaching car:

114

> "I that in heill was and gladness
> Am trublit now with great sickness
> And feblit with infirmitie:—
> Timor mortis conturbat me."

The car detects me and howls a warning. I hold my ground. The car could swing around, the road is wide and in any event a smooth surface is not absolutely necessary. But I hope, I believe that She will be aware of an obstacle in Her path, and tune in Her various amplifiers, and find me abnormal enough to stop for. Who, in SUM's world—who, even among the explorers that It has sent beyond in Its unappeasable hunger for data—would stand in a cold wildcountry dusk and shout while his harp snarls.

> "Our plesance here is all vain glory,
> This fals world is but transitory,
> The flesh is bruckle, the Feynd is slee:—
> Timor mortis conturbat me.
>
> The state of man does change and vary,
> Now sound, now sick, now blyth, now sary,
> Now dansand mirry, now like to die:—
> Timor mortis conturbat me.
>
> No state in Erd here standis sicker;
> As with the wynd wavis the wicker
> So wannis this world's vanitie:—
> Timor mortis conturbat me.—?"

The car draws alongside and sinks to the ground. I let my strings die away into the wind. The sky overhead and in the west is gray-purple; eastward it is quite dark and a few early stars peer forth. Here, down in the valley, shadows are heavy and I cannot see very well.

The canopy slides back. She stands erect in the chariot, thus looming over me. Her robe and cloak are black, fluttering like restless wings; beneath the cowl Her face is a white blur. I have seen it before, under full light, and in many thousands of pictures; but at this hour I cannot call it back to my mind, not entirely. I list sharp-sculptured profile and pale lips, sable hair and long green eyes, but these are nothing more than words.

"What are you doing?" She has a lovely low voice; but is

115

it, as oh, how rarely since SUM took Her to Itself, is it the least shaken? "What is that you were singing?"

My answer comes so strong that my skull resonates; for I am borne higher and higher on my tide. "Lady of Ours, I have a petition."

"Why did you not bring it before Me when I walked among men? Tonight I am homebound. You must wait till I ride forth with the new year."

"Lady of Ours, neither You nor I would wish living ears to hear what I have to say."

She regards me for a long while. Do I indeed sense fear also in Her? (Surely not of me. Her chariot is armed and armored, and would react with machine speed to protect Her should I offer violence. And should I somehow, incredibly, kill Her, or wound Her beyond chemosurgical repair, She of all beings has no need to doubt death. The ordinary bracelet cries with quite sufficient radio loudness to be heard by more than one thanatic station, when we die; and in that shielding the soul can scarcely be damaged before the Winged Heels arrive to bear it off to SUM. Surely the Dark Queen's circlet can call still farther, and is still better insulated, than any mortal's. And She will most absolutely be re-created. She has been, again and again; death and rebirth every seven years keep Her eternally young in the service of SUM. I have never been able to find out when She was first born.)

Fear, perhaps, of what I have sung and what I might speak?

At last She says—I can scarcely hear through the gusts and creakings in the trees—"Give me the Ring, then."

The dwarf robot which stands by Her throne when She sits among men appears beside Her and extends the massive dull-silver circle to me. I place my left arm within, so that my soul is enclosed. The tablet on the upper surface of the Ring, which looks so much like a jewel, slants away from me; I cannot read what flashes onto the bezel. But the faint glow picks Her features out of murk as She bends to look.

Of course, I tell myself, the actual soul is not scanned. That would take too long. Probably the bracelet which contains the soul has an identification code built in. The Ring sends this to an appropriate part of SUM, Which instantly sends back what is recorded under that code. I hope there is nothing more to it. SUM has not seen fit to tell us.

"What do you call yourself at the moment?" She asks.

A current of bitterness crosses my tide. "Lady of Ours,

why should You care? Is not my real name the number I got when I was allowed to be born?"

Calm descends once more upon Her. "If I am to evaluate properly what you say, I must know more about you than these few official data. Name indicates mood."

I too feel unshaken again, my tide running so strong and smooth that I might not know I was moving did I not see time recede behind me. "Lady of Ours, I cannot give You a fair answer. In this past year I have not troubled with names, or with much of anything else. But some people who knew me from earlier days call me Harper."

"What do you do besides make that sinister music?"

"These days, nothing, Lady of Ours. I've money to live out my life, if I eat sparingly and keep no home. Often I am fed and housed for the sake of my songs."

"What you sang is unlike anything I have heard since—" Anew, briefly, that robot serenity is shaken. "Since before the world was stabilized. You should not wake dead symbols, Harper. They walk through men's dreams."

"Is that bad?"

"Yes. The dreams become nightmares. Remember: mankind, every man who ever lived, was insane before SUM brought order, reason, and peace."

"Well, then," I say, "I will cease and desist if I may have my own dead wakened for me."

She stiffens. The tablet goes out. I withdraw my arm and the Ring is stored away by Her servant. So again She is faceless, beneath flickering stars, here at the bottom of this shadowed valley. Her voice falls cold as the air: "No one can be brought back to life before Resurrection Time is ripe."

I do not say, "What about You?" for that would be vicious. What did She think, how did She weep, when SUM chose Her of all the young on earth? What does She endure in Her centuries? I dare not imagine.

Instead, I smite my harp and sing, quietly this time:

> "Strew on her roses, roses,
> And never a spray of yew.
> In quiet she reposes:
> Ah! would that I did too."

The Dark Queen cries, "What are you doing? Are you really insane?" I go straight to the last stanza.

117

"Her cabin'd, ample Spirit
It flutter'd and fail'd for breath.
To-night it doth inherit
The vasty hall of Death."

I know why my songs strike so hard: because they bear dreads and passions that no one is used to—that most of us hardly know could exist—in SUM's ordered universe. But I had not the courage to hope She would be as torn by them as I see. Has She not lived with more darkness and terror than the ancients themselves could conceive? She calls, "Who has died?"

"She had many names, Lady of Ours," I say. "None was beautiful enough. I can tell You her number, though."

"Your daughter? I . . . sometimes I am asked if a dead child cannot be brought back. Not often, any more, when they go so soon to the crèche. But sometimes. I tell the mother she may have a new one: but if ever We started re-creating dead infants, at what age level could We stop?"

"No, this was my woman."

"Impossible!" Her tone seeks to be not unkindly but is, instead, well-nigh frantic. "You will have no trouble finding others. You are handsome, and your psyche is, is, is extraordinary. It burns like Lucifer."

"Do You remember the name Lucifer, Lady of Ours?" I pounce. "Then You are old indeed. So old that You must also remember how a man might desire only one woman, but her above the whole world and heaven."

She tries to defend Herself with a jeer: "Was that mutual, Harper? I know more of mankind than you do, and surely I am the last chaste woman in existence?"

"Now that she is gone, Lady, yes, perhaps You are. But we—Do You know how she died? We had gone to a wild-country area. A man saw her, alone, while I was off hunting gem rocks to make her a necklace. He approached her. She refused him. He threatened force. She fled. This was desert land, viper land, and she was barefoot. One of them bit her. I did not find her till hours later. By then the poison and the unshaded sun—She died quite soon after she told me what had happened and that she loved me. I could not get her body to chemosurgery in time for normal revival procedures. I had to let them cremate her and take her soul away to SUM."

"What right have you to demand her back, when no one else can be given their own?"

"The right that I love her, and she loves me. We are more necessary to each other than sun or moon. I do not think You could find another two people of whom this is so, Lady. And is not everyone entitled to claim what is necessary to his life? How else can society be kept whole?"

"You are being fantastic," She says thinly. "Let me go."

"No, Lady, I am speaking sober truth. But poor plain words won't serve me. I sing to You because then maybe You will understand." And I strike my harp anew; but it is more to her than Her that I sing.

> "If I had thought thou couldst have died,
> I might not weep for thee;
> But I forgot, when by thy side,
> That thou couldst mortal be:
> It never through my mind had past
> The time would e'er be o'er,
> And I on thee should look my last,
> And thou shouldst smile no more!"

"I cannot—" She falters. "I did not know—any such feelings—so strong—existed any longer."

"Now You do, Lady of Ours. And is that not an important datum for SUM?"

"Yes. If true." Abruptly She leans toward me. I see Her shudder in the murk, under the flapping cloak, and hear Her jaws clatter with cold. "I cannot linger here. But ride with Me. Sing to Me. I think I can bear it."

So much have I scarcely expected. But my destiny is upon me. I mount into the chariot. The canopy slides shut and we proceed.

The main cabin encloses us. Behind its rear door must be facilities for Her living on earth; this is a big vehicle. But here is little except curved panels. They are true wood of different comely grains: so She also needs periodic escape from our machine existence, does She? Furnishing is scant and austere. The only sound is our passage, muffled to a murmur for us; and, because their photomultipliers are not activated, the scanners show nothing outside but night. We huddle close to a glower, hands extended toward its fieriness. Our shoulders brush, our bare arms. Her skin is soft and Her hair falls loose

119

over the thrown-back cowl, smelling of the summer which is dead. What, is She still human?

After a timeless time, She says, not yet looking at me: "The thing you sang, there on the highroad as I came near— I do not remember it. Not even from the years before I became what I am."

"It is older than SUM," I answer, "and its truth will outlive It."

"Truth?" I see Her tense Herself. "Sing Me the rest."

My fingers are no longer too numb to call forth chords.

> "—Unto the Death gois all Estatis,
> Princis, Prelattis, and Potestatis,
> Baith rich and poor of all degree:—
> Timor mortis conturbat me.
>
> He takis the knichtis in to the field
> Enarmit under helm and scheild:
> Victor he is at all mellie:—
> Timor mortis conturbat me.
>
> That strong unmerciful tyrand
> Takis, on the mother's breast sowkand,
> The babe full of benignitio:—
> Timor mortis conturbat me.
>
> He takis the campion in the stour,
> The captain closit in the tour,
> The ladie in bour full of bewtie:—"

(There I must stop a moment.)

> "Timor mortis conturbat me.
>
> He sparis no lord for his piscence,
> Ha clerk for his intelligence;
> His awful straik may no man flee:—
> Timor mortis conturbat me."

She breaks me off, clapping hands to ears and half-shrieking, "No!"

I, grown unmerciful, pursue Her: "You understand now, do You not? You are not eternal either. SUM isn't. Not Earth, not sun, not stars. We hid from the truth. Every one

120

of us. I too, until I lost the one thing which made everything make sense. Then I had nothing left to lose, and could look with clear eyes. And what I saw was Death."

"Get out! Let Me alone!"

"I will not let the whole world alone, Queen, until I get her back. Give me her again, and I'll believe in SUM again. I'll praise It till men dance for joy to hear Its name."

She challenges me with wildcat eyes. "Do you think such matters to It?"

"Well," I shrug, "songs could be useful. They could help achieve the great objective sooner. Whatever that is. 'Optimization of total human activity'—wasn't that the program? I don't know if it still is. SUM has been adding to Itself so long. I doubt if You Yourself understand Its purposes, Lady of Ours."

"Don't speak as if It were alive," She says harshly. "It is a computer-effector complex. Nothing more."

"Are You certain?"

"I—Yes. It thinks, more widely and deeply than any human ever did or could; but It is not alive, not aware. It has no consciousness. That is one reason why It decided It needed Me."

"Be that as it may, Lady," I tell Her, "the ultimate result, whatever It finally does with us, lies far in the future. At present I care about that; I worry; I resent our loss of self-determination. But that's because only such abstractions are left to me. Give me back my Lightfoot, and she, not the distant future, will be my concern. I'll be grateful, honestly grateful, and You Two will know it from the songs I then choose to sing. Which, as I said, might be helpful to It."

"You are unbelievably insolent," She says without force.

"No, Lady, just desperate," I say.

The ghost of a smile touches Her lips. She leans back, eyes hooded, and murmurs, "Well, I'll take you there. What happens then, you realize, lies outside My power. My observations, My recommendations, are nothing but a few items to take into account, among billions. However . . . we have a long way to travel this night. Give me what data you think will help you, Harper."

I do not finish the Lament. Nor do I dwell in any other fashion on grief. Instead, as the hours pass, I call upon those who dealt with the joy (not the fun, not the short delirium, but the joy) that man and woman might once have of each other.

Knowing where we are bound, I too need such comfort.

And the night deepens, and the leagues fall behind us, and finally we are beyond habitation, beyond wildcountry, in the land where life never comes. By crooked moon and waning starlight I see the plain of concrete and iron, the missiles and energy projectors crouched like beasts, the robot aircraft wheeling aloft; and the lines, the relay towers, the scuttling beetle-shaped carriers, that whole transcendent nerve-blood-sinew by which SUM knows and orders the world. For all the flitting about, for all the forces which seethe, here is altogether still. The wind itself seems to have frozen to death. Hoarfrost is gray on the steel shapes. Ahead of us, tiered and mountainous, begins to appear the castle of SUM.

She Who rides with me does not give sign of noticing that my songs have died in my throat. What humanness She showed is departing; Her face is cold and shut, Her voice bears a ring of metal. She looks straight ahead. But She does speak to me for a little while yet:

"Do you understand what is going to happen? For the next half year I will be linked with SUM, integral, another component of It. I suppose you will see Me, but that will merely be My flesh. What speaks to you will be SUM."

"I know." The words must be forced forth. My coming this far is more triumph than any man in creation before me has won; and I am here to do battle for my Dancer-on-Moonglades; but nonetheless my heart shakes me, and is loud in my skull, and my sweat stinks.

I manage, though, to add: "You will be a part of It, Lady of Ours. That gives me hope."

For an instant She turns to me, and lays Her hand across mine, and something makes Her again so young and untaken that I almost forget the girl who died; and she whispers, "If you knew how I hope!"

The instant is gone, and I am alone among machines.

We must stop before the castle gate. The wall looms sheer above, so high and high that it seems to be toppling upon me against the westward march of the stars, so black and black that it does not only drink down every light, it radiates blindness. Challenge and response quiver on electronic bands I cannot sense. The outer-guardian parts of It have perceived a mortal aboard this craft. A missile launcher swings about to aim its three serpents at me. But the Dark Queen answers— She does not trouble to be peremptory—and the castle opens its jaws for us.

We descend. Once, I think, we cross a river. I hear a rushing and hollow echoing and see droplets glitter where they are cast onto the viewports and outlined against dark. They vanish at once: liquid hydrogen, perhaps, to keep certain parts near absolute zero?

Much later we stop and the canopy slides back. I rise with Her. We are in a room, or cavern, of which I can see nothing, for there is no light except a dull bluish phosphorescence which streams from every solid object, also from Her flesh and mine. But I judge the chamber is enormous, for a sound of great machines at work comes very remotely, as if heard through dream, while our own voices are swallowed up by distance. Air is pumped through, neither warm nor cold, totally without odor, a dead wind.

We descend to the floor. She stands before me, hands crossed on breast, eyes half shut beneath the cowl and not looking at me nor away from me. "Do what you are told, Harper," She says in a voice that has never an overtone, "Precisely as you are told." She turns and departs at an even pace. I watch Her go until I can no longer tell Her luminosity from the formless swirlings within my own eyeballs.

A claw plucks my tunic. I look down and am surprised to see that the dwarf robot has been waiting for me this whole time. How long a time that was, I cannot tell.

Its squat form leads me in another direction. Weariness crawls upward through me, my feet stumble, my lips tingle, lids are weighted and muscles have each their separate aches. Now and then I feel a jag of fear, but dully. When the robot indicates *Lie down here*, I am grateful.

The box fits me well. I let various wires be attached to me, various needles be injected which lead into tubes. I pay little attention to the machines which cluster and murmur around me. The robot goes away. I sink into blessed darkness.

I wake renewed in body. A kind of shell seems to have grown between my forebrain and the old animal parts. Far away I can feel the horror and hear the screaming and thrashing of my instincts; but awareness is chill, calm, logical. I have also a feeling that I slept for weeks, months, while leaves blew loose and snow fell on the upper world. But this may be wrong, and in no case does it matter. I am about to be judged by SUM.

The little faceless robot leads me off, through murmurous black corridors where the dead wind blows. I unsling my harp and clutch it to me, my sole friend and weapon. So the tranquillity of the reasoning mind which has been decreed for me cannot be absolute. I decide that It simply does not want to be bothered by anguish. (No; wrong; nothing so human-like; It has no desires; beneath that power to reason is nullity.)

At length a wall opens for us and we enter a room where She sits enthroned. The self-radiation of metal and flesh is not apparent here, for light is provided, a featureless white radiance with no apparent source. White, too, is the muted sound of the machines which encompass Her throne. White are Her robe and face. I look away from the multitudinous unwinking scanner eyes, into Hers, but She does not appear to recognize me. Does She even see me? Sum has reached out with invisible fingers of electromagnetic induction and taken Her back into Itself. I do not tremble or sweat—I cannot—but I square my shoulders, strike one plangent chord, and wait for It to speak.

It does, from some invisible place. I recognize the voice It has chosen to use: my own. The overtones, the inflections are true, normal, what I myself would use in talking as one reasonable man to another. Why not? In computing what to do about me, and in programming Itself accordingly, SUM must have used so many billion bits of information that adequate accent is a negligible sub-problem.

No . . . there I am mistaken again . . . SUM does not do things on the basis that It might as well do them as not. This talk with myself is intended to have some effect on me. I do not know what.

"Well," It says pleasantly, "you made quite a journey, didn't you? I'm glad. Welcome."

My instincts bare teeth to hear those words of humanity used by the unfeeling unalive. My logical mind considers replying with an ironic "Thank you," decides against it, and holds me silent.

"You see," SUM continues after a moment that whirrs, "you are unique. Pardon Me if I speak a little bluntly. Your sexual monomania is just one aspect of a generally atavistic, superstition-oriented personality. And yet, unlike the ordinary misfit, you're both strong and realistic enough to cope with the world. This chance to meet you, to analyze you while you rested, has opened new insights for Me on human psychophysiology. Which may lead to improved techniques for governing it and its evolution."

"That being so," I reply, "give me my reward."

124

"Now look here," SUM says in a mild tone, "you if anyone should know I'm not omnipotent. I was built originally to help govern a civilization grown too complex. Gradually, as My program of self-expansion progressed, I took over more and more decision-making functions. They were *given* to Me. People were happy to be relieved of responsibility, and they could see for themselves how much better I was running things than any mortal could. But to this day, My authority depends on a substantial consensus. If I started playing favorites, as by re-creating your girl, well, I'd have troubles."

"The consensus depends more on awe than on reason," I say. "You haven't abolished the gods, You've simply absorbed them into Yourself. If You choose to pass a miracle to me, your prophet singer—and I will be Your prophet if You do this—why, that strengthens the faith of the rest."

"So you think. But your opinions aren't based on any exact data. The historical and anthropological records from the past before Me are unquantitative. I've already phased them out of the curriculum. Eventually, when the culture's ready for such a move, I'll order them destroyed. They're too misleading. Look what they've done to you."

I grin into the scanner eyes. "Instead," I say, "people will be encouraged to think that before the world was, was SUM. All right. I don't care, as long as I get my girl back. Pass me a miracle, SUM, and I'll guarantee You a good payment."

"But I have no miracles. Not in your sense. You know how the soul works. The metal bracelet encloses a pseudo-virus, a set of giant protein molecules with tapes directly to the bloodstream and nervous system. They record the chromosome pattern, the synapse flash, the permanent changes, everything. At the owner's death, the bracelet is dissected out. The Winged Heels bring it here, and the information contained is transferred to one of My memory banks. I can use such a record to guide the growing of a new body in the vats: a young body, on which the former habits and recollections are imprinted. But you don't understand the complexity of the process, Harper. It takes Me weeks, every seven years, and very available biochemical facility, to re-create My human liaison. And the process isn't perfect, either. The pattern is affected by storage. You might say that this body and brain you see before you remembers each death. And those are short deaths. A longer one—man, use your sense. Imagine."

I can; and the shield between reason and feeling begins to crack. I had sung, of my darling dead:

125

"No motion has she now, no force;
She neither hears nor sees;
Roll'd round in earth's diurnal course,
With rocks, and stones, and trees."

Peace, at least. But if the memory-storage is not permanent but circulating; if, within those gloomy caverns of tubes and wire and outer-space cold, some remnant of her psyche must flit and flicker, alone, unremembering, aware of nothing but having lost life—No!

I smite the harp and shout so the room rings: "Give her back! Or I'll kill you!"

SUM finds it expedient to chuckle; and, horribly, the smile is reflected for a moment on the Dark Queen's lips, though otherwise She never stirs. "And how do you propose to do that?" It asks me.

It knows, I know, what I have in mind, so I counter: "How do You propose to stop me?"

"No need. You'll be considered a nuisance. Finally someone will decide you ought to have psychiatric treatment. They'll query My diagnostic outlet. I'll recommend certain excisions."

"On the other hand, since You've sifted my mind by now, and since You know how I've affected people with my songs—even the Lady yonder, even Her—wouldn't you rather have me working for You? With words like, 'O taste, and see, how gracious the Lord is; blessed is the man that trusteth in him. O fear the Lord, ye that are his saints: for they that fear him lack nothing.' I can make You into God."

"In a sense, I already am God."

"And in another sense not. Not yet." I can endure no more. "Why are we arguing? You made Your decision before I woke. Tell me and let me go!"

With an odd carefulness, SUM responds: "I'm still studying you. No harm in admitting to you, My knowledge of the human psyche is as yet imperfect. Certain areas won't yield to computation. I don't know precisely what you'd do, Harper. If to that uncertainty I added a potentially dangerous precedent—"

"Kill me, then. Let my ghost wander forever with hers, down in Your cryogenic dreams."

"No, that's also inexpedient. You've made yourself too conspicuous and controversial. Too many people know by now that you went off with the Lady." Is it possible that, behind steel and energy, a nonexistent hand brushes across a shadow face in puzzlement? My heartbeat is thick in the silence.

Suddenly It shakes me with decision: "The calculated probabilities do favor your keeping your promises and making yourself useful. Therefore I shall grant your request. However—"

I am on my knees. My forehead knocks on the floor until blood runs into my eyes. I hear through stormwinds:

"—testing must continue. Your faith in Me is not absolute; in fact, you're very skeptical of what you call My goodness. Without additional proof of your willingness to trust Me, I can't let you have the kind of importance which your getting your dead back from Me would give you. Do you understand?"

The question does not sound rhetorical. "Yes," I sob.

"Well, then," says my civilized, almost amiable voice, "I computed that you'd react much as you have done, and prepared for the likelihood. Your woman's body was re-created while you lay under study. The data which make personality are now being fed back into her neurones. She'll be ready to leave this place by the time you do.

"I repeat, though, there has to be a testing. The procedure is also necessary for its effect on you. If you're to be My prophet, you'll have to work pretty closely with Me; you'll have to undergo a great deal of reconditioning; this night we begin the process. Are you willing?"

"Yes, yes, yes, what must I do?"

"Only this: follow the robot out. At some point, she, your woman, will join you. She'll be conditioned to walk so quietly you can't hear her. Don't look back. Not once, until you're in the upper world. A single glance behind you will be an act of rebellion against Me, and a datum indicating you can't really be trusted . . . and that ends everything. Do you understand?"

"Is that all?" I cry. "Nothing more?"

"It will prove more difficult than you think," SUM tells me. My voice fades, as if into illimitable distances: "Farewell, worshipper."

The robot raises me to my feet. I stretch out my arms to the Dark Queen. Half-blinded with tears, I nonetheless see that She does not see me. "Goodbye," I mumble, and let the robot lead me away.

Our walking is long through those mirk miles. At first I am

in too much of a turmoil, and later too stunned, to know when or how we are bound. But later still, slowly, I become aware of my flesh and clothes and the robot's alloy, glimmering blue in blackness. Sounds and smells are muffled; rarely does another machine pass by, unheeding of us. (What work does SUM have for them?) I am so careful not to look behind me that my neck grows stiff.

Though it is not prohibited, is it, to lift my harp past my shoulder, in the course of strumming a few melodies to keep up my courage, and see if perchance a following illumination is reflected in this polished wood?

Nothing. Well, her second birth must take time—O SUM, be careful of her!—and then she must be led through many tunnels, no doubt, before she makes rendevous with my back. Be patient, Harper.

Sing. Welcome her home. No, these hollow spaces swallow all music; and she is as yet in that trance of death from which only the sun and my kiss can wake her; if, indeed, she has joined me yet. I listen for other footfalls than my own.

Surely we haven't much farther to go. I ask the robot, but of course I get no reply. Make an estimate. I know about how fast the chariot traveled coming down . . . The trouble is, time does not exist here. I have no day, no stars, no clock but my heartbeat and I have lost the count of that. Nevertheless, we must come to the end soon. What purpose would be served by walking me through this labyrinth till I die?

Well, if I am totally exhausted at the outer gate, I won't make undue trouble when I find no Rose-in-Hand behind me.

No, now that's ridiculous. If SUM didn't want to heed my plea, It need merely say so. I have no power to inflict physical damage on Its parts.

Of course, It might have plans for me. It did speak of reconditioning. A series of shocks, culminating in that last one, could make me ready for whatever kind of gelding It intends to do.

Or It might have changed Its mind. Why not? It was quite frank about an uncertainty factor in the human psyche. It may have re-evaluated the probabilities and decided: better not to serve my desire.

Or It may have tried, and failed. It admitted the recording process is imperfect. I must not expect quite the Gladness I knew; she will always be a little haunted. At best. But suppose the tank spawned a body with no awareness behind the eyes? Or a monster? Suppose, at this instant, I am being followed by a half-rotten corpse?

No! Stop that! SUM would know, and take corrective measures.

Would It? *Can It?*

I comprehend how this passage through night, where I never look to see what follows me, how this is an act of submission and confession. I am saying, with my whole existent being, that SUM is all-powerful, all-wise, all-good. To SUM I offer the love I came to win back. Oh, It looked more deeply into me than ever I did myself.

But I shall not fail.

Will SUM though? If there has indeed been some grisly error . . . let me not find it out under the sky. Let her, my only, not. For what then shall we do? Could I lead her here again, knock on the iron gate, and cry, "Master, You have given me a thing unfit to exist. Destroy it and start over?" For what might the wrongness be? Something so subtle, so pervasive, that it does not show in any way save my slow, resisted discovery that I embrace a zombie? Doesn't it make better sense to look—make certain while she is yet drowsy with death—use the whole power of SUM to correct what may be awry?

No, SUM wants me to believe that It makes no mistakes. I agreed to that price. And to much else . . . I don't know how much else, I am daunted to imagine, but that word "recondition" is ugly . . . Does not my woman have some rights in the matter too? Shall we not at least ask her if she wants to be the wife of a prophet; shall we not, hand in hand, ask SUM what the price of her life is to her?

Was that a footfall? Almost, I whirl about. I check myself and stand shaking; names of hers break from my lips. The robot urges me on.

Imagination. It wasn't her step. I am alone. I will always be alone.

The halls wind upward. Or so I think; I have grown too weary for much kinesthetic sense. We cross the sounding river and I am bitten to the bone by the cold which blows upward around the bridge, and I may not turn about to offer the naked newborn woman my garment. I lurch through endless chambers where machines do meaningless things. She hasn't seen them before. Into what nightmare has she risen; and why don't I, who wept into her dying senses that I loved her, why don't I look at her, why don't I speak?

Well, I could talk to her. I could assure the puzzled mute dead that I have come to lead her back into sunlight. Could I not? I asked the robot. It does not reply. I cannot remember if I may speak to her. If indeed I was ever told. I stumble forward.

I crash into a wall and fall bruised. The robot's claw closes on my shoulder. Another arm gestures. I see a passageway, very long and narrow, through the stone. I will have to crawl through. At the end, at the end, the door is swinging wide. The dear real dusk of Earth pours through into this darkness. I am blinded and deafened.

Do I hear her cry out? Was that the final testing; or was my own sick, shaken mind betraying me; or is there a destiny which, like SUM with us, makes tools of suns and SUM? I don't know. I know only that I turned, and there she stood. Her hair flowed long, loose, past the remembered face from which the trance was just departing, on which the knowing and the love of me had just awakened—flowed down over the body that reached forth arms, that took one step to meet me and was halted.

The great grim robot at her own back takes her to it. I think it sends lightning through her brain. She falls. It bears her away.

My guide ignores my screaming. Irresistible, it thrusts me out through the tunnel. The door clangs in my face. I stand before the wall which is like a mountain. Dry snow hisses across concrete. The sky is bloody with dawn; stars still gleam in the west, and arc lights are scattered over the twilight plain of the machines.

Presently I go dumb. I become almost calm. What is there left to have feelings about? The door is iron, the wall is stone fused into one basaltic mass. I walk some distance off into the wind, turn around, lower my head and charge. Let my brains be smeared across Its gate; the pattern will be my hieroglyphic for hatred.

I am seized from behind. The force that stops me must needs be bruisingly great. Released, I crumple to the ground before a machine with talons and wings. My voice from it says, "Not here. I'll carry you to a safe place."

"What more can You do to me?" I croak.

"Release you. You won't be restrained or molested on any orders of Mine."

"Why not?"

"Obviously you're going to appoint yourself My enemy
130

forever. This is an unprecedented situation, a valuable chance to collect data."

"You tell me this, You warn me, deliberately?"

"Of course. My computation is that these words will have the effect of provoking your utmost effort."

"You won't give her again? You don't want my love?"

"Not under the circumstances. Too uncontrollable. But your hatred should, as I say, be a useful experimental tool."

"I'll destroy You," I say.

It does not deign to speak further. Its machine picks me up and flies off with me. I am left on the fringes of a small town farther south. Then I go insane.

I do not much know what happens during that winter, nor care. The blizzards are too loud in my head. I walk the ways of Earth, among lordly towers, under neatly groomed trees, into careful gardens, over bland, bland campuses. I am unwashed, uncombed, unbarbered; my tatters flap about me and my bones are near thrusting through the skin; folk do not like to meet these eyes sunken so far into this skull, and perhaps for that reason they give me to eat. I sing to them.

> "From the hag and hungry goblin
> That into rags would rend ye
> And the spirit that stan' by the naked man
> In the Book of Moons defend ye!
> That of your five sound senses
> You never be forsaken
> Nor travel from yourselves with Tom
> Abroad to beg your bacon."

Such things perturb them, do not belong in their chrome-edged universe. So I am often driven away with curses, and sometimes I must flee those who would arrest me and scrub my brain smooth. An alley is a good hiding place, if I can find one in the oldest part of a city; I crouch there and yowl with the cats. A forest is also good. My pursuers dislike to enter any place where any wildness lingers.

But some feel otherwise. They have visited parklands, preserves, actual wildcountry. Their purpose was overconscious—measured, planned savagery, and a clock to tell them when they must go home—but at least they are not afraid of silences and unlighted nights. As spring returns, certain among them begin to follow me. They are merely curious, at first. But slowly, month by month, especially among the younger ones, my madness begins to call to something in them.

> "With an host of furious fancies
> Whereof I am commander
> With a burning spear, and a horse of air,
> To the wilderness I wander.
> By a knight of ghosts and shadows
> I summoned am to tourney
> Ten leagues beyond the wide world's edge.
> Me thinks it is no journey."

They sit at my feet and listen to me sing. They dance, crazily, to my harp. The girls bend close, tell me how I fascinate them, invite me to copulate. This I refuse, and when I tell them why they are puzzled, a little frightened maybe, but often they strive to understand.

For my rationality is renewed with the hawthorn blossoms. I bathe, have my hair and beard shorn, find clean raiment and take care to eat what my body needs. Less and less do I rave before anyone who will listen; more and more do I seek solitude, quietness, under the vast wheel of the stars, and think.

What is man? Why is man? We have buried such questions; we have sworn they are dead—that they never really existed, being devoid of empirical meaning—and we have dreaded that they might raise the stones we heaped on them, rise and walk the world again of nights. Alone, I summon them to me. They cannot hurt their fellow dead, among whom I now number myself.

I sing to her who is gone. The young people hear and wonder. Sometimes they weep.

> "Fear no more the heat o' the sun,
> Nor the furious winter's rages;
> Thou thy worldly task hast done,
> Home art gone, and ta'en thy wages:
> Golden lads and girls all must
> As chimney-sweepers, come to dust."

"But this is not so!" they protest. "We will die and sleep a while, and then we will live forever in SUM."

I answer as gently as may be: "No. Remember I went

there. So I know you are wrong. And even if you were right, it would not be right that you should be right."

"What?"

"Don't you see, it is not right that a thing should be the lord of man. It is not right that we should huddle through our whole lives in fear of finally losing them. You are not parts in a machine, and you have better ends than helping the machine run smoothly."

I dismiss them and stride off, solitary again, into a canyon where a river clangs, or onto some gaunt mountain peak. No revelation is given me. I climb and creep toward the truth.

Which is that SUM must be destroyed, not in revenge, not in hate, not in fear, simply because the human spirit cannot exist in the same reality as It.

But what, then, is our proper reality? And how shall we attain to it?

I return with my songs to the lowlands. Word about me has gone widely. They are a large crowd who follow me down the highroad until it has changed into a street.

"The Dark Queen will soon come to these parts," they tell me. "Abide till She does. Let Her answer those questions you put to us, which make us sleep so badly."

"Let me retire to prepare myself," I say. I go up a long flight of steps. The people watch from below, dumb with awe, till I vanish. Such few as were in the building depart. I walk down vaulted halls, through hushed high-ceilinged rooms full of tables, among shelves made massive by books. Sunlight slants dusty through the windows.

The half memory has plagued me of late: once before, I know not when, this year of mine also took place. Perhaps in this library I can find the tale that—casually, I suppose, in my abnormal childhood—I read. For man is older than SUM: wiser, I swear; his myths hold more truth than Its mathematics. I spend three days and most of three nights in my search. There is scant sound but the rustling of leaves between my hands. Folk place offerings of food and drink at the door. They tell themselves they do so out of pity, or curiosity, or to avoid the nuisance of having me die in an unconventional fashion. But I know better.

At the end of the three days I am little further along. I have too much material; I keep going off on sidetracks of beauty and fascination. (Which SUM means to eliminate.) My education was like everyone else's, science, rationality, good sane adjustment. (SUM writes our curricula, and the

133

teaching machines have direct connections to It.) Well, I can make some of my lopsided training work for me. My reading has given me sufficient clues to prepare a search program. I sit down before an information retrieval console and run my fingers across its keys. They make a clattery music.

Electron beams are swift hounds. Within seconds the screen lights up with words, and I read who I am.

It is fortunate that I am a fast reader. Before I can press the Clear button, the unreeling words are wiped out. For an instant the screen quivers with formlessness, then appears.

I HAD NOT CORRELATED THESE DATA WITH THE FACTS CONCERNING YOU. THIS INTRODUCES A NEW INDETERMINATE QUANTITY INTO THE COMPUTATIONS.

The nirvana which has come upon me (yes, I found that word among the old books, and how portentous it is) is not passiveness, it is a tide more full and strong than that which bore me down to the Dark Queen those ages apast in wild-country. I say, as coolly as may be, "An interesting coincidence. If it is a coincidence." Surely sonic receptors are emplaced hereabouts.

EITHER THAT, OR A CERTAIN NECESSARY CONSEQUENCE OF THE LOGIC OF EVENTS.

The vision dawning within me is so blinding bright that I cannot refrain from answering, "Or a destiny, SUM?"

MEANINGLESS. MEANINGLESS. MEANINGLESS.

"Now why did You repeat Yourself in that way? Once would have sufficed. Thrice, though, makes an incantation. Are You by any chance hoping Your words will make me stop existing?"

I DO NOT HOPE. YOU ARE AN EXPERIMENT. IF I COMPUTE A SIGNIFICANT PROBABILITY OF YOUR CAUSING SERIOUS DISTURBANCE, I WILL HAVE YOU TERMINATED.

I smile. "SUM," I say, "I am going to terminate You." I lean over and switch off the screen. I walk out into the evening.

Not everything is clear to me yet, that I must say and do. But enough is that I can start preaching at once to those who have been waiting for me. As I talk, others come down the street, and hear, and stay to listen. Soon they number in the hundreds.

I have no immense new truth to offer them: nothing that I have not said before, although piecemeal and unsystematically; nothing they have not felt themselves, in the innermost darkness of their beings. Today, however, knowing who I am and therefore why I am, I can put these things in words. Speaking quietly, now and then drawing on some forgotten song to show my meaning, I tell them how sick and starved their lives are; how they have made themselves slaves; how the enslavement is not even to a conscious mind, but to an insensate inanimate thing which their own ancestors began; how that thing is not the centrum of exisence, but a few scraps of metal and bleats of energy, a few sad stupid patterns, adrift in unbounded space-time. Put not your faith in SUM, I tell them. SUM is doomed, even as you and I. Seek out mystery; what else is the whole cosmos but mystery? Live bravely, die and be done, and you will be more than any machine. You may perhaps be God.

They grow tumultuous. They shout replies, some of which are animal howls. A few are for me, most are opposed. That doesn't matter. I have reached into them, my music is being played on their nervestrings, and this is my entire purpose.

The sun goes down behind the buildings. Dusk gathers. The city remains unilluminated. I soon realize why. She is coming, the Dark Queen Whom they wanted me to debate with. From afar we hear Her chariot thunder. Folk wail in terror. They are not wont to do that either. They used to disguise their feelings from Her and themselves by receiving Her with grave sparse ceremony. Now they would flee if they dared. I have lifted the masks.

The chariot halts in the street. She dismounts, tall and shadowy cowled. The people make way before Her like water before a shark. She climbs the stairs to face me. I see for the least instant that Her lips are not quite firm and Her eyes abrim with tears. She whispers, too low for anyone else to hear, "Oh, Harper, I'm sorry."

"Come join me," I invite. "Help me set the world free."

"No. I cannot. I have been too long with It." She straightens. Imperium descends upon Her. Her voice rises for everyone to hear. The little television robots flit close, bat shapes in the twilight, that the whole planet may witness my defeat. "What is this freedom you rant about?" She demands.

"To feel," I say. "To venture. To wonder. To become men again."

"To become beasts, you mean. Would you demolish the machines that keep us alive?"

"Yes. We must. Once they were good and useful, but we

135

let them grow upon us like a cancer, and now nothing but destruction and a new beginning can save us."

"Have you considered the chaos?"

"Yes. It too is necessary. We will not be men without the freedom to know suffering. In it is also enlightenment. Through it we travel beyond ourselves, beyond earth and stars, space and time, to Mystery."

"So you maintain that there is some undefined ultimate vagueness behind the measurable universe?" She smiles into the bat eyes. We have each been taught, as children, to laugh on hearing sarcasms of this kind. "Please offer me a little proof."

"No." I say. "Prove to me instead, beyond any doubt, that there is *not* something we cannot understand with words and equations. Prove to me likewise that I have no right to seek for it.

"The burden of proof is on You Two, so often have You lied to us. In the name of rationality, You resurrected myth. The better to control us! In the name of liberation, You chained our inner lives and castrated our souls. In the name of service, You bound and blinkered us. In the name of achievement, You held us to a narrower round than any swine in its pen. In the name of beneficence, You created pain, and horror, and darkness beyond darkness." I turn to the people. "I went there. I descended into the cellars. I know!"

"He found that SUM would not pander to his special wishes, at the expense of everyone else," cries the Dark Queen. Do I hear shrillness in her voice? "Therefore he claims SUM is cruel."

"I saw my dead," I tell them. "She will not rise again. Nor yours, nor you. Not ever, SUM will not, cannot raise us. In Its house is death indeed. We must seek life and rebirth elsewhere, among the mysteries."

She laughs aloud and points to my soul bracelet, glimmering faintly in the gray-blue thickening twilight. Need She say anything?

"Will someone give me a knife and an ax?" I ask.

The crowd stirs and mumbles. I smell their fear. Street lamps go on, as if they could scatter more than this corner of the night which is rolling upon us. I fold my arms and wait. The Dark Queen says something to me. I ignore Her.

The tools pass from hand to hand. He who brings them up the stairs comes like a flame. He kneels at my feet and lifts

136

what I have desired. The tools are good ones, a broad-bladed hunting knife and a long double-bitted ax.

Before the world, I take the knife in my right hand and slash beneath the bracelet on my left wrist. The connections to my inner body are cut. Blood flows, impossibly brilliant under the lamps. It does not hurt; I am too exalted.

The Dark Queen shrieks, "You meant it! Harper, Harper!"

"There is no life in SUM," I say. I pull my hand through the circle and cast the bracelet down so it rings.

A voice of brass: *"Arrest that maniac for correction. He is deadly dangerous."*

The monitors who have stood on the fringes of the crowd try to push through. They are resisted. Those who seek to help them encounter fists and fingernails.

I take the ax and smash downward. The bracelet crumples. The organic material within, starved of my secretions, exposed to the night air, withers.

I raise the tools, ax in right hand, knife in bleeding left. "I seek eternity where it is to be found," I call. "Who goes with me?"

A score or better break loose from the riot, which is already calling forth weapons and claiming lives. They surround me with their bodies. Their eyes are the eyes of prophets. We make haste to seek a hiding place, for one military robot has appeared and others will not be long in coming. The tall engine strides to stand guard over Our Lady, and this is my last glimpse of Her.

My followers do not reproach me for having cost them all they were. They are mine. In me is the godhead which can do no wrong.

And the war is open, between me and SUM. My friends are few, my enemies many and mighty. I go about the world as a fugitive. But always I sing. And always I find someone who will listen, will join us, embracing pain and death like a lover.

With the Knife and the Ax I take their souls. Afterward we hold for them the ritual of rebirth. Some go thence to become outlaw missionaries; most put on facsimile bracelets and return home, to whisper my word. It makes little difference to me. I have no haste, who own eternity.

For my word is of what lies beyond time. My enemies say I call forth ancient bestialities and lunacies; that I would bring civilization down in ruin; that it matters not a madman's giggle to me whether war, famine, and pestilence will

137

again scour the earth. With these accusations I am satisfied. The language of them shows me that here, too, I have re-awakened anger. And that emotion belongs to us as much as any other. More than the others, maybe, in the autumn of mankind. We need a gale, to strike down SUM and everything It stands for. Afterward will come the winter of barbarism.

And after that the springtime of a new and (perhaps) more human civilization. My friends seem to believe this will come in their very lifetimes: peace, brotherhood, enlightenment, sanctity. I know otherwise. I have been in the depths. The wholeness of mankind, which I am bringing back, has its horrors.

When one day

> the Eater of the Gods returns
> the Wolf breaks his chain
> the Horsemen ride forth
> the Age ends
> the Beast is reborn

then SUM will be destroyed; and you, strong and fair, may go back to earth and rain.

I shall await you.

My aloneness is nearly ended, Daybright. Just one task remains. The god must die, that his followers may believe he is raised from the dead and lives forever. Then they will go on to conquer the world.

There are those who say I have spurned and offended them. They too, borne on the tide which I raised, have torn out their machines souls and seek in music and ecstasy to find a meaning for existence. But their creed is a savage one, which has taken them into wildcountry, where they ambush the monitors sent against them and practice cruel rites. They believe that the final reality is female. Nevertheless, messengers of theirs have approached me with the suggestion of a mystic marriage. This I refuse; my wedding was long ago, and will be celebrated again when this cycle of the world has closed.

Therefore they hate me. But I have said I will come and talk to them.

I leave the road at the bottom of the valley and walk singing up the hill. Those few I let come this far with me have been told to abide my return. They shiver in the sunset; the vernal equinox is three days away. I feel no cold myself. I stride exultant among briars and twisted ancient apple trees. If my bare feet leave a little blood in the snow, that is good. The ridges around are dark with forest, which waits like the skeleton dead for leaves to be breathed across it again. The eastern sky is purple, where stands the evening star. Overhead, against blue, cruises an early flight of homebound geese. Their calls drift faintly down to me. Westward, above me and before me, smolders redness. Etched black against it are the women.

Frederik Pohl and C. M. Kornbluth

Now it is time to tell you why the thirty-first was the most magnificent convention ever to meet anywhere, any time, and in any field. I had published my novel *The Gods Themselves* (Doubleday) in 1972, and it was up for consideration for a Hugo.

As you all know, I am dreadfully short on Hugos. After I had listed my justifiable complaints in that respect in Volume One, attempts were made to rectify it. I got a Hugo for my science articles in 1963, and a Hugo, in retrospect, for my Foundation novels in 1966, but I wanted to win something current, if you know what I mean. *The Gods Themselves* had already taken the Nebula award for that year, and an honest pride in my craft (as opposed to the simple greed with which others approach these awards) made me wish the Hugo as well.

Lester del Rey was toastmaster that year. He twisted and turned in his efforts to delay the inevitable but was finally forced, grudgingly, to announce that victory was mine. I got it—a beautiful Hugo, which is prominently displayed in my living room along with the other two.

I'm not yet *completely* satisfied but I'll get to that in the Afterword.

At the Torcon, there were seated along with myself and Janet, Barbara and Ben Bova, Carol and Fred Pohl, and Gordon Dickson. First I had won in the novel category and brought my Hugo gleefully back to the table. Then Fred won in the short story category and brought back two, one for himself and one in the name of Cyril Kornbluth. Then Ben won in the editor category and brought back his.

Four Hugos sat there resplendent on that one table and I felt revolted that we had not made a clean sweep. I turned to sweet, innocent Gordie and said, censoriously, "Your non-Hugo presence at this table disgraces us. Aren't you ashamed?"

He hung his head and pretended to wipe a tear from his eye but I know phoniness when I see it. He wasn't crying. He won in the short story category with "Soldier, Ask Not" at the twenty-third convention in London, in 1965—this is included in Volume Two—and of course, he's let it go to his head.

Personally, I can't stand people without humility. I'm surprised more people don't model themselves on me. I take great pride in the extent of my humility.

I was pleased, by the way, that Cyril was in this way recorded in the archives as a Hugo winner. He died on March 21, 1958, at the age of thirty-six. Had he lived a normal lifespan, he would undoubtedly have won a number of Hugos of his own.

THE MEETING

Harry Vladek was too large a man for his Volkswagen, but he was too poor a man to trade it in, and as things were going he was going to stay that way a long time. He applied the brakes carefully ("master cylinder's leaking like a sieve, Mr. Vladek. What's the use of just fixing up the linings?"—but the estimate was a hundred and twenty-eight dollars, and where was it going to come from?) and parked in the neatly graveled lot. He squeezed out of the door, the upsetting telephone call from Dr. Nicholson on his mind, locked the car up, and went into the school building.

The Parent-Teachers Association of the Bingham County School for Exceptional Children was holding its first meeting of the term. Of the twenty people already there, Vladek knew only Mrs. Adler, the principal, or headmistress, or owner of the school. She was the one he needed to talk to most, he thought. Would there be any chance to see her privately? Right now she sat across the room at her scuffed golden-oak desk in a posture chair, talking in low, rapid tones with a gray-haired woman in a tan suit. A teacher? She seemed too old to be a parent, although his wife had told him some of the kids seemed to be twenty or more.

It was 8:30 and the parents were still driving up to the school, a converted building that had once been a big country house—almost a mansion. The living room was full of elegant reminders of that. *Two* chandeliers. Intricate vineleaf molding on the plaster above the dropped ceiling. The pink-veined, white-marble fireplace, unfortunately prominent because of the unsuitable andirons, too cheap and too small, that now stood in it. Golden-oak, sliding double doors to the hall. And visible through them a grim, fireproof staircase of concrete and steel. They must, Vladek thought, have had to rip out a beautiful wooden thing to install the fireproof stairs for compliance with the state school laws.

People kept coming in, single men, single women, and occasionally a couple. He wondered how the couples managed their baby-sitting problem. The subtitle on the school's letterhead was "an institution for emotionally disturbed and cerebrally damaged children capable of education." Harry's nine-year-old Thomas was one of the emotionally disturbed ones. With a taste of envy he wondered if cerebrally damaged children could be baby-sat by any reasonably competent grown-up. Thomas could not. The Vladeks had not had an evening out together since he was two, so that tonight Margaret was holding the fort at home, no doubt worrying herself sick about the call from Dr. Nicholson, while Harry was representing the family at the PTA.

As the room filled up, chairs were getting scarce. A young couple was standing at the end of the row near him, looking around for a pair of empty seats. "Here," he said to them. "I'll move over." The woman smiled politely and the man said thanks. Emboldened by an ashtray on the empty seat in front of him, Harry pulled out his pack of cigarettes and offered it to them, but it turned out they were nonsmokers. Harry lit up anyway, listening to what was going on around him.

Everybody was talking. One woman asked another, "How's the gall bladder? Are they going to take it out after all?" A heavy balding man said to a short man with bushy sideburns, "Well, my accountant says the tuition's medically deductible if the school is for psycho*somatic*, not just for psycho. That we've got to clear up." The short man told him positively, "Right, but all you need is a doctor's letter: he recommends the school, refers the child to the school." And a very young woman said intensely, "Dr. Shields was very optimistic, Mrs. Clerman. He says without a doubt the thyroid will make

142

Georgie accessible. And then——" A light-coffee-colored black man in an aloha shirt told a plump woman, "He really pulled a wingding over the weekend, two stitches in his face, busted my fishing pole in three places." And the woman said, "They get so bored. My little girl has this thing about crayons, so that rules out coloring books altogether. You wonder what you can do."

Harry finally said to the young man next to him, "My name's Vladek. I'm Tommy's father. He's in the beginners group."

"That's where ours is," said the young man. "He's Vern. Six years old. Blond like me. Maybe you've seen him."

Harry did not try very hard to remember. The two or three times he had picked Tommy up after class he had not been able to tell one child from another in the great bustle of departure. Coats, handkerchiefs, hats, one little girl who always hid in the supply closet and a little boy who never wanted to go home and hung onto the teacher. "Oh, yes," he said politely.

The young man introduced himself and his wife; they were named Murray and Celia Logan. Harry leaned over the man to shake the wife's hand, and she said, "Aren't you new here?"

"Yes. Tommy's been in the school a month. We moved in from Elmira to be near it." He hesitated, then added, "Tommy's nine, but the reason he's in the beginners group is that Mrs. Adler thought it would make the adjustment easier."

Logan pointed to a suntanned man in the first row. "See that fellow with the glasses? He moved here from *Texas*. Of course, he's got money."

"It must be a good place," Harry said questioningly.

Logan grinned, his expression a little nervous.

"How's your son?" Harry asked.

"That little rascal," said Logan. "Last week I got him another copy of the *My Fair Lady* album, I guess he's used up four or five of them, and he goes around singing 'luv-er-ly, luv-er-ly.' But *look* at you? No."

"Mine doesn't talk," said Harry.

Mrs. Logan said judiciously, "Ours talks. Not *to* anybody, though. It's like a wall."

"I know," said Harry, and pressed. "Has, ah, has Vern shown much improvement with the school?"

Murray Logan pursed his lips. "I would say, yes. The bed-

143

wetting's not too good, but life's a great deal smoother in some ways. You know, you don't hope for a dramatic break-through. But in little things, day by day, it goes smoother. Mostly smoother. Of course there are setbacks."

Harry nodded, thinking of seven years of setbacks, and two years of growing worry and puzzlement before that. He said, "Mrs. Adler told me that, for instance, a special outbreak of destructiveness might mean something like a plateau in speech therapy. So the child fights it and breaks out in some other direction."

"That too," said Logan, "but what I meant—Oh, they're starting."

Vladek nodded, stubbing out his cigarette and absent-mind-edly lighting another. His stomach was knotting up again. He wondered at these other parents, who seemed so safe and well, untouched. Wasn't it the same with them as with Margaret and himself? And it had been a long time since either of them had felt the world comfortable around them, even without Dr. Nicholson pressing for a decision. He forced himself to lean back and look as tranquil as the others.

Mrs. Adler was tapping her desk with a ruler. "I think everybody who is coming is here," she said. She leaned against the desk and waited for the room to quiet down. She was short, dark, plump, and surprisingly pretty. She did not look at all like a competent professional. She looked so unlike her role that, in fact, Harry's heart had sunk three months ago when their correspondence about admitting Tommy had been climaxed by the long trip from Elmira for the interview. He had expected a steel-gray lady with rimless glasses, a Valkyrie in a white smock like the nurse who had held wriggling, screaming Tommy while waiting for the suppository to quiet him down for his first EEG, a disheveled old fraud, he didn't know what. Anything except this pretty young woman. Another blind alley, he had thought in despair. Another, after a hundred too many already. First, "Wait for him to outgrow it." He doesn't. Then, "We must reconcile ourselves to God's will." But you don't want to. Then give him the prescription three times a day for three months. And it doesn't work. Then chase around for six months with the Child Guidance Clinic to find out it's only letterheads and one circuit-riding doctor who doesn't have time for anything. Then, after four dreary, weepy weeks of soul-searching, the State Training School, and find out it has an eight-year waiting list. Then the private custodial school, and find they're fifty-five hundred dollars a year—without medical treatment!—and where do you get fifty-five hundred dollars a year? And all the time everybody warns you, as if you didn't know it: "Hurry! Do something! Catch it early! This is the critical stage! Delay is fatal!" And then this soft-looking little woman; how could she do anything?

She had rapidly shown him how. She had questioned Margaret and Harry incisively, turned to Tommy, rampaging through the same room like a rogue bull, and turned his rampage into a game. In three minutes he was happily experimenting with an indestructible old windup cabinet Victrola, and Mrs. Adler was saying to the Vladeks, "Don't count on a miracle cure. There isn't any. But improvements, yes, and I think we can help Tommy."

Perhaps she had, thought Vladek bleakly. Perhaps she was helping as much as anyone ever could.

Meanwhile, Mrs. Adler had quickly and pleasantly welcomed the parents, suggested they remain for coffee and get to know each other, and introduced the PTA president, a Mrs. Rose, tall, prematurely gray and very executive. "This being the first meeting of the term," she said, "there are no minutes to be read, so we'll get to the committee work reports. What about the transportation problem, Mr. Baer?"

The man who got up was old. More than sixty; Harry wondered what it was like to have your life crowned with a late retarded child. He wore all the trappings of success—a four hundred dollar suit, an electronic wristwatch, a large gold fraternal ring. In a slight German accent he said, "I was to the district school board and they are not cooperating. My lawyer looked it up and the trouble is all one word. What the law says, the school board may, that is the word, may, reimburse parents of handicapped children for transportation to private schools. Not shall, you understand, but may. They were very frank with me. They said they just didn't want to spend the money. They have the impression we're all rich people here."

Slight sour laughter around the room.

"So my lawyer made an appointment, and we appeared before the full board and presented the case—we don't care, reimbursement, a school bus, anything so we can relieve the transportation burden a little. The answer was no." He shrugged and remained standing, looking at Mrs. Rose, who said:

"Thank you, Mr. Baer. Does anybody have any suggestions?"

A woman said angrily, "Put some heat on them. We're all voters!"

A man said, "Publicity, that's right. The principle is perfectly clear in the law, one taxpayer's child is supposed to get the same service as another taxpayer's child. We should write letters to the papers."

Mr. Baer said, "Wait a minute. Letters, I don't think mean anything, but I've got a public relations firm. I'll tell them to take a little time off my food specialties and use it for the school. They can use their own know-how, how to do it. They're the experts."

This was moved, seconded, and passed, while Murray Logan whispered to Vladek, "He's Marijane Garlic Mayonnaise. He had a twelve-year-old girl in very bad shape that Mrs. Adler helped in her old private class. He bought this building for her, along with a couple of other parents."

Harry Vladek was musing over how it felt to be a parent who could buy a building for a school that would help your child, while the committee reports continued. Some time later, to Harry's dismay, the business turned to financing, and there was a vote to hold a fund-raising theater party for which each couple with a child in the school would have to sell "at least" five pairs of orchestra seats at sixty dollars a pair. Let's get this straightened out now, he thought, and put up his hand.

"My name is Harry Vladek," he said when he was recognized, "and I'm brand new here. In the school and in the county. I work for a big insurance company, and I was lucky enough to get a transfer here so my boy can go to the school. But I just don't know anybody yet that I can sell tickets to for sixty dollars. That's an awful lot of money for my kind of people."

Mrs. Rose said, "It's an awful lot of money for most of us. You can get rid of your tickets, though. We've got to. It doesn't matter if you try a hundred people and ninety-five say no just as long as the others say yes."

He sat down, already calculating. Well, Mr. Crine at the office. He was a bachelor and he did go to the theater. Maybe work up an office raffle for another pair. Or two pairs. Then there was, let's see, the real estate dealer who had sold them the house, the lawyer they'd used for the closing . . .

Well. It had been explained to him that the tuition, while decidedly not nominal, eighteen hundred dollars a year in fact, did not cover the cost per child. Somebody had to pay for the speech therapist, the dance therapist, the full-time psychologist, and the part-time psychiatrist, and all the others, and it might as well be Mr. Crine at the office. And the lawyer.

And half an hour later Mrs. Rose looked at the agenda, checked off an item and said, "That seems to be all for tonight. Mr. and Mrs. Perry brought us some very nice cookies, and we all know that Mrs. Howe's coffee is out of this world. They're in the beginners room, and we hope you'll all stay to get acquainted. The meeting is adjourned."

Harry and the Logans joined the polite surge to the beginners room, where Tommy spent his mornings. "There's Miss Hackett," said Celia Logan. That was the beginners' teacher. She saw them and came over, smiling. Harry had seen her only in a tentlike smock, her armor against chocolate milk, finger paints, and sudden jets from the "water play" corner of the room. Without it she was handsomely middle-aged in a green pants suit.

"I'm glad you parents have met," she said. "I wanted to tell you that your little boys are getting along nicely. They're forming a sort of conspiracy against the others in the class. Vern swipes their toys and gives them to Tommy."

"He *does?*" cried Logan.

"Yes, indeed. I think he's beginning to relate. And, Mr. Vladek, Tommy's taken his thumb out of his mouth for minutes at a time. At least half a dozen times this morning, without my saying a word."

Harry said excitedly, "You know, I thought I noticed he was tapering off. I couldn't be sure. You're positive about that?"

"Absolutely," she said. "And I bluffed him into drawing a face. He gave me that glare of his when the others were drawing, so I started to take the paper away. He grabbed it back and scribbled a kind of Picasso-ish face in one second flat. I wanted to save it for Mrs. Vladek and you, but Tommy got it and shredded it in that methodical way he has."

"I wish I could have seen it," said Vladek.

"There'll be others. I can see the prospect of real improvement in your boys," she said, including the Logans in her smile. "I have a private case afternoons that's really tricky. A

147

nine-year-old boy, like Tommy. He's not bad except for one thing. He thinks Donald Duck is out to get him. His parents somehow managed to convince themselves for two years that he was kidding them, in spite of three broken TV picture tubes. Then they went to a psychiatrist and learned the score. Excuse me, I want to talk to Mrs. Adler."

Logan shook his head and said, "I guess we could be worse off, Vladek. Vern giving something to another boy! How do you like that?"

"I like it," his wife said radiantly.

"And did you hear about that other boy? Poor kid. When I hear about something like that . . . And then there was the Baer girl. I always think it's worse when it's a little girl because, you know, you worry with little girls that somebody will take advantage, but our boys'll make out, Vladek. You heard what Miss Hackett said."

Harry was suddenly impatient to get home to his wife. "I don't think I'll stay for coffee, or do they expect you to?"

"No, no, leave when you like."

"I have a half-hour drive," he said apologetically and went through the golden-oak doors, past the ugly but fireproof staircase, out onto the graveled parking lot. His real reason was that he wanted very much to get home before Margaret fell asleep so he could tell her about the thumb-sucking. Things were happening, definite things, after only a month. And Tommy drew a face. And Miss Hackett said . . .

He stopped in the middle of the lot. He had remembered about Dr. Nicholson, and besides, what was it, exactly, that Miss Hackett had said? Anything about a normal life? Not anything about a cure? "Real improvement," she said, but improvement how far?

He lit a cigarette, turned, and plowed his way back through the parents to Mrs. Adler. "Mrs. Adler," he said, "may I see you just for a moment?"

She came with him immediately out of earshot of the others. "Did you enjoy the meeting, Mr. Vladek?"

"Oh, sure. What I wanted to see you about is that I have to make a decision. I don't know what to do. I don't know who to go to. It would help a lot if you could tell me, well, what are Tommy's chances?"

She waited a moment before she responded. "Are you considering committing him, Mr. Vladek?" she demanded.

"No; it's not exactly that. It's—well, what can you tell me,

148

Mrs. Adler? I know a month isn't much. But is he ever going to be like everybody else?"

He could see from her face that she had done this before and had hated it. She said patiently, " 'Everybody else,' Mr. Vladek, includes some terrible people who just don't happen, technically, to be handicapped. Our objective isn't to make Tommy like 'everybody else.' It's just to help him to become the best and most rewarding Tommy Vladek he can."

"Yes, but what's going to happen later on? I mean, if Margaret and I—if anything happens to us?"

She was suffering. "There is simply no way to know, Mr. Vladek," she said gently. "I wouldn't give up hope. But I can't tell you to expect miracles."

Margaret wasn't asleep; she was waiting up for him, in the small living room of the small new house. "How was he?" Vladek asked, as each of them had asked the other on returning home for seven years.

She looked as though she had been crying, but she was calm enough. "Not too bad. I had to lie down with him to get him to go to bed. He took his gland gunk well, though. He licked the spoon."

"That's good," he said and told her about the drawing of the face, about the conspiracy with little Vern Logan, about the thumb-sucking. He could see how pleased she was, but she only said, "Dr. Nicholson called again."

"I told him not to bother you!"

"He didn't bother me, Harry. He was very nice. I promised him you'd call him back."

"It's eleven o'clock, Margaret. I'll call him in the morning."

"No, I said tonight, no matter what time. He's waiting, and he said to be sure and reverse the charges."

"I wish I'd never answered the son of a bitch's letter," he burst out and then, apologetically, "Is there any coffee? I didn't stay for it at the school."

She had put the water on to boil when she heard the car whine into the driveway, and the instant coffee was already in the cup. She poured it and said, "You have to talk to him, Harry. He has to know tonight."

"Know tonight! Know tonight," he mimicked savagely. He scalded his lips on the coffee cup and said, "What do you want me to do, Margaret? How do I make a decision like this? Today I picked up the phone and called the company

149

psychologist, and when his secretary answered, I said I had the wrong number. I didn't know what to say to him."

"I'm not trying to pressure you, Harry. But he has to know."

Vladek put down the cup and lit his fiftieth cigarette of the day. The little dining room—it wasn't that, it was a half breakfast alcove off the tiny kitchen, but they called it a dining room even to each other—was full of Tommy. The new paint on the wall where Tommy had peeled off the cups-and-spoons wallpaper. The Tommy-proof latch on the stove. The one odd aqua seat that didn't match the others on the kitchen chairs, where Tommy had methodically gouged it with the handle of his spoon. He said, "I know what my mother would tell me, talk to the priest. Maybe I should. But we've never even been to Mass here."

Margaret sat down and helped herself to one of his cigarettes. She was still a good-looking woman. She hadn't gained a pound since Tommy was born, although she usually looked tired. She said, carefully and straightforwardly, "We agreed, Harry. You said you would talk to Mrs. Adler, and you've done that. We said if she didn't think Tommy would ever straighten out we'd talk to Dr. Nicholson. I know it's hard on you, and I know I'm not much help. But I don't know what to do, and I have to let you decide."

Harry looked at his wife, lovingly and hopelessly, and at that moment the phone rang. It was, of course, Dr. Nicholson.

"I haven't made a decision," said Harry Vladek at once. "You're rushing me, Dr. Nicholson."

The distant voice was calm and assured. "No, Mr. Vladek, it's not me that's rushing you. The other boy's heart gave out an hour ago. That's what's rushing you."

"You mean he's dead?" cried Vladek.

"He's on the heart-lung machine, Mr. Vladek. We can hold him for at least eighteen hours, maybe twenty-four. The brain is all right. We're getting very good waves on the oscilloscope. The tissue match with your boy is satisfactory. Better than satisfactory. There's a flight out of JFK at six fifteen in the morning, and I've reserved space for yourself, your wife, and Tommy. You'll be met at the airport. You can be here by noon, so we have time. Only just time, Mr. Vladek. It's up to you now."

Vladek said furiously, "I can't decide that! Don't you understand? I don't know how."

150

"I do understand, Mr. Vladek," said the distant voice and, strangely, Vladek thought, it seemed he did. "I have a suggestion. Would you like to come down anyhow? I think it might help you to see the other boy, and you can talk to his parents. They feel they owe you something even for going this far, and they want to thank you."

"Oh, no!" cried Vladek.

The doctor went on, "All they want is for their boy to have a life. They don't expect anything but that. They'll give you custody of the child—your child, yours and theirs. He's a very fine little boy, Mr. Vladek. Eight years old. Reads beautifully. Makes model airplanes. They let him ride his bike because he was sensible and reliable, and the accident wasn't his fault. The truck came right up on the sidewalk and hit him."

Harry was trembling. "That's like giving me a bribe," he said harshly. "That's telling me I can trade Tommy in for somebody smarter and nicer."

"I didn't mean it that way, Mr. Vladek. I only wanted you to know the kind of a boy you can save."

"You don't even know the operation's going to work!"

"No," agreed the doctor. "Not positively. I can tell you that we've transplanted animals, including primates, and human cadavers, and one pair of terminal cases, but you're right, we've never had a transplant into a well body. I've shown you all the records, Mr. Vladek. We went over them with your own doctor when we first talked about this possibility, five months ago. This is the first case since then when the match was close and there was a real hope for success, but you're right, it's still unproved. Unless you help us prove it. For what it's worth, I think it will work. But no one can be sure."

Margaret had left the kitchen, but Vladek knew where she was from the scratchy click in the earpiece: in the bedroom, listening on the extension phone. He said at last, "I can't say now, Dr. Nicholson. I'll call you back in—in half an hour. I can't do any more than that right now."

"That's a great deal, Mr. Vladek. I'll be waiting right here for your call."

Harry sat down and drank the rest of his coffee. You had to be an expert in a lot of things to get along, he was thinking. What did he know about brain transplants? In one way, a lot. He knew that the surgery part was supposed to be straightforward, but the tissue rejection was the problem, but Dr. Nicholson thought he had that licked. He knew that every doctor he had talked to, and he had now talked to seven of them, had agreed that medically it was probably sound enough, and that every one of them had carefully clammed up when he got the conversation around to whether it was right. It was his decision, not theirs, they all said, sometimes just by their silence. But who was he to decide?

Margaret appeared in the doorway. "Harry. Let's go upstairs and look at Tommy."

He said harshly, "Is that supposed to make it easier for me to murder my son?"

She said, "We talked that out, Harry, and we agreed it isn't murder. Whatever it is. I only think that Tommy ought to be with us when we decide, even if he doesn't know what we're deciding."

The two of them stood next to the outsize crib that held their son, looking in the night light at the long fair lashes against the chubby cheeks and the pouted lips around the thumb. Reading. Model airplanes. Riding a bike. Against a quick sketch of a face and the occasional, cherished, tempestuous, bruising flurry of kisses.

Vladek stayed there the full half hour and then, as he had promised, went back to the kitchen, picked up the phone and began to dial.

Science fiction writers are born, not made. That, at least, is the way I feel about it. My ambition to write science fiction stretches almost as far back as I can remember, and so it must be with lots of other people.

Many times I get letters in crayon on large sheets of widely ruled paper that say:

> Dear Dr. Asimov:
>
> I am in the first grade and I would like to write science fiction. Can you tell me how to copyright my manuscripts? Also give me the name of five editors who will discuss my stories with me and guarantee, under bond, that they will not steal my ideas. Please write back. I am five years old.

Incidentally, I have noticed that everyone under the age of twenty says "Please write back." I have had to look up the word "reply" in the dictionary to make sure that it hasn't been lost or misplaced and, by heaven, it's still there.

As another proof of my contention, I remember little Bobby Silverberg in the days when he was still unbearded and publishing no more than two or three science fiction stories a month, and little Harlan Ellison in the days when he was still biting unwary passers-by on the knee (or on the lower thigh if he stood on tiptoe).

Naturally, then, every time a new name comes up in science fiction, I sigh and think: Another young snot-nose kid coming up to take the bread out of my mouth.

Consequently, when I was at the thirty-first convention and someone offered to introduce me to that new sensation, R.A. Lafferty, I was all prepared to meet some downy-cheeked grade-school youngster and was all set to pat his head and say, graciously, that I hoped he would continue to write successful science fiction after he had grown up.

Imagine, then, my horror when I was introduced to a fine gentleman, well-stricken in years.

That really puts the cherry on it—when middle-aged people, who should be playing golf or something, enter the field and also try to take the bread out of my mouth.

He was about the last of them.

What? The last of the great individualists? The last of the true creative geniuses of the century? The last of the sheer precursors?

No. No. He was the last of the dolts.

Kids were being born smarter all the time when he came along, and they would be so forever more. He was about the last dumb kid ever born.

Even his mother had to admit that Albert was a slow child. What else can you call a boy who doesn't begin to talk till he is four years old, who won't learn to handle a spoon till he is six, who can't operate a doorknob till he is eight? What else can you say about one who put his shoes on the wrong feet and walked in pain? And who had to be told to close his mouth after yawning?

Some things would always be beyond him—like whether it was the big hand or the little hand of the clock that told the hours. But this wasn't something serious. He never did care what time it was.

When, about the middle of his ninth year, Albert made a breakthrough at telling his right hand from his left, he did it by the most ridiculous set of mnemonics ever put together. It had to do with the way a dog turns around before lying down, the direction of whirlpools and whirlwinds, the side a cow is milked from and a horse is mounted from, the direction of twist of oak and sycamore leaves, the maze patterns of rock moss and of tree moss, the cleavage of limestone, the direction of a hawk's wheeling, of a shrike's hunting, and of a snake's coiling (remembering that the mountain boomer is an exception, and that it isn't a true snake), the lay of cedar fronds and of balsam fronds, the twist of a hole dug by a skunk and by a badger (remembering pungently that skunks

154

sometimes use old badger holes). Well, Albert finally learned to remember which was right and which was left, but an observant boy would have learned his right hand from his left without all that nonsense.

Albert never learned to write a readable hand. To get by in school he cheated. From a bicycle speedometer, a midget motor, tiny eccentric cams, and batteries stolen from his grandfather's hearing aid, Albert made a machine to write for him. It was small as a doodlebug and fitted onto a pen or pencil so that Albert could conceal it with his fingers. It formed the letters beautifully as Albert had set the cams to follow a copybook model. He triggered the different letters with keys no bigger than whiskers. Sure it was crooked, but what else can you do when you're too dumb to learn how to write passably?

Albert couldn't figure at all. He had to make another machine to figure for him. It was a palm-of-the-hand thing that would add and subtract and multiply and divide. The next year when he was in the ninth grade they gave him algebra, and he had to devise a flipper to go on the end of his gadget to work quadratic and simultaneous equations. If it weren't for such cheating Albert wouldn't have gotten any marks at all in school.

He had another difficulty when he came to his fifteenth year. People, that is an understatement. There should be a stronger word than "difficulty" for it. Albert was afraid of girls.

What to do?

"I will build me a machine that is not afraid of girls," Albert said. He set to work on it. He had it nearly finished when a thought came to him: "But no machine is afraid of girls. How will this help me?"

His logic was at fault and analogy broke down. He did what he always did. He cheated.

He took the programming rollers out of an old player piano in the attic, found a gear case that would serve, used magnetized sheets instead of perforated music rolls, fed a copy of *Wormwood's Logic* into the matrix, and he had a logic machine that would answer questions.

"What's the matter with me that I'm afraid of girls?" Albert asked his logic machine.

"Nothing the matter with you," the logic machine told

155

him. "It's logical to be afraid of girls. They seem pretty spooky to me too."

"But what can I do about it?"

"Wait for time and circumstances. They sure are slow. Unless you want to cheat—"

"Yes, yes, what then?"

"Build a machine that looks just like you, Albert, and talks just like you. Only make it smarter than you are, and not bashful. And, ah, Albert, there's a special thing you'd better put into it in case things go wrong. I'll whisper it to you. It's dangerous."

So Albert made Little Danny, a dummy who looked like him and talked like him, only he was smarter and not bashful. He filled Little Danny with quips from *Mad Magazine* and from *Quip,* and then they were set.

Albert and Little Danny went to call on Alice.

"Why, he's wonderful," Alice said. "Why can't you be like that, Albert? Aren't you wonderful, Little Danny. Why do you have to be so stupid, Albert, when Little Danny is so wonderful?"

"I, uh, uh, I don't know," Albert said. "Uh, uh, uh."

"He sounds like a fish with the hiccups," Little Danny said.

"You do, Albert, really you do!" Alice screamed. "Why can't you say smart things like Little Danny does, Albert? Why are you so stupid?"

This wasn't working out very well, but Albert kept on with it. He programmed Little Danny to play the ukulele and to sing. He wished that he could program himself to do it. Alice loved everything about Little Danny, but she paid no attention to Albert. And one day Albert had had enough.

"Wha-wha-what do we need with this dummy?" Albert asked. "I just made him to am- to amu- to make you laugh. Let's go off and leave him."

"Go off with you, Albert?" Alice asked. "But you're so stupid. I tell you what. Let's you and me go off and leave Albert, Little Danny. We can have more fun without him."

"Who needs him?" Little Danny asked. "Get lost, buster."

Albert walked away from them. He was glad that he'd taken his logic machine's advice as to the special thing to be built into Little Danny. Albert walked fifty steps. A hundred.

"Far enough," Albert said, and he pushed a button in his pocket.

Nobody but Albert and his logic machine ever did know what that explosion was. Tiny wheels out of Little Danny and

156

small pieces of Alice rained down a little later, but there weren't enough fragments for anyone to identify.

Albert had learned one lesson from his logic machine: never make anything that you can't unmake.

Well, Albert finally grew to be a man, in years at least. He would always have something about him of a very awkward teen-ager. And yet he fought his own war against those who were teen-agers in years, and he defeated them completely. There was enmity between them forever. Albert hadn't been a very well-adjusted adolescent, and he hated the memory of it. And nobody ever mistook him for an adjusted man.

Albert was too awkward to earn a living at an honest trade. He was reduced to peddling his little tricks and contrivances to shysters and promoters. But he did back into a sort of fame, and he did become burdened with wealth.

He was too stupid to handle his own monetary affairs, but he built an actuary machine to do his investing and he became rich by accident. He built the damned thing too good and he regretted it.

Albert became one of that furtive group that has saddled us with all the mean things in our history. There was that Punic who couldn't learn the rich variety of hieroglyphic characters and who devised the crippled short alphabet for wan-wits. There was the nameless Arab who couldn't count beyond ten and who set up the ten-number system for babies and idiots. There was the double-Dutchman with his movable type who drove fine copy out of the world. Albert was of their miserable company.

Albert himself wasn't much good for anything. But he had in himself the low knack for making machines that were good at everything.

His machines did a few things. You remember that anciently there was smog in the cities. Oh, it could be drawn out of the air easily enough. All it took was a tickler. Albert made a tickler machine. He would set it fresh every morning. It would clear the air in a circle three hundred yards around his hovel and gather a little over a ton of residue every twenty-four hours. This residue was rich in large polysyllabic molecules which one of his chemical machines could use.

"Why can't you clear all the air?" the people asked him.

"This is as much of the stuff as Clarence Deoxyribonucleiconibus needs every day," Albert said. That was the name of this particular chemical machine.

157

"But we die of the smog," the people said. "Have mercy on us."

"Oh, all right," Albert said. He turned it over to one of his reduplicating machines to make as many copies as were necessary.

You remember that once there was a teen-ager problem? You remember when those little buggers used to be mean? Albert got enough of them. There was something ungainly about them that reminded him too much of himself. He made a teen-ager of his own. It was rough. To the others it looked like one of themselves, the ring in the left ear, the dangling side-locks, the brass knucks and the long knife, the guitar pluck to jab in an eye. But it was incomparably rougher than the human teen-agers. It terrorized all in the neighborhood and made them behave, and dress like real people. And there was one thing about the teen-age machine that Albert made: it was made of such polarized metal and glass that it was invisible except to teen-ager eyes.

"Why is your neighborhood different?" the people asked Albert. "Why are there such good and polite teen-agers in your neighborhood and such mean ones everywhere else? It's as though something had spooked all those right around here."

"Oh, I thought I was the only one who didn't like the regular kind," Albert said.

"Oh, no, no," the people answered him. "If there is anything at all you can do about them—"

So Albert turned his mostly invisible teen-ager machine over to one of his reduplicating machines to make as many copies as were necessary, and set one up in every neighborhood. From that day till this the teen-agers have all been good and polite and a little bit frightened. But there is no evidence of what keeps them that way except an occasional eye dangling from the jab of an invisible guitar pluck.

So the two most pressing problems of the latter part of the twentieth century were solved, but accidentally, and to the credit of no one.

As the years went by, Albert felt his inferiority most when in the presence of his own machines, particularly those in the form of men. Albert just hadn't their urbanity or sparkle or wit. He was a clod beside them, and they made him feel it.

Why not? One of Albert's devices sat in the President's

Cabinet. One of them was on the High Council of World-Watchers that kept the peace everywhere. One of them presided at Riches Unlimited, that private-public-international instrument that guaranteed reasonable riches to everyone in the world. One of them was the guiding hand in the Health and Longevity Foundation which provided those things to everyone. Why should not such splendid and successful machines look down on their shabby uncle who had made them?

"I'm rich by a curious twist," Albert said to himself one day, "and honored through a mistake in circumstance. But there isn't a man or a machine in the world who is really my friend. A book here tells how to make friends, but I can't do it that way. I'll make one my own way."

So Albert set out to make a friend.

He made Poor Charles, a machine as stupid and awkward and inept as himself.

"Now I will have a companion," Albert said, but it didn't work. Add two zeros together and you still have zero. Poor Charles was too much like Albert to be good for anything.

Poor Charles! Unable to think, he made a—(but wait a moleskin-gloved minute here, Colonel, this isn't going to work at all)—he made a machi—(but isn't this the same blamed thing all over again?)—he made a machine to think for him and to—

Hold it, hold it! That's enough. Poor Charles was the only machine that Albert ever made that was dumb enough to do a thing like that.

Well, whatever it was, the machine that Poor Charles made was in control of the situation and of Poor Charles when Albert came onto them accidentally. The machine's machine, the device that Poor Charles had constructed to think for him, was lecturing Poor Charles in a humiliating way.

"Only the inept and deficient will invent," that damned machine's machine was droning. "The Greeks in their high period did not invent. They used neither adjunct power nor instrumentation. They used, as intelligent men or machines will always use, slaves. They did not descend to gadgets. They, who did the difficult with ease, did not seek the easier way.

"But the incompetent will invent. The insufficient will invent. The depraved will invent. And knaves will invent."

Albert, in a seldom fit of anger, killed them both. But he knew that the machine of his machine had spoken the truth.

159

Albert was very much cast down. A more intelligent man would have had a hunch as to what was wrong. Albert had only a hunch that he was not very good at hunches and would never be. Seeing no way out, he fabricated a machine and named it Hunchy.

In most ways this was the worst machine he ever made. In building it he tried to express something of his unease for the future. It was an awkward thing in mind and mechanism, a misfit.

Albert's more intelligent machines gathered around and hooted at him while he put it together.

"Boy! Are you lost!" they taunted. "That thing is a primitive! To draw its power from the ambient! We talked you into throwing that away twenty years ago and setting up coded power for all of us."

"Uh—someday there may be social disturbances and all centers of power seized," Albert stammered. "But Hunchy would be able to operate if the whole world were wiped smooth."

"It isn't even tuned to our information matrix," they jibed. "It's worse than Poor Charles. That stupid thing practically starts from scratch."

"Maybe there'll be a new kind of itch for it," said Albert.

"It's not even housebroken!" the urbane machines shouted their indignation. "Look at that! Some sort of primitive lubrication all over the floor."

"Remembering my childhood, I sympathize," Albert said.

"What's it good for?" they demanded.

"Ah—it gets hunches," Albert mumbled.

"Duplication!" they shouted. "That's all you're good for yourself, and not very good at that. We suggest an election to replace you as—pardon our laughter—the head of these enterprises."

"Boss, I've got a hunch how we can block them there," the unfinished Hunchy whispered.

"They're bluffing," Albert whispered back. "My first logic machine taught me never to make anything that I can't unmake. I've got them there and they know it. I wish I could think up things like that myself."

"Maybe there will come an awkward time and I will be good for something," Hunchy said.

Only once, and that rather late in life, did a sort of honesty flare up in Albert. He did one thing (and it was a dismal

160

failure) on his own. That was the night of the year of the double millennium when Albert was presented with the Finnerty-Hochmann Trophy, the highest award that the intellectual world could give. Albert was certainly an odd choice for it, but it had been noticed that almost every basic invention for thirty years could be traced back to him or to the devices with which he had surrounded himself.

You know the trophy. Atop it was Eurema, the synthetic Greek goddess of invention, with arms spread as if she would take flight. Below this was a stylized brain cut away to show the convoluted cortex. And below this was the coat of arms of the Academicians: Ancient Scholar rampant (argent); the Anderson Analyzer sinister (gules); the Mondeman Space-Drive dexter (vair). It was a fine work by Groben, his ninth period.

Albert had a speech composed for him by his speech-writing machine, but for some reason he did not use it. He went on his own, and that was disaster. He got to his feet when he was introduced, and he stuttered and spoke nonsense!

"Ah—only the sick oyster produces nacre," he said, and they all gaped at him. What sort of beginning for a speech was that? "Or do I have the wrong creature?" Albert asked weakly.

"Eurema doesn't look like that!" Albert gawked out and pointed suddenly at the trophy. "No, no, that isn't her at all. Eurema walks backward and is blind. And her mother is a brainless hulk."

Everybody was watching him with pained expression.

"Nothing rises without a leaven," Albert tried to explain, "but the yeast is itself a fungus and a disease. You be regularizers all, splendid and supreme! But you cannot live without the irregulars. You will die, and who will tell you that you are dead? When there are no longer any deprived or insufficient, *who will invent?* What will you do when there is none of us defectives left? Who will leaven your lump then?"

"Are you unwell?" the master of ceremonies asked him quietly. "Should you not make an end to it? People will understand."

"Of course I'm unwell. Always have been," Albert said. "What good would I be otherwise? You set the ideal that all should be healthy and well adjusted. No! No! Were we all well adjusted, we would ossify and die. The world is kept healthy only by some of the unhealthy minds lurking in it. The first implement made by man was not a scraper or celt

161

or stone knife. It was a crutch, and it wasn't devised by a hale man."

"Perhaps you should rest," a functionary said in a low voice, for this sort of rambling nonsense talk had never been heard at an awards dinner before.

"Know you," said Albert, "that it is not the fine bulls and wonderful cattle who make the new paths. Only a crippled calf makes a new path. In everything that survives there must be an element of the incongruous. Hey, you know the woman who said, 'My husband is incongruous, but I never liked Washington in the summertime.'"

Everybody gazed at him in stupor.

"That's the first joke I ever made," Albert said lamely. "My joke-making machine makes them a lot better than I do." He paused and gaped, and gulped a big breath.

"Dolts!" he croaked out fiercely then. "What will you do for dolts when the last of us is gone? How will you survive without us?"

Albert had finished. He gaped and forgot to close his mouth. They led him back to his seat. His publicity machine explained that Albert was tired from overwork, and then that machine passed around copies of the speech that Albert was supposed to have given.

It had been an unfortunate episode. How noisome it is that the innovators are never great men, and that the great men are never good for anything but just being great men.

In that year a decree went forth from Caesar that a census of the whole country should be taken. The decree was from Cesare Panebianco, the President of the country. It was the decimal year proper for the census, and there was nothing unusual about the decree. Certain provisions, however, were made for taking a census of the drifters and decrepits who were usually missed, to examine them and to see why they were so. It was in the course of this that Albert was picked up. If any man ever looked like a drifter and decrepit, it was Albert.

Albert was herded in with other derelicts, set down at a table, and asked tortuous questions. As:

"What is your name?"

He almost muffed that one, but he rallied and answered, "Albert."

"What time is it by that clock?"

They had him in his old weak spot. Which hand was which? He gaped and didn't answer.

"Can you read?" they asked him.

"Not without my—" Albert began. "I don't have with me my—No, I can't read very well by myself."

"Try."

They gave him a paper to mark up with true and false questions. Albert marked them all true, believing that he would have half of them right. But they were all false. The regularized people were partial to falsehood. Then they gave him a supply-the-word test on proverbs.

"———is the best policy" didn't mean a thing to him. He couldn't remember the names of the companies that he had his own policies with.

"A ——— in time saves nine" contained more mathematics than Albert could handle.

"There appear to be six unknowns," he told himself, "and only one positive value, nine. The equating verb 'saves' is a vague one. I cannot solve this equation. I am not even sure that it is an equation. If only I had with me my—"

But he hadn't any of his gadgets or machines with him. He was on his own. He left half a dozen other proverb fill-ins blank. Then he saw a chance to recoup. Nobody is so dumb as not to know one answer if enough questions are asked.

"———is the mother of invention," it said.

"Stupidity," Albert wrote in his weird ragged hand. Then he sat back in triumph. "I know that Eurema and her mother," he snickered. "Man, how I do know them!"

But they marked him wrong on that one too. He had missed every answer to every test. They began to fix him a ticket to a progressive booby hatch where he might learn to do something with his hands, his head being hopeless.

A couple of Albert's urbane machines came down and got him out of it. They explained that, while he was a drifter and a derelict, yet he was a rich drifter and derelict, and that he was even a man of some note.

"He doesn't look it, but he really is—pardon our laughter—a man of some importance," one of the fine machines explained. "He has to be told to close his mouth after he has yawned, but for all that he is the winner of the Finnerty-Hochmann Trophy. We will be responsible for him."

Albert was miserable as his fine machines took him out, especially when they asked that he walk three or four steps behind them and not seem to be with them. They gave him some pretty rough banter and turned him into a squirming worm of a man. Albert left them and went to a little hide-out he kept.

"I'll blow my crawfishing brains out," he swore. "The humiliation is more than I can bear. Can't do it myself, though. I'll have to have it done."

He set to work building a device in his hide-out.

"What you doing, boss?" Hunchy asked him. "I had a hunch you'd come here and start building something."

"I'm building a machine to blow my pumpkin-picking brains out," Albert shouted. "I'm too yellow to do it myself."

"Boss, I got a hunch there's something better to do. Let's have some fun."

"Don't believe I know how to," Albert said thoughtfully. "I built a fun machine once to do it for me. He had a real revel till he flew apart, but he never seemed to do anything for me."

"This fun will be for you and me, boss. Consider the world spread out. What is it?"

"It's a world too fine for me to live in any longer," Albert said. "Everything and all the people are perfect, and all alike. They're at the top of the heap. They've won it all and arranged it all neatly. There's no place for a clutter-up like me in the world. So I get out."

"Boss, I've got a hunch that you're seeing it wrong. You've got better eyes than that. Look again, real canny, at it. Now what do you see?"

"Hunchy, Hunchy, is that possible? Is that really what it is? I wonder why I never noticed it before. That's the way of it, though, now that I look closer.

"Six billion patsies waiting to be took! Six billion patsies without a defense of any kind! A couple of guys out for some fun, man, they could mow them down like fields of Albert-Improved Concho Wheat!"

"Boss, I've got a hunch that this is what I was made for. The world sure had been getting stuffy. Let's tie into it and eat off the top layer. Man, we can cut a swath."

"We'll inaugurate a new era!" Albert gloated. "We'll call it the Turning of the Worm. We'll have fun, Hunchy. We'll gobble them up like goobers. How come I never saw it like that before? Six billion patsies!"

The twenty-first century began on this rather odd note.

32nd CONVENTION
WASHINGTON

James Tiptree, Jr.

And this brings us to the thirty-second convention at Washington in 1974.

Pleasant memories! It was at the twenty-first convention at Washington in 1963 that I got my first Hugo, and it was also then that I absented myself long enough to take a tour through the White House, while it was still Camelot.

The thirty-second convention was a monster, though. There were some four thousand people in attendance, and I'm not sure that's entirely a good thing. It was almost impossible to see old friends because between any two of the true conventioneers there were a thousand strangers. Now back at the thirteenth convention at Cleveland in 1955, when I was guest of honor, the total attendance was three hundred. (Lester del Rey says it's because I was guest of honor that the attendance was that low, but, as we all know, Lester will say anything—and constantly does.)

The thirty-second convention was so enormous that I can't honestly tell you whether Tiptree was there, and if he was there, whether I met him. All I can remember clearly is the banquet at which Andy Offutt (I think he spells his name in lower case but I can't bring myself to do that) labored manfully under considerable difficulties to keep things going.

Tip and I have, however, corresponded, and on the basis of that correspondence, I can tell you Tip's a very nice person. Not only does he praise my science articles (sterling evidence of good taste on his part) but he invariably urges me not to answer, being fully aware of how incredibly busy I am. Of *course* I answer. He's not going to be politer than I am.

Incidentally, the thirty-second convention may be the most populous world science fiction convention I ever attended, but there were others that were even more spectacular, if that's the word I want.

In February 1976 there was a "Star Trek" convention (well, a variety of science fiction convention at that) at the New York Hilton in which the number of tickets sold far outweighed the space available. The entire population of New York City, I believe, bought tickets and all came to the convention. I walked in on the particular day they all came, gazed in horror at the crystallization of humanity (believe me, everyone was wedged in), and when I turned to leave found that thousands had crystallized behind me. It took me half an hour to diffuse out into the street again.

THE GIRL WHO WAS PLUGGED IN

Listen, zombie. Believe me. What I could tell you—you with your silly hands leaking sweat on your growth-stocks portfolio. One-ten lousy hacks of AT&T on twenty-point margin and you think you're Evil Knievel. AT&T? You doubleknit dummy, how I'd love to show you something.

Look, dead daddy, I'd say. See for instance that rotten girl?

In the crowd over there, that one gaping at her gods. One rotten girl in the city of the future. (That's what I said.) Watch.

She's jammed among bodies, craning and peering with her soul yearning out of her eyeballs. Love! Oo-ooh, love them! Her gods are coming out of a store called Body East. Three youngbloods, larking along loverly. Dressed like simple street-people but . . . smashing. See their great eyes swivel above their nosefilters, their hands lift shyly, their inhumanly tender lips melt? The crowd moans. Love! This whole boiling megacity, this whole fun future world loves its gods.

You don't believe gods, dad? Wait. Whatever turns you on, there's a god in the future for you, custom-made. Listen to this mob. "I touched his foot. Ow-oow, I TOUCHED Him!"

Even the people in the GTX tower up there love the gods—in their own way and for their own reasons.

The funky girl on the street, she just loves. Grooving on their beautiful lives, their mysterioso problems. No one ever told her about mortals who love a god and end up as a tree

167

or a sighing sound. In a million years it'd never occur to her that her gods might love her back.

She's squashed against the wall now as the godlings come by. They move in a clear space. A holocam bobs above but its shadow never falls on them. The store display screens are magically clear of bodies as the gods glance in and a beggar underfoot is suddenly alone. They give him a token. "Aaa-aah!" goes the crowd.

Now one of them flashes some wild new kind of timer and they all trot to catch a shuttle, just like people. The shuttle stops for them—more magic. The crowd sighs, closing back. The gods are gone.

(In a room far from—but not unconnected to—the GTX tower a molecular flipflop closes too, and three account tapes spin.)

Our girl is still stuck by the wall while guards and holocam equipment pull away. The adoration's fading from her face. That's good, because now you can see she's the ugly of the world. A tall monument to pituitary dystrophy. No surgeon would touch her. When she smiles, her jaw—it's half purple—almost bites her left eye out. She's also quite young, but who could care?

The crowd is pushing her along now, treating you to glimpses of her jumbled torso, her mismatched legs. At the corner she strains to send one last fond spasm after the god-lings' shuttle. Then her face reverts to its usual expression of dim pain and she lurches onto the moving walkway, stum-bling into people. The walkway junctions with another. She crosses, trips and collides with the casualty rail. Finally she comes out into a little place called a park. The sportshow is working, a basketball game in 3-di is going on right overhead. But all she does is squeeze onto a bench and huddle there while a ghostly free-throw goes by her ear.

After that nothing at all happens except a few furtive hand-mouth gestures which don't even interest her bench-mates.

But you're curious about the city? So ordinary after all, in the FUTURE?

Ah, there's plenty to swing with here—and it's not all that *far* in the future, dad. But pass up the sci-fi stuff for now, like for instance the holovision technology that's put TV and radio in museums. Or the worldwide carrier field bouncing down from satellites, controlling communication and transport systems all over the globe. That was a spin-off from asteroid mining, pass it by. We're watching that girl.

I'll give you just one goodie. Maybe you noticed on the sportshow or the streets? No commercials. No ads.

That's right. NO ADS. An eyeballer for you.

Look around. Not a billboard, sign, slogan, jingle, skywrite, blurb, sublimflash, in this whole fun world. Brand names? Only in those ticky little peep-screens on the stores and you could hardly call that advertising. How does that finger you?

Think about it. That girl is still sitting there.

She's parked right under the base of the GTX tower as a matter of fact. Look way up and you can see the sparkles from the bubble on top, up there among the domes of godland. Inside that bubble is a boardroom. Neat bronze shield on the door: Global Transmissions Corporation—not that that means anything.

I happen to know there's six people in that room. Five of them technically male, and the sixth isn't easily thought of as a mother. They are absolutely unremarkable. Those faces were seen once at their nuptials and will show again in their obituaries and impress nobody either time. If you're looking for the secret Big Blue Meanies of the world, forget it. I know. Zen, do I know! Flesh? Power? Glory? You'd horrify them.

What they do like up there is to have things orderly, especially their communications. You could say they've dedicated their lives to that, to freeing the world from garble. Their nightmares are about hemorrhages of information: channels screwed up, plans misimplemented, garble creeping in. Their gigantic wealth only worries them, it keeps opening new vistas of disorder. Luxury? They wear what their tailors put on them, eat what their cooks serve them. See that old boy there—his name is Isham—he's sipping water and frowning as he listens to a databall. The water was prescribed by his medistaff. It tastes awful. The databall also contains a disquieting message about his son, Paul.

But it's time to go back down, far below to our girl. Look!

She's toppled over sprawling on the ground.

A tepid commotion ensues among the bystanders. The consensus is she's dead, which she disproves by bubbling a little. And presently she's taken away by one of the superb ambulances of the future, which are a real improvement over ours when one happens to be around.

At the local bellevue the usual things are done by the usual team of clowns aided by a saintly mop-pusher. Our girl revives enough to answer the questionnaire without which you can't die, even in the future. Finally she's cast up, a pumped-out hulk of a cot in the long, dim ward.

Again nothing happens for a while except that her eyes leak a little from the understandable disappointment of finding herself still alive.

But somewhere one GTX computer has been tickling another, and toward midnight something does happen. First comes an attendant who pulls screens around her. Then a man in a business doublet comes daintily down the ward. He motions the attendant to strip off the sheet and go.

The groggy girl-brute heaves up, big hands clutching at bodyparts you'd pay not to see.

"Burke? P. Burke, is that your name?"

"Y-yes." Croak. "Are you . . . policeman?"

"No. They'll be along shortly, I expect. Public suicide's a felony."

". . . I'm sorry."

He has a 'corder in his hand. "No family, right?"

"No."

"You're seventeen. One year city college. What did you study?"

"La-languages."

"H'm. Say something."

Unintelligible rasp.

He studies her. Seen close, he's not so elegant. Errand-boy type.

"Why did you try to kill yourself?"

She stares at him with dead-rat dignity, hauling up the gray sheet. Give him a point, he doesn't ask twice.

"Tell me, did you see Breath this afternoon?"

Dead as she nearly is, that ghastly love-look wells up. Breath is the three young gods, a loser's cult. Give the man another point, he interprets her expression.

"How would you like to meet them?"

The girl's eyes bug out grotesquely.

"I have a job for someone like you. It's hard work. If you did well you'd be meeting Breath and stars like that all the time."

Is he insane? She's deciding she really did die.

"But it means you never see anybody you know again. Never, *ever*. You will be legally dead. Even the police won't know. Do you want to try?"

It all has to be repeated while her great jaw slowly sets. *Show me the fire I walk through.* Finally P. Burke's prints are in his 'corder, the man holding up the rancid girl-body without a sign of distaste. It makes you wonder what else he does.

And then—THE MAGIC. Sudden silent trot of litter-bearers tucking P. Burke into something quite different from a bellevue stretcher, the oiled slide into the daddy of all luxury ambulances—real flowers in that holder!—and the long jarless rush to nowhere. Nowhere is warm and gleaming and kind with nurses. (Where did you hear that money can't buy genuine kindness?) And clean clouds folding P. Burke into bewildered sleep.

. . . Sleep which merges into feedings and washings and more sleeps, into drowsy moments of afternoon where midnight should be, and gentle businesslike voices and friendly (but very few) faces, and endless painless hyposprays and peculiar numbnesses. And later comes the steadying rhythm of days and nights, and a quickening which P. Burke doesn't identify as health, but only knows that the fungus place in her armpit is gone. And then she's up and following those few new faces with growing trust, first tottering, then walking strongly, all better now, clumping down the short hall to the tests, tests, tests, and the other things.

And here is our girl, looking—

If possible, worse than before. (You thought this was Cinderella transistorized?)

The disimprovement in her looks comes from the electrode jacks peeping out of her sparse hair, and there are other meldings of flesh and metal. On the other hand, that collar and spinal plate are really an asset; you won't miss seeing that neck.

P. Burke is ready for training in her new job.

The training takes place in her suite, and is exactly what you'd call a charm course. How to walk, sit, eat, speak, blow her nose, how to stumble, to urinate, to hiccup—DELICIOUSLY. How to make each nose-blow or shrug delightfully, subtly different from any ever spooled before. As the man said, it's hard work.

But P. Burke proves apt. Somewhere in that horrible body is a gazelle, a houri who would have been buried forever without this crazy chance. See the ugly duckling go!

Only it isn't precisely P. Burke who's stepping, laughing, shaking out her shining hair. How could it be? P. Burke is doing it all right, but she's doing it through something. The something is to all appearances a live girl. (You were warned, this is the FUTURE.)

When they first open the big cryocase and show her her new body she says just one word. Staring, gulping, "How?"

Simple, really. Watch P. Burke in her sack and scuffs stump down the hall beside Joe, the man who supervises the technical part of her training. Joe doesn't mind P. Burke's looks, he hasn't noticed them. To Joe, system matrices are beautiful.

They go into a dim room containing a huge cabinet like a one-man sauna and a console for Joe. The room has a glass wall that's all dark now. And just for your information, the whole shebang is five hundred feet underground near what used to be Carbondale, Pa.

Joe opens the sauna-cabinet like a big clamshell standing on end with a lot of funny business inside. Our girl shucks her shift and walks into it bare, totally unembarrassed. *Eager.* She settles in face-forward, butting jacks into sockets. Joe closes it carefully onto her humpback. Clunk. She can't see in there or hear or move. She hates this minute. But how she loves what comes next!

Joe's at his console and the lights on the other side of the glass wall come up. A room is on the other side, all fluff and kicky bits, a girly bedroom. In the bed is a small mound of silk with a rope of yellow hair hanging out.

The sheet stirs and gets whammed back flat.

Sitting up in the bed is the darlingest girl child you've EVER seen. She quivers—porno for angels. She sticks both her little arms straight up, flips her hair, looks around full of sleepy pazazz. Then she can't resist rubbing her hands down over her minibreasts and belly. Because, you see, it's the godawful P. Burke who is sitting there hugging her perfect girl-body, looking at you out of delighted eyes.

Then the kitten hops out of bed and crashes flat on the floor.

From the sauna in the dim room comes a strangled noise. P. Burke, trying to rub her wired-up elbow is suddenly smothered in *two* bodies, electrodes jerking in her flesh. Joe juggles inputs, crooning into his mike. The flurry passes; it's all right.

In the lighted room the elf gets up, casts a cute glare at the glass wall and goes into a transparent cubicle. A bathroom, what else? She's a live girl, and live girls have to go to the

172

bathroom after a night's sleep even if their brains are in a sauna cabinet in the next room. And P. Burke isn't in that cabinet, she's in the bathroom. Perfectly simple, if you have the glue for that closed training circuit that's letting her run her neural system by remote control.

Now let's get one thing clear. P. Burke does not *feel* her brain is in the sauna room, she feels she's in that sweet little body. When you wash your hands, do you feel the water is running on your brain? Of course not. You feel the water on your hand, although the "feeling" is actually a potential-pattern flickering over the electrochemical jelly between your ears. And it's delivered there via the long circuits from your hands. Just so, P. Burke's brain in the cabinet feels the water on her hands in the bathroom. The fact that the signals have jumped across space on the way in makes no difference at all. If you want the jargon, it's known as eccentric projection or sensory reference and you've done it all your life. Clear?

Time to leave the honey-pot to her toilet training—she's made a booboo with the toothbrush, because P. Burke can't get used to what she sees in the mirror—

But wait, you say. Where did that girl-body come from?

P. Burke asks that too, dragging out the words.

"They grow 'em," Joe tells her. He couldn't care less about the flesh department. "PDs. Placental decanters. Modified embryos, see? Fit the control implants in later. Without a Remote Operator it's just a vegetable. Look at the feet—no callus at all." (He knows because they told him.)

"Oh . . . oh, she's incredible . . ."

"Yeah, a neat job. Want to try walking-talking mode today? You're coming on fast."

And she is. Joe's reports and the reports from the nurse and the doctor and style man go to a bushy man upstairs who is some kind of medical cybertech but mostly a project administrator. His reports in turn go—to the GTX boardroom? Certainly not, did you think this is a *big* thing? His reports just go up. The point is, they're green, very green. P. Burke promises well.

So the bushy man—Doctor Tesla—has procedures to initiate. The little kitten's dossier in the Central Data Bank, for instance. Purely routine. And the phase-in schedule which will put her on the scene. This is simple: a small exposure in an off-network holoshow.

Next he has to line out the event which will fund and target her. That takes budget meetings, clearances, coordinations. The Burke project begins to recruit and grow. And there's the messy business of the name, which always gives Doctor Tesla an acute pain in the bush.

The name comes out weird, when it's suddenly discovered that Burke's "P." stands for "Philadelphia." Philadelphia? The astrologer grooves on it. Joe thinks it would help identification. The semantics girl references *brotherly love, Liberty-Bell, main-line, low teratogenesis,* blah-blah. Nicknames Philly? Pala? Pooty? Delphi? Is it good, bad? Finally "Delphi" is gingerly declared goodo. ("Burke" is replaced by something nobody remembers.)

Coming along now. We're at the official checkout down in the underground suite, which is as far as the training circuits reach. The bushy Doctor Tesla is there, braced by two budgetary types and a quiet fatherly man whom he handles like hot plasma.

Joe swings the door wide and she steps shyly in.

Their little Delphi, fifteen and flawless.

Tesla introduces her around. She's child-solemn, a beautiful baby to whom something so wonderful has happened you can feel the tingles. She doesn't smile, she . . . brims. That brimming joy is all that shows of P. Burke, the forgotten hulk in the sauna next door. But P. Burke doesn't know she's alive—it's Delphi who lives, every warm inch of her.

One of the budget types lets go a libidinous snuffle and freezes. The fatherly man, whose name is Mr. Cantle, clears his throat.

"Well, young lady, are you ready to go to work?"

"Yes sir," gravely from the elf.

"We'll see. Has anybody told you what you're going to do for us?"

"No, sir." Joe and Tesla exhale quietly.

"Good." He eyes her, probing for the blind brain in the room next door.

"Do you know what *advertising* is?"

He's talking dirty, hitting to shock. Delphi's eyes widen and her little chin goes up. Joe is in ecstasy at the complex expressions P. Burke is getting through. Mr. Cantle waits.

"It's, well, it's when they used to tell people to buy things." She swallows. "It's not allowed."

"That's right." Mr. Cantle leans back, grave. "Advertising as it used to be is against the law. *A display other than the legitimate use of the product, intended to promote its sale.* In former times every manufacturer was free to tout his wares

174

any way, place or time he could afford. All the media and most of the landscape was taken up with extravagant competing displays. The thing became uneconomic. The public rebelled. Since the so-called Huckster Act, sellers have been restrained to, I quote, displays in or on the product itself, visible during its legitimate use or in on-premise sales." Mr. Cantle leans forward. "Now tell me, Delphi, why do people buy one product rather than another?"

"Well . . ." Enchanting puzzlement from Delphi. "They, um, they see them and like them, or they hear about them from somebody?" (Touch of P. Burke there; she didn't say, from a friend.)

"Partly. Why did *you* buy your particular body-lift?"

"I never had a body-lift, sir."

Mr. Cantle frowns; what gutters do they drag for these Remotes?

"Well, what brand of water do you drink?"

"Just what was in the faucet, sir," says Delphi humbly. "I—I did try to boil it—"

"Good God." He scowls; Tesla stiffens. "Well, what did you boil it in? A cooker?"

The shining yellow head nods.

"What *brand* of cooker did you buy?"

"I didn't buy it, sir," says frightened P. Burke through Delphi's lips. "But—I know the best kind! Ananga has a Burnbabi, I saw the name when she—"

"Exactly!" Cantle's fatherly beam comes back strong; the Burnbabi account is a strong one, too. "You saw Ananga using one so you thought it must be good, eh? And it is good or a great human being like Ananga wouldn't be using it. Absolutely right. And now, Delphi, you know what you're going to be doing for us. You're going to show some products. Doesn't sound very hard, does it?"

"Oh, no, sir . . ." Baffled child's stare; Joe gloats.

"And you must never, *never* tell anyone what you're doing." Cantle's eyes bore for the brain behind this seductive child.

"You're wondering why we ask you to do this, naturally. There's a very serious reason. All those products people use, foods and healthaids and cookers and cleaners and clothes and car—they're all made by *people*. Somebody put in years of hard work designing and making them. A man comes up with a fine new idea for a better product. He has to get a factory and machinery, and hire workmen. Now. What happens

175

if people have no way of hearing about his product? Word-of-mouth is far too slow and unreliable. Nobody might ever stumble onto his new product or find out how good it was, right? And then he and all the people who worked for him—they'd go bankrupt, right? So, Delphi, there has to be *some way* that large numbers of people can get a look at a good new product, right? How? By letting people see you using it. You're giving that man a chance."

Delphi's little head is nodding in happy relief.

"Yes, sir, I do see now—but sir, it seems so sensible, why don't they let you—"

Cantle smiles sadly.

"It's an overreaction, my dear. History goes by swings. People overreact and pass harsh unrealistic laws which attempt to stamp out an essential social process. When this happens, the people who understand have to carry on as best they can until the pendulum swings back." He sighs. "The Huckster Laws are bad, inhuman laws, Delphi, despite their good intent. If they were strictly observed they would wreak havoc. Our economy, our society would be cruelly destroyed. We'd be back in caves!" His inner fire is showing; if the Huckster Laws were strictly enforced he'd be back punching a databank.

"It's our duty, Delphi. Our solemn social duty. We are not breaking the law. You will be using the product. But people wouldn't understand, if they knew. They would become upset, just as you did. So you must be very, very careful not to mention any of this to anybody."

(And somebody will be very, very carefully monitoring Delphi's speech circuits.)

"Now we're all straight, aren't we? Little Delphi here"—He is speaking to the invisible creature next door—"Little Delphi is going to live a wonderful, exciting life. She's going to be a girl people watch. And she's going to be using fine products people will be glad to know about and helping the good people who make them. Yours will be a genuine social contribution." He keys up his pitch; the creature in there must be older.

Delphi digests this with ravishing gravity.

"But sir, how do I—?"

"Don't worry about a thing. You'll have people behind you whose job it is to select the most worthy products for you to use. Your job is just to do as they say. They'll show you what

176

outfits to wear to parties, what suncars and viewers to buy and so on. That's all you have to do."

Parties—clothes—suncars! Delphi's pink mouth opens. In P. Burke's starved seventeen-year-old head the ethics of product sponsorship float far away.

"Now tell me in your own words what your job is, Delphi."

"Yes sir. I—I'm to go to parties and buy things and use them as they tell me, to help the people who work in factories."

"And what did I say was so important?"

"Oh—I shouldn't let anybody know, about the things."

"Right." Mr. Cantle has another paragraph he uses when the subject shows, well, immaturity. But he can sense only eagerness here. Good. He doesn't really enjoy the other speech.

"It's a lucky girl who can have all the fun she wants while doing good for others, isn't it?" He beams around. There's a prompt shuffling of chairs. Clearly this one is go.

Joe leads her out, grinning. The poor fool thinks they're admiring her coordination.

It's out into the world for Delphi now, and at this point the up-channels get used. On the administrative side account schedules are opened, subprojects activated. On the technical side the reserved bandwidth is cleared. (That carrier field, remember?) A new name is waiting for Delphi, a name she'll never hear. It's a long string of binaries which have been quietly cycling in a GTX tank ever since a certain Beautiful Person didn't wake up.

The name winks out of cycle, dances from pulses into modulations of modulations, whizzes through phasing, and shoots into a giga-band beam racing up to a synchronous satellite poised over Guatemala. From there the beam pours twenty thousand miles back to earth again, forming an all-pervasive field of structured energics supplying tuned demand-points all over the CanAm quadrant.

With that field, if you have the right credit rating you can sit at a GTX console and operate a tuned ore-extractor in Brazil. Or—if you have some simple credentials like being able to walk on water—you could shoot a spool into the network holocam shows running day and night in every home and dorm and rec. site. Or you could create a continentwide traffic jam. Is it any wonder GTX guards those inputs like a sacred trust?

Delphi's "name" appears as a tiny analyzable nonredundancy in the flux, and she'd be very proud if she knew about it. It would strike P. Burke as magic; P. Burke never even understood robotcars. But Delphi is in no sense a robot. Call her a waldo if you must. The fact is she's just a girl, a real live girl with her brain in an unusual place. A simple real-time on-line system with plenty of bit-rate—even as you and you.

The point of all this hardware, which isn't very much hardware in this society, is so Delphi can walk out of that underground suite, a mobile demand-point draining an omnipresent fieldform. And she does—eighty-nine pounds of tender girl flesh and blood with a few metallic components, stepping out into the sunlight to be taken to her new life. A girl with everything going for her including a meditech escort. Walking lovely, stopping to widen her eyes at the big antennae system overhead.

The mere fact that something called P. Burke is left behind down underground has no bearing at all. P. Burke is totally unselfaware and happy as a clam in its shell. (Her bed has been moved into the waldo cabinet room now.) And P. Burke isn't in the cabinet; P. Burke is climbing out of an airvan in a fabulous Colorado beef preserve and her name is Delphi. Delphi is looking at live Charolais steers and live cottonwoods and aspens gold against the blue smog and stepping over live grass to be welcomed by the reserve super's wife.

The super's wife is looking forward to a visit from Delphi and her friends and by a happy coincidence there's a holo-cam outfit here doing a piece for the nature nuts.

You could write the script yourself now, while Delphi learns a few rules about structural interferences and how to handle the tiny time lag which results from the new forty-thousand-mile parenthesis in her nervous system. That's right—the people with the leased holocam rig naturally find the gold aspen shadows look a lot better on Delphi's flank than they do on a steer. And Delphi's face improves the mountains too, when you can see them. But the nature freaks aren't quite as joyful as you'd expect.

"See you in Barcelona, kitten," the head man says sourly as they pack up.

"Barcelona?" echoes Delphi with that charming little subliminal lag. She sees where his hand is and steps back.

"Cool, it's not her fault," another man says wearily. He knocks back his grizzled hair. "Maybe they'll leave in some of the gut."

Delphi watches them go off to load the spools on the GTX transport for processing. Her hand roves over the breast the man had touched. Back under Carbondale, P. Burke has discovered something new about her Delphi-body.

About the difference between Delphi and her own grim carcass.

She's always known Delphi has almost no sense of taste or smell. They explained that: only so much bandwidth. You don't have to taste a suncar, do you? And the slight overall dimness of Delphi's sense of touch—she's familiar with that, too. Fabrics that would prickle P. Burke's own hide feel like a cool plastic film to Delphi.

But the blank spots. It took her a while to notice them. Delphi doesn't have much privacy; investments of her size don't. So she's slow about discovering there's certain definite places where her beastly P. Burke body *feels* things that Delphi's dainty flesh does not. H'mm! Channel space again, she thinks—and forgets it in the pure bliss of being Delphi.

You ask how a girl could forget a thing like that? Look. P. Burke is about as far as you can get from the concept *girl*. She's a female, yes—but for her, sex is a four-letter word spelled P-A-I-N. She isn't quite a virgin. You don't want the details; she'd been about twelve and the freak-lovers were bombed blind. When they came down they threw her out with a small hole in her anatomy and a mortal one elsewhere. She dragged off to buy her first and last shot and she can still hear the clerk's incredulous guffaws.

Do you see why Delphi grins, stretching her delicious little numb body in the sun she faintly feels? Beams, saying, "Please, I'm ready now."

Ready for what? For Barcelona like the sour man said, where his nature-thing is now making it strong in the amateur section of the Festival. A winner! Like he also said, a lot of strip-mines and dead fish have been scrubbed but who cares with Delphi's darling face so visible?

So it's time for Delphi's face and her other delectabilities to show on Barcelona's Playa Neuva. Which means switching her channel to the EurAf synchsat.

They ship her at night so the nanosecond transfer isn't even noticed by that insignificant part of Delphi that lives five hundred feet under Carbondale, so excited the nurse has to make sure she eats. The circuit switches while Delphi "sleeps," that is, while P. Burke is out of the waldo cabinet. The next time she plugs in to open Delphi's eyes it's no dif-

179

ferent—do you notice which relay boards your phone calls go through?

And now for the event that turns the sugarcube from Colorado into the PRINCESS.

Literally true, he's a prince, or rather an Infante of an old Spanish line that got shined up in the Neomonarchy. He's also eighty-one, with a passion for birds—the kind you see in zoos. Now it suddenly turns out that he isn't poor at all. Quite the reverse; his old sister laughs in their tax lawyer's face and starts restoring the family hacienda while the Infante totters out to court Delphi. And little Delphi begins to live the life of the gods.

What do gods do? Well, everything beautiful. But (remember Mr. Cantle?) the main point is Things. Ever see a god empty-handed? You can't be a god without at least a magic girdle or an eight-legged horse. But in the old days some stone tablets or winged sandals or a chariot drawn by virgins would do a god for life. No more! Gods make it on novelty now. By Delphi's time the hunt for new god-gear is turning the earth and seas inside-out and sending frantic fingers to the stars. And what gods have, mortals desire.

So Delphi starts on a Euromarket shopping spree squired by her old Infante, thereby doing her bit to stave off social collapse.

Social what? Didn't you get it, when Mr. Cantle talked about a world where advertising is banned and fifteen billion consumers are glued to their holocam shows? One capricious self-powered god can wreck you.

Take the nose-filter massacre. Years, the industry sweated years to achieve an almost invisible enzymatic filter. So one day a couple of pop-gods show up wearing nose-filters like *big purple bats*. By the end of the week the whole market is screaming for purple bats. Then it switched to bird-heads and skulls, but by the time the industry retooled the crazies had dropped bird-heads and gone to injection globes. Blood!

Multiply that by a million consumer industries and you can see why it's economic to have a few controllable goods. Especially with the beautiful hunk of space R&D the Peace Department laid out for, and which the taxpayers are only too glad to have taken off their hands by an outfit like GTX which everybody knows is almost a public trust.

And so you—or rather, GTX—find a creature like P. Burke and give her Delphi. And Delphi helps keep things *or-*

derly, she does what you tell her to. Why? That's right, Mr. Cantle never finished his speech.

But here come the tests of Delphi's button-nose twinkling in the torrent of news and entertainment. And she's noticed. The feedback shows a flock of viewers turning up the amps when this country baby gets tangled in her new colloidal body-jewels. She registers at a couple of major scenes, too, and when the Infante gives her a suncar, little Delphi trying out suncars is a tiger. There's a solid response in high-credit country. Mr. Cantle is humming his happy tune as he cancels a Benelux subnet option to guest her on a nude cook-show called Work Venus.

And now for the superposh old-world wedding! The hacienda has Moorish baths and six-foot silver candelabra and real black horses and the Spanish Vatican blesses them. The final event is a grand gaucho ball with the old prince and his little Infanta on a bowered balcony. She's a spectacular doll of silver lace, wildly launching toy doves at her new friends whirling by below.

The Infante beams, twitches his old nose to the scent of her sweet excitement. His doctor has been very helpful. Surely now, after he has been so patient with the suncars and all the nonsense—

The child looks up at him, saying something incomprehensible about "breath." He makes out that she's complaining about the three singers she had begged for.

"They've changed!" she marvels. "Haven't they changed? They're so dreary. I'm so happy now!"

And Delphi falls fainting against a gothic vargueno.

Her American duenna rushes up, calls help. Delphi's eyes are open, but Delphi isn't there. The duenna pokes among Delphi's hair, slaps her. The old prince grimaces. He has no idea what she is beyond an excellent solution to his tax problems, but he had been a falconer in his youth. There comes to his mind the small pinioned birds which were flung up to stimulate the hawks. He pockets the veined claw to which he had promised certain indulgences and departs to design his new aviary.

And Delphi also departs with her retinue to the Infante's newly discovered yacht. The trouble isn't serious. It's only that five thousand miles away and five hundred feet down P. Burke has been doing it too well.

They've always known she has terrific aptitude. Joe says he never saw a Remote take over so fast. No disorientations, no rejections. The psychomed talks about self-alienation. She's going into Delphi like a salmon to the sea.

She isn't eating or sleeping, they can't keep her out of the body-cabinet to get her blood moving, there are necroses under her grisly sit-down. Crisis!

So Delphi gets a long "sleep" on the yacht and P. Burke gets it pounded through her perforated head that she's endangering Delphi. (Nurse Fleming thinks of that, thus alienating the psychomed.)

They rig a pool down there (Nurse Fleming again) and chase P. Burke back and forth. And she loves it. So naturally when they let her plug in again Delphi loves it too. Every noon beside the yacht's hydrofoils darling Delphi clips along in the blue sea they've warned her not to drink. And every night around the shoulder of the world an ill-shaped thing in a dark burrow beats its way across a sterile pool.

So presently the yacht stands up on its foils and carries Delphi to the program Mr. Cantle has waiting. It's long-range; she's scheduled for at least two decades' product life. Phase One calls for her to connect with a flock of young ultra-riches who are romping loose between Brioni and Djakarta where a competitor named PEV could pick them off.

A routine luxgear op, see; no politics, no policy angles, and the main budget items are the title and the yacht which was idle anyway. The storyline is that Delphi goes to accept some rare birds for her prince—who cares? The *point* is that the Haiti area is no longer radioactive and look!—the gods are there. And so are several new Carib West Happy Isles which can afford GTX rates, in fact two of them are GTX subsids.

But you don't want to get the idea that all these newsworthy people are wired-up robbies, for pity's sake. You don't need many if they're placed right. Delphi asks Joe about that when he comes down to Baranquilla to check her over. (P. Burke's own mouth hasn't said much for a while.)

"Are there many like me?"

"Nobody's like you, buttons. Look, are you still getting that Van Allen warble?"

"I mean, like Davy. Is he a Remote?"

(Davy is the lad who is helping her collect the birds. A sincere redhead who needs a little more exposure.)

"Davy? He's one of Matt's boys, some psychojob. They haven't any channel."

"What about the real ones? Djuma van O, or Ali, or Jim Ten?"

"Djuma was born with a pile of GTX basic where her brain should be, she's nothing but a pain. Jimsy does what his astrologer tells him. Look, peanut, where do you get the idea you aren't real? You're the realest. Aren't you having joy?"

"Oh, Joe!" Flinging her little arms around him and his analyzer grids. "Oh, *me gusto mucho, muchissimo!*"

"Hey, hey." He pets her yellow head, folding the analyzer.

Three thousand miles north and five hundred feet down a forgotten hulk in a body-waldo glows.

And is she having joy. To waken out of the nightmare of being P. Burke and find herself a peri, a star-girl? On a yacht in paradise with no more to do than adorn herself and play with toys and attend revels and greet her friends—her, P. Burke, having friends!—and turn the right way for the holo-cams? Joy!

And it shows. One look at Delphi and the viewers know: DREAMS CAN COME TRUE.

Look at her riding pillions on Davy's sea-bike, carrying an apoplectic macaw in a silver hoop. *Oh, Morton, let's go there this winter!* Or learning the Japanese chinchona from that Kobe group, in a dress that looks like a blowtorch rising from one knee, and which should sell big in Texas. *Morton, is that real fire?* Happy, happy little girl!

And Davy. He's her pet and her baby and she loves to help him fix his red-gold hair. (P. Burke marveling, running Delphi's fingers through the curls.) Of course Davy is one of Matt's boys—not impotent exactly, but very *very* low drive. (Nobody knows exactly what Matt does with his bitty budget but the boys are useful and one or two have made names.) He's perfect for Delphi; in fact the psychomed lets her take him to bed, two kittens in a basket. Davy doesn't mind the fact that Delphi "sleeps" like the dead. That's when P. Burke is out of the body-waldo up at Carbondale, attending to her own depressing needs.

A funny thing about that. Most of her sleepy-time Delphi's just a gently ticking lush little vegetable waiting for P. Burke to get back on the controls. But now and again Delphi all by herself smiles a bit or stirs in her "sleep." Once she breathed a sound: "Yes."

Under Carbondale P. Burke knows nothing. She's asleep too, dreaming of Delphi, what else? But if the bushy Dr. Tesla had heard that single syllable his bush would have turned snow-white. Because Delphi is TURNED OFF.

He doesn't. Davy is too dim to notice and Delphi's staff boss, Hopkins, wasn't monitoring.

And they've all got something else to think about now, because the cold-fire dress sells half a million copies, and not only in Texas. The GTX computers already know it. When they correlate a minor demand for macaws in Alaska the problem comes to human attention: Delphi is something special.

It's a problem, see, because Delphi is targeted on a limited consumer bracket. Now it turns out she has mass-pop potential—those macaws in *Fairbanks*, man!—it's like trying to shoot mice with an ABM. A whole new ball game. Dr. Tesla and the fatherly Mr. Cantle start going around in headquarters circles and buddy-lunching together when they can get away from a seventh-level weasel boy who scares them both.

In the end it's decided to ship Delphi down to the GTX holocam enclave in Chile to try a spot on one of the mainstream shows. (Never mind why an Infanta takes up acting.) The holocam complex occupies a couple of mountains where an observatory once used the clear air. Holocam total-environment shells are very expensive and electronically super-stable. Inside them actors can move freely without going off-register and the whole scene or any selected part will show up in the viewer's home in complete 3-di, so real you can look up their noses and much denser than you get from mobile rigs. You can blow a tit ten feet tall when there's no molecular skiffle around.

The enclave looks—well, take everything you know about Hollywood-Burbank and throw it away. What Delphi sees coming down is a neat giant mushroom-farm, domes of all sizes up to monsters for the big games and stuff. It's orderly. The idea that art thrives on creative flamboyance has long been torpedoed by proof that what art needs is computers. Because this showbiz has something TV and Hollywood never had—*automated inbuilt viewer feedback*. Samples, ratings, critics, polls? Forget it. With that carrier field you can get real-time response-sensor readouts from every receiver in the world, served up at your console. That started as a thingie to give the public more influence on content.

Yes.

Try it, man. You're at the console. Slice to the sex-age-educ-econ-ethno-cetera audience of your choice and start. You can't miss. Where the feedback warms up, give 'em more of that. Warm—warmer—*hot!* You've hit it—the secret itch under those hides, the dream in those hearts. You don't need to know its name. With your hand controlling all the input and your eye reading all the response you can make them a god ... and somebody'll do the same for you.

But Delphi just sees rainbows, when she gets through the degaussing ports and the field relay and takes her first look at the insides of those shells. The next thing she sees is a team of shapers and technicians descending on her, and millisecond timers everywhere. The tropical leisure is finished. She's in gigabuck mainstream now, at the funnel maw of the unceasing hose that's pumping the sight and sound and flesh and blood and sobs and laughs and dreams of *reality* into the world's happy head. Little Delphi is going plonk into a zillion homes in prime time and nothing is left to chance. Work!

And again Delphi proves apt. Of course it's really P. Burke down under Carbondale who's doing it, but who remembers that carcass? Certainly not P. Burke, she hasn't spoken through her own mouth for months. Delphi doesn't even recall dreaming of her when she wakes up.

As for the show itself, don't bother. It's gone on so long no living soul could unscramble the plotline. Delphi's trial spot has something to do with a widow and her dead husband's brother's amnesia.

The flap comes after Delphi's spots begin to flash out along the world-hose and the feedback appears. You've guessed it, of course. Sensational! As you'd say, they IDENTIFY.

The report actually says something like InskinEmp with a string of percentages meaning that Delphi not only has it for anybody with a Y-chromosome, but also for women and every thing in between. It's the sweet supernatural jackpot, the million-to-one.

Remember your Harlow? A sexpot, sure. But why did bitter hausfraus in Gary and Memphis know that the vanilla-ice-cream goddess with the white hair and crazy eyebrows was *their baby girl*? And write loving letters to Jean warning her that their husbands weren't good enough for her? Why? The GTX analysts don't know either, but they know what to do with it when it happens.

(Back in his bird sanctuary the old Infante spots it without benefit of computers and gazes thoughtfully at his bride in widow's weeds. It might, he feels, be well to accelerate the completion of his studies.)

The excitement reaches down to the burrow under Carbondale where P. Burke gets two medical exams in a week and a chronically inflamed electrode is replaced. Nurse Fleming also gets an assistant who doesn't do much nursing but is very interested in access doors and identity tabs.

And in Chile little Delphi is promoted to a new home up among the stars' residential spreads and a private jitney to carry her to work. For Hopkins there's a new computer terminal and a full-time schedule man. What is the schedule crowded with?

Things.

And here begins the trouble. You probably saw that coming too.

"What does she think she is, a goddam *consumer rep?*" Mr. Cantle's fatherly face in Carbondale contorts.

"The girl's upset," Miss Fleming says stubbornly. "She *believes* that, what you told her about helping people and good new products."

"They are good products," Mr. Cantle snaps automatically, but his anger is under control. He hasn't got where he is by irrelevant reactions.

"She says the plastic gave her a rash and the glo-pills made her dizzy."

"Good god, she shouldn't swallow them," Doctor Tesla puts in agitatedly.

"You told her she'd use them," persists Miss Fleming. Mr. Cantle is busy figuring how to ease this problem to the weasel-faced young man. What, was it a goose that lays golden eggs?

Whatever he says to level Seven, down in Chile the offending products vanish. And a symbol goes into Delphi's tank matrix, one that means roughly *Balance unit resistance against PR index.* This means that Delphi's complaints will be endured as long as her Pop Response stays above a certain level. (What happens when it sinks need not concern us.) And to compensate, the price of her exposure-time rises again. She's a regular on the show now and response is still climbing.

See her under the sizzling lasers, in a holocam shell set up as a walkway accident. (The show is guesting an acupuncture school expert.)

"I don't think this new body-lift is safe," Delphi's saying. "It's made a funny blue spot on me—look, Mr. Vere."

She wiggles to show where the mini-grav pak that imparts a delicious sense of weightlessness is attached.

186

"So don't leave it *on*, Dee. With your meat—watch that deck-spot, it's starting to synch."

"But if I don't wear it it isn't honest. They should insulate it more or something, don't you see?"

The show's beloved old father, who is the casualty, gives a senile snigger.

"I'll tell them," Mr. Vere mutters. "Look now, as you step back bend like this so it just shows, see? And hold two beats."

Obediently Delphi turns, and through the dazzle her eyes connect with a pair of strange dark ones. She squints. A quite young man is lounging alone by the port, apparently waiting to use the chamber.

Delphi's used by now to young men looking at her with many peculiar expressions, but she isn't used to what she gets here. A jolt of something somber and knowing. *Secrets.*

"Eyes! Eyes, Dee!"

She moves through the routine, stealing peeks at the stranger. He stares back. He knows something.

When they let her go she comes shyly to him.

"Living wild, kitten." Cool voice, hot underneath.

"What do you mean?"

"Dumping on the product. You trying to get dead?"

"But it isn't right," she tells him. "They don't know, but I do, I've been wearing it."

His cool is jolted.

"You're out of your head."

"Oh, they'll see I'm right when they check it," she explains. "They're just so busy. When I tell them—"

He is staring down at little flower-face. His mouth opens, closes. "What are you doing in this sewer anyway? Who are you?"

Bewilderedly she says, "I'm Delphi."

"Holy Zen."

"What's wrong. Who are you, please?"

Her people are moving her out now, nodding at him.

"Sorry we ran over, Mister Uhunh," the script girl says.

He mutters something but it's lost as her convoy bustles her toward the flower-decked jitney.

(Hear the click of an invisible ignition-train being armed?)

"Who was he?" Delphi asks her hair man.

The hair man is bending up and down from his knees as he works.

"Paul. Isham. Three," he says and puts a comb in his mouth.

"Who's that? I can't see."

He mumbles around the comb, meaning "Are you jiving?" Because she has to be, in the middle of the GTX enclave.

Next day there's a darkly smoldering face under a turban-towel when Delphi and the show's paraplegic go to use the carbonated pool.

She looks.

He looks.

And the next day, too.

(Hear that automatic sequencer cutting in? The system couples, the fuels begin to travel.)

Poor old Isham senior. You have to feel sorry for a man who values order: when he begets young, genetic information is still transmitted in the old ape way. One minute it's a happy midget with a rubber duck—look around and here's this huge healthy stranger, opaquely emotional, running with God knows who. Questions are heard where there's nothing to question, and eruptions claiming to be moral outrage. When this is called to Papa's attention—it may take time, in that boardroom—Papa does what he can, but without immortality-juice the problem is worrisome.

And young Paul Isham is a bear. He's bright and articulate and tender-souled and incessantly active and he and his friends are choking with appallment at the world their fathers made. And it hasn't taken Paul long to discover that _his_ father's house has many mansions and even the GTX computers can't relate everything to everything else. He noses out a decaying project which adds up to something like Sponsoring Marginal Creativity (the free-lance team that "discovered" Delphi was one such grantee). And from there it turns out that an agile lad named Isham can get his hands on a viable packet of GTX holocam facilities.

So here he is with his little band, way down the mushroom-farm mountain, busily spooling a show which has no relation to Delphi's. It's built on bizarre techniques and unsettling distortions pregnant with social protest. An _underground_ expression to you.

All this isn't unknown to his father, of course, but so far it has done nothing more than deepen Isham senior's apprehensive frown.

Until Paul connects with Delphi.

And by the time Papa learns this, those invisible hyper-

188

golics have exploded, the energy-shells are rushing out. For Paul, you see, is the genuine article. He's serious. He dreams. He even reads—for example, *Green Mansions*—and he wept fiercely when those fiends burned Rima alive.

When he hears that some new GTX pussy is making it big he sneers and forgets it. He's busy. He never connects the name with this little girl making her idiotic, doomed protest in the holocam chamber. This strangely simple little girl.

And she comes and looks up at him and he sees Rima, lost Rima the enchanted bird girl, and his unwired human heart goes twang.

And Rima turns out to be Delphi.

Do you need a map? The angry puzzlement. The rejection of the dissonance Rima-hustling-for-GTX-My-Father. Garbage, cannot be. The loitering around the pool to confirm the swindle . . . dark eyes hitting on blue wonder, jerky words exchanged in a peculiar stillness . . . the dreadful reorganization of the image into Rima-Delphi *in my Father's tentacles*—

You don't need a map.

Nor for Delphi either, the girl who loved her gods. She's seen their divine flesh close now, heard their unamplified voices call her name. She's played their god-games, worn their garlands. She's even become a goddess herself, though she doesn't believe it. She's not disenchanted, don't think that. She's still full of love. It's just that some crazy kind of *hope* hasn't—

Really you can skip all this, when the loving little girl on the yellow-brick road meets a Man. A real human male burning with angry compassion and grandly concerned with human justice, who reaches for her with real male arms and—boom! She loves him back with all her heart.

A happy trip, see?

Except.

Except that it's really P. Burke five thousand miles away who loves Paul. P. Burke the monster, down in a dungeon, smelling of electrode-paste. A caricature of a woman burning, melting, obsessed with true love. Trying over twenty-double-thousand miles of hard vacuum to reach her beloved through the girl-flesh numbed by an invisible film. Feeling his arms around the body he thinks is hers, fighting through shadows to give herself to him. Trying to taste and smell him through beautiful dead nostrils, to love him back with a body that goes dead in the heart of the fire.

Perhaps you get P. Burke's state of mind?

She has phases. The trying, first. And the shame. The SHAME. *I am not what thou lovest.* And the fiercer trying. And the realization that there is no, no way, none. Never. *Never.* . . . A bit delayed, isn't it, her understanding that the bargain she made was forever? P. Burke should have noticed those stories about mortals who end up as grasshoppers.

You see the outcome—the funneling of all this agony into one dumb protoplasmic drive to fuse with Delphi. To leave, to close out the beast she is chained to. *To become Delphi.*

Of course it's impossible.

However her torments have an effect on Paul. Delphi-as Rima is a potent enough love object, and liberating Delphi's mind requires hours of deeply satisfying instruction in the rottenness of it all. Add in Delphi's body worshipping his flesh, burning in the fire of P. Burke's savage heart—do you wonder Paul is involved?

That's not all.

By now they're spending every spare moment together and some that aren't so spare.

"Mister Isham, would you mind staying out of this sports sequence? The script calls for Davy here."

(Davy's still around, the exposure did him good.)

"What's the difference?" Paul yawns. "It's just an ad. I'm not blocking that thing."

Shocked silence at his two-letter word. The script girl swallows bravely.

"I'm sorry, sir, our directive is to do the *social sequence* exactly as scripted. We're having to respool the segments we did last week, Mister Hopkins is very angry with me."

"Who the hell is Hopkins? Where is he?"

"Oh, please, Paul. *Please.*"

Paul unwraps himself, saunters back. The holocam crew nervously check their angles. The GTX boardroom has a foible about having things *pointed* at them and theirs. Cold shivers, when the image of an Isham nearly went onto the world beam beside that Dialadinner.

Worse yet. Paul has no respect for the sacred schedules which are now a full-time job for ferret boy up at headquarters. Paul keeps forgetting to bring her back on time and poor Hopkins can't cope.

So pretty soon the boardroom data-ball has an urgent personal action-tab for Mr. Isham senior. They do it the gentle way, at first.

190

"I can't today, Paul."

"Why not?"

"They say I have to, it's *very* important."

He strokes the faint gold down on her narrow back. Under Carbondale, Pa., a blind mole-woman shivers.

"Important. Their importance. Making more gold. Can't you see? To them you're just a thing to get scratch with. A *huckster*. Are you going to let them screw you, Dee? Are you?"

"Oh, Paul—"

He doesn't know it but he's seeing a weirdie; Remotes aren't hooked up to flow tears.

"Just say no, Dee. No. Integrity. You have to."

"But they say, it's my job—"

"You won't believe I can take care of you, Dee, baby, baby, you're letting them rip us. You have to choose. Tell them, no."

"Paul . . . I w-will . . ."

And she does. Brave little Delphi (insane P. Burke). Saying "No, please, I promised, Paul."

They try some more, still gently.

"Paul, Mr. Hopkins told me the reason they don't want us to be together so much. It's because of who you are, your father."

She thinks her father is like Mr. Cantle, maybe.

"Oh great. Hopkins. I'll fix him. Listen, I can't think about Hopkins now. Ken came back today, he found out something."

They are lying on the high Andes meadow watching his friends dive their singing kites.

"Would you believe, on the coast the police have *electrodes in their heads*?"

She stiffens in his arms.

"Yeah, weird. I thought they only used PPs on criminals and the army. Don't you see, Dee—something has to be going on. Some movement. Maybe somebody's organizing. How can we find out?" He pounds the ground behind her. "We should make *contact*! If we could only find out."

"The, the news?" she asks distractedly.

"The news." He laughs. "There's nothing in the news except what they want people to know. Half the country could burn up and nobody would know it if they didn't want. Dee, can't you take what I'm explaining to you? They've got the whole world programmed! Total control of communication.

191

They've got everybody's mind wired in to think what they show them and want what they give them and they give them what they're programmed to want—you can't break in or out of it, you can't get *hold* of it anywhere. I don't think they even have a plan except to keep things going round and round—and God knows what's happening to the people or the earth or the other planets, maybe. One great big vortex of lies and garbage pouring round and round getting bigger and bigger and nothing can ever change. If people don't wake up soon we're through!"

He pounds her stomach, softly.

"You have to break out, Dee."

"I'll try, Paul, I will—"

"You're mine. They can't have you."

And he goes to see Hopkins, who is indeed cowed.

But that night up under Carbondale the fatherly Mr. Cantle goes to see P. Burke.

P. Burke? On a cot in a utility robe like a dead camel in a tent, she cannot at first comprehend that he is telling *her* to break it off with Paul. P. Burke has never seen Paul. *Delphi* sees Paul. The fact is, P. Burke can no longer clearly recall that she exists apart from Delphi.

Mr. Cantle can scarcely believe it either but he tries.

He points out the futility, the potential embarrassment for Paul. That gets a dim stare from the bulk on the bed. Then he goes into her duty to GTX, her job, isn't she grateful for the opportunity, etcetera. He's very persuasive.

The cobwebby mouth of P. Burke opens and croaks.

"No."

Nothing more seems to be forthcoming.

Mr. Cantle isn't dense, he knows an immovable obstacle when he bumps one. He also knows an irresistible force: GTX. The simple solution is to lock the waldo-cabinet until Paul gets tired of waiting for Delphi to wake up. But the cost, the schedules! And there's something odd here . . . he eyes the corporate asset hulking on the bed and his hunch-sense prickles.

You see, Remotes don't love. They don't have real sex, the circuits designed that out from the start. So it's been assumed that it's *Paul* who is diverting himself or something with the pretty little body in Chile. P. Burke can only be doing what comes natural to any ambitious gutter-meat. It hasn't oc-curred to anyone that they're dealing with the real hairy thing whose shadow is blasting out of every holoshow on earth.

192

Love?

Mr. Cantle frowns. The idea is grotesque. But his instinct for the fuzzy line is strong; he will recommend flexibility.

And so, in Chile:

"Darling, I don't have to work tonight! And Friday too—isn't that right, Mr. Hopkins?"

"Oh, great. When does she come up for parole?"

"Mr. Isham, please be reasonable. Our schedule—surely your own production people must be needing you?"

This happens to be true. Paul goes away. Hopkins stares after him wondering distastefully why an Isham wants to ball a waldo. (How sound are those boardroom belly-fears—garble creeps, creeps in!) It never occurs to Hopkins that an Isham might not know what Delphi is.

Especially with Davy crying because Paul has kicked him out of Delphi's bed.

Delphi's bed is under a real window.

"Stars," Paul says sleepily. He rolls over, pulling Delphi on top. "Are you aware that this is one of the last places on earth where people can see the stars? Tibet, too, maybe."

"Paul . . ."

"Go to sleep. I want to see you sleep."

"Paul, I . . . I sleep so *hard*, I mean, it's a joke how hard I am to wake up. Do you mind?"

"Yes."

But finally, fearfully, she must let go. So that five thousand miles north a crazy spent creature can crawl out to gulp concentrates and fall on her cot. But not for long. It's pink dawn when Delphi's eyes open to find Paul's arms around her, his voice saying rude, tender things. He's been kept awake. The nerveless little statue that was her Delphi-body nuzzled him in the night.

Insane hope rises, is fed a couple of nights later when he tells her she called his name in her sleep.

And that day Paul's arms keep her from work and Hopkins' wails go up to headquarters where the sharp-faced lad is working his sharp tailbone off packing Delphi's program. Mr. Cantle defuses that one. But next week it happens again, to a major client. And ferret-face has connections on the technical side.

Now you can see that when you have a field of complexly heterodyned energy modulations tuned to a demand-point like Delphi there are many problems of standwaves and lashback and skiffle of all sorts which are normally balanced out with ease by the technology of the future. By the same token they can be delicately unbalanced too, in ways that feed back into the waldo operator with striking results.

"Darling—what the hell! What's wrong? DELPHI!"

Helpless shrieks, writhings. Then the Rima-bird is lying wet and limp in his arms, her eyes enormous.

"I . . . I wasn't supposed to . . ." she gasps faintly. "They told me not to . . ."

"Oh my god—*Delphi*."

And his hard fingers are digging in her thick yellow hair. Electronically knowledgeable fingers. They freeze.

"You're a *doll*! You're one of those. PP implants. They control you. I should have known. Oh God, I should have known."

"No, Paul," she's sobbing. "No, no, no—"

"Damn them. Damn them, what they've done—you're not *you*—"

He's shaking her, crouching over her in the bed and jerking her back and forth, glaring at the pitiful beauty.

"No!" She pleads (it's not true, that dark bad dream back there). "I'm Delphi!"

"My father. Filth, pigs—damn them, damn them, damn them."

"No, no," she babbles. "They were good to me—" P. Burke underground mouthing, "They were good to me—AAH-AAAAH!"

Another agony skewers her. Up north the sharp young man wants to make sure this so-tiny interference works. Paul can scarcely hang onto her, he's crying too. "I'll kill them."

His Delphi, a wired-up slave! Spikes in her brain, electronic shackles in his bird's heart. Remember when those savages burned Rima alive?

"I'll *kill* the man that's doing this to you."

He's still saying it afterward but she doesn't hear. She's sure he hates her now, all she wants is to die. When she finally understands that the fierceness is tenderness she thinks it's a miracle. *He knows—and he still loves!*

How can she guess that he's got it a little bit wrong?

You can't blame Paul. Give him credit that he's even heard about pleasure-pain implants and snoops, which by their nature aren't mentioned much by those who know them most intimately. That's what he thinks is being used on Delphi, something to *control* her. And to listen—he burns at the unknown ears in their bed.

Of waldo-bodies and objects like P. Burke he has heard nothing.

So it never crosses his mind as he looks down at his violated bird, sick with fury and love, that he isn't holding *all* of her. Do you need to be told the mad resolve jelling in him now?

To free Delphi.

How? Well, he is after all Paul Isham III. And he even has an idea where the GTX neurolab is. In Carbondale.

But first things have to be done for Delphi, and for his own stomach. So he gives her back to Hopkins and departs in a restrained and discreet way. And the Chile staff is grateful and do not understand that his teeth don't normally show so much.

And a week passes in which Delphi is a very good, docile little ghost. They let her have the load of wildflowers Paul sends and the bland loving notes. (He's playing it coony.) And up in headquarters weasel boy feels that *his* destiny has clicked a notch onward and floats the word up that he's handy with little problems.

And no one knows what P. Burke thinks in any way whatever, except that Miss Fleming catches her flushing her food down the can and next night she faints in the pool. They haul her out and stick her with IVs. Miss Fleming frets, she's seen expressions like that before. But she wasn't around when crazies who called themselves Followers of the Fish looked through flames to life everlasting. P. Burke is seeing Heaven on the far side of death, too. Heaven spelled P-a-u-l, but the idea's the same. *I will die and be born again in Delphi.*

Garbage, electronically speaking. No way.

Another week and Paul's madness has become a plan. (Remember, he does have friends.) He smolders, watching his love paraded by her masters. He turns out a scorching sequence for his own show. And finally, politely, he requests from Hopkins a morsel of his bird's free time, which duly arrives.

"I thought you didn't *want* me any more," she's repeating as they wing over mountain flanks in Paul's suncar. "Now you *know*—"

"Look at me!"

His hand covers her mouth and he's showing her a lettered card.

DON'T TALK THEY CAN HEAR EVERYTHING WE SAY.

I'M TAKING YOU AWAY NOW.

She kisses his hand. He nods urgently, flipping the card.

DON'T BE AFRAID. I CAN STOP THE PAIN IF THEY TRY TO HURT YOU.

With his free hand he shakes out a silvery scrambler-mesh on a power pack. She is dumbfounded.

THIS WILL CUT THE SIGNALS AND PROTECT YOU DARLING.

She's staring at him, her head going vaguely from side to side, No.

"Yes!" He grins triumphantly. "Yes!"

For a moment she wonders. That powered mesh will cut off the field, all right. It will also cut off Delphi. But he is *Paul*. Paul is kissing her, she can only seek him hungrily as he sweeps the suncar through a pass.

Ahead is an old jet ramp with a shiny bullet waiting to go. (Paul also has credits and a Name.) The little GTX patrol courier is built for nothing but speed. Paul and Delphi wedge in behind the pilot's extra fuel tank and there's no more talking when the torches start to scream.

They're screaming high over Quito before Hopkins starts to worry. He wastes another hour tracking the beeper on Paul's suncar. The suncar is sailing a pattern out to sea. By the time they're sure it's empty and Hopkins gets on the hot flue to headquarters the fugitives are a sourceless howl about Carib West.

Up at headquarters weasel boy gets the squeal. His first impulse is to repeat his previous play but then his brain snaps to. This one is too hot. Because, see, although in the long run they can make P. Burke do anything at all except maybe *live*, instant emergencies can be tricky. And—Paul Isham III.

"Can't you order her back?"

They're all in the GTX tower monitor station, Mr. Cantle and ferret-face and Joe and a very neat man who is Mr. Isham senior's personal eyes and ears.

"No sir," Joe says doggedly. "We can read channels, particularly speech, but we can't interpolate organized patterns. It takes the waldo op to send one-to-one—"

"What are they saying?"

"Nothing at the moment, sir." The console jockey's eyes are closed. "I believe they are, ah, embracing."

"They're not answering," a traffic monitor says. "Still heading zero zero three zero—due north, sir."

"You're certain Kennedy is alerted not to fire on them?" the neat man asks anxiously.

"Yes, sir."

"Can't you just turn her off?" The sharp-faced lad is angry. "Pull that pig out of the controls!"

"If you cut the transmission cold you'll kill the Remote," Joe explains for the third time. "Withdrawal has to be phased right, you have to fade over to the Remote's own autonomics. Heart, breathing, cerebellum would go blooey. If you pull Burke out you'll probably finish her too. It's a fantastic cybersystem, you don't want to do that."

"The investment," Mr. Cantle shudders.

Weasel boy puts his hand on the console jock's shoulder, it's the contact who arranged the No-no effect for him.

"We can at least give them a warning signal, sir." He licks his lips, gives the neat man his sweet ferret smile. "We know that does no damage."

Joe frowns, Mr. Cantle sighs. The neat man is murmuring into his wrist. He looks up. "I am authorized," he says reverently, "I am authorized to, ah, direct a signal. If this is the only course. But minimal, minimal."

Sharp-face squeezes his man's shoulder.

In the silver bullet shrieking over Charleston Paul feels Delphi arch in his arms. He reaches for the mesh, hot for action. She thrashes, pushing at his hands, her eyes roll. She's afraid of that mesh despite the agony. (And she's right.) Frantically Paul fights her in the cramped space, gets it over her head. As he turns the power up she burrows free under his arm and the spasm fades.

"They're calling you again, Mister Isham!" the pilot yells.

"Don't answer. Darling, keep this over your head damn it how can I—"

An AX90 barrels over their nose, there's a flash.

"Mister Isham! Those are Air Force jets!"

"Forget it," Paul shouts back. "They won't fire. Darling, don't be afraid."

Another AX90 rocks them.

"Would you mind pointing your pistol at my head where they can see it, sir?" the pilot howls.

Paul does so. The AX90s take up escort formation around them. The pilot goes back to figuring how he can collect from GTX too, and after Goldsboro AB the escort peels away.

"Holding the same course," Traffic is reporting to the

group around the monitor. "Apparently they've taken on enough fuel to bring them to towerport here."

"In that case it's just a question of waiting for them to dock." Mr. Cantle's fatherly manner revives a bit.

"Why can't they cut off that damn freak's life-support," the sharp young man fumes. "It's ridiculous."

"They're working on it," Cantle assures him.

What they're doing, down under Carbondale, is arguing.

Miss Fleming's watchdog has summoned the bushy man to the waldo room.

"Miss Fleming, you will obey orders."

"You'll kill her if you try that, sir. I can't believe you meant it, that's why I didn't. We've already fed her enough sedative to affect heart action; if you cut any more oxygen she'll die in there."

The bushy man grimaces. "Get Doctor Quine here fast."

They wait, staring at the cabinet in which a drugged, ugly madwoman fights for consciousness, fights to hold Delphi's eyes open.

High over Richmond the silver pod starts a turn. Delphi is sagged into Paul's arm, her eyes swim up to him.

"Starting down now, baby. It'll be over soon, all you have to do is stay alive, Dee."

". . . Stay alive . . ."

The traffic monitor has caught them. "Sir! They've turned off for Carbondale—Control has contact—"

"Let's go."

But the headquarters posse is too late to intercept the courier wailing into Carbondale. And Paul's friends have come through again. The fugitives are out through the freight dock and into the neurolab admin port before the guard gets organized. At the elevator Paul's face plus his handgun get them in.

"I want Doctor—what's his name, Dee? Dee!"

". . . Tesla . . ." She's reeling on her feet.

"Doctor Tesla. Take me down to Tesla, fast."

Intercoms are squalling around them as they whoosh down, Paul's pistol in the guard's back. When the door slides open the bushy man is there.

"I'm Tesla."

"I'm Paul Isham. *Isham*. You're going to take your flaming implants out of this girl—now. Move!"

"What?"

"You heard me. Where's your operating room? Go!"

"But—"

"Move! Do I have to burn somebody?"

Paul waves the weapon at Dr. Quine, who has just appeared.

"No, no," says Tesla hurriedly. "But I can't, you know. It's impossible, there'll be nothing left."

"You screaming well can, right now. You mess up and I'll kill you," says Paul murderously. "Where is it, there? And wipe the feke that's on her circuits now."

He's backing them down the hall, Delphi heavy on his arm.

"Is this the place, baby? Where they did it to you?"

"Yes," she whispers, blinking at a door. "Yes . . ."

Because it is, see. Behind that door is the very suite where she was born.

Paul herds them through it into a gleaming hall. An inner door opens and a nurse and a gray man rush out. And freeze.

Paul sees there's something special about that inner door. He crowds them past it and pushes it open and looks in.

Inside is a big mean-looking cabinet with its front door panels ajar.

And inside the cabinet is a poisoned carcass to whom something wonderful, unspeakable, is happening. Inside is P. Burke the real living woman who knows that HE is there, coming closer—Paul whom she had fought to reach through forty thousand miles of ice—PAUL is here!—is yanking at the waldo doors—

The doors tear open and a monster rises up.

"Paul darling!" croaks the voice of love and the arms of love reach for him.

And he responds.

Wouldn't you, if a gaunt she-golem flab-naked and spouting wires and blood came at you clawing with metal studded paws—

"Get away!" He knocks wires.

It doesn't much matter which wires, P. Burke has so to speak her nervous system hanging out. Imagine somebody jerking a handful of your medulla—

She crashes onto the floor at his feet, flopping and roaring *"PAUL-PAUL-PAUL"* in rictus.

It's doubtful he recognizes his name or sees her life coming out of her eyes at him. And at the last it doesn't go to him. The eyes find Delphi, fainting by the doorway, and die.

Now of course Delphi is dead, too.

There's total silence as Paul steps away from the thing by his foot.

"You killed her," Tesla says. "That was her."

"Your control." Paul is furious, the thought of that monster fastened into little Delphi's brain nauseates him. He sees her crumpling and holds out his arms. Not knowing she is dead.

And Delphi comes to him.

One foot before the other, not moving very well—but moving. Her darling face turns up. Paul is distracted by the terrible quiet, and when he looks down he sees only her tender little neck.

"Now you get the implants out," he warns them. Nobody moves.

"But, she's dead," Miss Fleming whispers wildly.

Paul feels Delphi's life under his hand, they're talking about their monster. He aims his pistol at the gray man.

"You. If we aren't in your surgery when I count three I'm burning off this man's leg."

"Mr. Isham," Tesla says desperately, "you have just killed the person who animated the body you call Delphi. Delphi herself is dead. If you release your arm you'll see what I say is true."

The tone gets through. Slowly Paul opens his arms, looks down.

"Delphi?"

She totters, sways, stays upright. Her face comes slowly up.

"Paul . . ." Tiny voice.

"Your crotty tricks," Paul snarls at them. "Move!"

"Look at her eyes," Dr. Quine croaks.

They look. One of Delphi's pupils fills the iris, her lips writhe weirdly.

"Shock." Paul grabs her to him. "*Fix* her!" He yells at them, aiming at Tesla.

"For God's sake . . . bring it in the lab." Tesla quavers.

"Goodbye-bye," says Delphi clearly. They lurch down the hall, Paul carrying her, and meet a wave of people.

Headquarters has arrived.

Joe takes one look and dives for the waldo room, running into Paul's gun.

"Oh no, you don't."

Everybody is yelling. The little thing in his arm stirs, says plaintively, "I'm Delphi."

And all through the ensuing jabber and ranting she hangs

on, keeps it up, the ghost of P. Burke or whatever whispering crazily, "Paul . . . Paul . . . Please, I'm Delphi . . . Paul?"

"I'm here, darling, I'm here." He's holding her in the nursing bed. Tesla talks, talks, talks unheard.

"Paul . . . don't sleep . . ." the ghost-voice whispers. Paul is in agony, he will not accept, WILL NOT believe.

Tesla runs down.

And then near midnight Delphi says roughly, "Ag-ag-ag—" and slips onto the floor, making a rough noise like a seal.

Paul screams. There's more of the *ag-ag* business and more gruesome convulsive disintegrations, until by two in the morning Delphi is nothing but a warm little bundle of vegetative functions hitched to some expensive hardware—the same that sustained her before her life began. Joe has finally persuaded Paul to let him at the waldo-cabinet. Paul stays by her long enough to see her face change in a dreadfully alien and coldly convincing way, and then he stumbles out bleakly through the group in Tesla's office.

Behind him Joe is working wet-faced, sweating to reintegrate the fantastic complex of circulation, respiration, endocrines, mid-brain homeostases, the patterned flux that was a human being—it's like saving an orchestra abandoned in midair. Joe is also crying a little; he alone had truly loved P. Burke. P. Burke, now a dead pile on a table, was the greatest cybersystem he has ever known, and he never forgets her.

The end, really.

You're curious?

Sure, Delphi lives again. Next year she's back on the yacht getting sympathy for her tragic breakdown. But there's a different chick in Chile, because while Delphi's new operator is competent, you don't get two P. Burkes in a row—for which GTX is duly grateful.

The real belly-bomb of course is Paul. He was *young*, see. Fighting abstract wrong. Now life has clawed into him and he goes through gut rage and grief and grows in human wisdom and resolve. So much so that you won't be surprised, some time later, to find him—where?

In the GTX boardroom, dummy. Using the advantage of his birth to radicalize the system. You'd call it "boring from within."

That's how he put it, and his friends couldn't agree more. It gives them a warm, confident feeling to know that Paul is up there. Sometimes one of them who's still around runs into him and gets a big hello.

And the sharp-faced lad?

Oh, he matures too. He learns fast, believe it. For instance, he's the first to learn that an obscure GTX research unit is actually getting something with their loopy temporal anomalizer project. True, he doesn't have a physics background, and he's bugged quite a few people. But he doesn't really learn about that until the day he stands where somebody points him during a test run—and wakes up lying on a newspaper headlined NIXON UNVEILS PHASE TWO.

Lucky he's a fast learner.

Believe it, zombie. When I say growth I mean *growth*. Capital appreciation. You can stop sweating. There's a great future there.

Here's Harlan. We can't have a Hugo winners volume without Harlan, can we?

There seems to be an odd feeling about Harlan and me. A lot of the readers think we are annoyed with each other. Nothing can be further from the truth. We love each other.

It's just that neither can resist the other's physiognomy. I can't resist short and he can't resist plump. So we each talk about our irresistibles in the other's presence. It's a harmless little hobby we have, and we both laugh very heartily about it.

For instance, earlier this year I introduced Harlan at a Manhattan hall where he was going to read a couple of his stories (and if you haven't heard him read his stories, you're missing something great—good as he is as a writer, he's even better as a reader). As I stood up to perform the introduction, with a smile of Judeo-Christian benevolence on my face, I heard him mutter behind me, "Here comes a short joke."

How could he think that of me? Nothing like that had ever entered my mind. It was my every intention to comment on his rangy build and his loose-limbed lankiness. Of course, however, he set me off. I couldn't help it. I told of the festivities at Harlan's birth and how every fairy in the land had been invited, all except the wicked fairy, Diabola, who had been overlooked by accident. At the height of the celebration she appeared in a swirl of sulfur fumes, stood over the crib of Baby Harlan, and said, "All right, you rotten creep, you have a choice—talent or tall."

Would I have said that if he hadn't put short jokes into my head? Of course not.

But we have to end our little game. It's gotten away from us. You see, no one can go fifteen rounds of insult with Harlan, except me. (He goes easy on me out of love.) One of the games at conventions is to have us get up on the stage and give each other the Don Rickles treatment. And we did that at the thirty-second convention in Washington. Each of us was on a separate platform with four thousand people in

203

between us and we proceeded to make unflattering comments about each other.

No, I guess it wasn't a dignified and conservative thing to do. Worse yet, the sulfur fumes of the wicked fairy, Diabola, got into Harlan in his crib, and he is very apt to use sulfurous language, and he did on this occasion.

What we didn't know was that there was a newspaperman on the scene, and he was horrified. He had never *heard* language like that. He had a little girl who sat next to him translate some of the expressions and he blushed furiously. Well, it got written up in the paper, and Harlan and I agreed that the conventions just weren't private enough any more and we quit.

Too bad. The world is getting old.

THE DEATHBIRD

1

This is a test. Take notes. This will count as three fourths of your final grade. Hints: remember, in chess, kings cancel each other out and cannot occupy adjacent squares, are therefore all-powerful and totally powerless, cannot affect one another, produce stalemate. Hinduism is a polytheistic religion; the sect of Atman worships the divine spark of life within Man; in effect saying, "Thou art God." Provisos of equal time are not served by one viewpoint having media access to two hundred million people in prime time while opposing viewpoints are provided with a soap-box on the corner. Not everyone tells the truth. Operational note: these sections may be taken out of numerical sequence: rearrange to suit yourself for optimum clarity. Turn over your test papers and begin.

Uncounted layers of rock pressed down on the magma pool. White-hot with the bubbling ferocity of the molten nickel-iron core, the pool spat and shuddered, yet did not pit or char or smoke or damage in the slightest the smooth and reflective surfaces of the strange crypt.

Nathan Stack lay in the crypt—silent, sleeping.

A shadow passed through rock. Through shale, through coal, through marble, through mica schist, through quartzite; through miles-thick deposits of phosphates, through diatomaceous earth, through feldspars, though diorite; through faults and folds, through anticlines and monoclines, through dips and synclines; through hellfire; and came to the ceiling of the great cavern and passed through; and saw the magma pool and dropped down; and came to the crypt. The shadow.

A triangular face with a single eye peered into the crypt, saw Stack, and laid four-fingered hands on the crypt's cool surface. Nathan Stack woke at the touch, and the crypt became transparent; he woke though the touch had not been upon his body. His soul felt the shadowy pressure and he opened his eyes to see the leaping brilliance of the world-core around him, to see the shadow with its single eye staring in at him.

The serpentine shadow enfolded the crypt; its darkness flowed upward again, through the Earth's mantle, toward the crust, toward the surface of the cinder, the broken toy that was the Earth.

When they reached the surface, the shadow bore the crypt to a place where the poison winds did not reach, and caused it to open.

Nathan Stack tried to move, and moved only with difficulty. Memories rushed through his head of other lives, many other lives, as many other men, then the memories slowed and melted into a background tone that could be ignored.

The shadow thing reached down a hand and touched Stack's naked flesh. Gently, but firmly, the thing helped him to stand, and gave him garments, and a neck-pouch that contained a short knife and a warming-stone and other things. He offered his hand, and Stack took it, and after two hundred and fifty thousand years sleeping in the crypt, Nathan Stack stepped out on the face of the sick planet Earth.

Then the thing bent low against the poison winds and began walking away. Nathan Stack, having no other choice, bent forward and followed the shadow creature.

<h2 style="text-align:center">3</h2>

A messenger had been sent for Dira and he had come as quickly as the meditations would permit. When he reached the Summit, he found the fathers waiting, and they took him gently into their cove, where they immersed themselves and began to speak.

"We've lost the arbitration," the coil-father said. "It will be necessary for us to go and leave it to him."

Dira could not believe it. "But didn't they listen to our arguments, to our logic?"

The fang-father shook his head sadly and touched Dira's shoulder. "There were . . . accommodations to be made. It was their time. So we must leave."

The coil-father said, "We've decided you will remain. One was permitted, in caretakership. Will you accept our commission?"

It was a very great honor but Dira began to feel the loneliness even as they told him they would leave. Yet he accepted. Wondering why they had selected *him*, of all their people. There were reasons, there were always reasons, but he could not ask. And so he accepted the honor, with all its attendant sadness, and remained behind when they left.

The limits of his caretakership were harsh, for they insured he could not defend himself against whatever slurs or legends would be spread, nor could he take action unless it became clear the trust was being breached by the other—who now held possession. And he had no threat save the Deathbird. A final threat that could be used only when final measures were needed: and therefore too late.

But he was patient. Perhaps the most patient of all his people.

Thousands of years later, when he saw how it was destined to go, when there was no doubt left how it would end, he understood *that* was the reason he had been chosen to stay behind.

But it did not help the loneliness.

Nor could it save the Earth. Only Stack could do that.

1 Now the serpent was more subtil than any beast of the field which the LORD God had made. And he said unto the woman, Yea, hath God said, Ye shall not eat of every tree of the garden?

2 And the woman said unto the serpent, We may eat of the fruit of the trees of the garden:

3 But of the fruit of the tree which is in the midst of the garden, God hath said, Ye shall not eat of it, neither shall ye touch it, lest ye die.

4 And the serpent said unto the woman, Ye shall not surely die:

5 (Omitted)

6 And when the woman saw that the tree was good for food, and that it was pleasant to the eyes, and a tree to be desired to make one wise, she took of the fruit thereof, and did eat, and gave also unto her husband with her; and he did eat.

7 (Omitted)

8 (Omitted)

9 And the LORD God called unto Adam, and said unto him, Where art thou?

10 (Omitted)

11 And he said, Who told thee that thou wast naked? Hast thou eaten of the tree, whereof I commanded thee that thou shouldst not eat?

12 And the man said, The woman whom thou gavest to be with me, she gave me of the tree, and I did eat.

13 And the LORD God said unto the woman, What is this that thou hast done? And the woman said, The serpent beguiled me, and I did eat.

14 And the LORD God said unto the serpent, Because thou hast done this, thou art cursed above all cattle, and above every beast of the field; upon thy belly shalt thou go, and dust shalt thou eat all the days of thy life:

15 And I will put enmity between thee and the woman, and between thy seed and her seed; it shall bruise thy head, and thou shalt bruise his heel.

GENESIS——3:1—15

(Give 5 points per right answer.)

1. Melville's *Moby Dick* begins, "Call me Ishmael." We say it is told in the *first* person. In what person is Genesis told? From whose viewpoint?

2. Who is the "good guy" in this story? Who is the "bad guy"? Can you make a strong case for reversal of the roles?

3. Traditionally, the apple is considered to be the fruit the serpent offered to Eve. But apples are not endemic to the Near East. Select one of the following, more logical substitutes, and discuss how myths come into being and are corrupted over long periods of time: olive, fig, date, pomegranate.

4. Why is the word LORD always in capitals and the name God always capitalized? Shouldn't the serpent's name be capitalized, as well? If no, why?

5. If God created everything (see *Genesis*, Chap. 1), why did he create problems for himself by creating a serpent who would lead his creations astray? Why did God create a tree he did not want Adam and Eve to know about, and then go out of his way to warn them against it?

6. Compare and contrast Michelangelo's Sistine Chapel ceiling panel of the *Expulsion from Paradise* with Bosch's *Garden of Earthly Delights.*

7. Was Adam being a gentleman when he placed blame on Eve? Who was Quisling? Discuss "narking" as a character flaw.

8. God grew angry when he found out he had been defied. If God is omnipotent and omniscient, didn't he know? Why couldn't he find Adam and Eve when they hid?

9. If God had not wanted Adam and Eve to taste the fruit of the forbidden tree, why didn't he warn the serpent? Could God have prevented the serpent from tempting Adam and Eve? If yes, why didn't he? If no, discuss the possibility the serpent was as powerful as God.

10. Using examples from two different media journals, demonstrate the concept of "slanted news."

5

The poison winds howled and tore at the powder covering the land. Nothing lived there. The winds, green and deadly, dived out of the sky and raked the carcass of the Earth, seeking, seeking: anything moving, anything still living. But there was nothing. Powder. Talc. Pumice.

And the onyx spire of the mountain toward which Nathan Stack and the shadow thing had moved, all that first day. When night fell they dug a pit in the tundra and the shadow thing coated it with a substance thick as glue that had been in Stack's neck-pouch. Stack had slept the night fitfully, clutching the warming-stone to his chest and breathing through a filter tube from the pouch.

Once he had awakened, at the sound of great batlike creatures flying overhead; he had seen them swooping low, coming in flat trajectories across the wasteland toward his pit in the earth. But they seemed unaware that he—and the shadow thing—lay in the hole. They defecated thin, phosphorescent stringers that fell glowing through the night and were lost on the plains; then the creatures swooped upward and were whirled away on the winds. Stark resumed sleeping with difficulty.

In the morning, frosted with an icy light that gave everything a blue tinge, the shadow thing scrabbled its way out of the choking powder and crawled along the ground, then lay flat, fingers clawing for purchase in the whiskaway surface. Behind it, from the powder, Stack bore toward the surface, reached up a hand and trembled for help.

The shadow creature slid across the ground, fighting the winds that had grown stronger in the night, back to the soft place that had been their pit, to the hand thrust up through the powder. It grasped the hand, and Stack's fingers tightened convulsively. Then the crawling shadow exerted pressure and pulled the man from the treacherous pumice.

Together they lay against the earth, fighting to see, fighting to draw breath without filling their lungs with suffocating death.

"Why is it like this . . . what *happened?*" Stack screamed against the wind. The shadow creature did not answer, but it looked at Stack for a long moment and then, with very careful movements, raised its hand, held it up before Stack's eyes and slowly, making claws of the fingers, closed the four fingers into a cage, into a fist, into a painfully tight ball that said more eloquently than words: *destruction.*

Then they began to crawl toward the mountain.

6

The onyx spire of the mountain rose out of hell and struggled toward the shredded sky. It was monstrous arrogance. Nothing should have tried that climb out of desolation. But the black mountain had tried, and succeeded.

It was like an old man. Seamed, ancient, dirt caked in striated lines, autumnal, lonely; black and desolate, piled strength upon strength. It would *not* give in to gravity and pressure and death. It struggled for the sky. Ferociously alone, it was the only feature that broke the desolate line of the horizon.

In another twenty-five million years the mountain might be worn as smooth and featureless as a tiny onyx offering to the deity night. But though the powder plains swirled and the poison winds drove the pumice against the flanks of the pinnacle, thus far their scouring had only served to soften the edges of the mountain's profile, as though divine intervention had protected the spire.

Lights moved near the summit.

7

Stack learned the nature of the phosphorescent strings excreted onto the plain the night before by the batlike creatures. They were spores that became, in the wan light of day, strange bleeder plants.

All around them as they crawled through the dawn, the little live things sensed their warmth and began thrusting shoots up through the talc. As the fading red ember of the dying sun climbed painfully into the sky, the bleeding plants were already reaching maturity.

Stack cried out as one of the vine tentacles fastened around his ankle, holding him. A second looped itself around his neck.

Thin films of berry-black blood coated the vines, leaving rings on Stack's flesh. The rings burned terribly.

The shadow creature slid on its belly and pulled itself back to the man. Its triangular head came close to Stack's neck, and it bit into the vine. Thick black blood spurted as the vine parted, and the shadow creature rasped its razor-edged teeth back and forth till Stack was able to breathe again. With a violent movement Stack folded himself down and around, pulling the short knife from the neck-pouch. He sawed through the vine tightening inexorably around his ankle. It screamed as it was severed, in the same voice Stack had heard from the skies the night before. The severed vine writhed away, withdrawing into the talc.

Stack and the shadow thing crawled forward once again, low, flat, holding onto the dying earth: toward the mountain. High in the bloody sky, the Deathbird circled.

8

On their own world, they had lived in luminous, oily-walled caverns for millions of years, evolving and spreading their race through the universe. When they had had enough of empire-building, they turned inward, and much of their time was spent in the intricate construction of songs of wisdom, and the designating of fine worlds for many races.

There were other races that designed, however. And when there was a conflict over jurisdiction, an arbitration was called, adjudicated by a race whose *raison d'être* was impartiality and cleverness in unraveling knotted threads of claim and counterclaim. Their racial honor, in fact, depended on the flawless application of these qualities. Through the centuries they had refined their talents in more and more sophisticated arenas of arbitration until the time came when they were the final authority. The litigants were compelled to abide by the judgments, not merely because the decisions were always wise and creatively fair, but because the judges' race would, if its decisions were questioned as suspect, destroy itself. In the holiest place on their world they had erected a religious machine. It could be activated to emit a tone that would shatter their crystal carapaces. They were a race of exquisite cricket-like creatures, no larger than the thumb of a man. They were treasured throughout the civilized worlds, and their loss would have been catastrophic. Their honor and their value were never questioned. All races abided by their decisions.

So Dira's people gave over jurisdiction to that certain world, and went away, leaving Dira with only the Deathbird, a special caretakership the adjudicators had creatively woven into their judgment.

211

There is recorded one last meeting between Dira and those who had given him his commission. There were readings that could not be ignored—had, in fact, been urgently brought to the attention of the fathers of Dira's race by the adjudicators—and the Great Coiled One came to Dira at the last possible moment to tell him of the mad thing into whose hands this world had been given, to tell Dira of what the mad thing could do.

The Great Coiled One—whose rings were loops of wisdom acquired through centuries of gentleness and perception and immersed meditations that had brought forth lovely designs for many worlds—he who was the holiest of Dira's race, honored Dira by coming to *him*, rather than commanding Dira to appear.

We have only one gift to leave them, he said. *Wisdom. This mad one will come, and he will lie to them, and he will tell them: created he them. And we will be gone, and there will be nothing between them and the mad one but you. Only you can give them the wisdom to defeat him in their own good time.* Then the Great Coiled One stroked the skin of Dira with ritual affection, and Dira was deeply moved and could not reply. Then he was left alone.

The mad one came, and interposed himself, and Dira gave them wisdom, and time passed. His name became other than Dira, it became Snake, and the new name was despised: but Dira could see the Great Coiled One had been correct in his readings. So Dira made his selection. A man, one of them, and gifted him with the spark.

All of this is recorded somewhere. It is history.

9

The man was not Jesus of Nazareth. He may have been Simon. Not Genghis Khan, but perhaps a foot soldier in his horde. Not Aristotle, but possibly one who sat and listened to Socrates in the agora. Neither the shambler who discovered the wheel nor the link who first ceased painting himself blue and applied the colors to the walls of the cave. But one near them, somewhere near at hand. The man was not Richard *Coeur de Lion*, Rembrandt, Richelieu, Rasputin, Robert Fulton or the Mahdi. Just a man. With the spark.

10

Once, Dira came to the man. Very early on. The spark was there, but the light needed to be converted to energy. So Dira came to the man, and did what had to be done before the mad one knew of it, and when the mad one discovered that Dira, the Snake, had made contact, he quickly made explanations.

This legend has come down to us as the fable of *Faust.*
TRUE or FALSE?

11

Light converted to energy, thus:

In the fortieth year of his five hundredth incarnation, all-unknowing of the eons of which he had been part, the man found himself wandering in a terribly dry place under a thin, flat burning disc of sun. He was a Berber tribesman who had never considered shadows save to relish them when they provided shade. The shadow came to him, sweeping down across the sands like the *khamsin* of Egypt, the *simoom* of Asia Minor, the *harmattan*, all of which he had known in his various lives, none of which he remembered. The shadow came over him like the *sirocco.*

The shadow stole the breath from his lungs and the man's eyes rolled up in his head. He fell to the ground and the shadow took him down and down, through the sands, into the Earth.

Mother Earth.

She lived, this world of trees and rivers and rocks with deep stone thoughts. She breathed, had feelings, dreamed dreams, gave birth, laughed and grew contemplative for millennia. This great creature swimming in the sea of space.

What a wonder, thought the man, for he had never understood that the Earth was his mother, before this. He had never understood, before this, that the Earth had a life of its own, at once a part of mankind and quite separate from mankind. A mother with a life of her own.

Dira, Snake, shadow . . . took the man down and let the spark of light change itself to energy as the man became one with the Earth. His flesh melted, and became quiet, cool soil. His eyes glowed with the light that shines in the darkest centers of the planet and he saw the way the mother cared for her young: the worms, the roots of plants, the rivers that cascaded for miles over great cliffs in enormous caverns, the bark of trees. He was taken once more to the bosom of that great Earth mother, and understood the joy of her life.

Remember this, Dira said to the man.

What a wonder, the man thought . . .

. . . and was returned to the sands of the desert, with no remembrance of having slept with, loved, enjoyed the body of his natural mother.

12

They camped at the base of the mountain, in a greenglass cave; not deep but angled sharply so the blown pumice could not reach them. They put Nathan Stack's stone in a fault in the cave's floor, and the heat spread quickly, warming them. The shadow thing with its triangular head sank back in shadow and closed its eye and sent its hunting instinct out for food. A shriek came back on the wind.

Much later, when Nathan Stack had eaten, when he was reasonably content and well-fed, he stared into the shadows and spoke to the creature sitting there.

"How long was I down there . . . how long was the sleep?"

The shadow thing spoke in whispers. *A quarter of a million years.*

Stack did not reply. The figure was beyond belief. The shadow creature seemed to understand.

In the life of a world no time at all.

Nathan Stack was a man who could make accommodations. He smiled quickly and said, "I must have been tired."

The shadow did not respond.

"I don't understand very much of this. It's pretty damned frightening. To die, then to wake up . . . here. Like this."

You did not die. You were taken, put down here. By the end you will understand everything, I promise you.

"Who put me down there?"

I did. I came and found you when the time was right, and I put you down there.

"Am I still Nathan Stack?"

If you wish.

"But *am* I Nathan Stack?"

You always were. You had many other names, many other bodies, but the spark was always yours. Stack seemed about

214

to speak, and the shadow creature added, *You were always on your way to being who you are.*

"But what *am* I? Am I still Nathan Stack, dammit?"

If you wish.

"Listen: you don't seem too sure about that. You came and got me, I mean I woke up and there you were; now who should know better than you what my name is?"

You have had many names in many times. Nathan Stack is merely the one you remember. You had a very different name long ago, at the start, when I first came to you.

Stack was afraid of the answer, but he asked, "What was my name then?"

Ish-lilith. Husband of Lilith. Do you remember her?

Stack thought, tried to open himself to the past, but it was as unfathomable as the quarter of a million years through which he had slept in the crypt.

"No. But there were other women, in other times."

Many. There was one who replaced Lilith.

"I don't remember."

Her name . . . does not matter. But when the mad one took her from you and replaced her with the other . . . then I knew it would end like this. The Deathbird.

"I don't mean to be stupid, but I haven't the faintest idea what you're talking about."

Before it ends, you will understand everything.

"You said that before," Stack paused, stared at the shadow creature for a long time only moments long, then, "What was your name?"

Before I met you my name was Dira.

He said it in his native tongue. Stack could not pronounce it.

"Before you met me. What is it now?"

Snake.

Something slithered past the mouth of the cave. It did not stop, but it called out with the voice of moist mud sucking down into a quagmire.

"Why did you put *me* down there? Why did you come to me in the first place? What spark? Why can't I remember these other lives or who I was? What do you want from me?"

You should sleep. It will be a long climb. And cold.

"I slept for two hundred and fifty thousand years, I'm hardly tired," Stack said. "Why did you pick me?"

Later. Now sleep. Sleep has other uses.

Darkness deepened around Snake, seeped out around the

215

cave, and Nathan Stack lay down near the warming-stone, and the darkness took him.

13

SUPPLEMENTARY READING

This is an essay by a writer. It is clearly an appeal to the emotions. As you read it ask yourself how it applies to the subject under discussion. What is the writer trying to say? Does he succeed in making his point? Does this essay cast light on the point of the subject under discussion? After you have read this essay, using the reverse side of your test paper, write your own essay (500 words or less) on the loss of a loved one. If you have never lost a loved one, fake it.

AHBHU

Yesterday my dog died. For eleven years Ahbhu was my closest friend. He was responsible for my writing a story about a boy and his dog that many people have read. He was not a pet, he was a person. It was impossible to anthropomorphize him, he wouldn't stand for it. But he was so much his own kind of creature, he had such a strongly formed personality, he was so determined to share his life with only those he chose, that it was also impossible to think of him as simply a dog. Apart from those canine characteristics into which he was locked by his species, he comported himself like one of a kind.

We met when I came to him at the West Los Angeles Animal Shelter. I'd wanted a dog because I was lonely and I'd remembered when I was a little boy how my dog had been a friend when I had no other friends. One summer I went away to camp and when I returned I found a rotten old neighbor lady from up the street had had my dog picked up and gassed while my father was at work. I crept into the woman's back yard that night and found a rug hanging on the clothesline. The rug beater was hanging from a post. I stole it and buried it.

At the Animal Shelter there was a man in line ahead of me. He had brought in a puppy only a week or so old. A Puli, a Hungarian sheep dog; it was a sad-looking little thing. He had too many in the litter and had brought in this one to either be taken by someone else, or to be put to sleep. They took the dog inside and the man behind the counter called

216

my turn. I told him I wanted a dog and he took me back inside to walk down the line of cages.

In one of the cages the little Puli that had just been brought in was being assaulted by three larger dogs who had been earlier tenants. He was a little thing, and he was on the bottom, getting the stuffing knocked out of him. But he was struggling mightily. The runt of the litter.

"Get him out of there!" I yelled. "I'll take him, I'll take him, get him out of there!"

He cost two dollars. It was the best two bucks I ever spent.

Driving home with him, he was lying on the other side of the front seat, staring at me. I had had a vague idea what I'd name a pet, but as I stared at him, and he stared back at me, I suddenly was put in mind of the scene in Alexander Korda's 1939 film *The Thief of Bagdad*, where the evil vizier, played by Conrad Veidt, had changed Ahbhu, the little thief, played by Sabu, into a dog. The film had superimposed the human over the canine face for a moment so there was an extraordinary look of intelligence in the face of the dog. The little Puli was looking at me with that same expression. "Ahbhu," I said.

He didn't react to the name, but then he couldn't have cared less. But that was his name, from that time on.

No one who ever came into my house was unaffected by him. When he sensed someone with good vibrations, he was right there, lying at their feet. He loved to be scratched, and despite years of admonitions he refused to stop begging for scraps at table, because he found most of the people who had come to dinner at my house were patsies, unable to escape his woebegone Jackie-Coogan-as-the-Kid look.

But he was a certain barometer of bums, as well. On any number of occasions when I found someone I liked, and Ahbhu would have nothing to do with him or her, it always turned out the person was a wrongo. I took to noting his attitude toward newcomers, and I must admit it influenced my own reactions. I was always wary of someone Ahbhu shunned.

Women with whom I had had unsatisfactory affairs would nonetheless return to the house from time to time—to visit the dog. He had an intimate circle of friends, many of whom had nothing to do with me, and numbering among their company some of the most beautiful actresses in Hollywood. One exquisite lady used to send her driver to pick him up for Sunday afternoon romps at the beach.

I never asked him what happened on those occasions. He didn't talk.

Last year he started going downhill, though I didn't realize it because he maintained the manner of a puppy almost to the end. But he began sleeping too much, and he couldn't hold down his food—not even the Hungarian meals prepared for him by the Magyars who lived up the street. And it became apparent to me something was wrong with him when he got scared during the big Los Angeles earthquake last year. Ahbhu wasn't afraid of anything. He attacked the Pacific Ocean and walked tall around vicious cats. But the quake terrified him and he jumped up in my bed and threw his forelegs around my neck. I was very nearly the only victim of the earthquake to die from animal strangulation.

He was in and out of the veterinarian's shop all through the early part of this year, and the idiot always said it was his diet.

Then one Sunday when he was out in the backyard, I found him lying at the foot of the porch stairs, covered with mud, vomiting so heavily all he could bring up was bile. He was matted with his own refuse and he was trying desperately to dig his nose into the earth for coolness. He was barely breathing. I took him to a different vet.

At first they thought it was just old age . . . that they could pull him through. But finally they took X-rays and saw the cancer had taken hold in his stomach and liver.

I put off the day as much as I could. Somehow I just couldn't conceive of a world that didn't have him in it. But yesterday I went to the vet's office and signed the euthanasia papers.

"I'd like to spend a little time with him, before," I said.

They brought him in and put him on the stainless steel examination table. He had grown so thin. He'd always had a pot-belly and it was gone. The muscles in his hind legs were weak, flaccid. He came to me and put his head into the hollow of my armpit. He was trembling violently. I lifted his head and he looked at me with that comic face I'd always thought made him look like Lawrence Talbot, the Wolf Man. He knew. Sharp as hell right up to the end, hey old friend? He knew, and he was scared. He trembled all the way down to his spiderweb legs. This bouncing ball of hair that, when lying on a dark carpet, could be taken for a sheepskin rug, with no way to tell at which end head and which end tail. So thin. Shaking, knowing what was going to happen to him. But still a puppy.

I cried and my eyes closed as my nose swelled with the crying, and he buried his head in my arms because we hadn't

218

done much crying at one another. I was ashamed of myself not to be taking it as well as he was.

"I got to, pup, because you're in pain and you can't eat. I *got* to." But he didn't want to know that.

The vet came in, then. He was a nice guy and he asked me if I wanted to go away and just let it be done.

Then Ahbhu came up out of there and *looked* at me.

There is a scene in Kazan's *Viva Zapata* where a close friend of Zapata's, Brando's, has been condemned for conspiring with the *Federales*. A friend that had been with Zapata since the mountains, since the *revolución* had begun. And they come to the hut to take him to the firing squad, and Brando starts out, and his friend stops him with a hand on his arm, and he says to him with great friendship, "Emiliano, do it yourself."

Ahbhu looked at me and I know he was just a dog, but if he could have spoken wtih human tongue he could not have said more eloquently than he did with a look, *don't leave me with strangers.*

So I held him as they laid him down and the vet slipped the lanyard up around his right foreleg and drew it tight to bulge the vein, and I held his head and he turned it away from me as the needle went in. It was impossible to tell the moment he passed over from life to death. He simply laid his head on my hand, his eyes fluttered shut and he was gone.

I wrapped him in a sheet with the help of the vet, and I drove home with Ahbhu on the seat beside me, just the way we had come home eleven years before. I took him out in the backyard and began digging his grave. I dug for hours, crying and mumbling to myself, talking to him in the sheet. It was a very neat, rectangular grave with smooth sides and all the loose dirt scooped out by hand.

I laid him down in the hole and he was so tiny in there for a dog who had seemed to be so big in life, so furry, so funny. And I covered him over and when the hole was packed full of dirt I replaced the neat divot of grass I'd scalped off at the start. And that was all.

But I couldn't send him to strangers.

THE END

QUESTIONS FOR DISCUSSION

1. Is there any significance to the reversal of the word god being dog? If so, what?
2. Does the writer try to impart human qualities to

a non-human creature? Why? Discuss anthropo-
morphism in the light of the phrase, "Thou art
God."
3. Discuss the love the writer shows in this essay.
Compare and contrast it with other forms of love:
the love of a man for a woman, a mother for a
child, a son for a mother, a botanist for plants,
an ecologist for the Earth.

14

In his sleep, Nathan Stack talked.
"Why did you pick me? Why me . . ."

15

Like the Earth, the Mother was in pain.

The great house was very quiet. The doctor had left, and
the relatives had gone into town for dinner. He sat by the side
of her bed and stared down at her. She looked gray and old
and crumpled; her skin was a soft ashy hue of moth-dust. He
was crying softly.

He felt her hand on his knee, and looked up to see her
staring at him. "You weren't supposed to catch me," he said.

"I'd be disappointed if I hadn't," she said. Her voice was
very thin, very smooth.

"How is it?"

"It hurts. Ben didn't dope me too well."

He bit his lower lip. The doctor had used massive doses,
but the pain was more massive. She gave little starts as tremors
of sudden agony hit her. Impacts. He watched the life leaking
out of her eyes.

"How is your sister taking it?"

He shrugged. "You know Charlene. She's sorry, but it's all
pretty intellectual to her."

His mother let a tiny ripple of a smile move her lips. "It's a
terrible thing to say, Nathan, but your sister isn't the most
likeable woman in the world. I'm glad you're here." She
paused, thinking, then added, "It's just possible your father
and I missed something from the gene pool. Charlene isn't
whole."

"Can I get you something? A drink of water?"

"No. I'm fine."

He looked at the ampoule of narcotic pain killer. The

syringe lay mechanical and still on a clean towel beside it. He felt her eyes on him. She knew what he was thinking. He looked away.

"I would kill for a cigarette," she said.

He laughed. At sixty-five, both legs gone, what remained of her left side paralyzed, the cancer spreading like deadly jelly toward her heart, she was still the matriarch. "You can't have a cigarette, so forget it."

"Then why don't you use that hypo and let me out of here?"

"Shut up, Mother."

"Oh, for Christ's sake, Nathan. It's hours if I'm lucky. Months if I'm not. We've had this conversation before. You know I always win."

"Did I ever tell you you were a bitchy old lady?"

"Many times, but I love you anyhow."

He got up and walked to the wall. He could not walk through it, so he went around the inside of the room.

"You can't get away from it."

"Mother, Jesus! Please!"

"All right. Let's talk about the business."

"I couldn't care less about the business right now."

"Then what should we talk about? The lofty uses to which an old lady can put her last moments?"

"You know, you're really ghoulish. I think you're enjoying this in some sick way."

"What other way is there to enjoy it."

"An adventure."

"The biggest. A pity your father never had the chance to savor it."

"I hardly think he'd have savored the feeling of being stamped to death in a hydraulic press."

Then he thought about it, because that little smile was on her lips again. "Okay, he probably would have. The two of you were so unreal, you'd have sat there and discussed it and analyzed the pulp."

"And you're our son."

He was, and he was. And he could not deny it, nor had he ever. He was hard and gentle and wild just like them, and he remembered the days in the jungle beyond Brasilia, and the hunt in the Cayman Trench, and the other days working in the mills alongside his father, and he knew when his moment came he would savor death as she did.

"Tell me something. I've always wanted to know. Did Dad kill Tom Golden?"

"Use the needle and I'll tell you."

"I'm a Stack. I don't bribe."

"I'm a Stack, and know what a killing curiosity you've got. Use the needle and I'll tell you."

He walked widdershins, around the room. She watched him, eyes bright as the mill vats.

"You old bitch."

"Shame, Nathan. You know you're not the son of a bitch. Which is more than your sister can say. Did I ever tell you she wasn't your father's child?"

"No, but I knew."

"You'd have liked her father. He was Swedish. Your father liked him."

"Is that why Dad broke both his arms?"

"Probably. But I never heard the Swede complain. One night in bed with me in those days was worth a couple of broken arms. Use the needle."

Finally, while the family was between the entree and the dessert, he filled the syringe and injected her. Her eyes widened as the stuff smacked her heart, and just before she died she rallied all her strength and said, "A deal's a deal. Your father didn't kill Tom Golden, I did. You're a hell of a man, Nathan, and you fought us the way we wanted, and we both loved you more than you could know. Except, dammit, you cunning s.o.b., you do know, don't you?"

"I know," he said, and she died; and he cried; and that was the extent of the poetry in it.

16

He knows we are coming.

They were climbing the northern face of the onyx mountain. Snake had coated Nathan Stack's feet with the thick glue and, though it was hardly a country walk, he was able to keep a foothold and pull himself up. Now they had paused to rest on a spiral ledge, and Snake had spoken for the first time of what waited for them where they were going.

"He?"

Snake did not answer. Stack slumped against the wall of the ledge. At the lower slopes of the mountain they had encountered slug-like creatures that had tried to attach themselves to Stack's flesh, but when Snake had driven them off they had returned to sucking the rocks. They had not come near the shadow creature. Farther up, Stack could see the

222

lights that flickered at the summit; he had felt fear that crawled up from his stomach. A short time before they had come to this ledge they had stumbled past a cave in the mountain where the bat creatures slept. They had gone mad at the presence of the man and the Snake and the sounds they had made sent waves of nausea through Stack. Snake had helped him and they had gotten past. Now they had stopped and Snake would not answer Stack's questions.

We must keep climbing.

"Because he knows we're here." There was a sarcastic rise in Stack's voice.

Snake started moving. Stack closed his eyes. Snake stopped and came back to him. Stack looked up at the one-eyed shadow.

"Not another step."

There is no reason why you should not know.

"Except, friend, I have the feeling you aren't going to tell me anything."

It is not yet time for you to know.

"Look: just because I haven't asked, doesn't mean I don't want to know. You've told me things I shouldn't be able to handle . . . all kinds of crazy things . . . I'm as old as, as . . . I don't know *how* old, but I get the feeling you've been trying to tell me I'm Adam . . ."

That is so.

". . . uh." He stopped rattling and stared back at the shadow creature. Then, very softly, accepting even more than he had thought possible, he said, "Snake." He was silent again. After a time he asked, "Give me another dream and let me know the rest of it?"

You must be patient. The one who lives at the top knows we are coming but I have been able to keep him from perceiving your danger to him only because you do not know yourself.

"Tell me this, then: does he *want* us to come up . . . the one on the top?"

He allows it. Because he doesn't know.

Stack nodded, resigned to following Snake's lead. He got to his feet and performed an elaborate butler's motion, *after you, Snake.*

And Snake turned, his flat hands sticking to the wall of the ledge, and they climbed higher, spiraling upward toward the summit.

223

The Deathbird swooped, then rose toward the Moon. There was still time.

17

Dira came to Nathan Stack near sunset, appearing in the board room of the industrial consortium Stack had built from the empire bequeathed him by his family.

Stack sat in the pneumatic chair that dominated the conversation pit where top-level decisions were made. He was alone. The others had left hours before and the room was dim with only the barest glow of light from hidden banks that shone through the soft walls.

The shadow creature passed through the walls—and at his passage they became rose quartz, then returned to what they had been. He stood staring at Nathan Stack, and for long moments the man was unaware of any other presence in the room.

You have to go now, Snake said.

Stack looked up, his eyes widened in horror, and through his mind flitted the unmistakable image of Satan, fanged mouth smiling, horns gleaming with scintillas of light as though seen through crosstar filters, rope tail with its spade-shaped pointed tip thrashing, large cloven hoofs leaving burning imprints in the carpet, eyes as deep as pools of oil, the pitchfork, the satin-lined cape, the hairy legs of a goat, talons. He tried to scream but the sound dammed up in his throat.

No, Snake said, *that is not so. Come with me, and you will understand.*

There was a tone of sadness in the voice. As though Satan had been sorely wronged. Stack shook his head violently.

There was no time for argument. The moment had come, and Dira could not hesitate. He gestured and Nathan Stack rose from the pneumatic chair, leaving behind something that looked like Nathan Stack asleep, and he walked to Dira and Snake took him by the hand and they passed through rose quartz and went away from there.

Down and down Snake took him.

The Mother was in pain. She had been sick for eons, but it had reached the point where Snake knew it would be terminal, and the Mother knew it, too. But she would hide her child, she would intercede in her own behalf and hide him away deep in her bosom where no one, not even the mad one, could find him.

Dira took Stack to Hell.

It was a fine place.

Warm and safe and far from the probing of mad ones.

And the sickness raged on unchecked. Nations crumbled, the oceans boiled and then grew cold and filmed over with scum, the air became thick with dust and killing vapors, flesh ran like oil, the skies grew dark, the sun blurred and became dull. The Earth moaned.

The planets suffered and consumed themselves, beasts became crippled and went mad, trees burst into flame and from their ashes rose glass shapes that shattered in the wind. The Earth was dying; a long, slow, painful death.

In the center of the Earth, in the fine place, Nathan Stack slept. *Don't leave me with strangers.*

Overhead, far away against the stars, the Deathbird circled and circled, waiting for the word.

18

When they reached the highest peak, Nathan Stack looked across through the terrible burning cold and the ferocious grittiness of the demon wind and saw the sanctuary of always, the cathedral of forever, the pillar of remembrance, the haven of perfection, the pyramid of blessings, the toyshop of creation, the vault of deliverance, the monument of longing, the receptacle of thoughts, the maze of wonder, the catafalque of despair, the podium of pronouncements and the kiln of last attempts.

On a slope that rose to a star pinnacle, he saw the home of the one who dwelled here—lights flashing and flickering, lights that could be seen far off across the deserted face of the planet—and he began to suspect the name of the resident.

Suddenly everything went red for Nathan Stack. As though a filter had been dropped over his eyes, the black sky, the flickering lights, the rocks that formed the great plateau on which they stood, even Snake became red, and with the color came pain. Terrible pain that burned through every channel of Stack's body, as though his blood had been set afire. He screamed and fell to his knees, the pain crackling through his brain, following every nerve and blood vessel and ganglion and neural track. His skull flamed.

Fight him, Snake said. *Fight him!*

I can't, screamed silently through Stack's mind, the pain too great even to speak. Fire licked and leaped and he felt the delicate tissues of thought shriveling. He tried to focus his thoughts on ice. He clutched for salvation at ice, chunks of ice, mountains of ice, swimming icebergs of ice half-buried in frozen water, even as his soul smoked and smoldered. *Ice!* He thought of millions of particles of hail rushing, falling, thundering against the firestorm eating his mind, and there was a spit of steam, a flame that went out, a corner that grew cool . . . and he took his stand in that corner, thinking ice, thinking blocks and chunks and monuments of ice, edging them out to widen the circle of coolness and safety. Then the flames began to retreat, to slide back down the channels, and he sent ice after them, snuffing them, burying them in ice and chill waters that raced after the flames and drove them out.

When he opened his eyes, he was still on his knees, but he could think again, and the red surfaces had become normal again.

He will try again. You must be ready.

"Tell me *everything!* I can't go through this without knowing, I need help! Tell me, Snake, tell me now!"

You can help yourself. You have the strength. I gave you the spark.

. . . and the second derangement struck!

The air turned shaverasse and he held dripping chunks of unclean rova in his jowls, the taste making him weak with nausea. His pods withered and drew up into his shell and as the bones cracked he howled with strings of pain that came so fast they were almost one. He tried to scuttle away, but his eyes magnified the shatter of light that beat against him. Facets of his eyes cracked and the juice began to bubble out. The pain was unbelievable.

Fight him!

Stack rolled onto his back, sending out cilia to touch the earth, and for an instant he realized he was seeing through the eyes of another creature, another form of life he could not even describe. But he was under an open sky and that produced fear, he was surrounded by air that had become deadly and *that* produced fear, he was going blind and *that* produced fear, he was . . . he was a man . . . he fought back against the feeling of being some other thing . . . he was a *man* and he would not feel fear, he would stand.

He rolled over, withdrew his cilia, and struggled to lower

226

his pods. Broken bones grated and pain thundered through his body. He forced himself to ignore it, and finally the pods were down and he was breathing and he felt his head reeling . . .

And when he opened his eyes he was Nathan Stack again.

. . . and the third derangement struck:

Hopelessness.

Out of unending misery he came back to be Stack.

. . . and the fourth derangement struck:

Madness.

Out of raging lunacy he fought his way to be Stack.

. . . and the fifth derangement, and the sixth, and the seventh, and the plagues, and the whirlwinds, and the pools of evil, and the reduction in size and accompanying fall forever through submicroscopic hells, and the things that fed on him from inside, and the twentieth, and the fortieth, and the sound of his voice screaming for release, and the voice of Snake always beside him, whispering *Fight him!*

Finally it stopped.

Quickly, now.

Snake took Stack by the hand and half-dragging him they raced to the great palace of light and glass on the slope, shining brightly under the star pinnacle, and they passed under an arch of shining metal into the ascension hall. The portal sealed behind them.

There were tremors in the walls. The inlaid floors of jewels began to rumble and tremble. Bits of high and faraway ceilings began to drop. Quaking, the palace gave one hideous shudder and collapsed around them.

Now, Snake said. *Now you will know everything!*

And everything forgot to fall. Frozen in mid-air, the wreckage of the palace hung suspended above them. Even the air ceased to swirl. Time stood still. The movement of the Earth was halted. Everything held utterly immobile as Nathan Stack was permitted to understand all.

19

MULTIPLE CHOICE (Counts for ½ your final grade.)

1. **God is:**
    A. **An invisible spirit with a long beard.**
    B. **A small dog dead in a hole.**
    C. **Everyman.**

    D. The Wizard of Oz.
2. **Nietzsche wrote "God is dead." By this did he mean:**
    A. Life is pointless.
    B. Belief in supreme deities has waned.
    C. There never was a God to begin with.
    D. Thou art God.
3. **Ecology is another name for:**
    A. Mother love.
    B. Enlightened self-interest.
    C. A good health salad with Granola.
    D. God.
4. **Which of these phrases most typifies the profoundest love:**
    A. Don't leave me with strangers.
    B. I love you.
    C. God is love.
    D. Use the needle.
5. **Which of these powers do we usually associate with God:**
    A. Power.
    B. Love.
    C. Humanity.
    D. Docility.

20

None of the above.

Starlight shone in the eyes of the Deathbird and its passage through the night cast a shadow on the Moon.

21

Nathan Stack raised his hands and around them the air was still as the palace fell crashing. They were untouched. *Now you know all there is to know*, Snake said, sinking to one knee as though worshipping. There was no one there to worship but Nathan Stack.

"Was he always mad?"

From the first.

"Then those who gave our world to him were mad, and your race was mad to allow it."

Snake had no answer.

"Perhaps it was supposed to be like this," Stack said.

He reached down and lifted Snake to his feet, and he touched the shadow creature's sleek triangular head. "Friend," he said.

Snake's race was incapable of tears. He said, *I have waited longer than you can know for that word.*

"I'm sorry it comes at the end."

Perhaps it was supposed to be like this.

Then there was a swirling of air, a scintillation in the ruined palace, and the owner of the mountain, the owner of the ruined Earth came to them in a burning bush.

AGAIN, SNAKE? AGAIN YOU ANNOY ME?

The time for toys is ended.

NATHAN STACK YOU BRING TO STOP ME? *I* SAY WHEN THE TIME IS ENDED. *I* SAY, AS I'VE ALWAYS SAID.

Then, to Nathan Stack:

GO AWAY. FIND A PLACE TO HIDE UNTIL I COME FOR YOU.

Stack ignored the burning bush. He waved his hand and the cone of safety in which they stood vanished. "Let's find him, first, then I know what to do."

The Deathbird sharpened its talons on the night wind and sailed down through emptiness toward the cinder of the Earth.

22

Nathan Stack had once contracted pneumonia. He had lain on the operating table as the surgeon made the small incision in the chest wall. Had he not been stubborn, had he not continued working around the clock while the infection developed into empyema, he would never have had to go under the knife, even for an operation as safe as a thoracotomy. But he was a Stack, and so he lay on the operating table as the rubber tube was inserted into the chest cavity to drain off the pus in the pleural cavity, and heard someone speak his name.

NATHAN STACK.

He heard it, from far off, across an Arctic vastness; heard it echoing over and over, down an endless corridor; as the knife sliced.

NATHAN STACK.

He remembered Lilith, with hair the color of dark wine. He remembered taking hours to die beneath a rock slide as

229

his hunting companions in the pack ripped apart the remains of the bear and ignored his grunted moans for help. He remembered the impact of the crossbow bolt as it ripped through his hauberk and split his chest and he died at Agincourt. He remembered the icy water of the Ohio as it closed over his head and the flatboat disappearing without his mates noticing his loss. He remembered the mustard gas that ate his lungs as he tried to crawl toward a farmhouse near Verdun. He remembered looking directly into the flash of the bomb and feeling the flesh of his face melt away. He remembered Snake coming to him in the board room and husking him like corn from his body. He remembered sleeping in the molten core of the Earth for a quarter of a million years.

Across the dead centuries he heard his mother pleading with him to set her free, to end her pain. *Use the needle.* Her voice mingled with the voice of the Earth crying out in endless pain at her flesh that had been ripped away, at her rivers turned to arteries of dust, at her rolling hills and green fields slagged to greenglass and ashes. The voices of his mother and the mother that was Earth became one, and mingled to become Snake's voice telling him he was the one man in the world—the last man in the world—who could end the terminal case the Earth had become.

Use the needle. Put the suffering Earth out of its misery. *It belongs to you now.*

Nathan Stack was secure in the power he contained. A power that far outstripped that of gods or Snakes or mad creators who stuck pins in their creations, who broke their toys.

YOU CAN'T. I WON'T LET YOU.

Nathan Stack walked around the burning bush as it crackled impotently in rage. He looked at it almost pityingly, remembering the Wizard of Oz with his great and ominous disembodied head floating in mist and lightning, and the poor little man behind the curtain turning the dials to create the effects. Stack walked around the effect, knowing he had more power than this sad, poor thing that had held his race in thrall since before Lilith had been taken from him.

He went in search of the mad one who capitalized his name.

23

Zarathustra descended alone from the mountains, encountering no one. But when he came into the forest, all at once there stood before him an old man who had left his holy cottage to look for roots in the woods. And thus spoke the old man to Zarathustra.

"No stranger to me is this wanderer: many years ago he passed this way. Zarathustra he was called, but he has changed. At that time you carried your ashes to the mountains; would you now carry your fire into the valleys? Do you not fear to be punished as an arsonist?

"Zarathustra has changed, Zarathustra has become a child, Zarathustra is an awakened one; what do you now want among the sleepers? You lived in your solitude as in the sea, and the sea carried you. Alas, would you now climb ashore? Alas, would you again drag your own body?"

Zarathustra answered: "I love man."

"Why," asked the saint, "did I go into the forest and the desert? Was it not because I loved man all-too-much? Now I love God; man I love not. Man is for me too imperfect a thing. Love of man would kill me."

"And what is the saint doing in the forest?" asked Zarathustra.

The saint answered: "I make songs and sing them; and when I make songs, I laugh, cry, and hum: thus I praise God. With singing, crying, laughing, and humming, I praise the god who is my god. But what do you bring us as a gift?"

When Zarathustra had heard these words he bade the saint farewell and said: "What could I have to give you? But let me go quickly lest I take something from you!" And thus they separated, the old one and the man, laughing as two boys laugh.

But when Zarathustra was alone he spoke thus to his heart: "Could it be possible? This old saint in the forest had not yet heard anything of this, that *God is dead!*"

24

Stack found the mad one wandering in the forest of final moments. He was an old, tired man, and Stack knew with a wave of his hand he could end it for this god in a moment. But what was the reason for it? It was even too late for revenge. It had been too late from the start. So he let the old one go his way, wandering in the forest, mumbling to himself, I WON'T LET YOU DO IT, in the voice of a cranky child; mumbling pathetically, OH, PLEASE, I DON'T

WANT TO GO TO BED YET, I'M NOT YET DONE
PLAYING.

And Stack came back to Snake, who had served his func-
tion and protected Stack until Stack had learned that he was
more powerful than the God he'd worshipped all through the
history of Men. He came back to Snake and their hands
touched and the bond of friendship was sealed at last, at the
end.

Then they worked together and Nathan Stack used the
needle with a wave of his hands, and the Earth could not sigh
with relief as its endless pain was ended . . . but it did sigh,
and it settled in upon itself, and the molten core went out,
and the winds died, and from high above them Stack heard
the fulfillment of Snake's final act; he heard the descent of
the Deathbird.

"What was your name?" Stack asked his friend.

Dira.

And the Deathbird settled down across the tired shape of
the Earth, and it spread its wings wide, and brought them
over and down, and enfolded the Earth as a mother enfolds
her weary child. Dira settled down on the amethyst floor of
the dark-shrouded palace, and closed his single eye with gratitude. To sleep at last, at the end.

All this, as Nathan Stack stood watching. He was the last,
at the end, and because he had come to own—if even for a
few moments—that which could have been his from the start,
had he but known, he did not sleep but stood and watched.
Knowing at last, at the end, that he had loved and done no
wrong.

25

The Deathbird closed its wings over the Earth until at last,
at the end, there was only the great bird crouched over the
dead cinder. Then the Deathbird raised its head to the star-
filled sky and repeated the sigh of loss the Earth had felt at
the end. Then its eyes closed, it tucked its head carefully under its wing, and all was night.

Far away, the stars waited for the cry of the Deathbird to
reach them so final moments could be observed at last, at the
end, for the race of Men.

26

THIS IS FOR MARK TWAIN

Here's the other story by Ursula. She wasn't at Toronto for her novella award and she wasn't at Washington for her short story award and I still haven't met her.

I did see her picture once.

It came about this way . . . Every once in a while, some newspaper or magazine decides that a feature article on science fiction should be prepared. This generally strikes us old pros with consternation. We would *like* to see science fiction dealt with appropriately, but our notion of the appropriate and that of the various members of the news media rarely match. Too many of the non-science-fiction people of the press have some vague memory of wrist-radios in a Dick Tracy comic strip or once saw a Flash Gordon episode and that's all.

To be sure, this is not always so. Once at a local convention in New York, a reporter from the New York *Post* approached me and asked if he could interview me in connection with a story he was writing on the convention.

"Why?" I said. "Can't you make fun of us without interviewing me?"

He said, quite seriously, "Why don't you read my story tomorrow and see if that's my intention."

So I thought: Yes, I'm prejudging him, and I shouldn't.

I answered his questions straightforwardly and he wrote a nice article that treated us well.

That's the exception that keeps us hoping—and then hurting. A weekly newsmagazine did a feature article on science fiction and lots of us co-operated, out of hope. I was interviewed for an hour and a half. So was Ben Bova. So was Judy-Lynn del Rey. So were lots of good and honest people.

But nothing of it showed in the final article, which hung us up for laughs and let us twist slowly, slowly in the wind. The general impression was that science fiction was essentially a twelve-year-old boy wearing Spock ears.

In this article there was a picture of Ursula smoking a pipe.

I understand that Ursula does smoke a pipe, and why not? I hate tobacco and I think anyone who smokes is a dolt, but

233

I'm a feminist and I will maintain to my dying breath that women have, and what's more *should* have, fully as much capacity for dolthood as men do.

I do not believe, however, that the picture was run for the sake of supporting feminism. Rather, I suspect it was included because the magazine thought it would help demonstrate how nutty science fiction people were.

Alas!

12

THE ONES WHO WALK AWAY FROM OMELAS

(Variations on a Theme by William James)

With a clamor of bells that set the swallows soaring, the Festival of Summer came to the city Omelas, bright-towered by the sea. The rigging of the boats in harbor sparkled with flags. In the streets between houses with red roofs and painted walls, between old moss-grown gardens and under avenues of trees, past great parks and public buildings, processions moved. Some were decorous: old people in long stiff robes of mauve and gray, grave master workmen, quiet, merry women carrying their babies and chatting as they walked. In other streets the music beat faster, a shimmering of gong and tambourine, and the people went dancing, the procession was a dance. Children dodged in and out, their high calls rising like the swallows' crossing flights over the music and the singing. All the processions wound toward the north side of the city, where on the great watermeadow called the Green Fields boys and girls, naked in the bright air, with mudstained feet and ankles and long, lithe arms, exercised their restive horses before the race. The horses wore no gear at all but a halter without bit. Their manes were braided with streamers of silver, gold, and green. They blew out their nostrils and pranced and boasted to one another; they were vastly excited, the horse being the only animal who has adopted our ceremonies as his own. Far off to the north and west the mountains stood up half-encircling Omelas on her bay. The air of morning was so clear that the snow still crowning the Eighteen Peaks burned with white-gold fire across the miles of sunlit air, under the dark blue of the sky. There was just enough wind to make the banners that marked the race course snap and flutter now and then. In the silence of the broad green meadows one could hear the music winding through the city streets, farther and nearer and ever approaching, a cheerful faint sweetness of the air that from time to time trembled and gathered together and broke out into the great joyous clanging of the bells.

Joyous! How is one to tell about joy? How describe the citizens of Omelas?

They were not simple folk, you see, though they were happy. But we do not say the words of cheer much any more. All smiles have become archaic. Given a description such as this one tends to make certain assumptions. Given a description such as this one tends to look next for the King, mounted on a splendid stallion and surrounded by his noble knights, or perhaps in a golden litter borne by great-muscled slaves. But there was no king. They did not use swords, or keep slaves. They were not barbarians. I do not know the rules and laws of their society, but I suspect that they were singularly few. As they did without monarchy and slavery, so they also got on without the stock exchange, the advertisement, the secret police, and the bomb. Yet I repeat that these were not simple folk, not dulcet shepherds, noble savages, bland utopians. They were not less complex than we. The trouble is that we have a bad habit, encouraged by pedants and sophisticates, of considering happiness as something rather stupid. Only pain is intellectual, only evil interesting. This is the treason of the artist: a refusal to admit the banality of evil and the terrible boredom of pain. If you can't lick 'em, join 'em. If it hurts, repeat it. But to praise despair is to condemn delight, to embrace violence is to lose hold of everything else. We have almost lost hold; we can no longer describe a happy man, nor make any celebration of joy. How can I tell you about the people of Omelas? They were not naive and happy children—though their children were, in fact, happy. They were mature, intelligent, passionate adults whose lives were not wretched. O miracle! But I wish I could describe it better. I wish I could convince you. Omelas sounds in my words like a city in a fairytale, long ago and far away, once upon a time. Perhaps it would be best if you imagined it as your own fancy bids, assuming it will rise to the occasion, for certainly I cannot suit you all. For instance, how about technology? I think that there would be no cars or helicopters in and above the streets; this follows from the fact that the people of Omelas are happy people. Happiness is based on a just discrimination of what is necessary, what is neither necessary nor destructive, and what is destructive. In the middle category, however—that of the unnecessary but un-destructive, that of comfort, luxury, exuberance, etc.—they could perfectly well have central heating, subway trains, washing machines, and all kinds of marvelous devices not yet invented here, floating lightsources, fuelless power, a cure for the common cold. Or they could have none of that: it doesn't matter. As you like it. I incline to think that people from towns up and down the coast have been coming in to Omelas during the last days before the Festival on very fast little trains and doubledecked trams, and that the train station of Omelas is actually the handsomest building in town, though plainer than the magnificent Farmers Market. But even granted trains, I fear that Omelas so far strikes some of you as goody-goody. Smiles, bells, parades, horses, bleh. If so, please add an orgy. If an orgy would help, don't hesitate. Let us not, however, have temples from which issue beautiful nude priests and priestesses already half in ecstasy and ready to copulate with whosoever, man or woman, lover or stranger, desires union with the deep godhead of the blood, although that was my first idea. But really it would be better not to have any temples in Omelas—at least, not manned temples. Religion yes, clergy no. Surely the beautiful nudes can just wander about, offering themselves like divine soufflés to the hunger of the needy and the rapture of the flesh. Let them join the processions. Let tambourines be struck above the copulations, and the glory of desire be proclaimed upon the gongs, and (a not unimportant point) let the offspring of these delightful rituals be beloved and looked after by all. One thing I know there is none of in Omelas is guilt. But what else should there be? I thought at first there were no drugs, but that is puritanical. For those who like it, the faint insistent sweetness of *drooz* may perfume the ways of the city, *drooz* which first brings a great lightness and brilliance to the mind and limbs, and then after some hours a dreamy languor, and wonderful visions at last of the very arcana and

236

inmost secrets of the Universe, as well as exciting the pleasure of sex beyond all belief; and it is not habit-forming. For more modest tastes I think there ought to be beer. What else, what else belongs in the joyous city? The sense of victory, surely, the celebration of courage. But as we did without clergy, let us do without soldiers. The joy built upon successful slaughter is not the right kind of joy; it will not do; it is fearful and it is trivial. A boundless and generous contentment, a magnanimous triumph felt not against some outer enemy but in communion with the finest and fairest in the souls of all men everywhere and the splendor of the world's summer: this is what swells the hearts of the people of Omelas, and the victory they celebrate is that of life. I really don't think many of them need to take *drooz*.

Most of the processions have reached the Green Fields by now. A marvelous smell of cooking goes forth from the red and blue tents of the provisioners. The faces of small children are amiably sticky; in the benign gray beard of a man a couple of crumbs of rich pastry are entangled. The youths and girls have mounted their horses and are beginning to group around the starting line of the course. An old woman, small, fat, and laughing, is passing out flowers from a basket, and tall young men wear her flowers in their shining hair. A child of nine or ten sits at the edge of the crowd, alone, playing on a wooden flute. People pause to listen, and they smile, but they do not speak to him, for he never ceases playing and never sees them, his dark eyes wholly rapt in the sweet, thin magic of the tune.

He finishes, and slowly lowers his hands holding the wooden flute.

As if that little private silence were the signal, all at once a trumpet sounds from the pavilion near the starting line: imperious, melancholy, piercing. The horses rear on their slender legs, and some of them neigh in answer. Sober-faced, the young riders stroke the horses' necks and soothe them, whispering, "Quiet, quiet, there my beauty, my hope . . ." They begin to form in rank along the starting line. The crowds along the race course are like a field of grass and flowers in the wind. The Festival of Summer has begun.

Do you believe? Do you accept the festival, the city, the joy? No? Then let me describe one more thing.

In a basement under one of the beautiful buildings of Omelas, or perhaps in the cellar of one of its spacious private homes, there is a room. It has one locked door, and no window. A little light seeps in dustily between cracks in the boards, secondhand from a cobwebbed window somewhere across the cellar. In one corner of the little room a couple of mops, with stiff, clotted, foul-smelling heads, stand near a rusty bucket. The floor is dirt, a little damp to the touch, as cellar dirt usually is. The room is about three paces long and two wide: a mere broom closet or disused toolroom. In the room a child is sitting. It might be a boy or a girl. It looks about six, but actually is nearly ten. It is feebleminded. Perhaps it was born defective, or perhaps it has become imbecile through fear, malnutrition, and neglect. It picks its nose and occasionally fumbles vaguely with its toes or genitals, as it sits hunched in the corner farthest from the bucket and the two mops. It is afraid of the mops. It finds them horrible. It shuts its eyes, but it knows the mops are still standing there; and the door is locked; and nobody will come. The door is always locked, and nobody ever comes, except that sometimes—the child has no understanding of time or interval—sometimes the door rattles terribly and opens, and a person, or several people, are there. One of them may come in and kick the child to make it stand up. The others never come close, but peer in at it with frightened, disgusted eyes. The food bowl and the water jug are hastily filled, the door is locked, the eyes disappear. The people at the door never say anything, but the child, who has not always lived in the toolroom, and can remember sunlight and its mother's voice, sometimes speaks. "I will be good," it says. "Please let me out. I will be good!" They never answer. The child used to scream for help at night, and cry a good deal, but now it only makes a kind of whining, "eh-haa, eh-haa," and it speaks less and less often. It is so thin there are no calves to its legs; its belly protrudes; it lives on a half-bowl of cornmeal and grease a day. It is naked. Its buttocks and thighs are a mass of festered sores, as it sits in its own excrement continually.

They all know it is there, all the people of Omelas. Some of them have come to see it, others are content merely to know it is there. They all know that it has to be there. Some of them understand why, and some do not, but they all understand that their happiness, the beauty of their city, the tenderness of their friendships, the health of their children, the wisdom of their scholars, the skill of their makers, even the abundance of their harvest and the kindly weathers of their skies, depend wholly on this child's abominable misery.

This is usually explained to children when they are between eight and twelve, whenever they seem capable of understanding; and most of those who come to see the child are young people, though often enough an adult comes, or comes back, to see the child. No matter how well the matter has been explained to them, these young spectators are always shocked and sickened at the sight. They feel disgust, which they had thought themselves superior to. They feel anger, outrage, impotence, despite all the explanations. They would like to do something for the child. But there is nothing they can do. If the child were brought up into the sunlight out of that vile place, if it were cleaned and fed and comforted, that would be a good thing, indeed; but if it were done, in that day and hour all the prosperity and beauty and delight of Omelas would wither and be destroyed. Those are the terms. To exchange all the goodness and grace of every life in Omelas for that single, small improvement: to throw away the happiness of thousands for the chance of the happiness of one: that would be to let guilt within the walls indeed.

The terms are strict and absolute; there may not even be a kind word spoken to the child.

Often the young people go home in tears, or in a tearless rage, when they have seen the child and faced this terrible paradox. They may brood over it for weeks or years. But as time goes on they begin to realize that even if the child could be released, it would not get much good of its freedom: a vague pleasure of warmth and food, no doubt, but little more. It is too degraded and imbecile to know any real joy. It has been afraid too long ever to be free of fear. Its habits are too uncouth for it to respond to humane treatment. Indeed after so long it would probably be wretched without walls about it to protect it, and darkness for its eyes, and its own excrement to sit in. Their tears at the bitter injustice dry when they begin to perceive the terrible justice of reality, and to accept it. Yet it is their tears and anger, the trying of their generosity and the acceptance of their helplessness, which are perhaps the true source of the splendor of their lives. Theirs is no vapid, irresponsible happiness. They know that they, like the child, are not free. They know compassion. It is the existence of the child, and their knowledge of its existence, that makes possible the nobility of their architecture, the poignancy of their music, the profundity of their science. It is because of the child that they are so gentle with children. They know that if the wretched one were not there sniveling in the dark, the other one, the flute player, could make no joyful music as the young riders line up in their beauty for the race in the sunlight of the first morning of summer.

Now do you believe in them? Are they not more credible? But there is one more thing to tell, and this is quite incredible.

At times one of the adolescent girls or boys who go to see the child does not go home to weep or rage, does not, in fact, go home at all. Sometimes also a man or woman much older falls silent for a day or two, and then leaves home. These people go out into the street, and walk down the street alone. They keep walking, and walk straight out of the city of Omelas, through the beautiful gates. They keep walking across the farmlands of Omelas. Each one goes alone, youth or girl, man or woman. Night falls; the traveler must pass down village streets, between the houses with yellow-lit windows, and on out into the darkness of the fields. Each alone, they go west or north, toward the mountains. They go on. They leave Omelas, they walk ahead into the darkness, and they do not come back. The place they go toward is a place even less imaginable to most of us than the city of happiness. I cannot describe it at all. It is possible that it does not exist. But they seem to know where they are going, the ones who walk away from Omelas.

33rd CONVENTION
MELBOURNE

George R. R. Martin

The first convention was held in New York in 1939 (and I was there, by the way). It was the brainchild of Sam Moskowitz, who gets very little credit for having originated this grand and fruitful concept, and who is for this and for many other reasons one of my favorite science fiction people. It was Sam who placed the adjective "World" on the convention, though there were few people who attended who came from a distance of more than a hundred miles from New York. (Forrest J. Ackerman came from Los Angeles, but Forrie would have come from Mars, if he'd had to.)

The first twenty-two world conventions were held in the United States (well, one of them was in Canada), and it was not till the twenty-third, in 1965, that a world convention was held overseas, in London. The twenty-eighth convention was in Heidelberg in 1970, the first one in a non-English-speaking country. And the thirty-third was in Melbourne in 1975, for the first time in the Southern Hemisphere.

We're getting there. Someday there's got to be a World Science Fiction Convention on the moon—except that will raise a problem with the familiar names usually given the conventions. Thus, conventions in Toronto are "Torcons," those in Washington are "Discons," those in New York are "Nycons" and so on. A convention on the moon should be a "Lunacon" but that is the title given the annual science fiction convention held in New York at Easter time. We'll have to call the moon convention the Selenocon.

But I'll never be at these far-out conventions. I wonder if George R. R. Martin was at the thirty-third. If I had been there I might have met him—if he had been there. As it is, I haven't met him anywhere. The only thing I know about him is that Ben Bova calls him George Railroad Martin.

Which brings up the importance of names. A memorable name is usually thought to be useful to a writer, who, after all, depends on instant recognition to help sales. George Martin is a very bland name; add the R.R. and it gains flavor. Change Ed Smith to E. E. Smith, Ph.D., and you have the best-known science fiction name of the 1930s. Or think how dull Jack Campbell would be in comparison with John W. Campbell, Jr.

Yet is that so? Jack Williamson got along. So did Jack Vance. In the last analysis it's the stories that count. You can call yourself Abdul Alhazred, if you want to, or even Fyodor Dostoevski, but if your stories consistently stink, so will your name.

And if your stories are good, your name will glow, however dull it might be intrinsically—even if it be something as ordinary and commonplace as Isaac Asimov.

A SONG FOR LYA

The cities of the Shkeen are old, older far than man's, and the great rust-red metropolis that rose from their sacred hill country had proved to be the oldest of them all. The Shkeen city had no name. It needed none. Though they built cities and towns by the hundreds and the thousands, the hill city had no rivals. It was the largest in size and population, and it was alone in the sacred hills. It was their Rome, Mecca, Jerusalem; all in one. It was *the* city, and all Shkeen came to it at last, in the final days before Union.

That city had been ancient in the days before Rome fell, had been huge and sprawling when Babylon was still a dream. But there was no feel of age to it. The human eye saw only miles and miles of low, red-brick domes; small hummocks of dried mud that covered the rolling hills like a rash. Inside they were dim and nearly airless. The rooms were small and the furniture crude.

Yet it was not a grim city. Day after day it squatted in those scrubby hills, broiling under a hot sun that sat in the sky like a weary orange melon; but the city teemed with life: smells of cooking, the sounds of laughter and talk and children running, the bustle and sweat of brickmen repairing the domes, the bells of the Joined ringing in the streets. The Shkeen were a lusty and exuberant people, almost childlike.

243

Certainly there was nothing about them that told of great age or ancient wisdom. This is a young race, said the signs, this is a culture in its infancy.

But that infancy had lasted more than fourteen thousand years.

The human city was the real infant, less than ten Earth years old. It was built on the edge of the hills, between the Shkeen metropolis and the dusty brown plains where the spaceport had gone up. In human terms, it was a beautiful city: open and airy, full of graceful archways and glistening fountains and wide boulevards lined by trees. The buildings were wrought of metal and colored plastic and native woods, and most of them were low in deference to Shkeen architecture. Most of them . . . the Administration Tower was the exception, a polished blue steel needle that split a crystal sky.

You could see it for miles in all directions. Lyanna spied it even before we landed, and we admired it from the air. The gaunt skyscrapers of Old Earth and Baldur were taller, and the fantastic webbed cities of Arachne were far more beautiful—but that slim blue Tower was still imposing enough as it rose unrivaled to its lonely dominance above the sacred hills.

The spaceport was in the shadow of the Tower, easy walking distance. But they met us anyway. A low-slung scarlet aircar sat purring at the base of the ramp as we disembarked, with a driver lounging against the stick. Dino Valcarenghi stood next to it, leaning on the door and talking to an aide.

Valcarenghi was the planetary administrator, the boy wonder of the sector. Young, of course, but I'd known that. Short, and good-looking, in a dark, intense way, with black hair that curled thickly against his head and an easy, genial smile.

He flashed us that smile then, when we stepped off the ramp, and reached to shake hands. "Hi," he began, "I'm glad to see you." There was no nonsense with formal introductions. He knew who we were, and we knew who he was, and Valcarenghi wasn't the kind of man who put much stock in ritual.

Lyanna took his hand lightly in hers, and gave him her vampire look: big, dark eyes opened wide and staring, thin mouth lifted in a tiny faint smile. She's a small girl, almost waiflike, with short brown hair and a child's figure. She can look very fragile, very helpless. When she wants to. But she rattles people with that look. If they know Lya's a telepath, they figure she's poking around amid their innermost secrets.

244

Actually she's playing with them. When Lyanna is *really* reading, her whole body goes stiff and you can almost see her tremble. And those big, soul-sucking eyes get narrow and hard and opaque.

But not many people know that, so they squirm under her vampire eyes and look the other way and hurry to release her hand. Not Valcarenghi, though. He just smiled and stared back, then moved on to me.

I *was* reading when I took his hand—my standard operating procedure. Also a bad habit, I guess, since it's put some promising friendships into an early grave. My talent isn't equal to Lya's. But it's not as demanding, either. I read emotions. Valcarenghi's geniality came through strong and genuine. With nothing behind it, or at least nothing that was close enough to the surface for me to catch.

We also shook hands with the aide, a middle-aged blond stork named Nelson Gourlay. Then Valcarenghi ushered everybody into the aircar and we took off. "I imagine you're tired," he said after we were airborne, "so we'll save the tour of the city and head straight for the Tower. Nelse will show you your quarters, then you can join us for a drink, and we'll talk over the problem. You've read the materials I sent?"

"Yes," I said. Lya nodded. "Interesting background, but I'm not sure why we're here."

"We'll get to that soon enough," Valcarenghi replied. "I ought to be letting you enjoy the scenery." He gestured toward the window, smiled, and fell silent.

So Lya and I enjoyed the scenery, or as much as we could enjoy during the five-minute flight from spaceport to tower. The aircar was whisking down the main street at treetop level, stirring up a breeze that whipped the thin branches as we went by. It was cool and dark in the interior of the car, but outside the Shkeen sun was riding toward noon, and you could see the heat waves shimmering from the pavement. The population must have been inside huddled around their air-conditioners, because we saw very little traffic.

We got out near the main entrance to the Tower and walked through a huge, sparkling-clean lobby. Valcarenghi left us then to talk to some underlings. Gourlay led us into one of the tubes and we shot up fifty floors. Then we waltzed past a secretary into another, private tube, and climbed some more.

Our rooms were lovely, carpeted in cool green, and paneled with wood. There was a complete library there, mostly

245

Earth classics bound in snythaleather, with a few novels from Baldur, our home world. Somebody had been researching our tastes. One of the walls of the bedroom was tinted glass, giving a panoramic view of the city far below us, with a control that could darken it for sleeping.

Gourlay showed it to us dutifully, like a dour bellhop. I read him briefly though, and found no resentment. He was nervous, but only slightly. There was honest affection there for someone. Us? Valcarenghi?

Lya sat down on one of the twin beds. "Is someone bringing our luggage?" she asked.

Gourlay nodded. "You'll be well taken care of," he said. "Anything you want, ask."

"Don't worry, we will," I said. I dropped to the second bed, and gestured Gourlay to a chair. "How long you been here?"

"Six years," he said, taking the chair gratefully and sprawling out all over it. "I'm one of the veterans. I've worked under four administrators now. Dino, and Stuart before him, and Gustaffson before *him*. I was even under Rockwood a few months."

Lya perked up, crossing her legs under her and leaning forward. "That was all Rockwood lasted, wasn't it?"

"Right," Gourlay said. "He didn't like the planet, took a quick demotion to assistant administrator someplace else. I didn't care much, to tell the truth. He was the nervous type, always giving orders to prove who was boss."

"And Valcarenghi?" I asked.

Gourlay made a smile look like a yawn. "Dino? Dino's OK, the best of the lot. He's good, knows he's good. He's only been here two months, but he's gotten a lot done, and he's made a lot of friends. He treats the staff like people, calls everybody by his first name, all that stuff. People like that."

I was reading, and I read sincerity. It was Valcarenghi that Gourlay was affectionate toward, then. He believed what he was saying.

I had more questions, but I didn't get to ask them. Gourlay got up suddenly. "I really shouldn't stay," he said. "You want to rest, right? Come up to the top in about two hours and we'll go over things with you. You know where the tube is?"

We nodded, and Gourlay left. I turned to Lyanna. "What do you think?"

She lay back on the bed and considered the ceiling. "I don't know," she said. "I wasn't reading. I wonder why they've had so many administrators. And why they wanted us."

"We're Talented," I said, smiling. With the capital, yes. Lyanna and I have been tested and registered as psi Talents, and we have the licenses to prove it.

"Uh-huh," she said, turning on her side and smiling back at me. Not her vampire half-smile this time. Her sexy little girl smile.

"Valcarenghi wants us to get some rest," I said. "It's probably not a bad idea."

Lya bounced out of bed. "OK," she said, "but these twins have got to go."

"We could push them together."

She smiled again. We pushed them together.

And we *did* get some sleep. Eventually.

Our luggage was outside the door when we woke. We changed into fresh clothes, old casual stuff, counting on Valcarenghi's notorious lack of pomp. The tube took us to the top of the Tower.

The office of the planetary administrator was hardly an office. There was no desk, none of the usual trappings. Just a bar and lush blue carpets that swallowed us ankle high, and six or seven scattered chairs. Plus lots of space and sunlight, with Shkea laid out at our feet beyond the tinted glass. All four walls this time.

Valcarenghi and Gourlay were waiting for us, and Valcarenghi did the bartending chores personally. I didn't recognize the beverage, but it was cool and spicy and aromatic, with a real sting to it. I sipped it gratefully. For some reason I felt I needed a lift.

"Shkeen wine," Valcarenghi said, smiling, in answer to an unasked question. "They've got a name for it, but I can't pronounce it yet. But give me time. I've only been here two months, and the language is rough."

"You're learning Shkeen?" Lya asked, surprised. I knew why. Shkeen is rough on human tongues, but the natives learned Terran with stunning ease. Most people accepted that happily, and just forgot about the difficulties of cracking the alien language.

"It gives me an insight into the way they think," Valcarenghi said. "At least that's the theory." He smiled.

I read him again, although it was more difficult. Physical contact makes things sharper. Again, I got a simple emotion,

247

close to the surface—pride this time. With pleasure mixed in. I chalked that up to the wine. Nothing beneath.

"However you pronounce the drink, I like it," I said.

"The Shkeen produce a wide variety of liquors and food-stuffs," Gourlay put in. "We've cleared many for export already, and we're checking others. Market should be good."

"You'll have a chance to sample more of the local produce this evening," Valcarenghi said. "I've set up a tour of the city, with a stop or two in Shkeentown. For a settlement of our size, our night life is fairly interesting. I'll be your guide."

"Sounds good," I said. Lya was smiling too. A tour was unusually considerate. Most Normals feel uneasy around Talents, so they rush us in to do whatever they want done, then rush us out again as quickly as possible. They certainly don't socialize with us.

"Now—the problem," Valcarenghi said, lowering his drink and leaning forward in the chair. "You read about the Cult of the Union?"

"A Shkeen religion," Lya said.

"*The* Shkeen religion," corrected Valcarenghi. "Every one of them is a believer. This is a planet without heretics."

"We read the materials you sent on it," Lya said. "Along with everything else."

"What do you think?"

I shrugged. "Grim. Primitive. But no more than any number of others I've read about. The Shkeen aren't very advanced, after all. There were religions on Old Earth that included human sacrifice."

Valcarenghi shook his head, and looked toward Gourlay.

"No, you don't understand," Gourlay started, putting his drink down on the carpet. "I've been studying their religion for six years. It's like no other in history. Nothing on Old Earth like it, no sir. Nor in any other race we've encountered.

"And Union, well, it's wrong to compare it to human sacrifice, just wrong. The Old Earth religions sacrificed one or two unwilling victims to appease their gods. Killed a handful to get mercy for the millions. And the handful generally protested. The Shkeen don't work it that way. The Greeshka takes *everyone*. And they go willingly. Like lemmings they march off to the caves to be eaten alive by those parasites. Every Shkeen is Joined at forty, and goes to Final Union before he's fifty."

I was confused. "All right," I said. "I see the distinction, I guess. But so what? Is this the problem? I imagine that Union

248

is rough on the Shkeen, but that's their business. Their religion is no worse than the ritual cannibalism of the Hrangans, is it?"

Valcarenghi finished his drink and got up, heading for the bar. As he poured himself a refill, he said, almost casually, "As far as I know, Hrangan cannibalism has claimed no human converts."

Lya looked startled. I felt startled. I sat up and stared. "What?"

Valcarenghi headed back to his seat, glass in hand. "Human converts have been joining the Cult of the Union. Dozens of them are already Joined. None of them have achieved full Union yet, but that's only a question of time." He sat down, and looked at Gourlay. So did we.

The gangling blond aide picked up the narrative. "The first convert was about seven years ago. Nearly a year before I got here, two and a half after Shkea was discovered and the settlement built. Guy named Magly. Psi-psych, worked closely with the Shkeen. He was it for two years. Then another in '08, more than next year. And the rate's been climbing ever since. There was one big one. Phil Gustaffson."

Lya blinked. "The planetary administrator?"

"The same," said Gourlay. "We've had a lot of administrators. Gustaffson came in after Rockwood couldn't stand it. He was a big, gruff old guy. Everybody loved him. He'd lost his wife and kids on his last assignment, but you'd never have known it. He was always hearty, full of fun. Well, he got interested in the Shkeen religion, started talking to them. Talked to Magly and some of the other converts too. Even went to see a Greeshka. That shook him up real bad for a while. But finally he got over it, went back to his researches. I worked with him, but I never guessed what he had in mind. A little over a year ago, he converted. He's Joined now. Nobody's ever been accepted that fast. I hear talk in Shkeentown that he may even be admitted to Final Union, rushed right in. Well, Phil was administrator here longer than anybody else. People liked him, and when he went over, a lot of his friends followed. The rate's way up now."

"Not quite one percent, and rising," Valcarenghi said. "That seems low, but remember what it means. One percent of the people in my settlement are choosing a religion that includes a very unpleasant form of suicide."

Lya looked from him to Gourlay and back again. "Why hasn't this been reported?"

"It should have been," Valcarenghi said. "But Stuart succeeded Gustaffson, and he was scared stiff of a scandal. There's no law against humans adopting an alien religion, so Stuart defined it as a nonproblem. He reported the conversion rate routinely, and nobody higher up ever bothered to make the correlation and remember just what all these people were converting *to*."

I finished my drink, set it down. "Go on," I said to Valcarenghi.

"I define the situation as a problem," he said. "I don't care how few people are involved, the idea that human beings would allow the Greeshka to consume them alarms me. I've had a team of psychs on it since I took over, but they're getting nowhere. I needed Talent. I want you two to find out *why* these people are converting. Then I'll be able to deal with the situation."

The problem was strange, but the assignment seemed straightforward enough. I read Valcarenghi to be sure. His emotions were a bit more complex this time, but not much. Confidence above all: he was sure we could handle the problem. There was honest concern there, but no fear, and not even a hint of deception. Again, I couldn't catch anything below the surface. Valcarenghi kept his hidden turmoil well hidden, if he had any.

I glanced at Lyanna. She was sitting awkwardly in her chair, and her fingers were wrapped very tightly around her wine glass. Reading. Then she loosened up and looked my way and nodded.

"All right," I said. "I think we can do it."

Valcarenghi smiled. "That I never doubted," he said. "It was only a question of whether you *would*. But enough of business for tonight. I've promised you a night on the town, and I always try to deliver on my promises. I'll meet you downstairs in the lobby in a half-hour."

Lya and I changed into something more formal back in our room. I picked a dark blue tunic, with white slacks and a matching mesh scarf. Not the height of fashion, but I was hoping that Shkea would be several months behind the times. Lya slipped into a silky white skintight with a tracery of thin blue lines that flowed over her in sensuous patterns in response to her body heat. The lines were definitely lecherous, accentuating her thin figure with a singleminded determination. A blue raincape completed the outfit.

"Valcarenghi's funny," she said as she fastened it.

"Oh?" I was struggling with the sealseam on my tunic, which refused to seal. "You catch something when you read him?"

"No," she said. She finished attaching the cape and admired herself in the mirror. Then she spun toward me, the cape swirling behind her. "That's it. He was thinking what he was saying. Oh, variations in the wording, of course, but nothing important. His mind was on what we were discussing, and behind that there was only a wall." She smiled. "Didn't get a single one of his deep dark secrets."

I finally conquered the sealseam. "Tsk," I said. "Well, you get another chance tonight."

That got me a grimace. "The hell I do. I don't read people on off-time. It isn't fair. Besides, it's such a strain. I wish I could catch thoughts as easily as you do feelings."

"The price of Talent," I said. "You're more Talented, your price is higher." I rummaged in our luggage for a raincape, but I didn't find anything that went well, so I decided not to wear one. Capes were out, anyway. "I didn't get much on Valcarenghi either. You could have told as much by watching his face. He must be a very disciplined mind. But I'll forgive him. He serves good wine."

Lya nodded. "Right! That stuff did me good. Got rid of the headache I woke up with."

"The altitude," I suggested. We headed for the door.

The lobby was deserted, but Valcarenghi didn't keep us waiting long. This time he drove his own aircar, a battered black job that had evidently been with him for a while. Gourlay wasn't the sociable type, but Valcarenghi had a woman with him, a stunning auburn-haired vision named Laurie Blackburn. She was even younger than Valcarenghi—mid-twenties, by the look of her.

It was sunset when we took off. The whole far horizon was a gorgeous tapestry in red and orange, and a cool breeze was blowing in from the plains. Valcarenghi left the coolers off and opened the car windows, and we watched the city darken into twilight as we drove.

Dinner was at a plush restaurant with Baldurian decor—to make us feel comfortable, I guessed. The food, however, was very cosmopolitan. The spices, the herbs, the *style* of cooking were all Baldur. The meats and vegetables were native. It made for an interesting combination. Valcarenghi ordered for all four of us, and we wound up sampling about a dozen different dishes. My favorite was a tiny Shkeen bird that they cooked in sourtang sauce. There wasn't very much of it, but what there was tasted great. We also polished off three bottles of wine during the meal: more of the Shkeen stuff we'd sampled that afternoon, a flask of chilled Veltaar from Baldur, and some real Old Earth Burgundy.

The tale warmed up quickly; Valcarenghi was a born story-teller and an equally good listener. Eventually, of course, the conversation got around to Shkea and the Shkeen. Laurie led it there. She'd been on Shkea for about six months, working toward an advanced degree in extee anthropology. She was trying to discover why the Shkeen civilization had remained frozen for so many millennia.

"They're older than we are, you know," she told us. "They had cities before men were using tools. It should have been spacetraveling Shkeen that stumbled on primitive men, not the other way around."

"Aren't there theories on that already?" I asked.

"Yes, but none of them is universally accepted," she said. "Cullen cites a lack of heavy metals, for example. A factor, but is it the *whole* answer? Von Hamrin claims the Shkeen didn't get enough competition. No big carnivores on the planet, so there was nothing to breed aggressiveness into the race. But he's come under a lot of fire. Shkea isn't all *that* idyllic; if it were, the Shkeen never would have reached their present levels. Besides, what's the Greeshka if not a carnivore? It *eats* them, doesn't it?"

"What do you think?" Lya asked.

"I think it had something to do with the religion, but I haven't worked it all out yet. Dino's helping me talk to people and the Shkeen are open enough, but research isn't easy." She stopped suddenly and looked at Lya hard. "For me, anyway. I imagine it'd be easier for you."

We'd heard that before. Normals often figure that Talents have unfair advantages, which is perfectly understandable. We do. But Laurie wasn't resentful. She delivered her statement in a wistful, speculative tone, instead of etching it in verbal acid.

Valcarenghi leaned over and put an arm around her. "Hey," he said. "Enough shop talk. Robb and Lya shouldn't be worrying about the Shkeen until tomorrow."

Laurie looked at him, and smiled tentatively. "OK," she said lightly. "I get carried away. Sorry."

"That's OK," I told her. "It's an interesting subject. Give us a day and we'll probably be getting enthusiastic too."

Lya nodded agreement, and added that Laurie would be the first to know if our work turned up anything that would support her theory. I was hardly listening. I know it's not polite to read Normals when you're out with them socially, but there are times I can't resist. Valcarenghi had his arm around Laurie and had pulled her toward him gently. I was curious.

So I took a quick, guilty reading. He was very high—slightly drunk, I guess, and feeling very confident and protective. The master of the situation. But Laurie was a jumble—uncertainty, repressed anger, a vague fading hint of fright. And love, confused but very strong. I doubted that it was for me or Lya. She loved Valcarenghi.

I reached under the table, searching for Lya's hand, and found her knee. I squeezed it gently and she looked at me and smiled. She wasn't reading, which was good. It bothered me that Laurie loved Valcarenghi, though I didn't know why, and I was just as glad that Lya didn't see my discontent.

We finished off the last of the wine in short order, and Valcarenghi took care of the whole bill. Then he rose. "Onward!" he announced. "The night is fresh, and we've got visits to make."

So we made visits. No holoshows or anything that drab, although the city had its share of theaters. A casino was next on the list. Gambling was legal on Shkea, of course, and Valcarenghi would have legalized it if it weren't. He supplied the chips and I lost some for him, as did Laurie. Lya was barred from playing; her Talent was too strong. Valcarenghi won big; he was a superb mindspin player, and pretty good at the traditional games too.

Then came a bar. More drinks, plus local entertainment which was better than I would have expected.

It was pitch black when we got out, and I assumed that the expedition was nearing its end. Valcarenghi surprised us. When we got back to the car, he reached under the controls, pulled out a box of sober-ups, and passed them around.

"Hey," I said. "You're driving. Why do I need this? I just barely got up here."

"I'm about to take you to a genuine Shkeen cultural event, Robb," he said. "I don't want you making rude comments or throwing up on the natives. Take your pill."

I took my pill, and the buzz in my head began to fade. Valcarenghi already had the car airborne. I leaned back and put my arm around Lya, and she rested her head on my shoulder. "Where are we going?" I asked.

"Shkeentown," he replied, never looking back, "to their Great Hall. There's a Gathering tonight, and I figured you'd be interested."

"It will be in Shkeen, of course," Laurie said, "but Dino can translate for you. I know a little of the language too, and I'll fill in whatever he misses."

Lya looked excited. We'd read about Gatherings, of course, but we hardly expected to go see one on our first day of Shkea. The Gatherings were a species of religious rite; a mass confessional of sorts for pilgrims who were about to be admitted to the ranks of the Joined. Pilgrims swelled the hill city daily, but Gatherings were conducted only three or four times a year when the numbers of those-about-to-be-Joined climbed high enough.

The aircar streaked almost soundlessly through the brightly lit settlement, passing huge fountains that danced with a dozen colors and pretty ornamental arches that flowed like liquid fire. A few other cars were airborne, and here and there we flew above pedestrians strolling the city's broad malls. But most people were inside, and light and music flooded from many of the homes we passed.

Then, abruptly, the character of the city began to change. The level ground began to roll and heave, hills rose before us and then behind us, and the lights vanished. Below, the malls gave way to unlit roads of crushed stone and dust, and the domes of glass and metal done in fashionable mock-Shkeen yielded to their older brick brothers. The Shkeen city was quieter than its human counterpart; most of the houses were darkly silent.

Then, ahead of us, a hummock appeared that was larger than the others—almost a hill in itself, with a big arched door and a series of slitlike windows. And light leaked from this one, and noise, and there were Shkeen outside.

I suddenly realized that, although I'd been on Shkea for nearly a day, this was the first sight I'd caught of the Shkeen. Not that I could see them all that clearly from an aircar at night. But I did see them. They were smaller than men—the tallest was around five feet—with big eyes and long arms. That was all I could tell from above.

Valcarenghi put the car down alongside the Great Hall, and we piled out. Shkeen were trickling through the arch from several directions, but most of them were already inside.

We joined the trickle, and nobody even looked twice at us, except for one character who hailed Valcarenghi in a thin, squeaky voice and called him Dino. He had friends even here.

The interior was one huge room, with a great crude platform built in the center and an immense crowd of Shkeen circling it. The only light was from torches that were stuck in grooves along the walls, and on high poles surrounding the platform. Someone was speaking, and every one of those great, bulging eyes was turned his way. We four were the only humans in the Hall.

The speaker, outlined brightly by the torches, was a fat, middle-aged Shkeen who moved his arms slowly, almost hypnotically, as he talked. His speech was a series of whistles, wheezes, and grunts, so I didn't listen very closely. He was much too far away to read. I was reduced to studying his appearance, and that of other Shkeen near me. All of them were hairless, as far as I could see, with softish-looking orange skin that was creased by a thousand tiny wrinkles. They wore simple shifts of crude, multicolored cloth, and I had difficulty telling male from female.

Valcarenghi leaned over toward me and whispered, careful to keep his voice low. "The speaker is a farmer," he said. "He's telling the crowd how far he's come, and some of the hardships of his life."

I looked around. Valcarenghi's whisper was the only sound in the place. Everyone else was dead quiet, eyes riveted on the platform, scarcely breathing. "He's saying that he has four brothers," Valcarenghi told me. "Two have gone on to Final Union, one is among the Joined. The other is younger than himself, and now owns the farm." He frowned. "The speaker will never see his farm again," he said, more loudly, "but he's happy about it."

"Bad crops?" asked Lya, smiling irreverently. She'd been listening to the same whisper. I gave her a stern look.

The Shkeen went on. Valcarenghi stumbled after him. "Now he's telling his crimes, all the things he's done that he's ashamed of, his blackest soul-secrets. He's had a sharp tongue at times, he's vain, once he actually struck his younger brother. Now he speaks of his wife, and the other women he has known. He has betrayed her many times, copulating with others. As a boy, he mated with animals for he feared females. In recent years he has grown incapable, and his brother has serviced his wife."

On and on and on it went, in incredible detail, detail that was both startling and frightening. No intimacy went untold, no secret was left undisturbed. I stood and listened to Valcarenghi's whispers, shocked at first, finally growing bored with the squalor of it all. I began to get restless. I wondered briefly if I knew any human half so well as I now knew this great fat Shkeen. Then I wondered whether Lyanna, with her Talent, knew anyone half so well. It was almost as if the speaker wanted all of us to live through his life right here and now.

His speech lasted for what seemed hours, but finally it began to wind up. "He speaks now of Union," Valcarenghi whispered. "He will be Joined, he is joyful about it, he has craved it for so long. His misery is at an end, his aloneness will cease, soon he shall walk the streets of the sacred city and peal his joy with the bells. And then Final Union, in the years to come. He will be with his brothers in the afterlife."

"No, Dino." This whisper was Laurie. "Quit wrapping human phrases around what he says. He will be his brothers, he says. The phrase also implies they will be him."

Valcarenghi smiled. "OK, Laurie. If you say so . . ."

Suddenly the fat farmer was gone from the platform. The crowd rustled, and another figure took his place: much shorter, wrinkled excessively, one eye a great gaping hole. He began to speak, haltingly at first, then with greater skill.

"This one is a brickman, he has worked many domes, he lives in the sacred city. His eye was lost many years ago, when he fell from a dome and a sharp stick poked into him. The pain was very great, but he returned to work within a year, he did not beg for premature Union, he was very brave, he is proud of his courage. He has a wife, but they never had offspring, he is sad of that, he cannot talk to his wife easily, they are apart even when together and she weeps at night, he is sad of that too, but he has never hurt her and . . ."

It went on for hours again. My restlessness stirred again, but I cracked down on it—this was too important. I let myself get lost in Valcarenghi's narration, and the story of the one-eyed Shkeen. Before long, I was riveted as closely to the tale as the aliens around me. It was hot and stuffy and all but airless in the dome, and my tunic was getting sooty and soaked by sweat, some of it from the creatures who pressed around me. But I hardly noticed.

The second speaker ended as had the first, with a long praise of the joy of being Joined and the coming of Final

Union. Toward the end, I hardly even needed Valcarenghi's translation—I could hear the happiness in the voice of the Shkeen, and see it in his trembling figure. Or maybe I was reading, unconsciously. But I can't read at that distance—unless the target is emoting very hard.

A third speaker ascended the platform, and spoke in a voice louder than the others. Valcarenghi kept pace. "A woman this time," he said. "She has carried eight children for her man, she has four sisters and three brothers, she has farmed all her life, she . . ."

Suddenly her speech seemed to peak, and she ended a long sequence with several sharp, high whistles. Then she fell silent. The crowd, as one, began to respond with whistles of their own. An eerie, echoing music filled the Great Hall, and the Shkeen around us all began to sway and whistle. The woman looked out at the scene from a bent and broken position.

Valcarenghi started to translate, but he stumbled over something. Laurie cut in before he could backtrack. "She has now told them of great tragedy," she whispered. "They whistle to show their grief, their oneness with her pain."

"Sympathy, yes," said Valcarenghi, taking over again. "When she was young, her brother grew ill, and seemed to be dying. Her parents told her to take him to the sacred hills, for they could not leave the younger children. But she shattered a wheel on her cart through careless driving, and her brother died upon the plains. He perished without Union. She blames herself."

The Shkeen had begun again. Laurie began to translate, leaning close to us and using a soft whisper. "Her brother died, she is saying again. She faulted him, denied him Union, now he is sundered and alone and gone without . . . without . . ."

"Afterlife," said Valcarenghi. "Without afterlife."

"I'm not sure that's entirely right," Laurie said. "That concept is . . ."

Valcarenghi waved her silent. "Listen," he said. He continued to translate.

We listened to her story, told in Valcarenghi's increasingly hoarse whisper. She spoke longest of all, and her story was the grimmest of the three. When she finished, she too was replaced. But Valcarenghi put a hand on my shoulder and beckoned toward the exit.

The cool night air hit like ice water, and I suddenly realized that I was drenched with sweat. Valcarenghi walked quickly toward the car. Behind us, the speaking was still in progress, and the Shkeen showed no signs of tiring.

"Gatherings go on for days, sometimes weeks," Laurie told us as we climbed inside the aircar. "The Shkeen listen in shifts, more or less—they try terribly to hear every word, but exhaustion gets to them sooner or later and they retire for brief rests, then return for more. It is a great honor to last through an entire Gathering without sleep."

Valcarenghi shot us aloft. "I'm going to try that someday," he said. "I've never attended for more than a couple of hours, but I think I could make it if I fortified myself with drugs. We'll get more understanding between human and Shkeen if we participate more fully in their rituals."

"Oh," I said. "Maybe Gustaffson felt the same way."

Valcarenghi laughed lightly. "Yes, well, I don't intend to participate *that* fully."

The trip home was a tired silence. I'd lost track of time but my body insisted that it was almost dawn. Lya, curled up under my arm, looked drained and empty and only half-awake. I felt the same way.

We left the aircar in front of the Tower, and took the tubes up. I was past thinking. Sleep came very, very quickly.

I dreamed that night. A good dream, I think, but it faded with the coming of the light, leaving me empty and feeling cheated. I lay there, after waking, with my arm around Lya and my eyes on the ceiling, trying to recall what the dream had been about. But nothing came.

Instead, I found myself thinking about the Gathering, running it through again in my head. Finally I disentangled myself and climbed out of bed. We'd darkened the glass, so the room was still pitch black. But I found the controls easily enough, and let through a trickle of late morning light.

Lya mumbled some sort of sleepy protest and rolled over, but made no effort to get up. I left her alone in the bedroom and went out to our library, looking for a book on the Shkeen—something with a little more detail than the material we'd been sent. No luck. The library was meant for recreation, not research.

I found a viewscreen and punched up to Valcarenghi's office. Gourlay answered. "Hello," he said. "Dino figured you'd be calling. He's not here right now. He's out arbitrating a trade contract. What do you need?"

"Books," I said, my voice still a little sleepy. "Something on the Shkeen."

"That I can't do," Gourlay said. "Are none, really. Lots of papers and studies and monographs, but no full-fledged books. I'm going to write one, but I haven't gotten to it yet. Dino figured I could be your resource, I guess."

"Oh."

"Got any questions?"

I searched for a question, found none. "Not really," I said, shrugging. "I just wanted general background, maybe some more information on Gatherings."

"I can talk to you about that later," Gourlay said. "Dino figured you'd want to get to work today. We can bring people to the Tower, if you'd like, or you can get out to them."

"We'll go out," I said quickly. Bringing subjects in for interviews fouls up everything. They get all anxious, and that covers up any emotions I might want to read, and they *think* on different things, too, so Lyanna has trouble.

"Fine," said Gourlay. "Dino put an aircar at your disposal. Pick it up down in the lobby. Also, they'll have some keys for you, so you can come straight up here to the office without bothering with the secretaries and all."

"Thanks," I said. "Talk to you later." I flicked off the viewscreen and walked back to the bedroom.

Lya was sitting up, the covers around her waist. I sat down next to her and kissed her. She smiled, but didn't respond. "Hey," I said. "What's wrong?"

"Headache," she replied. "I thought sober-ups were supposed to get rid of hangovers."

"That's the theory. Mine worked pretty well." I went to the closet and began looking for something to wear. "We should have headache pills around here someplace. I'm sure Dino wouldn't forget anything that obvious."

"Umpf. Yes. Throw me some clothes."

I grabbed one of her coveralls and tossed it across the room. Lya stood up and slipped into it while I dressed, then went off to the washroom.

"Better," she said. "You're right, he didn't forget medicines."

"He's the thorough sort."

She smiled. "I guess. Laurie knows the language better, though. I read her. Dino made a couple of mistakes in that translation last night."

I'd guessed at something like that. No discredit to Valcarenghi; he was working on a four-month handicap, from what they'd said. I nodded. "Read anything else?"

"No. I tried to get those speakers, but the distance was too much." She came up and took my hand. "Where are we going today?"

"Shkeentown," I said. "Let's try to find some of these Joined. I didn't notice any at the Gathering."

"No. Those things are for Shkeen about-to-be-Joined."

"So I hear. Let's go."

We went. We stopped at the fourth level for a late breakfast in the Tower cafeteria, then got our aircar pointed out to us by a man in the lobby. A sporty green four-seater, very common, very inconspicuous.

I didn't take the aircar all the way into the Shkeen city, figuring we'd get more of the feel of the place if we went through on foot. So I dropped down just beyond the first range of hills, and we walked.

The human city had seemed almost empty, but Shkeentown lived. The crushed-rock streets were full of aliens, hustling back and forth busily, carrying loads of bricks and baskets of fruit and clothing. There were children everywhere, most of them naked: fat balls of orange energy that ran around us in circles, whistling and grunting and grinning, tugging at us every once in a while. The kids looked different from the adults. They had a few patches of reddish hair, for one thing, and their skins were still smooth and unwrinkled. They were the only ones who really paid any attention to us. The adult Shkeen just went about their business, and gave us an occasional friendly smile. Humans were obviously not all that uncommon in the streets of Shkeentown.

Most of the traffic was on foot, but small wooden carts were also common. The Shkeen draft animal looked like a big green dog that was about to be sick. They were strapped to the carts in pairs, and they whined constantly as they pulled. So, naturally, men called them whiners. In addition to whining, they also defecated constantly. That, with odors from the food peddled in baskets and the Shkeen themselves, gave the city a definite pungency.

There was noise too, a constant clamor. Kids whistling, Shkeen talking loudly with grunts and whimpers and squeaks, whiners whining and their carts rattling over the rocks. Lya and I walked through it all silently, hand in hand, watching and listening and smelling and . . . reading.

I was wide open when I entered Shkeentown, letting everything wash over me as I walked, unfocused but receptive. I was the center of a small bubble of emotion—feelings rushed up at me as Shkeen approached, faded as they walked away, circled around and around with the dancing children. I swam in a sea of impressions. And it startled me.

It startled me because it was all so familiar. I'd read aliens before. Sometimes it was difficult, sometimes it was easy, but it was never pleasant. The Hrangans have sour minds, rank with hate and bitterness, and I feel unclean when I come out. The Fyndii feel emotions so palely that I can scarcely read them at all. The Damoosh are . . . *different*. I read them strongly, but I can't find names for the feelings I read.

But the Shkeen—it was like walking down a street on Baldur. No wait—more like one of the Lost Colonies, when a human settlement has fallen back into barbarism and forgotten its origins. Human emotions rage there, primal and strong and real, but less sophisticated than on Old Earth or Baldur. The Shkeen were like that: primitive, maybe, but very understandable. I read joy and sorrow, envy, anger, whimsy, bitterness, yearning, pain. The same heady mixture that engulfs me everywhere, when I open myself to it.

Lya was reading, too. I felt her hand tense in mine. After a while, it softened again. I turned to her, and she saw the question in my eyes.

"They're people," she said. "They're like us."

I nodded. "Parallel evolution, maybe. Shkea might be an older Earth, with a few minor differences. But you're right. They're more human than any other race we've encountered in space." I considered that. "Does that answer Dino's question? If they're like us, it follows that their religion would be more appealing than a *really* alien one."

"No, Robb," Lya said. "I don't think so. Just the reverse. If they're like us, it doesn't make sense that *they'd* go off so willingly to die. See?"

She was right, of course. There was nothing suicidal in the emotions I'd read, nothing unstable, nothing really abnormal. Yet every one of the Shkeen went off to Final Union in the end.

"We should focus on somebody," I said. "This blend of thought isn't getting us anywhere." I looked around to find a subject, but just then I heard the bells begin.

They were off to the left somewhere, nearly lost in the city's gentle roar. I tugged Lya by the hand, and we ran down the street to find them, turning left at the first gap in the orderly row of domes.

The bells were still ahead, and we kept running, cutting through what must have been somebody's yard, and climbing over a low bush fence that bristled with sweethorns. Beyond that was another yard, a dung pit, more domes, and finally a street. It was there we found the bell-ringers.

There were four of them, all Joined, wearing long gowns of bright red fabric that trailed in the dust, with great bronze bells in either hand. They rang the bells constantly, their long arms swinging back and forth, the sharp, clanging notes filling the street. All four were elderly, as Shkeen go—hairless and pinched up with a million tiny wrinkles. But they smiled very widely, and the younger Shkeen that passed smiled at them.

On their heads rode the Greeshka.

I'd expected to find the sight hideous. I didn't. It was faintly disquieting, but only because I knew what it meant. The parasites were bright blobs of crimson goo, ranging in size from a pulsing wart on the back of one Shkeen skull to a great sheet of dripping, moving red that covered the head and shoulders of the smallest like a living cowl. The Greeshka lived by sharing the nutrients in the Shkeen bloodstream, I knew.

And also by slowly—oh so slowly—consuming its host.

Lya and I stopped a few yards from them, and watched them ring. Her face was solemn, and I think mine was. All of the others were smiling, and the songs that the bells sang were songs of joy. I squeezed Lyanna's hand tightly. "Read," I whispered.

We read.

Me: I read bells. Not the sound of bells, no, no, but the *feel* of bells, the *emotion* of bells, the bright clanging joy, the hooting-shouting-ringing loudness, the song of the Joined, the togetherness and the sharing of it all. I read what the Joined felt as they pealed their bells, their happiness and anticipation, their ecstasy in telling others of their clamorous contentment. And I read love, coming from them in great hot waves, passionate possessive love of a man and woman together, not the weak watery affection of the human who "loves" his brothers. This was real and fervent and it burned almost as it washed over me and surrounded me. They loved themselves, and they loved all Shkeen, and they loved the Greeshka, and they loved each other, and they loved us. They

262

loved us. They loved *me*, as hotly and wildly as Lya loved me. And with love I read belonging, and sharing. They four were all apart, all distinct, but they thought as one almost, and they belonged to the Greeshka, and they were all *together* and linked although each was still himself and none could read the others as I read them.

And Lyanna? I reeled back from them, and shut myself off, and looked at Lya. She was white-faced, but smiling. "They're beautiful," she said, her voice very small and soft and wondering. Drenched in love, I still remembered how much I loved *her*, and how I was part of her and her of me.

"What—what did you read?" I asked, my voice fighting the continued clangor of the bells.

She shook her head, as if to clear it. "They love us," she said. "You must know that, but oh, I felt it, they *do* love us. And it's so *deep*. Below that love there's more love, and below that more, and on and on forever. Their minds are so deep, so open. I don't think I've ever read a human that deeply. Everything is right at the surface, right there, their whole lives and all their dreams and feelings and memories and oh—I just took it in, swept it up with a reading, a glance. With men, with humans, it's so much work. I have to dig, I have to fight, and even then I don't get down very far. You know, Robb, you know. Oh, *Robb!*" And she came to me and pressed tight against me, and I held her in my arms. The torrent of feeling that had washed over me must have been a tidal wave for her. Her Talent was broader and deeper than mine, and now she was shaken. I read her as she clutched me, and I read love, great love, and wonder and happiness, but also fear, nervous fear swirling through it all.

Around us, the ringing suddenly stopped. The bells, one by one, ceased to swing, and the four Joined stood in silence for a brief second. One of the other Shkeen nearby came up to them with a huge, cloth-covered basket. The smallest of the Joined threw back the cloth, and the aroma of hot meatrolls rose in the street. Each of the Joined took several from the basket, and before long they were all crunching away happily, and the owner of the rolls was grinning at them. Another Shkeen, a small nude girl, ran up and offered them a flask of water, and they passed it around without comment.

"What's going on?" I asked Lya. Then, even before she told me, I remembered. Something from the literature that Valcarenghi had sent. The Joined did no work. Forty Earthyears they lived and toiled, but from First Joining to Final

263

Union there was only joy and music, and they wandered the streets and rang their bells and talked and sang, and other Shkeen gave food and drink. It was an honor to feed a Joined, and the Shkeen who had given up his meatrolls was radiating pride and pleasure.

"Lya," I whispered, "can you read them now?"

She nodded against my chest and pulled away and stared at the Joined, her eyes going hard and then softening again. She looked back at me. "It's different," she said, curious.

"How?"

She squinted in puzzlement. "I don't know. I mean, they still love us, and all. But now their thoughts are, well, sort of more human. There are levels, you know, and digging isn't easy, and there are hidden things, things they hide even from themselves. It's not all open like it was. They're thinking about the food now and how good it tastes. It's all very vivid. I could taste the rolls myself. But it's not the same."

I had an inspiration. "How many minds are there?"

"Four," she said. "Linked somehow, I think. But not really." She stopped, confused, and shook her head. "I mean, they sort of feel each other's emotions, like you do, I guess. But not thoughts, not the detail. I can read them, but they don't read each other. Each one is distinct. They were closer before, when they were ringing, but they were always individuals."

I was slightly disappointed. "Four minds then, not one?"

"Umpf, yes. Four."

"And the Greeshka?" My other bright idea. If the Greeshka had minds of their own . . .

"Nothing," Lya said. "Like reading a plant, or a piece of clothing. Not even yes-I-live."

That was disturbing. Even lower animals had some vague consciousness of life—the feeling Talents called yes-I-live—usually only a dim spark that it took a major Talent to see. But Lya *was* a major Talent.

"Let's talk to them," I said. She nodded, and we walked up to where the Joined were munching their meatrolls. "Hello," I said awkwardly, wondering how to address them. "Can you speak Terran?"

Three of them looked at me without comprehension. But the fourth one, the little one whose Greeshka was a rippling red cape, bobbed his head up and down. "Yesh," he said, in a piping-thin voice.

I suddenly forgot what I was going to ask, but Lyanna

came to my rescue. "Do you know of human Joined?" she said.

He grinned. "All Joined are one," he said.

"Oh," I said. "Well, yes, but do you know any who look like us? Tall, you know, with hair and skin that's pink or brown or something?" I came to another awkward halt, wondering just how *much* Terran the old Shkeen knew, and eyeing his Greeshka a little apprehensively.

His head bobbled from side to side. "Joined are all different, but all are one, all are shame. Shome look ash you. Would you Join?"

"No, thanks," I said. "Where can I find a human Joined?"

He bobbled his head some more. "Joined shing and ring and walk the shacred city."

Lya had been reading. "He doesn't know," she told me. "The Joined just wander and play their bells. There's no pattern to it, nobody keeps track. It's all random. Some travel in groups, some alone, and new groups form every time two bunches meet."

"We'll have to search," I said.

"Eat," the Shkeen told us. He reached into the basket on the ground and his hands came out with two steaming meatrolls. He pressed one into my hand, one in Lya's.

I looked at it dubiously. "Thank you," I told him. I pulled at Lya with my free hand and we walked off together. The Joined grinned at us as we left, and started ringing once more before we were halfway down the street.

The meatroll was still in my hand, its crust burning my fingers. "Should I eat this?" I asked Lya.

She took a bite out of hers. "Why not? We had them last night in the restaurant, right? And I'm sure Valcarenghi would've warned us if the native food was poisonous."

That made sense, so I lifted the roll to my mouth and took a bite as I walked. It was hot, and also *hot*, and it wasn't a bit like the meatrolls we'd sampled the previous night. Those had been golden, flaky things, seasoned gently with orange-spice from Baldur. The Shkeen version was crunchy, and the meat inside dripped grease and burned my mouth. But it was good, and I was hungry, and the roll didn't last long.

"Get anything else when you read the small guy?" I asked Lya around a mouthful of hot roll.

She swallowed, and nodded. "Yes, I did. He was happy, even more than the rest. He's older. He's near Final Union, and he's very thrilled about it." She spoke with her old easy

265

manner; the after effects of reading the Joined seemed to have faded.

"Why?" I was musing out loud. "He's going to *die*. Why is he so happy about it?"

Lya shrugged. "He wasn't thinking in any great analytical detail, I'm afraid."

I licked my fingers to get rid of the last of the grease. We were at a crossroads, with Shkeen bustling by us in all directions, and now we could hear more bells on the wind. "More Joined," I said. "Want to look them up?"

"What would we find out? That we don't already know? We need a *human* Joined."

"Maybe one of this batch *will* be human."

I got Lya's withering look. "Ha. What are the odds?"

"All right," I conceded. It was now late afternoon. "Maybe we'd better head back. Get an earlier start tomorrow. Besides, Dino is probably expecting us for dinner."

Dinner, this time, was served in Valcarenghi's office, after a little additional furniture had been dragged in. His quarters, it turned out, were on the level below, but he preferred to entertain upstairs where his guests could enjoy the spectacular Tower view.

There were five of us, all told: me and Lya, Valcarenghi and Laurie, plus Gourlay. Laurie did the cooking, supervised by master chef Valcarenghi. We had beefsteaks, bred on Shkea from Old Earth stock, plus a fascinating blend of vegetables that included mushrooms from Old Earth, groundpips from Baldur, and Shkeen sweethorns. Dino liked to experiment and the dish was one of his inventions.

Lya and I gave a full report on the day's adventures, interrupted only by Valcarenghi's sharp, perceptive questioning. After dinner, we got rid of tables and dishes and sat around drinking Veltaar and talking. This time Lya and I asked the questions, with Gourlay supplying the biggest chunk of the answers. Valcarenghi listened from a cushion on the floor, one arm around Laurie, the other holding his wine glass. We were not the first Talents to visit Shkea, he told us. Nor the first to claim the Shkeen were manlike.

"Suppose that means something," he said. "But I don't know. They're *not* men, you know. No, sir. They're much more social, for one thing. Great little city builders from way back, always in towns, always surrounding themselves with others. And they're more communal than man, too. Cooperate in all sorts of things, and they're big on sharing. Trade, for instance—they see that as mutual sharing."

Valcarenghi laughed. "You can say that again. I just spent the whole day trying to work out a trade contract with a group of farmers who hadn't dealt with us before. It's not easy, believe me. They give us as much of their stuff as we ask for, if they don't need it themselves and no one else has asked for it earlier. But then they want to get whatever *they* ask for in the future. They expect it, in fact. So every time we deal we've got a choice; hand them a blank check, or go through an incredible round of talks that ends with them convinced that we're totally selfish."

Lya wasn't satisfied. "What about sex?" she demanded. "From the stuff you were translating last night, I got the impression they're monogamous."

"They're confused about sex relationships," Gourlay said. "It's very strange. Sex is sharing, you see, and it's good to share with everyone. But the sharing has to be real and meaningful. That creates problems."

Laurie sat up, attentive. "I've studied the point," she said quickly. "Shkeen morality insists they love *everybody*. But they can't do it, they're too human, too possessive. They wind up in monogamous relationships, because a really deep sex-sharing with one person is better than a million shallow physical things, in their culture. The ideal Shkeen would sex-share with everyone, with each of the unions being just as deep, but they can't achieve that ideal."

I frowned. "Wasn't somebody guilty last night over betraying his wife?"

Laurie nodded eagerly. "Yes, but the guilt was because his other relationships caused his sharing with his wife to diminish. *That* was the betrayal. If he'd been able to manage it without hurting his older relationship, the sex would have been meaningless. And, if all of the relationships have been real love-sharing, it would have been a plus. His wife would have been proud of him. It's quite an achievement for a Shkeen to be in a multiple union that works."

"And one of the greatest Shkeen crimes is to leave another alone," Gourlay said. "Emotionally alone. Without sharing."

I mulled over that, while Gourlay went on. The Shkeen had little crime, he told us. Especially no violent crime. No murders, no beatings, no prisons, no wars in their long, empty history.

"They're a race without murderers," Valcarenghi said.

267

"Which may explain something. On Old Earth, the same cultures that had the highest suicide rates often had the lowest murder rates, too. And the Shkeen suicide rate is one hundred percent."

"They kill animals," I said.

"Not part of the Union," Gourlay replied. "The Union embraces all that thinks, and its creatures may not be killed. They do not kill Shkeen, or humans, or Greeshka."

Lya looked at me, then at Gourlay. "The Greeshka don't think," she said. "I tried to read them this morning and got nothing but the minds of the Shkeen they rode. Not even a yes-I-live."

"We've known that, but the point's always puzzled me," Valcarenghi said, climbing to his feet. He went to the bar for more wine, brought out a bottle, and filled our glasses. "A truly mindless parasite, but an intelligent race like the Shkeen are enslaved by it. Why?"

The new wine was good and chilled, a cold trail down my throat. I drank it, and nodded, remembering the flood of euphoria that had swept over us earlier that day. "Drugs," I said, speculatively. "The Greeshka must produce an organic pleasure drug. The Shkeen submit to it willingly and die happy. The joy is real, believe me. We felt it."

Lyanna looked doubtful, though, and Gourlay shook his head adamantly. "No, Robb. Not so. We've experimented on the Greeshka, and . . ."

He must have noticed my raised eyebrows. He stopped.

"How did the Shkeen feel about that?" I asked.

"Didn't tell them. They wouldn't have liked it, not at all. Greeshka's just an animal, but it's their God. Don't fool around with God, you know. We refrained for a long time, but when Gustaffson went over, old Stuart had to know. His orders. We didn't get anywhere, though. No extracts that might be a drug, no secretions, nothing. In fact, the Shkeen are the *only* native life that submits so easily. We caught a whiner, you see, and strapped it down, and let a Greeshka link up. Then, couple hours later, we yanked the straps. Damn whiner was furious, screeching and yelping, attacking the thing on its head. Nearly clawed its own skull to ribbons before it got it off."

"Maybe only the Shkeen are susceptible?" I said. A feeble rescue attempt.

"Not quite," said Valcarenghi, with a small, thin smile. "There's us."

Lya was strangely silent in the tube, almost withdrawn. I assumed she was thinking about the conversation. But the door to our suite had barely slid shut behind us when she turned toward me and wrapped her arms around me.

I reached up and stroked her soft brown hair, slightly startled by the hug. "Hey," I muttered, "what's wrong?"

She gave me her vampire look, big-eyed and fragile. "Make love to me, Robb," she said with a soft sudden urgency. "Please. Make love to me now."

I smiled, but it was a puzzled smile, not my usual lecherous bedroom grin. Lya generally comes on impish and wicked when she's horny, but now she was all troubled and vulnerable. I didn't quite get it.

But it wasn't a time for questions, and I didn't ask any. I just pulled her to me wordlessly and kissed her hard, and we walked together to the bedroom.

And we made love, *really* made love, more than poor Normals can do. We joined our bodies as one, and I felt Lya stiffen as her mind reached out to mine. And as we moved together I was opening myself to her, drowning myself in the flood of love and need and fear that was pouring from her.

Then, quickly as it had begun, it ended. Her pleasure washed over me in a raw red wave. And I joined her on the crest, and Lya clutched me tightly, her eyes shrunk up small as she drank it all in.

Afterwards, we lay there in the darkness and let the stars of Shkea pour their radiance through the window. Lya huddled against me, her head on my chest, while I stroked her.

"That was good," I said in a drowsy-dreamy voice, smiling in the star-filled darkness.

"Yes," she replied. Her voice was soft and small, so small I barely heard it. "I love you, Robb," she whispered.

"Uh-huh," I said. "And I love you."

She pulled loose of my arm and rolled over, propping her head on a hand to stare at me and smile. "You do," she said. "I read it. I know it. And you know how much I love you, too, don't you?"

I nodded, smiling. "Sure."

"We're lucky, you know. The Normals have only words. Poor little Normals. How can they *tell*, with just words? How can they *know*? They're always apart from each other, trying to reach each other and failing. Even when they make love,

269

even when they come, they're always apart. They must be very lonely."

There was something . . . disturbing . . . in that. I looked at Lya, into her bright happy eyes, and thought about it. "Maybe," I said, finally. "But it's not that bad for them. They don't know any other way. And they try, they love too. They bridge the gap sometimes."

"Only a look and a voice, then darkness again and a silence," Lya quoted, her voice sad and tender. "We're luckier, aren't we? We have so much more."

"We're luckier," I echoed. And I reached out to read her too. Her mind was a haze of satisfaction, with a gentle scent of wistful, lonely longing. But there was something else, way down, almost gone now, but still faintly detectable.

I sat up slowly. "Hey," I said. "You're worried about something. And before, when we came in, you were scared. What's the matter?"

"I don't know, really," she said. She sounded puzzled and she *was* puzzled; I read it there. "I *was* scared, but I don't know why. The Joined, I think. I kept thinking about how much they loved me. They didn't even *know* me, but they loved me so much, and they understood—it was almost like what we have. It—I don't know. It bothered me. I mean, I didn't think I could ever be loved that way, except by you. And they were so *close,* so together. I felt kind of lonely, just holding hands and talking. I wanted to be close to *you* that way. After the way they were all sharing and everything, being alone just seemed empty. And frightening. You know?"

"I know," I said, touching her lightly again, with hand and mind. "I understand. We do understand each other. We're together almost as they are, as Normals can't ever be."

Lya nodded, and smiled, and hugged me. We went to sleep in each other's arms.

Dreams again. But again, at dawn, the memory stole away from me. It was all very annoying. The dream had been pleasant, comfortable. I wanted it back, and I couldn't even remember what it was. Our bedroom, washed by harsh daylight, seemed drab compared to the splendors of my lost vision.

Lya woke after me, with another headache. This time she had the pills on hand, by the bedstand. She grimaced and took one.

"It must be the Shkeen wine," I told her. "Something about it takes a dim view of your metabolism."

She pulled on a fresh coverall and scowled at me. "Ha. We were drinking Veltaar last night, remember? My father gave me my first glass of Veltaar when I was nine. It never gave me headaches before."

"A first!" I said, smiling.

"It's not funny," she said. "It hurts."

I quit kidding, and tried to read her. She was right. It *did* hurt. Her whole forehead throbbed with pain. I withdrew quickly before I caught it too.

"All right," I said. "I'm sorry. The pills will take care of it, though. Meanwhile, we've got work to do."

Lya nodded. She'd never let anything interfere with work yet.

The second day was a day of manhunt. We got off to a much earlier start, had a quick breakfast with Gourlay, then picked up our aircar outside the Tower. This time we didn't drop down when we hit Shkeentown. We wanted a human Joined, which meant we had to cover a lot of ground. The city was the biggest I'd ever seen, in area at any rate, and the thousand-odd human cultists were lost among millions of Shkeen. And, of those humans, only about half were actually Joined yet.

So we kept the aircar low, and buzzed up and down the dome-dotted hills like a floating rollercoaster, causing quite a stir in the streets below us. The Shkeen had seen aircars before, of course, but it still had some novelty value, particularly to the kids, who tried to run after us whenever we flashed by. We also panicked a whiner, causing him to upset the cart full of fruit he was dragging. I felt guilty about that, so I kept the car higher afterwards.

We spotted Joined all over the city, singing, eating, walking—and ringing those bells, those eternal bronze bells. But for the first three hours, all we found were Shkeen Joined. Lya and I took turns driving and watching. After the excitement of the previous day, the search was tedious and tiring.

Finally, however, we found something: a large group of Joined, ten of them, clustered around a bread cart behind one of the steeper hills. Two were taller than the rest.

We landed on the other side of the hill and walked around to meet them, leaving our aircar surrounded by a crowd of Shkeen children. The Joined were still eating when we arrived. Eight of them were Shkeen of various sizes and hues,

Greeshka pulsing atop their skulls. The other two were human.

They wore the same long red gowns as the Shkeen, and they carried the same bells. One of them was a big man, with loose skin that hung in flaps, as if he'd lost a lot of weight recently. His hair was white and curly, his face marked by a broad smile and laugh wrinkles around his eyes. The other was a thin, dark weasel of a man with a big hooked nose.

Both of them had Greeshka sucking at their skulls. The parasite riding the weasel was barely a pimple, but the older man had a lordly specimen that dripped down beyond his shoulders and into the back of the gown.

Somehow, this time, it *did* look hideous.

Lyanna and I walked up to them, trying hard to smile, not reading—at least at first. They smiled at us as we approached. Then they waved.

"Hello," the weasel said cheerily when we got there. "I've never seen you. Are you new on Shkea?"

That took me slightly by surprise. I'd been expecting some sort of garbled mystic greeting, or maybe no greeting at all. I was assuming that somehow the human converts would have abandoned their humanity to become mock-Shkeen. I was wrong.

"More or less," I replied. And I read the weasel. He was genuinely pleased to see us, and just bubbled with contentment and good cheer. "We've been hired to talk to people like you." I'd decided to be honest about it.

The weasel stretched his grin farther than I thought it would go. "I am Joined, and happy," he said. "I'll be glad to talk to you. My name is Lester Kamenz. What do you want to know, brother?"

Lya, next to me, was going tense. I decided I'd let her read in depth while I asked questions. "When did you convert to the Cult?"

"Cult?" Kamenz said.

"The Union."

He nodded, and I was struck by the grotesque similarity of his bobbing head and that of the elderly Shkeen we'd seen yesterday. "I have always been in the Union. You are in the Union. All that thinks is in the Union."

"Some of us weren't told," I said. "How about you? When did you realize you were in the Union?"

"A year ago, Old Earth time. I was admitted to the ranks of the Joined only a few weeks ago. The First Joining is a

272

joyful time. I am joyful. Now I will walk the streets and ring my bells until the Final Union."

"What did you do before?"

"Before?" A short vague look. "I ran machines once. I ran computers, in the Tower. But my life was empty, brother. I did not know I was in the Union, and I was alone. I had only machines, cold machines. Now I am Joined. Now I am"—again he searched—"not alone."

I reached into him, and found the happiness still there, with love. But now there was an ache too, a vague recollection of past pain, the stink of unwelcome memories. Did these fade? Maybe the gift the Greeshka gave its victims was oblivion, sweet mindless rest and end of struggle. Maybe.

I decided to try something. "That thing on your head," I said, sharply. "It's a parasite. It's drinking your blood right now, feeding on it. As it grows, it will take more and more of the things *you* need to live. Finally it will start to eat your tissue. Understand? It will *eat* you. I don't know how painful it will be, but however it feels, at the end you'll be *dead*. Unless you come back to the Tower now, and have the surgeons remove it. Or maybe you could remove it yourself. Why don't you try? Just reach up and pull it off. Go ahead."

I'd expected—what? Rage? Horror? Disgust? I got none of these. Kamenz just stuffed bread in his mouth and smiled at me, and all I read was his love and joy and a little pity.

"The Greeshka does not kill," he said finally. "The Greeshka gives joy and happy Union. Only those who have no Greeshka die. They are . . . alone. Oh, forever alone." Something in his mind trembled with sudden fear, but it faded quickly.

I glanced at Lya. She was stiff and hard-eyed, still reading. I looked back and began to phrase another question. But suddenly the Joined began to ring. One of the Shkeen started it off, swinging his bell up and down to produce a single sharp clang. Then his other hand swung, then the first again, then the second, then another Joined began to ring, then still another, and then they were all swinging and clanging and the noise of their bells was smashing against my ears as the joy and the love and the feel of the bells assaulted my mind once again.

I lingered to savor it. The love there was breathtaking, awesome, almost frightening in its heat and intensity, and there was so much sharing to frolic in and wonder at, such a soothing-calming-exhilarating tapestry of good feelings. Something happened to the Joined when they rang, something touched them and lifted them and gave them a glow, something strange and glorious that mere Normals could not hear in their harsh clanging music. I was no Normal, though. I could hear it.

I withdrew reluctantly, slowly. Kamenz and the other human were both ringing vigorously now, with broad smiles and glowing twinkling eyes that transfigured their faces. Lyanna was still tense, still reading. Her mouth was slightly open, and she trembled where she stood.

I put an arm around her and waited, listening to the music, patient. Lya continued to read. Finally, after minutes, I shook her gently. She turned and studied me with hard, distant eyes. Then blinked. And her eyes widened and she came back, shaking her head and frowning.

Puzzled, I looked into her head. Strange and stranger. It was a swirling fog of emotion, a dense moving blend of more feelings than I'd care to put a name to. No sooner had I entered than I was lost, lost and uneasy. Somewhere in the fog there was a bottomless abyss lurking to engulf me. At least it felt that way.

"Lya," I said. "What's wrong?"

She shook her head again, and looked at the Joined with a look that was equal parts fear and longing. I repeated my question.

"I—I don't know," she said. "Robb, let's not talk now. Let's go. I want time to think."

"OK," I said. What was going on here? I took her hand and we walked slowly around the hill to the slope where we'd left the car. Shkeen kids were climbing all over it. I chased them, laughing. Lya just stood there, her eyes gone all faraway on me. I wanted to read her again, but somehow I felt it would be an invasion of privacy.

Airborne, we streaked back toward the Tower, riding higher and faster this time. I drove, while Lya sat beside me and stared out into the distance.

"Did you get anything useful?" I asked her, trying to get her mind back on the assignment.

"Yes. No. Maybe." Her voice sounded distracted, as if only part of her was talking to me. "I read their lives, both of them. Kamenz was a computer programmer, as he said. But he wasn't very good. An ugly little man with an ugly little personality, no friends, no sex, no nothing. Lived by himself, avoided the Shkeen, didn't like them at all. Didn't even like people, really. But Gustaffson got through to him, somehow. He ignored Kamenz' coldness, his bitter little cuts, his cruel jokes. He didn't retaliate, you know? After a while, Kamenz came to like Gustaffson, to admire him. They were never really friends in any normal sense, but still Gustaffson was the nearest thing to a friend that Kamenz had."

She stopped suddenly. "So he went over with Gustaffson?" I prompted, glancing at her quickly. Her eyes still wandered.

"No, not at first. He was still afraid, still scared of the Shkeen and terrified of the Greeshka. But later, with Gustaffson gone, he began to realize how empty his life was. He worked all day with people who despised him and machines that didn't care, then sat alone at night reading and watching holoshows. Not life, really. He hardly touched the people around him. Finally he went to find Gustaffson, and wound up converted. Now . . ."

"Now . . . ?"

She hesitated. "He's happy, Robb," she said. "He really is. For the first time in his life, he's happy. He'd never known love before. Now it fills him."

"You got a lot," I said.

"Yes." Still the distracted voice, the lost eyes. "He was open, sort of. There were levels, but digging wasn't as hard as it usually is—as if his barriers were weakening, coming down almost . . ."

"How about the other guy?"

She stroked the instrument panel, staring only at her hand. "Him? That was Gustaffson . . ."

And that, suddenly, seemed to wake her, to restore her to the Lya I knew and loved. She shook her head and looked at me, and the aimless voice became an animated torrent of words. "Robb, listen, that was *Gustaffson*, he's been Joined over a year now, and he's going on to Final Union within a week. The Greeshka has accepted him, and he wants it, you know? He really does, and—and—oh Robb, he's *dying!*"

"Within a week, according to what you just said."

"No. I mean yes, but that's not what I mean. Final Union isn't death, to him. He believes it, all of it, the whole religion. The Greeshka is his god, and he's going to join it. But before, and now, he was dying. He's got the Slow Plague, Robb. A terminal case. It's been eating at him from inside for fifteen years now. He got it back on Nightmare, in the swamps, when his family died. That's no world for people, but he was there, the administrator over a research base, a short-term thing. They lived on Thor; it was only a visit, but the ship crashed. Gustaffson got all wild and tried to reach them before the end, but he grabbed a faulty pair of skinthins, and the spores got through. And they were all dead when he got there. He had an awful lot of pain, Robb. From the Slow Plague, but more from the loss. He really loved them, and it was never the same after. They gave him Shkea as a reward, kind of, to take his mind off the crash, but he still thought of it all the time. I could see the picture, Robb. It was vivid. He couldn't forget it. The kids were inside the ship, safe behind the walls, but the life system failed and choked them to death. But his wife—oh, Robb—she took some skinthins and tried to go for help, and outside those *things*, those big wrigglers they have on Nightmare—?"

I swallowed hard, feeling a little sick. "The eater-worms," I said, dully. I'd read about them, and seen holos. I could imagine the picture that Lya'd seen in Gustaffson's memory, and it wasn't at all pretty. I was glad I didn't have her Talent.

"They were still—still—when Gustaffson got there. You know. He killed them all with a screech gun."

I shook my head. "I didn't think things like that really went on."

"No," Lya said. "Neither did Gustaffson. They'd been so—so *happy* before that, before the thing on Nightmare. He loved her, and they were really close, and his career had been almost charmed. He didn't have to go to Nightmare, you know. He took it because it was a challenge, because nobody else could handle it. That gnaws at him, too. And he remembers all the time. He—they—" Her voice faltered. "They thought they were *lucky*," she said, before falling into silence.

There was nothing to say to that. I just kept quiet and drove, thinking, feeling a blurred, watered-down version of what Gustaffson's pain must have been like. After a while, Lya began to speak again.

"It was all there, Robb," she said, her voice softer and slower and more thoughtful once again. "But he was at peace. He still remembered it all, and the way it had hurt, but it didn't bother him as it had. Only now he was sorry they weren't with him. He was sorry that they died without Final Union. Almost like the Shkeen woman, remember? The one at the Gathering? With her brother?"

"I remember," I said.

"Like that. And his mind was open, too. More than Kamenz, much more. When he rang, the levels all vanished, and everything was right at the surface, all the love and pain and everything. His whole life, Robb. I shared his whole life with him, in an instant. And all his thoughts, too . . . he's seen the caves of Union . . . he went down once, before he converted. I . . ."

More silence, settling over us and darkening the car. We were close to the end of Shkeentown. The Tower slashed the sky ahead of us, shining in the sun. And the lower domes and archways of the glittering human city were coming into view.

"Robb," Lya said. "Land here. I have to think a while, you know? Go back without me. I want to walk among the Shkeen a little."

I glanced at her, frowning. "Walk? It's a long way back to the Tower, Lya."

"I'll be all right. Please. Just let me think a bit."

I read her. The thought fog had returned, denser than ever, laced through with the colors of fear. "Are you sure?" I said. "You're scared, Lyanna. Why? What's wrong? The eaterworms are a long way off."

She just looked at me, troubled. "Please, Robb," she repeated.

I didn't know what else to do, so I landed.

And I, too, thought, as I guided the aircar home. Of what Lyanna had said, and read—of Kamenz and Gustaffson. I kept my mind on the problem we'd been assigned to crack. I tried to keep it off Lya, and whatever was bothering her. That would solve itself, I thought.

Back at the Tower, I wasted no time. I went straight up to Valcarenghi's office. He was there, alone, dictating into a machine. He shut it off when I entered.

"Hi, Robb," he began. "Where's Lya?"

"Out walking. She wanted to think. I've been thinking, too. And I believe I've got your answer."

He raised his eyebrows, waiting.

I sat down. "We found Gustaffson this afternoon, and Lya read him. I think it's clear why he went over. He was a broken man, inside, however much he smiled. The Greeshka gave him an end to his pain. And there was another convert with him, a Lester Kamenz. He'd been miserable, too, a pathetic lonely man with nothing to live for. Why *shouldn't* he convert? Check out the other converts, and I bet you'll find a pattern. The most lost and vulnerable, the failures, the isolated—those will be the ones that turned to Union."

Valcarenghi nodded. "OK, I'll buy that," he said. "But our psychs guessed that long ago, Robb. Only it's no answer, not really. Sure, the converts on the whole have been a messed-up crew, I won't dispute that. But why turn to the Cult of the Union? The psychs can't answer that. Take Gustaffson now. He was a strong man, believe me. I never knew him personally, but I knew his career. He took some rough assignments, generally for the hell of it, and beat them. He could have had the cushy jobs, but he wasn't interested. I've heard about the incident on Nightmare. It's famous, in a warped sort of way. But Phil Gustaffson wasn't the sort of man to be beaten, even by something like that. He snapped out of it very quickly, from what Nelse tells me. He came to Shkea and really set the place in order, cleaning up the mess that Rockwood had left. He pushed through the first real trade contract we ever got, *and* he made the Shkeen understand what it meant, which isn't easy.

"So here he is, this competent, talented man, who's made a career of beating tough jobs and handling men. He's gone through a personal nightmare, but it hasn't destroyed him. He's as tough as ever. And suddenly he turns to the Cult of the Union, signs up for a grotesque suicide. Why? For an end to his pain, you say? An interesting theory, but there are other ways to end pain. Gustaffson had years between Nightmare and the Greeshka. He never ran away from pain then. He didn't turn to drink, or drugs, or any of the usual outs. He didn't head back to Old Earth to have a psi-psych clean up his memories—and believe me, he could've gotten it paid for, if he'd wanted it. The colonial office would have done anything for him, after Nightmare. He went on, swallowed his pain, rebuilt. Until suddenly he converts.

"His pain made him more vulnerable, yes, no doubt of it. But something else brought him over—something that Union offered, something he couldn't get from wine or memory wipe. The same's true of Kamenz, and the others. They had other outs, other ways to vote no on life. They passed them up. But they chose Union. You see what I'm getting at?"

I did, of course. My answer was no answer at all, and I realized it. But Valcarenghi was wrong too, in parts.

"Yes," I said. "I guess we've still got some reading to do." I smiled wanly. "One thing, though. Gustaffson hadn't really beaten his pain, not ever. Lya was very clear on that. It was inside him all the time, tormenting him. He just never let it come out."

278

"That's victory, isn't it?" Valcarenghi said. "If you bury your hurts so deep that no one can tell you have them?"

"I don't know. I don't think so. But . . . anyway, there was more. Gustaffson has the Slow Plague. He's dying. He's been dying for years."

Valcarenghi's expression flickered briefly. "That I didn't know, but it just bolsters my point. I've read that some eighty percent of Slow Plague victims opt for euthanasia, if they happen to be on a planet where it's legal. Gustaffson was a planetary administrator. He could have *made* it legal. If he passed up suicide for all those years, why choose it now?"

I didn't have an answer for that. Lyanna hadn't given me one, if she had one. I didn't know where we could find one either, unless . . .

"The caves," I said suddenly. "The caves of Union. We've got to witness a Final Union. There must be something about it, something that accounts for the conversions. Give us a chance to find out what it is."

Valcarenghi smiled. "All right," he said. "I can arrange it. I expected it would come to that. It's not pleasant, though, I'll warn you. I've gone down myself, so I know what I'm talking about."

"That's OK," I told him. "If you think reading Gustaffson was any fun, you should have seen Lya when she was through. She's out now trying to walk it off." That, I'd decided, must have been what was bothering her. "Final Union won't be any worse than those memories of Nightmare, I'm sure."

"Fine, then. I'll set it up for tomorrow. I'm going with you, of course. I don't want to take any chances on anything happening to you."

I nodded. Valcarenghi rose. "Good enough," he said. "Meanwhile, let's think about more interesting things. You have any plans for dinner?"

We wound up eating at a mock-Shkeen restaurant run by humans, in the company of Gourlay and Laurie Blackburn. The talk was mostly social noises—sports, politics, art, old jokes, that sort of thing. I don't think there was a mention of the Shkeen or the Greeshka all evening.

Afterwards, when I got back to our suite, I found Lyanna waiting for me. She was in bed, reading one of the handsome volumes from our library, a book of Old Earth poetry. She looked up when I entered.

"Hi," I said. "How was your walk?"

"Long." A smile creased her pale, small face, then faded. "But I had time to think. About this afternoon, and yesterday, and about the Joined. And us."

"Us?"

"Robb, do you love me?" The question was delivered almost matter-of-factly, in a voice full of question. As if she didn't know. As if she really didn't know.

I sat down on the bed and took her hand and tried to smile. "Sure," I said. "You know that, Lya."

"I did. I do. You love me, Robb, really you do. As much as a human can love. But . . ." She stopped. She shook her head and closed her book and sighed. "But we're still apart, Robb. We're still apart."

"What *are* you talking about?"

"This afternoon. I was so confused afterwards, and scared. I wasn't sure why, but I've thought about it. When I was reading, Robb—I was in there, with the Joined, sharing them and their love. I really was. And I didn't want to come out. I didn't want to leave them, Robb. When I did, I felt so isolated, so cut off."

"That's your fault," I said. "I tried to talk to you. You were too busy thinking."

"Talking? What good is talking? It's communication, I guess, but it is *really*? I used to think so, before they trained my Talent. After that, reading seemed to be the real communication, the real way to reach somebody else, somebody like you. But now I don't know. The Joined—when they ring—they're so *together*, Robb. All linked. Like us when we make love, almost. And they love each other, too. And they love us, so intensely. I felt—I don't know. But Gustaffson loves me as much as you do. No. He loves me more."

Her face was white as she said that, her eyes wide, lost, lonely. And me, I felt a sudden chill, like a cold wind blowing through my soul. I didn't say anything. I only looked at her, and wet my lips. And bled.

She saw the hurt in my eyes, I guess. Or read it. Her hand pulled at mine, caressed it. "Oh, Robb. Please. I don't mean to hurt you. It's not you. It's all of us. What do *we* have, compared to *them*?"

"I don't know what you're talking about, Lya." Half of me suddenly wanted to cry. The other half wanted to shout. I stifled both halves, and kept my voice steady. But inside I wasn't steady, I wasn't steady at all.

"Do you love me, Robb?" Again. Wondering.

"Yes!" Fiercely. A challenge.

"What does that mean?" she said.

"You know what it means," I said. "Dammit, Lya, *think!* Remember all we've had, all we've shared together. *That's* love, Lya. It is. We're the lucky ones, remember? You said that yourself. The Normals have only a touch and a voice, then back to their darkness. They can barely find each other. They're alone. Always. Groping. Trying, over and over, to climb out of their isolation booths, and failing, over and over. But not us, we found the way, we know each other as much as any human beings ever can. There's nothing I wouldn't tell you, or share with you. I've said that before, and you know it's true, you can read it in me. *That's love,* dammit. *Isn't it?"*

"I don't know," she said, in a voice so sadly baffled. Soundlessly, without even a sob, she began to cry. And while the tears ran in lonely paths down her cheeks, she talked. "Maybe that's love. I always thought it was. But now I don't know. If what we have is love, what was it I felt this afternoon, what was it I touched and shared in? Oh, Robb, I love you too. You know that. I try to share with you. I want to share what I read, what it was like. But I can't. We're cut off. I can't make you understand. I'm here and you're there and we can touch and make love and talk, but we're still apart. You see? You see? I'm alone. And this afternoon, I *wasn't."*

"You're not alone, dammit," I said suddenly. "I'm here." I clutched her hand tightly. "Feel? Hear? You're not alone!"

She shook her head, and the tears flowed on. "You don't understand, see? And there's no way I can make you. You said we know each other as much as any human beings ever can. You're right. But how much can human beings know each other? Aren't all of them cut off, really? Each alone in a big, dark, empty universe? We only trick ourselves when we think that someone else is there. In the end, in the cold lonely end, it's only us, by ourselves, in the blackness. Are you there, Robb? How do I know? Will you die with me, Robb? Will we be together then? Are we together *now?* You say we're luckier than the Normals. I've said it too. They have only a touch and voice, right? How many times have I quoted that? But what do *we* have? A touch and two voices, maybe. It's not enough anymore. I'm scared. Suddenly I'm scared."

She began to sob. Instinctively I reached out to her, wrapped her in my arms, stroked her. We lay back together, and she wept against my chest. I read her, briefly, and I read her pain, her sudden loneliness, her hunger, all aswirl in a darkening mindstorm of fear. And, though I touched her and caressed her and whispered—over and over—that it would be all right, that I was here, that she wasn't alone, I knew that it would not be enough. Suddenly there was a gulf between us, a great dark yawning thing that grew and grew, and I didn't know how to bridge it. And Lya, my Lya, was crying, and she needed me. And I needed her, but I couldn't get to her.

Then I realized that I was crying too.

We held each other, in silent tears, for what must have been an hour. But finally the tears ran out. Lya clutched her body to me so tightly I could hardly breathe, and I held her just as tightly.

"Robb," she whispered. "You said—you said we really know each other. All those times you've said it. And you say, sometimes, that I'm *right* for you, that I'm perfect."

I nodded, wanting to believe. "Yes. You are."

"No," she said, choking out the word, forcing it into the air, fighting herself to say it. "It's not *so*. I read you, yes. I can hear the words rattling around in your head as you fit a sentence together before saying it. And I listen to you scold yourself when you've done something stupid. And I see memories, some memories, and live through them with you. But it's all on the surface, Robb, all on the top. Below it, there's more, more of *you*. Drifting half-thoughts I don't quite catch. Feelings I can't put a name to. Passions you suppress, and memories even you don't know you have. Sometimes I can get to that level. Sometimes. If I really fight, if I drain myself to exhaustion. But when I get there, I know—I *know*—that there's another level below *that*. And more and more, on and on, down and down. I can't reach them, Robb, though they're part of you. I don't know you. I can't know you. You don't even know yourself, see? And me, do you know me? No. Even less. You know what I tell you, and I tell you the truth, but maybe not all. And you read my feelings, my surface feelings—the pain of a stubbed toe, a quick flash of annoyance, the pleasure I get when you're in me. Does that mean you know me? What of *my* levels, and levels? What about the things I don't even know myself? Do *you* know them? How, Robb, how?"

She shook her head again, with that funny little gesture she had whenever she was confused. "And you say I'm perfect, and that you love me. I'm so right for you. But *am* I? Robb,

282

I read your thoughts. I know when you want me to be sexy, so I'm sexy. I see what turns you on, so I do it. I know when you want me to be serious, and when you want me to joke. I know what kind of jokes to tell, too. Never the cutting kind, you don't like that, to hurt or see people hurt. You laugh *with* people not *at* them, and I laugh with you, and love you for your tastes. I know when you want me to talk, and when to keep quiet. I know when you want me to be your proud tigress, your tawny telepath, and when you want a little girl to shelter in your arms. And I *am* those things, Robb, because you want me to be, because I love you, because I can feel joy in your mind at every *right* thing that I do. I never set out to do it that way, but it happened. I didn't mind, I don't mind. Most of the time it wasn't even conscious. You do the same thing, too. I read it in you. You can't read as I do, so sometimes you guess wrong—you come on witty when I want silent understanding, or you act the strong man when I need a boy to mother. But you get it right sometimes, too. And you *try*, you always try.

"But it it really *you?* Is it really *me?* What if I wasn't perfect, you see, if I was just myself, with all my faults and the things you don't like out in the open? Would you love me *then?* I don't know. But Gustaffson would, and Kamenz. I know that, Robb. I saw it. I know *them.* Their levels . . . vanished. I *KNOW* them, and if I went back I could share with them, more than with you. And they know me, the real me, all of me, I think. And they love me. You see? *You see?"*

Did I see? I don't know. I was confused. Would I love Lya if she was "herself"? But what was "herself"? How was it different from the Lya I knew? I thought I loved Lya and would always love Lya—but what if the real Lya wasn't like my Lya? *What* did I love? The strange abstract concept of a human being, or the flesh and voice and personality that I thought of as Lya? I didn't know. I didn't know who Lya was, or who I was, or what the hell it all meant. And I was scared. Maybe I couldn't feel what she had felt that afternoon. But I knew what she was feeling then. I was alone, and I needed someone.

"Lya," I called. "Lya, let's try. We don't have to give up. We can reach each other. There's a way, our way. We've done it before. Come, Lya, come with me, come to me."

As I spoke, I undressed her, and she responded and her hands joined mine. When we were nude, I began to stroke her, slowly, and she me. Our minds reached out to each

283

other. Reached and probed as never before. I could feel her, inside my head, digging. Deeper and deeper. Down. And I opened myself to her, I surrendered, all the petty little secrets I had kept even from her, or tried to, now I yielded up to her everything I could remember, my triumphs and shames, the good moments and the pain, the times I'd hurt someone, the times I'd been hurt, the long crying sessions by myself, the fears I wouldn't admit, the prejudices I fought, the vanities I battled when the time struck, the silly boyish sins. All. Everything. I buried nothing. I hid nothing. I gave myself to her, to Lya, to *my* Lya. She had to know me.

And so, too, she yielded. Her mind was a forest through which I roamed, hunting down wisps of emotion, the fear and the need and the love at the top, the fainter things beneath, the half-formed whims and passions still deeper into the woods. I don't have Lya's Talent, I read only feelings, never thoughts. But I read thoughts then, for the first and only time, thoughts she threw at me because I'd never seen them before. I couldn't reach much, but some I got.

And as her mind opened to mine, so did her body. I entered her, and we moved together, bodies one, minds entwined, as close as human beings can join. I felt pleasure washing over me in great glorious waves, my pleasure, her pleasure, both together building on each other, and I rode the crest for an eternity as it approached a far distant shore. And finally as it smashed into that beach, we came together, and for a second—for a tiny, fleeting second—I could not tell which orgasm was mine, and which was hers.

But then it passed. We lay, bodies locked together, on the bed. In the starlight. But it was not a bed. It was the beach, the flat black beach, and there were no stars above. A thought touched me, a vagrant thought that was not mine. Lya's thought. We were on a plain, she was thinking, and I saw that she was right. The waters that had carried us here were gone, receded. There was only a vast flat blackness stretching away in all directions, with dim ominous shapes moving on either horizon. *We are here as on a darkling plain,* Lya thought. And suddenly I knew what those shapes were, and what poem she had been reading.

We slept.

I woke, alone.

The room was dark. Lya lay on the other side of the bed,

curled up, still asleep. It was late, near dawn I thought. But I wasn't sure. I was restless.

I got up and dressed in silence. I needed to walk somewhere, to think, to work things out. Where, though?

There was a key in my pocket. I touched it when I pulled on my tunic, and remembered. Valcarenghi's office. It would be locked and deserted at this time of night. And the view might help me think.

I left, found the tubes, and shot up, up, up to the apex of the Tower, the top of man's steel challenge to the Shkeen. The office was unlit, the furniture dark shapes in the shadows. There was only the starlight. Shkea is closer to the galactic center than Old Earth, or Baldur. The stars are a fiery canopy across the night sky. Some of them are very close, and they burn like red and blue-white fires in the awesome blackness above. In Valcarenghi's office, all the walls are glass. I went to one, and looked out. I wasn't thinking. Just feeling. And I felt cold and lost and little.

Then there was a soft voice behind me saying hello. I barely heard it.

I turned away from the window, but other stars leaped at me from the far walls. Laurie Blackburn sat in one of the low chairs, concealed by the darkness.

"Hello," I said. "I didn't mean to intrude. I thought no one would be here."

She smiled. A radiant smile in a radiant face, but there was no humor in it. Her hair fell in sweeping auburn waves past her shoulders, and she was dressed in something long and gauzy. I could see her gentle curves through its folds, and she made no effort to hide herself.

"I come up here a lot," she said. "At night, usually. When Dino's asleep. It's a good place to think."

"Yes," I said, smiling. "My thoughts, too."

"The stars are pretty, aren't they?"

"Yes."

"I think so. I—" Hesitation. Then she rose and came to me. "Do you love Lya?" she said.

A hammer of a question. Timed terribly. But I handled it well, I think. My mind was still on my talk with Lya. "Yes," I said. "Very much. Why?"

She was standing close to me, looking at my face, and past me, out to the stars. "I don't know. I wonder about love, sometimes. I love Dino, you know. He came here two months ago, so we haven't known each other long. But I love him al-

285

ready. I've never known anybody like him. He's kind, and considerate, and he does everything well. I've never seen him fail at anything he tried. Yet he doesn't seem driven, like some men. He wins so easily. He believes in himself a lot, and that's attractive. He's given me anything I could ask for, everything."

I read her, caught her love and worry and guessed. "Except himself," I said.

She looked at me, startled. Then she smiled. "I forgot. You're a Talent. Of course you know. You're right. I don't know what I worry about, but I do worry. Dino is so perfect, you know. I've told him—well, everything. All about me and my life. And he listens and understands. He's always receptive, he's there when I need him. But—"

"It's all one way," I said. It was a statement. I knew.

She nodded. "It's not that he keeps secrets. He doesn't. He'll answer any question I ask. But the answers mean nothing. I ask him what he fears, and he says nothing, and makes me believe it. He's very rational, very calm. He never gets angry, he never has. I asked him. He doesn't hate people, he thinks hate is bad. He's never felt pain, either, or he *says* he hasn't. Emotional pain, I mean. Yet he understands me when I talk about my life. Once he said his biggest fault was laziness. But he's not lazy at all, I know that. Is he really that perfect? He tells me he's always sure of himself, because he *knows* he's good, but he smiles when he says it, so I can't even accuse him of being vain. He says he believes in God, but he never talks about it. If you try to talk seriously, he'll listen patiently, or joke with you, or lead the conversation away. He says he loves me, but—"

I nodded. I knew what was coming.

It came. She looked at me, eyes begging. "You're a Talent," she said. "You've read him, haven't you? You know him? Tell me. Please tell me."

I was reading her. I could see how much she needed to know, how much she worried and feared, how much she loved. I couldn't lie to her. Yet it was hard to give her the answer I had to.

"I've read him," I said. Slowly. Carefully. Measuring out my words like precious fluids. "And you, you too. I saw your love, on that first night, when we ate together."

"And Dino?"

My words caught in my throat. "He's—funny, Lya said once. I can read his surface emotions easily enough. Below

286

that, nothing. He's very self-contained, walled off. Almost as if his only emotions are the ones he—*allows* himself to feel. I've felt his confidence, his pleasure. I've felt worry too, but never real fear. He's very affectionate toward you, very protective. He enjoys feeling protective."

"Is that all?" So hopeful. It hurt.

"I'm afraid it is. He's walled off, Laurie. He needs himself, only himself. If there's love in him, it's behind that wall, hidden. I can't read it. He thinks a lot of you, Laurie. But love—well, it's different. It's stronger and more unreasoning and it comes in crashing floods. And Dino's not like that, at least not out where I can read."

"Closed," she said. "He's closed to me. I opened myself to him, totally. But he didn't. I was always afraid—even when he was with me, I felt sometimes that he wasn't there at all—"

She sighed. I read her despair, her welling loneliness. I didn't know what to do. "Cry if you like," I told her, inanely. "Sometimes it helps. I know. I've cried enough in my time."

She didn't cry. She looked up, and laughed lightly. "No," she said. "I can't. Dino taught me never to cry. He said tears never solve anything."

A sad philosophy. Tears don't solve anything, maybe, but they're part of being human. I wanted to tell her so, but instead I just smiled at her.

She smiled back, and cocked her head. "You cry," she said suddenly, in a voice strangely delighted. "That's funny. That's more of an admission than I ever heard from Dino, in a way. Thank you, Robb. Thank you."

And Laurie stood on her toes and looked up, expectant. And I could read what she expected. So I took her and kissed her, and she pressed her body hard against mine. And all the while I thought of Lya, telling myself that she wouldn't mind, that she'd be proud of me, that she'd understand.

Afterwards, I stayed up in the office alone to watch the dawn come up. I was drained, but somehow content. The light that crept over the horizon was chasing the shadows before it, and suddenly all the fears that had seemed so threatening in the night were silly, unreasoning. We'd bridged it, I thought—Lya and I. Whatever it was, we'd handled it, and today we'd handle the Greeshka with the same ease, together.

When I got back to our room, Lya was gone.

"We found the aircar in the middle of Shkeentown," Valcarenghi was saying. He was cool, precise, reassuring. His voice told me, without words, that there was nothing to worry about. "I've got men out looking for her. But Shkeentown's a big place. Do you have any idea where she might have gone?"

"No," I said, dully. "Not really. Maybe to see some more Joined. She seemed—well, almost obsessed by them. I don't know."

"Well, we've got a good police force. We'll find her, I'm certain of that. But it may take a while. Did you two have a fight?"

"Yes. No. Sort of, but it wasn't a real fight. It was strange."

"I see," he said. But he didn't. "Laurie tells me you came up here last night, alone."

"Yes. I needed to think."

"All right," said Valcarenghi. "So let's say Lya woke up, decided she wanted to think too. You came up here. She took a ride. Maybe she just wants a day off to wander around Shkeentown. She did something like that yesterday, didn't she?"

"Yes."

"So she's doing it again. No problem. She'll probably be back well before dinner." He smiled.

"Why did she go without telling me, then? Or leaving a note, or *something*?"

"I don't know. It's not important."

Wasn't it, though? *Wasn't it?* I sat in the chair, head in my hands and a scowl on my face, and I was sweating. Suddenly I was very much afraid, of what I didn't know. I should never have left her alone, I was telling myself. While I was up here with Laurie, Lyanna woke alone in a darkened room, and—and—and *what?* And left.

"Meanwhile, though," Valcarenghi said, "we've got work to do. The trip to the caves is all set."

I looked up, disbelieving. "The caves? I can't go there, not now, not alone."

He gave a sigh of exasperation, exaggerated for effect. "Oh, come now, Robb. It's not the end of the world. Lya will be all right. She seemed to be a perfectly sensible girl, and I'm sure she can take care of herself. Right?"

I nodded.

288

"Meanwhile, we'll cover the caves. I still want to get to the bottom of this."

"It won't do any good," I protested. "Not without Lya. She's the major Talent. I—I just read emotions. I can't get down deep, as she can. I won't solve anything for you."

He shrugged. "Maybe not. But the trip is on, and we've got nothing to lose. We can always make a second run after Lya comes back. Besides, this should do you good, get your mind off this other business. There's nothing you can do for Lya now. I've got every available man out searching for her, and if they don't find her you certainly won't. So there's no sense dwelling on it. Just get back into action, keep busy." He turned, headed for the tube. "Come. There's an aircar waiting for us. Nelse will go too."

Reluctantly, I stood. I was in no mood to consider the problems of the Shkeen, but Valcarenghi's arguments made a certain amount of sense. Besides which, he'd hired Lyanna and me, and we still had obligations to him. I could try anyway, I thought.

On the ride out, Valcarenghi sat in the front with the driver, a hulking police sergeant with a face chiseled out of granite. He'd selected a police car this time so we could keep posted on the search for Lya. Gourlay and I were in the back seat together. Gourlay had covered our laps with a big map, and he was telling me about the caves of Final Union.

"Theory is the caves are the original home of the Greeshka," he said. "Probably true, makes sense. Greeshka are a lot bigger there. You'll see. The caves are all through the hills, away from our part of Shkeentown, where the country gets wilder. A regular little honeycomb. Greeshka in every one, too. Or so I've heard. Been in a few myself, Greeshka in all of *them*. So I believe what they say about the rest. The city, the sacred city, well, it was probably built *because* of the caves. Shkeen come here from all over the continent, you know, for Final Union. Here, this is the cave region." He took out a pen, and made a big circle in red near the center of the map. It was meaningless to me. The map was getting me down. I hadn't realized that the Shkeen city was so *huge*. How the hell could they find anyone who didn't want to be found?

Valcarenghi looked back from the front seat. "The cave we're going to is a big one, as these places go. I've been there before. There's no formality about Final Union, you understand. The Shkeen just pick a cave, and walk in, and lie

289

down on top of the Greeshka. They'll use whatever entrance is most convenient. Some of them are no bigger than sewer pipes, but if you went in far enough, theory says you'd run into a Greeshka, setting back in the dark and pulsing away. The biggest caves are lighted with torches, like the Great Hall, but that's just a frill. It doesn't play any real part in the Union."

"I take it we're going to one of them?" I said.

Valcarenghi nodded. "Right. I figured you'd want to see what a mature Greeshka is like. It's not pretty, but it's educational. So we need lighting."

Gourlay resumed his narrative then, but I tuned him out. I felt I knew quite enough about the Shkeen and the Greeshka, and I was still worried about Lyanna. After a while he wound down, and the rest of the trip was in silence. We covered more ground than we ever had before. Even the Tower—our shining steel landmark—had been swallowed by the hills behind us.

The terrain got rougher, rockier, and more overgrown, and the hills rose higher and wilder. But the domes went on and on and on, and there were Shkeen everywhere. Lya could be down there, I thought, lost among those teeming millions. Looking for what? Thinking what?

Finally we landed, in a wooded valley between two massive, rock-studded hills. Even here there were Shkeen, the red-brick domes rising from the undergrowth among the stubby trees. I had no trouble spotting the cave. It was halfway up one of the slopes, a dark yawn in the rock face, with a dusty road winding up to it.

We set down in the valley and climbed that road. Gourlay ate up the distance with long, gawky strides, while Valcarenghi moved with an easy, untiring grace, and the policeman plodded on stolidly. I was the straggler. I dragged myself up, and I was half-winded by the time we got to the cave mouth.

If I'd expected cave paintings, or an altar, or some kind of nature temple, I was sadly disappointed. It was an ordinary cave, with damp stone walls and low ceilings and cold, wet air. Cooler than most of Shkea, and less dusty, but that was about it. There was one long, winding passage through the rock, wide enough for the four of us to walk abreast yet low enough so Gourlay had to stoop. Torches were set along the walls at regular intervals, but only every fourth one or so was lit. They burned with an oily smoke that seemed to cling to the top of the cave and drift down into the depths before us. I wondered what was sucking it in.

After about ten minutes of walking, most of it down a barely perceptible incline, the passage led us out into a high, brightly lit room, with a vaulting stone roof that was stained sooty by torch smoke. In the room, the Greeshka.

Its color was a dull brownish red, like old blood, not the bright near-translucent crimson of the small creatures that clung to the skulls of the Joined. There were spots of black, too, like burns or soot stains on the vasty body. I could barely see the far side of the cave; the Greeshka was too huge, it towered above us so that there was only a thin crack between it and the roof. But it sloped down abruptly halfway across the chamber, like an immense jellied hill, and ended a good twenty feet from where we stood. Between us and the great bulk of the Greeshka was a forest of hanging, dangling red strands, a living cobweb of Greeshka tissue that came almost to our faces.

And it pulsed. As one organism. Even the strands kept time, widening and then contracting again, moving to a silent beat that was one with the great Greeshka behind them.

My stomach churned, but my companions seemed unmoved. They'd seen this before. "Come," Valcarenghi said, switching on a flashlight he'd brought to augment the torchlight. The light, twisting around the pulsing web, gave the illusion of some weird haunted forest. Valcarenghi stepped into that forest. Lightly. Swinging the light and brushing aside the Greeshka.

Gourlay followed him, but I recoiled. Valcarenghi looked back and smiled. "Don't worry," he said. "The Greeshka takes hours to attach itself, and it's easily removed. It won't grab you if you stumble against it."

I screwed up my courage, reached out, and touched one of the living strands. It was soft and wet, and there was a slimy feel to it. But that was all. It broke easily enough. I walked through it, reaching before me and bending and breaking the web to clear my path. The policeman walked silently behind me.

Then we stood on the far side of the web, at the foot of the great Greeshka. Valcarenghi studied it for a second, then pointed with his flashlight. "Look," he said. "Final Union."

I looked. His beam had thrown a pool of light around one of the dark spots, a blemish on the reddish hulk. I looked closer. There was a head in the blemish. Centered in the dark spot, with just the face showing, and even that covered by a thin reddish film. But the features were unmistakable. An elderly Shkeen, wrinkled and big-eyed, his eyes closed now. But smiling. Smiling.

I moved closer. A little lower and to the right, a few fingertips hung out of the mass. But that was all. Most of the body was already gone, sunken into the Greeshka, dissolved or dissolving. The old Shkeen was dead, and the parasite was digesting his corpse.

"Every one of the dark spots is a recent Union," Valcarenghi was saying, moving his light around like a pointer. "The spots fade in time, of course. The Greeshka is growing steadily. In another hundred years it will fill this chamber, and start up the passageway."

Then there was a rustle of movement behind us. I looked back. Someone else was coming through the web.

She reached us soon, and smiled. A Shkeen woman, old, naked, breasts hanging past her waist. Joined, of course. Her Greeshka covered most of her head and hung lower than her breasts. It was still bright and translucent from its time in the sun. You could see through it, to where it was eating the skin off her back.

"A candidate for Final Union," Gourlay said.

"This is a popular cave," Valcarenghi added in a low, sardonic voice.

The woman did not speak to us, nor we to her. Smiling, she walked past us. And lay down on the Greeshka.

The little Greeshka, the one that rode her back, seemed almost to dissolve on contact, melting away into the great cave creature, so the Shkeen woman and the great Greeshka were joined as one. After that, nothing. She just closed her eyes, and lay peacefully, seemingly asleep.

"What's happening?" I asked.

"Union," said Valcarenghi. "It'll be an hour before you'd notice anything, but the Greeshka is closing over her even now, swallowing her. A response to her body heat, I'm told. In a day she'll be buried in it. In two, like him—" The flash found the half-dissolved face above us.

"Can you read her?" Gourlay suggested. "Maybe that'd tell us something."

"All right," I said, repelled but curious. I opened myself. And the mindstorm hit.

But it's wrong to call it a mindstorm. It was immense and awesome and intense, searing and blinding and choking. But
292

it was peaceful too, and gentle with a gentleness that was more violent than human hate. It shrieked soft shrieks and siren calls and pulled at me seductively, and it washed over me in crimson waves of passion, and drew me to it. It filled me and emptied me all at once. And I heard the bells somewhere, clanging a harsh bronze song, a song of love and surrender and togetherness, of joining and union and never being alone.

Storm, mindstorm, yes, it was that. But it was to an ordinary mindstorm as a supernova is to a hurricane, and its violence was the violence of love. It loved me, that mindstorm, and it wanted me, and its bells called to me, and sang its love, and I reached to it and touched, wanting to be with it, wanting to link, wanting never to be alone again. And suddenly I was on the crest of a great wave once again, a wave of fire that washed across the stars forever, and this time I knew the wave would never end, this time I would not be alone afterwards upon my darkling plain.

But with that phrase I thought of Lya.

And suddenly I was struggling, fighting it, battling back against the sea of sucking love. I ran, ran, *ran, RAN* . . . and closed my minddoor and hammered shut the latch and let the storm flail and howl against it while I held it with all my strength, resisting. Yet the door began to buckle and crack.

I screamed. The door smashed open, and the storm whipped in and clutched at me, whirled me out and around and around. I sailed up to the cold stars but they were cold no longer, and I grew bigger and bigger until I *was* the stars and they were me, and I was Union, and for a single solitary glittering instant I was the universe.

Then nothing.

I woke up back in my room, with a headache that was trying to tear my skull apart. Gourlay was sitting on a chair reading one of our books. He looked up when I groaned.

Lya's headache pills were still on the bedstand. I took one hastily, then struggled to sit up in bed.

"You all right?" Gourlay asked.

"Headache," I said, rubbing my forehead. It *throbbed,* as if it was about to burst. Worse than the time I'd peered into Lya's pain. "What happened?"

He stood up. "You scared the hell out of us. After you began to read, all of a sudden you started trembling. Then you

293

walked right into the goddamn Greeshka. And you screamed. Dino and the sergeant had to drag you out. You were stepping right in the thing, and it was up to your knees. Twitching, too. Weird. Dino hit you, knocked you out."

He shook his head, started for the door. "Where are you going?" I said.

"To sleep," he said. "You've been out for eight hours or so. Dino asked me to watch you till you came to. OK, you came to. Now get some rest, and I will too. We'll talk about it tomorrow."

"I want to talk about it now."

"It's late," he said, as he closed the bedroom door. I listened to his footsteps on the way out. And I'm sure I heard the outer door lock. Somebody was clearly afraid of Talents who steal away into the night. I wasn't going anywhere.

I got up and went out for a drink. There was Veltaar chilling. I put away a couple of glasses quick, and ate a light snack. The headache began to fade. Then I went back to the bedroom, turned off the light and cleared the glass, so the stars would all shine through. Then back to sleep.

But I didn't sleep, not right away. Too much had happened. I had to think about it. The headache first, the incredible headache that ripped at my skull. Like Lya's. But Lya hadn't been through what I had. Or had she? Lya was a major Talent, much more sensitive than I was, with a greater range. Could that mindstorm have reached *this* far, over miles and miles? Late at night, when humans and Shkeen were sleeping and their thoughts dim? Maybe. And maybe my half-remembered dreams were pale reflections of whatever she had felt the same nights. But my dreams had been pleasant. It was waking that bothered me, waking and not remembering.

But again, had I had this headache when I slept? Or when I woke?

What the hell had happened? What was that thing, that reached me there in the cave, and pulled me to it? The Greeshka? It had to be. I hadn't even time to focus on the Shkeen woman, it *had* to be the Greeshka. But Lyanna had said that Greeshka had no minds, not even a yes-I-live . . .

It all swirled around me, questions on questions on questions, and I had no answers. I began to think of Lya then, to wonder where she was and why she'd left me. Was this what she had been going through? Why hadn't I understood? I missed her then. I needed her beside me, and she wasn't there. I was alone, and very aware of it.

I slept.

Long darkness then, but finally a dream, and finally I remembered. I was back on the plain again, the infinite darkling plain with its starless sky and black shapes in the distance, the plain Lya had spoken of so often. It was from one of her favorite poems. I was alone, forever alone, and I knew it. That was the nature of things. I was the only reality in the universe, and I was cold and hungry and frightened, and the shapes were moving toward me, inhuman and inexorable. And there was no one to call to, no one to turn to, no one to hear my cries. There never had been anyone. There never would be anyone.

Then Lya came to me.

She floated down from the starless sky, pale and thin and fragile, and stood beside me on the plain. She brushed her hair back with her hand, and looked at me with glowing wide eyes, and smiled. And I knew it was no dream. She was with me, somehow. We talked.

Hi, Robb.

Lya? Hi, Lya. Where are you? You left me.

I'm sorry. I had to. You understand, Robb. You have to. I didn't want to be here anymore, ever, in this place, this awful place. I would have been, Robb. Men are always here, but for brief moments.

A touch and a voice?

Yes, Robb. Then darkness again, and a silence. And the darkling plain.

You're mixing two poems, Lya. But it's OK. You knew them better than I do. But aren't you leaving out something? The earlier part. "Ah love, let us be true . . ."

Oh, Robb.

Where are you?

I'm—everywhere. But mostly in a cave. I was ready, Robb. I was already more open than the rest. I could skip the Gathering, and the Joining. My Talent made me used to sharing. It took me.

Final Union?

Yes.

Oh, Lya.

Robb. Please. Join us, join me. It's happiness, you know? Forever and forever, and belonging and sharing and being together. I'm in love, Robb, I'm in love with a billion billion people, and I know all of them better than I ever knew you, and they know me, all of me, and they love me. And it will last forever. Me. Us. The Union. I'm still me, but I'm them too, you see? And they're me. The Joined, the reading, opened me, and the Union called to me every night, because it loved me, you see? Oh, Robb, join us, join us. I love you.

The Union. The Greeshka, you mean. I love you, Lya. Please come back. It can't have absorbed you already. Tell me where you are. I'll come to you.

Yes, come to me. Come anywhere, Robb. The Greeshka is all one, the caves all connect under the hills, the little Greeshka are all part of the Union. Come to me and join me. Love me as you said you did. Join me. You're so far away, I can hardly reach you, even with the Union. Come and be one with us.

No. I will not be eaten. Please, Lya, tell me where you are.

Poor Robb. Don't worry, love. The body isn't important. The Greeshka needs it for nourishment, and we need the Greeshka. But, oh Robb, the Union isn't just the Greeshka, you see? The Greeshka isn't important, it doesn't even have a mind, it's just the link, the medium, the Union is the Shkeen. A million billion billion Shkeen, all the Shkeen that have lived and Joined in fourteen thousand years, all together and loving and belonging, immortal. It's beautiful, Robb, it's more than we had, much more, and we were the lucky ones, remember? We were! But this is better.

Lya. My Lya. I loved you. This isn't for you, this isn't for humans. Come back to me.

This isn't for humans? Oh, it IS! It's what humans have always been looking for, searching for, crying for on lonely nights. It's love, Robb, real love, and human love is only a pale imitation. You see?

No.

Come, Robb. Join. Or you'll be alone forever, alone on the plain, with only a voice and a touch to keep you going. And in the end when your body dies, you won't even have that. Just an eternity of empty blackness. The plain, Robb, forever and ever. And I won't be able to reach you, not ever. But it doesn't have to be . . .

No.

Oh, Robb. I'm fading. Please come.

No. Lya, don't go. I love you, Lya. Don't leave me.

I love you, Robb. I did. I really did . . .

And then she was gone. I was alone on the plain again. A

wind was blowing from somewhere, and it whipped her fading words away from me, out into the cold vastness of infinity.

In the cheerless morning, the outer door was unlocked. I ascended the tower and found Valcarenghi alone in his office. "Do you believe in God?" I asked him.

He looked up, smiled. "Sure." Said lightly. I was reading him. It was a subject he'd never thought about.

"I don't," I said. "Neither did Lya. Most Talents are atheists, you know. There was an experiment tried back on Old Earth fifty years ago. It was organized by a major Talent named Linnel, who was also devoutly religious. He thought that by using drugs, and linking together the minds of the world's most potent Talents, he could reach something he called the Universal Yes-I-Live. Also known as God. The experiment was a dismal failure, but *something* happened. Linnel went mad, and the others came away with only a vision of a vast, dark, uncaring nothingness, a void without reason or form or meaning. Other Talents have felt the same way, and Normals too. Centuries ago there was a poet named Arnold, who wrote of a darkling plain. The poem's in one of the old languages, but it's worth reading. It shows—fear, I think. Something basic in man, some dread of being alone in the cosmos. Maybe it's just fear of death, maybe it's more. I don't know. But it's primal. All men are forever alone, but they don't want to be. They're always searching, trying to make contact, trying to reach others across the void. Some people never succeed, some break through occasionally. Lya and I were lucky. But it's never permanent. In the end you're alone again, back on the darkling plain. You see, Dino? *Do you see?*"

He smiled an amused little smile. Not derisive—that wasn't his style—just surprised and disbelieving. "No," he said.

"Look again, then. Always people are reaching for something, for someone, searching. Talk, Talent, love, sex, it's all part of the same thing, the same search. And gods, too. Man invents gods because he's afraid of being alone, scared of an empty universe, scared of the darkling plain. That's why your men are converting, Dino, that's why people are going over. They've found God, or as much of a God as they're ever likely to find. The Union is a mass-mind, an immortal mass-mind, many in one, all love. The Shkeen don't die, dammit. No wonder they don't have the concept of an afterlife. They

297

know there's a God. Maybe it didn't create the universe, but it's love, pure love, and they say that God is love, don't they? Or maybe what we call love is a tiny piece of God. I don't care, whatever it is, the Union is it. The end of the search for the Shkeen, and for Man too. We're alike after all, we're so alike it hurts."

Valcarenghi gave his exaggerated sigh. "Robb, you're over-wrought. You sound like one of the Joined."

"Maybe that's just what I should be. Lya is. She's part of the Union now."

He blinked. "How do you know that?"

"She came to me last night in a dream."

"Oh. A dream."

"It was *true,* dammit. It's all true."

Valcarenghi stood, and smiled. "I believe you," he said. "That is, I believe that the Greeshka uses a psi-lure, a love lure if you will, to draw in its prey, something so powerful that it convinces men—even you—that it's God. Dangerous, of course. I'll have to think about this before taking action. We could guard the caves to keep humans out, but there are too many caves. And sealing off the Greeshka wouldn't help our relations with the Shkeen. But now it's my problem. You've done your job."

I waited until he was through. "You're wrong, Dino. This is real, no trick, no illusion. I *felt* it, and Lya too. The Greesh-ka hasn't even a yes-I-live, let alone a psi-lure strong enough to bring in Shkeen and men."

"You expect me to believe that God is an animal who lives in the caves of Shkea?"

"Yes."

"Robb, that's absurd, and you know it. You think the Shkeen have found the answer to the mysteries of creation. But look at them. The oldest civilized race in known space, but they've been stuck in the Bronze Age for fourteen thousand years. We came to *them.* Where are their spaceships? Where are their towers?"

"Where are our bells?" I said. "And our joy? They're happy, Dino. Are we? Maybe they've found what we're still looking for. Why the hell is man so driven, anyway? Why is he out to conquer the galaxy, the universe, whatever? Look-ing for God, maybe . . . ? Maybe. He can't find him any-where, though, so on he goes, on and on, always looking. But always back to the same darkling plain in the end."

"Compare the accomplishments. I'll take humanity's record."

"Is it worth it?"

"I think so." He went to the window, and looked out. "We've got the only Tower on their world," he said, smiling, as he looked down through the clouds.

"They've got the only God in our universe," I told him. But he only smiled.

"All right, Robb," he said, when he finally turned from the window. "I'll keep all this in mind. And we'll find Lyanna for you."

My voice softened. "Lya is lost," I said. "I know that now. I will be too, if I wait. I'm leaving tonight. I'll book passage on the first ship out to Baldur."

He nodded. "If you like. I'll have your money ready." He grinned. "And we'll send Lya after you, when we find her. I imagine she'll be a little miffed, but that's your worry."

I didn't answer. Instead I shrugged, and headed for the tube. I was almost there when he stopped me.

"Wait," he said. "How about dinner tonight? You've done a good job for us. We're having a farewell party anyway, Laurie and me. She's leaving too."

"I'm sorry," I said.

His turn to shrug. "What for? Laurie's a beautiful person, and I'll miss her. But it's no tragedy. There are other beautiful people. I think she was getting restless with Shkea, anyway."

I'd almost forgotten my Talent, in my heat and the pain of my loss. I remembered it now. I read him. There was no sorrow, no pain, just a vague disappointment. And below that, his wall. Always the wall, keeping him apart, this man who was a first-name friend to everyone and an intimate to none. And on it, it was almost as if there were a sign that read, THIS FAR YOU GO, AND NO FARTHER.

"Come up," he said. "It should be fun." I nodded.

I asked myself, when my ship lifted off, why I was leaving.

Maybe to return home. We have a house on Baldur, away from the cities, on one of the undeveloped continents with only wilderness for a neighbor. It stands on a cliff, above a high waterfall that tumbles endlessly down into a shaded green pool. Lya and I swam there often, in the sunlit days between assignments. And afterwards we'd lie down nude in the shade of the orangespice trees, and make love on a carpet of silver moss. Maybe I'm returning to that. But it won't be the same without Lya, lost Lya . . .

Lya whom I could still have. Whom I could have now. It would be easy, so easy. A slow stroll into a darkened cave, a short sleep. Then Lya with me for eternity, in me, sharing me, being me, and I her. Loving and knowing more of each other than men can ever do. Union and Joy, and no darkness again, ever. God. If I believed that, what I told Valcarenghi, then why did I tell Lya no?

Maybe because I'm not sure. Maybe I still hope, for something still greater and more loving than the Union, for the God they told me of so long ago. Maybe I'm taking a risk, because part of me still believes. But if I'm wrong . . . then the darkness, and the plain . . .

But maybe it's something else, something I saw in Valcarenghi, something that made me doubt what I had said. For man is more than Shkeen, somehow; there are men like Dino and Gourlay as well as Lya and Gustaffson, men who fear love and Union as much as they crave it. A dichotomy, then. Man has two primal urges, and the Shkeen only one? If so, perhaps there is a human answer, to reach and join and not be alone, and yet to still be men.

I do not envy Valcarenghi. He cries behind his wall, I think, and no one knows, not even he. And no one will ever know, and in the end he'll always be alone in smiling pain. No, I do not envy Dino.

Yet there is something of him in me, Lya, as well as much of you. And that is why I ran, though I loved you.

Laurie Blackburn was on the ship with me. I ate with her after liftoff, and we spent the evening talking over wine. Not a happy conversation, maybe, but a human one. Both of us needed someone, and we reached out.

Afterwards, I took her back to my cabin, and made love to her as fiercely as I could. Then, the darkness softened, we held each other and talked away the night.

"Adrift Just Off the Islets of Langerhans: Latitude 38° 54'
N, Longitude 77° 00' 13″ W"

What a story title!

John Campbell, when he was in his prime, liked short
titles, preferably one-word titles, because they fit on the cover
very nicely.

I liked short titles, too, preferably one-word titles, because
that made it easier for readers to discuss the story, and
helped in that word-of-mouth advertising which is the only
kind I'm ever likely to get.

Now look at Harlan's mistake—

One reader says enthusiastically to another, "I just read a
great story. You've got to read it."

"Oh boy, what's the name?"

"It's 'Adrift Off the—' I mean 'Adrift Just Off the Islands—uh—Islets of Something or Other' with some figures— Listen, this other story I read is called 'Nightfall,'
you've got to read it."

But don't get Harlan wrong. He's playing for other stakes.
He won the Hugo with it, didn't he? Well, the reason he won
this Hugo was that by the time they got through printing up
the title of this story there was no room to include the rest of
the nominees.*

Anyway, I had occasion to use Harlan recently. I was doing a murder mystery (*Murder at the ABA*, Doubleday,
1976) and I needed a hero. Since ABA stands for "American
Booksellers Association," I wanted someone who would
naturally attend such a meeting, and I chose a writer. I
wanted him to be fearfully intelligent so that he could solve
the murder, and fearfully courageous so he could beat off the
bad guys, and fearfully charming so he could get the girl, and
fearfully nice so he could interest the reader. And it couldn't
be me (my first thought) because I'm a character—an innocent bystander—in the book, so it had to be a friend of mine.

* One of which was a story of my very own entitled "That Thou Art Mindful of Him." My fault. I should have called it "Mindful," then they might
just barely have squeezed it in.

"Well," thought I to myself, "who do I know who is a writer, and who is fearfully intelligent, courageous, charming, and nice, and who is a friend of mine?"

That was easy. So I made my hero five feet two inches tall.†

Then I wrote to Harlan and asked if it would be all right. Harlan, who, underneath that assiduously cultivated outer armor composed exclusively of porcupine quills and crocodile scales, is the world's nicest pussycat, sent me a letter of permission and blessed the enterprise. I promptly stapled the letter to my contract.

My hero is named Darius Just and I love him—but not as much as I love Harlan.

ADRIFT JUST OFF THE ISLETS OF LANGERHANS: LATITUDE 38° 54′ N, LONGITUDE 77° 00′ 13″ W

As Moby Dick awoke one morning from uneasy dreams, he found himself changed in his bed of kelp into a monstrous Ahab.

Crawling in stages from the soggy womb of sheets, he stumbled into the kitchen and ran water into the teapot. There was lye in the corner of each eye. He put his head under the spigot and let the cold water rush around his cheeks.

Dead bottles littered the living room. One hundred and eleven empty bottles that had contained Robitussin and Romilar-CF. He padded through the debris to the front door and opened it a crack. Daylight assaulted him. "Oh, God," he murmured, and closed his eyes to pick up the folded newspaper from the stoop.

† Height note from Ellison proofing the galleys: All the rest about me is dead on the button true; I am a terrific person. Only the height is wrong. As I have pointed out to Isaac, both in person and in print, I am not 5′ 2″; I am 5′ 5″. This makes the tenth such correction. And I wuv you, too, Ike.
—H. E.

Once more in dusk, he opened the paper. The headline read: BOLIVIAN AMBASSADOR FOUND MURDERED, and the feature story heading column one detailed the discovery of the ambassador's body, badly decomposed, in an abandoned refrigerator in an empty lot in Secaucus, New Jersey.

The teapot whistled.

Naked, he padded toward the kitchen; as he passed the aquarium he saw that terrible fish was still alive, and this morning whistling like a bluejay, making tiny streams of bubbles that rose to burst on the scummy surface of the water. He paused beside the tank, turned on the light and looked in through the drifting eddies of stringered algae. The fish simply would not die. It had killed off every other fish in the tank—prettier fish, friendlier fish, livelier fish, even larger and more dangerous fish—had killed them all one by one, and eaten out the eyes. Now it swam the tank alone, ruler of its worthless domain.

He had tried to let the fish kill itself, trying every form of neglect short of outright murder by not feeding it; but the pale, worm-pink devil even thrived in the dark and filth-laden waters.

Now it sang like a bluejay. He hated the fish with a passion he could barely contain.

He sprinkled flakes from a plastic container, grinding them between thumb and forefinger as experts had advised him to do it, and watched the multi-colored granules of fish meal, roe, milt, brine shrimp, day-fly eggs, oatflour and egg yolk ride on the surface for a moment before the detestable fishface came snapping to the top to suck them down. He turned away, cursing and hating the fish. It would not die. Like him, it would not die.

In the kitchen, bent over the boiling water, he understood for the first time the true status of his situation. Though he was probably nowhere near the rotting outer edge of sanity, he could smell its foulness on the wind, coming in from the horizon; and like some wild animal rolling its eyes at the scent of carrion and the feeders thereon, he was being driven closer to lunacy every day, just from the smell.

He carried the teapot, a cup and two tea bags to the kitchen table and sat down. Propped open in a plastic stand used for keeping cookbooks handy while mixing ingredients, the Mayan Codex translations remained unread from the evening before. He poured the water, dangled the tea bags in the cup, and tried to focus his attention. The references to

Itzamna, the chief divinity of the Maya pantheon, and medicine, his chief sphere of influence, blurred. Ixtab, the goddess of suicide, seemed more apropos for this morning, this deadly terrible morning. He tried reading, but the words only went in, nothing happened to them, they didn't sing. He sipped tea and found himself thinking of the chill, full circle of the Moon. He glanced over his shoulder at the kitchen clock. Seven forty-four.

He shoved away from the table, taking the half-full cup of tea, and went into the bedroom. The impression of his body, where it had lain in tortured sleep, still indented the bed. There were clumps of blood-matted hair clinging to the manacles that he had riveted to metal plates in the headboard. He rubbed his wrists where they had been scored raw, slopping a little tea on his left forearm. He wondered if the Bolivian ambassador had been a piece of work he had tended to the month before.

His wrist watch lay on the bureau. He checked it. Seven forty-six. Slightly less than an hour and a quarter to make the meeting with the consultation service. He went into the bathroom, reached inside the shower stall and turned the handle till a fine needle-spray of icy water smashed the tiled wall of the stall. Letting the water run, he turned to the medicine cabinet for his shampoo. Taped to the mirror was an Ouchless Telfa finger bandage on which three lines had been neatly typed, in capitals:

THE WAY YOU WALK IS
THORNY, MY SON, THROUGH
NO FAULT OF YOUR OWN.

Then, opening the cabinet, removing a plastic bottle of herbal shampoo that smelled like friendly, deep forests, Lawrence Talbot resigned himself to the situation, turned and stepped into the shower, the merciless ice-laden waters of the Arctic pounding against his tortured flesh.

Suite 1544 of the Tishman Airport Center Building was a men's toilet. He stood against the wall opposite the door labeled MEN and drew the envelope from the inner breast pocket of his jacket. The paper was of good quality, the envelope crackled as he thumbed up the flap and withdrew the single sheet letter inside. It was the correct address, the correct floor, the correct suite. Suite 1544 was a men's toilet, nonetheless. Talbot started to turn away. It was a vicious joke; he found no humor in the situation; not in his present circumstances.

He took one step toward the elevators.

The door to the men's room shimmered, fogged over like a windshield in winter, and re-formed. The legend on the door had changed. It now read:

INFORMATION ASSOCIATES

Suite 1544 was the consultation service that had written the invitational letter on paper of good quality in response to Talbot's mail inquiry responding to a noncommittal but judiciously-phrased advertisement in *Forbes*.

He opened the door and stepped inside. The woman behind the teak reception desk smiled at him, and his glance was split between the dimples that formed and her legs, very nice, smooth legs, crossed and framed by the kneehole of the desk. "Mr. Talbot?"

He nodded. "Lawrence Talbot."

She smiled again. "Mr. Demeter will see you at once, sir. Would you like something to drink? Coffee? A soft drink?"

Talbot found himself touching his jacket where the envelope lay in an inner pocket. "No. Thank you."

She stood up, moving toward an inner office door, as Talbot said, "What do you do when someone tries to flush your desk?" He was not trying to be cute. He was annoyed. She turned and stared at him. There was silence in her appraisal, nothing more.

"Mr. Demeter is right through here, sir."

She opened the door and stood aside. Talbot walked past her, catching a scent of mimosa.

The inner office was furnished like the reading room of an exclusive men's club. Old money. Deep quiet. Dark, heavy woods. A lowered ceiling of acoustical tile on tracks, concealing a crawl space and probably electrical conduits. The pile rug of oranges and burnt umbers swallowed his feet to the ankles. Through a wall-sized window could be seen not the city that lay outside the building, but a panoramic view of Hanauma Bay, on the Koko Head side of Oahu. The pure aquamarine waves came in like undulant snakes, rose like cobras, crested out white, tunneled, and struck like asps at the blazing yellow beach. It was not a window; there were no windows in the office. It was a photograph. A deep, real pho-

305

tograph that was neither a projection nor a hologram. It was a wall looking out on another place entirely. Talbot knew nothing about exotic flora, but he was certain that the tall, razor-edged-leafed trees growing right down to beach's boundary were identical to those pictured in books depicting the Carboniferous period of the Earth before even the saurians had walked the land. What he was seeing had been gone for a very long time.

"Mr. Talbot. Good of you to come. John Demeter."

He came up from a wingback chair, extended his hand. Talbot took it. The grip was firm and cool. "Won't you sit down," Demeter said. "Something to drink? Coffee, perhaps, or a soft drink?" Talbot shook his head: Demeter nodded dismissal to the receptionist; she closed the door behind her, firmly, smoothly, silently.

Talbot studied Demeter in one long appraisal as he took the chair opposite the wingback. Demeter was in his early fifties, had retained a full and rich mop of hair that fell across his forehead in gray waves that clearly had not been touched up. His eyes were clear and blue, his features regular and jovial, his mouth wide and sincere. He was trim. The dark brown business suit was hand-tailored and hung well. He sat easily and crossed his legs, revealing black hose that went above his shins. His shoes were highly polished.

"That's a fascinating door, the one to your outer office," Talbot said.

"Do we talk about my door?" Demeter asked.

"Not if you don't want to. That isn't why I came here."

"I don't want to. So let's discuss your particular problem."

"Your advertisement. I was intrigued."

Demeter smiled reassuringly. "Four copywriters worked very diligently at the proper phraseology."

"It brings in business."

"The right kind of business."

"You slanted it toward smart money. Very reserved. Conservative portfolios, few glamors, steady climbers. Wise old owls."

Demeter steepled his fingers and nodded; an understanding uncle. "Directly to the core, Mr. Talbot: wise old owls."

"I need some information. Some special, certain information. How confidential is your service, Mr. Demeter?"

The friendly uncle, the wise old owl, the reassuring businessman understood all the edited spaces behind the question. He nodded several times. Then he smiled and said,

"That *is* a clever door I have, isn't it? You're absolutely right, Mr. Talbot."

"A certain understated eloquence."

"One hopes it answers more questions for our clients than it poses."

Talbot sat back in the chair for the first time since he had entered Demeter's office. "I think I can accept that."

"Fine. Then why don't we get to specifics. Mr. Talbot, you're having some difficulty dying. Am I stating the situation succinctly?"

"Gently, Mr. Demeter."

"Always."

"Yes. You're on the target."

"But you have some problems, some rather unusual problems."

"Inner ring."

Demeter stood up and walked around the room, touching an astrolabe on a bookshelf, a cut glass decanter on a sideboard, a sheaf of *London Times*es held together by a wooden pole. "We are only information specialists, Mr. Talbot. We can put you on to what you need, but the effectation is your problem."

"If I have the *modus operandi,* I'll have no trouble taking care of getting it done."

"You've put a little aside."

"A little."

"Conservative portfolio? A few glamors, mostly steady climbers?"

"Bullseye, Mr. Demeter."

Demeter came back and sat down again. "All right, then. If you'll take the time to very carefully write out *precisely* what you want—I know generally, from your letter, but I want this *precise,* for the contract—I think I can undertake to supply the data necessary to solving your problem."

"At what cost?"

"Let's decide what it is you want, first, shall we?"

Talbot nodded. Demeter reached over and pressed a call button on the smoking stand beside the wingback. The door opened. "Susan, would you show Mr. Talbot to the sanctum and provide him with writing materials." She smiled and stood aside, waiting for Talbot to follow her. "And bring Mr. Talbot something to drink if he'd like it . . . some coffee? A soft drink, perhaps?" Talbot did not respond to the offer.

"I might need some time to get the phraseology down just

307

right. I might have to work as diligently as your copywriters. It might take me a while. I'll go home and bring it in tomorrow."

Demeter looked troubled. "That might be inconvenient. That's why we provide a quiet place where you can think."

"You'd prefer I do it now."

"Inner ring, Mr. Talbot."

"You might be a toilet if I came back tomorrow."

"Bullseye."

"Let's go, Susan. Bring me a glass of orange juice if you have it." He preceded her through the door.

He followed her down the corridor at the far side of the reception room. He had not seen it before. She stopped at a door and opened it for him. There was an escritoire and a comfortable chair inside the small room. He could hear Muzak. "I'll bring you your orange juice," she said.

He went in and sat down. After a long time he wrote seven words on a sheet of paper.

Two months later, long after the series of visitations from silent messengers who brought rough drafts of the contract to be examined, who came again to take them away revised, who came again with counter-proposals, who came again to take away further revised versions, who came again—finally—with Demeter-signed finals, and who waited while he examined and initialed and signed the finals—two months later, the map came via the last, mute messenger. He arranged for the final installment of the payment to Information Associates that same day: he had ceased wondering where fifteen boxcars of maize—grown specifically as the Zuni nation had grown it—was of value.

Two days later, a small item on an inside page of the New York *Times* noted that fifteen boxcars of farm produce had somehow vanished off a railroad spur near Albuquerque. An official investigation had been initiated.

The map was very specific, very detailed; it looked accurate.

He spent several days with Grey's *Anatomy* and, when he was satisfied that Demeter and his organization had been worth the staggering fee, he made a phone call. The long distance operator turned him over to Inboard and he waited for the static-laden connection to be made. He insisted the Budapest operator on the other end let it ring twenty times, twice the number the phone company permitted per call. On
308

the twenty-first ring it was picked up. Miraculously, the background noise-level dropped and he heard Victor's voice as though it was across the room.

"Yes! Hello!" Impatient, surly as always.

"Victor . . . Larry Talbot."

"Where are you calling from?"

"The States. How are you?"

"Busy. What do you want?"

"I have a project. I want to hire you and your lab."

"Forget it. I'm coming down to final moments on a project and I can't be bothered now."

The imminence of hangup was in his voice. Talbot cut in quickly. "How long do you anticipate?"

"Till what?"

"Till you're clear."

"Another six months inside, eight to ten if it gets muddy. I said: forget it, Larry. I'm *not* available."

"At least let's talk."

"No."

"Am I wrong, Victor, or do you owe me a little?"

"After all this time you're calling in debts?"

"They only ripen with age."

There was a long silence in which Talbot heard dead space being pirated off their line. At one point he thought the other man had racked the receiver. Then, finally, "Okay, Larry. We'll *talk*. But you'll have to come to me; I'm too involved to be hopping any jets."

"That's fine. I have free time." A slow beat, then he added, "Nothing but free time."

"*After* the full moon, Larry." It was said with great specificity.

"Of course. I'll meet you at the last place we met, at the same time, on the thirtieth of this month. Do you remember?"

"I remember. That'll be fine."

"Thank you, Victor. I appreciate this."

There was no response.

Talbot's voice softened: "How is your father?"

"Goodbye, Larry," he answered, and hung up.

They met on the thirtieth of that month, at moonless midnight, on the corpse barge that plied between Buda and Pesht. It was the correct sort of night: chill fog moved in a pulsing curtain up the Danube from Belgrade.

They shook hands in the lee of a stack of cheap wooden coffins and, after hesitating awkwardly for a moment, they embraced like brothers. Talbot's smile was tight and barely discernible by the withered illumination of the lantern and the barge's running light as he said, "All right, get it said so I don't have to wait for the other shoe to drop."

Victor grinned and murmured ominously.

> "Even a man who is pure in heart
> "And says his prayers by night,
> "May become a wolf when the wolfbane blooms
> "And the Autumn moon shines bright."

Talbot made a face. "And other songs from the same album."

"Still saying your prayers at night?"

"I stopped that when I realized the damned thing didn't scan."

"Hey. We aren't here getting pneumonia just to discuss forced rhyme."

The lines of weariness in Talbot's face settled into a joyless pattern. "Victor, I need your help."

"I'll listen, Larry. Further than that it's doubtful."

Talbot weighed the warning and said, "Three months ago I answered an advertisement in *Forbes*, the business magazine. Information Associates. It was cleverly-phrased, very reserved, small box, inconspicuously placed. Except to those who knew how to read it. I won't waste your time on details but the sequence went like this: I answered the ad, hinting at my problem as circuitously as possible without being completely impenetrable. Vague words about important money. I had hopes. Well, I hit with this one. They sent back a letter calling a meet. Perhaps another false trail, was what I thought . . . God knows there've been enough of those."

Victor lit a Sobranie Black & Gold and let the pungent scent of the smoke drift away on the fog. "But you went."

"I went. Peculiar outfit, sophisticated security system; I had a strong feeling they came from, well, I'm not sure where . . . or when."

Victor's glance was abruptly kilowatts heavier with interest. "*When*, you say? Temporal travelers?"

"I don't know."

"I've been waiting for something like that, you know. It's

inevitable. And they'd certainly make themselves known eventually."

He lapsed into silence, thinking. Talbot brought him back sharply. "I don't know, Victor. I really don't. But that's not my concern at the moment."

"Oh. Right. Sorry, Larry. Go on. You met with them . . ."

"Man named Demeter. I thought there might be some clue there. The name. I didn't think of it at the time. The name Demeter, there was a florist in Cleveland, many years ago. But later, when I looked it up, Demeter, the Earth goddess, Greek mythology . . . no connection. At least, I don't think so.

"We talked. He understood my problem and said he'd undertake the commission. But he wanted it specific, what I required of him, wanted it specific for the contract—God knows how he would have enforced the contract, but I'm sure he could have—he had a *window*, Victor, it looked out on—"

Victor spun the cigarette off his thumb and middle finger, snapping it straight down into the blood-black Danube. "Larry, you're maundering."

Talbot's words caught in his throat. It was true. "I'm counting on you, Victor. I'm afraid it's putting my usual aplomb out of phase."

"All right, take it easy. Let me hear the rest of this and we'll see. Relax."

Talbot nodded and felt grateful. "I wrote out the nature of the commission. It was only seven words." He reached into his topcoat pocket and brought out a folded slip of paper. Victor unfolded the paper and read:

GEOGRAPHICAL COORDINATES
FOR LOCATION OF MY SOUL

Victor looked at the line of type long after he had absorbed its message. When he handed it back to Talbot, he wore a new, fresher expression. "You'll never give up, will you, Larry?"

"Did your father?"

"No." Great sadness flickered across the face of the man Talbot called Victor. "And," he added, tightly, after a beat, "he's been lying in a catatonia sling for sixteen years *because* he wouldn't give up." He lapsed into silence. Finally, softly, "It never hurts to know when to give up, Larry. Never hurts. Sometimes you've just got to leave it alone."

Talbot snorted softly with bemusement. "Easy enough for you to say, old chum. You're going to die."

"That wasn't fair, Larry."

"Then help me, dammit! I've gone further toward getting myself out of all this than I ever have. Now I need *you*. You've got the expertise."

"Have you sounded out 3M or Rand or even General Dynamics? They've got good people there."

"Damn you."

"Okay. Sorry. Let me think a minute."

The corpse barge cut through the invisible water, silent, fog-shrouded, without Charon, without Styx, merely a public service, a garbage scow of unfinished sentences, uncompleted errands, unrealized dreams. With the exception of these two, talking, the barge's supercargo had left decisions and desertions behind.

Then, Victor said, softly, talking as much to himself as to Talbot, "We could do it with microtelemetry. Either through direct microminiaturizing techniques or by shrinking a servomechanism package containing sensing, remote control, and guidance/manipulative/propulsion hardware. Use a saline solution to inject it into the bloodstream. Knock you out with 'Russian sleep' and/or tap into the sensory nerves so you'd perceive or control the device as if you were there . . . conscious transfer of point of view."

Talbot looked at him expectantly.

"No. Forget it," said Victor. "It won't do."

He continued to think. Talbot reached into the other's jacket pocket and brought out the Sobranies. He lit one and stood silently, waiting. It was always thus with Victor. He had to worm his way through the analytical labyrinth.

"Maybe the biotechnic equivalent: a tailored microorganism or slug . . . injected . . . telepathic link established. No. Too many flaws: possible ego/control conflict. Impaired perceptions. Maybe it could be a hive creature injected for multiple p.o.v." A pause, then, "No. No good."

Talbot drew on the cigarette, letting the mysterious Eastern smoke curl through his lungs. "How about . . . say, just for the sake of discussion," Victor said, "say the ego-id exists to some extent in each sperm. It's been ventured. Raise the consciousness in one cell and send it on a mission to . . . forget it, that's metaphysical bullshit. Oh, damn damn damn . . . this will take time and thought, Larry. Go away, let me think on it. I'll get back to you."

Talbot butted the Sobranie on the railing, and exhaled the final stream of smoke. "Okay, Victor. I take it you're interested sufficiently to work at it."

"I'm a scientist, Larry. That means I'm hooked. I'd have to be an idiot not to be . . . this speaks directly to what . . . to what my father . . ."

"I understand. I'll let you alone. I'll wait."

They rode across in silence, the one thinking of solutions, the other considering the problems. When they parted, it was with an embrace.

Talbot flew back the next morning, and waited through the nights of the full moon, knowing better than to pray. It only muddied the waters. And angered the gods.

When the phone rang, and Talbot lifted the receiver, he knew what it would be. He had known *every* time the phone had rung, for over two months. "Mr. Talbot? Western Union. We have a cablegram for you, from Moldava, Czechoslovakia."

"Please read it."

"It's very short, sir. It says, 'Come immediately. The trail has been marked.' It's signed, 'Victor.' "

He departed less than an hour later. The Learjet had been on the ready line since he had returned from Budapest, fuel tanks regularly topped-off and flight-plan logged. His suitcase had been packed for seventy-two days, waiting beside the door, visas and passport current, and handily stored in an inner pocket. When he departed, the apartment continued to tremble for some time with the echoes of his leaving.

The flight seemed endless, interminable; he *knew* it was taking longer than necessary.

Customs, even with high government clearances (all masterpieces of forgery) and bribes, seemed to be drawn out sadistically by the mustached trio of petty officials; secure, and reveling in their momentary power.

The overland facilities could not merely be called slow. They were reminiscent of the Molasses Man who cannot run till he's warmed-up and who, when he's warmed-up, grows too soft to run.

Expectedly, like the most suspenseful chapter of a cheap gothic novel, a fierce electrical storm suddenly erupted out of the mountains when the ancient touring car was within a few miles of Talbot's destination. It rose up through the steep mountain pass, hurtling out of the sky, black as a grave, and swept across the road obscuring everything.

The driver, a taciturn man whose accent had marked him as a Serbian, held the big saloon to the center of the road with the tenacity of a rodeo rider, hands at ten till and ten after midnight on the wheel.

"Mister Talbot."

"Yes?"

"It grow worse. Will I turn back?"

"How much farther?"

"Perhaps seven kilometer."

Headlights caught the moment of uprootment as a small tree by the roadside toppled toward them. The driver spun the wheel and accelerated. They rushed past as naked branches scraped across the boot of the touring car with the sound of fingernails on a blackboard. Talbot found he had been holding his breath. Death was beyond him, yet the menace of the moment denied that knowledge.

"I have to get there."

"Then I go on. Be at ease."

Talbot settled back. He could see the Serb smiling in the rear-view mirror. Secure, he stared out the window. Branches of lightning shattered the darkness, causing the surrounding landscape to assume ominous, unsettling shapes.

Finally, he arrived.

The laboratory, an incongruous modernistic cube—bone white against the—again—ominous basalt of the looming prominences—sat high above the rutted road. They had been climbing steadily for hours and now, like carnivores waiting for the most opportune moment, the Carpathians loomed all around them.

The driver negotiated the final mile and a half up the access road to the laboratory with difficulty: tides of dark, topsoil-and-twig-laden water rushed past them.

Victor was waiting for him. Without extended greetings he had an associate take the suitcase, and he hurried Talbot to the sub-ground floor theater where a half dozen technicians moved quickly at their tasks, plying between enormous banks of controls and a huge glass plate hanging suspended from guy-wires beneath the track-laden ceiling.

The mood was one of highly-charged expectancy; Talbot could feel it in the sharp, short glances the technicians threw him, in the way Victor steered him by the arm, in the uncanny racehorse readiness of the peculiar-looking machines around which the men and women swarmed. And he sensed in Victor's manner that something new and wonderful was about to be born in this laboratory. That perhaps . . . at last . . . after so terribly, lightlessly long . . . peace waited for him in this white-tiled room. Victor was fairly bursting to talk.

"Final adjustments," he said, indicating two female technicians working at a pair of similar machines mounted opposite each other on the walls facing the glass plate. To Talbot, they looked like laser projectors of a highly complex design. The women were tracking them slowly left and right on their gimbals, accompanied by soft electrical humming. Victor let Talbot study them for a long moment, then said, "Not lasers. *Grasers*. Gamma Ray Amplification by Stimulated Emission of Radiation. Pay attention to them, they're at least half the heart of the answer to your problem."

The technicians took sightings across the room, through the glass, and nodded at each other. Then the older of the two, a woman in her fifties, called to Victor.

"On line, Doctor."

Victor waved acknowledgment, and turned back to Talbot. "We'd have been ready sooner, but this damned storm. It's been going on for a week. It wouldn't have hampered us but we had a freak lightning strike on our main transformer. The power supply was on emergency for several days and it's taken a while to get everything up to peak strength again."

A door opened in the wall of the gallery to Talbot's right. It opened slowly, as though it was heavy and the strength needed to force it was lacking. The yellow baked enamel plate on the door said, in heavy black letters, in French, PER-SONNEL MONITORING DEVICES ARE REQUIRED BEYOND THIS ENTRANCE. The door swung fully open, at last, and Talbot saw the warning plate on the other side:

CAUTION
RADIATION
AREA

There was a three-armed, triangular-shaped design beneath the words. He thought of the Father, the Son, and the Holy Ghost. For no rational reason.

Then he saw the sign beneath, and had his rational reason: OPENING THIS DOOR FOR MORE THAN 30 SECONDS WILL REQUIRE A SEARCH AND SECURE.

Talbot's attention was divided between the doorway and what Victor had said. "You seem worried about the storm."

"Not worried," Victor said, "just cautious. There's no conceivable way it could interfere with the experiment, unless we had another direct hit, which I doubt—we've taken special precautions—but I wouldn't want to risk the power going out in the middle of the shot."

"The shot?"

"I'll explain all that. In fact, I *have* to explain it, so your mite will have the knowledge." Victor smiled at Talbot's confusion. "Don't worry about it." An old woman in a lab smock had come through the door and now stood just behind and to the right of Talbot, waiting, clearly, for their conversation to end so she could speak to Victor.

Victor turned his eyes to her. "Yes, Nadja?"

Talbot looked at her. An acid rain began falling in his stomach.

"Yesterday considerable effort was directed toward finding the cause of a high field horizontal instability," she said, speaking softly, tonelessly, a page of some specific status report. "The attendant beam blowup prevented efficient extraction." Eighty, if a day. Gray eyes sunk deep in folds of crinkled flesh the color of liver paste. "During the afternoon the accelerator was shut down to effect several repairs." Withered, weary, bent, too many bones for the sack. "The super pinger at C48 was replaced with a section of vacuum chamber; it had a vacuum leak." Talbot was in extreme pain. Memories came at him in ravening hordes, a dark wave of ant bodies gnawing at everything soft and folded and vulnerable in his brain. "Two hours of beam time were lost during the owl shift because a solenoid failed on a new vacuum valve in the transfer hall."

"Mother . . . ?" Talbot said, whispering hoarsely.

The old woman started violently, her head coming around and her eyes of settled ashes widening. "Victor," she said, terror in the word.

Talbot barely moved, and Victor took him by the arm and held him. "Thank you, Nadja; go down to target station B and log the secondary beams. Go right now."

She moved past them, hobbling, and quickly vanished through another door in the far wall, held open for her by one of the younger women.

Talbot watched her go, tears in his eyes.

"Oh my God, Victor. It was . . ."

316

"No, Larry, it wasn't."

"It was. So help me God it *was!* But *how*, Victor, tell me *how?*"

Victor turned him and lifted his chin with his free hand. "Look at me, Larry. *Damn it*, I said *look at me:* it wasn't. You're wrong."

The last time Lawrence Talbot had cried had been the morning he had awakened from sleep, lying under hydrangea shrubs in the botanical garden next to the Minneapolis Museum of Art, lying beside something bloody and still. Under his fingernails had been caked flesh and dirt and blood. That had been the time he learned about manacles and releasing oneself from them when in one state of consciousness, but not in another. Now he felt like crying. Again. With cause.

"Wait here a moment," Victor said. "Larry? Will you wait right here for me? I'll be back in a moment."

He nodded, averting his face, and Victor went away. While he stood there, waves of painful memory thundering through him, a door slid open into the wall at the far side of the chamber, and another white-smocked technician stuck his head into the room. Through the opening, Talbot could see massive machinery in an enormous chamber beyond. Titanium electrodes. Stainless steel cones. He thought he recognized it: a Cockroft-Walton pre-accelerator.

Victor came back with a glass of milky liquid. He handed it to Talbot.

"Victor—" the male technician called from the far doorway.

"Drink it," Victor said to Talbot, then turned to the technician.

"Ready to run."

Victor waved to him. "Give me about ten minutes, Karl, then take it up to the first phase shift and signal us." The technician nodded understanding and vanished through the doorway; the door slid out of the wall and closed, hiding the imposing chamberfull of equipment. "And that was part of the other half of the mystical, magical solution to your problem," the physicist said, smiling now like a proud father.

"What was that I drank?"

"Something to stabilize you. I can't have you hallucinating."

"I wasn't hallucinating. What was her name?"

"Nadja. You're wrong; you've never seen her before in

317

your life. Have I ever lied to you? How far back do we know each other? I need your trust if this is going to be all the way."

"I'll be all right." The milky liquid had already begun to work. Talbot's face lost its flush, his hands ceased trembling.

Victor was very stern suddenly, a scientist without the time for sidetracks; there was information to be imparted. "Good; for a moment I thought I'd spent a great deal of time preparing . . . well," and he smiled again, quickly. "Let me put it this way: I thought for a moment no one was coming to my party."

Talbot gave a strained, tiny chuckle, and followed Victor to a bank of television monitors set into rolling frame-stacks in a corner. "Okay. Let's get you briefed." He turned on sets, one after another, till all twelve were glowing, each one holding a scene of dull-finished and massive installations.

Monitor #1 showed an endlessly long underground tunnel painted eggshell white. Talbot had spent much of his two-month wait reading; he recognized the tunnel as a view down the "straightaway" of the main ring. Gigantic bending magnets in their shockproof concrete cradles glowed faintly in the dim light of the tunnel.

Monitor #2 showed the linac tunnel.

Monitor #3 showed the rectifier stack of the Cockroft-Walton pre-accelerator.

Monitor #4 was a view of the booster. Monitor #5 showed the interior of the transfer hall. Monitors #6 through #9 revealed three experimental target areas and, smaller in scope and size, an internal target area supporting the meson, neutrino and proton areas.

The remaining three monitors showed research areas in the underground lab complex, the final one of which was the main hall itself, where Talbot stood looking into twelve monitors, in the twelfth screen of which could be seen Talbot standing looking into twelve . . .

Victor turned off the sets.

All Talbot could think of was the old woman called Nadja. It *couldn't* be. "Larry! What did you see?"

"From what I could see," Talbot said, "that looked to be a particle accelerator. And it looked as big as CERN's proton synchrotron in Geneva."

Victor was impressed. "You've been doing some reading."

"It behooved me."

"Well, well. Let's see if I can impress *you*. CERN's accelerator reaches energies up to 33 BeV; the ring underneath this room reaches energies of 15 GeV."

"Giga meaning trillion."

"You have *been* reading up, haven't you! Fifteen *trillion* electron volts. There's simply no keeping secrets from you, is there, Larry?"

"Only one."

Victor waited expectantly.

"Can you do it?"

"Yes. Meteorology says the eye is almost passing over us. We'll have better than an hour, more than enough time for the dangerous parts of the experiment."

"But you *can* do it."

"Yes, Larry. I don't like having to say it twice." There was no hesitancy in his voice, none of the "yes but" equivocations he'd always heard before. Victor had found the trail.

"I'm sorry, Victor. Anxiety. But if we're ready, why do I have to go through an indoctrination?"

Victor grinned wryly and began reciting, "As your Wizard, I am about to embark on a hazardous and technically unexplainable journey to the upper stratosphere. To confer, converse, and otherwise hobnob with my fellow wizards."

Talbot threw up his hands. "No more."

"Okay, then. Pay attention. If I didn't have to, I wouldn't; believe me, nothing is more boring than listening to the sound of my own lectures. But your mite has to have all the data *you* have. So listen. Now comes the boring—but incredibly informative—explanation."

Western Europe's CERN—*Conseil Européen pour la Recherche Nucléaire*—had settled on Geneva as the site for their Big Machine. Holland lost out on the rich plum because it was common knowledge the food was lousy in the Lowlands. A small matter, but a significant one.

The Eastern Bloc's CEERN—*Conseil de l'Europe de l'Est pour la Recherche Nucléaire*—had been forced into selecting this isolated location high in the White Carpathians (over such likelier and more hospitable sites as Cluj in Rumania, Budapest in Hungary and Gdańsk in Poland) because Talbot's friend Victor had selected this site. CERN had had Dahl and Wideroë and Goward and Adams and Reich; CEERN had Victor. It balanced. He could call the tune.

So the laboratory had been painstakingly built to his specifications, and the particle accelerator dwarfed the CERN

Machine. It dwarfed the four-mile ring at the National Accelerator Lab in Batavia, Illinois. It was, in fact, the world's largest, most advanced "synchrophasotron."

Only seventy per cent of the experiments conducted in the underground laboratory were devoted to projects sponsored by CEERN. One hundred per cent of the staff of Victor's complex were personally committed to him, not to CEERN, not to the Eastern Bloc, not to philosophies or dogmas . . . to the man. So thirty per cent of the experiments run on the sixteen-mile-diameter accelerator ring were Victor's own. If CEERN knew—and it would have been difficult for them to find out—it said nothing. Seventy per cent of the fruits of genius was better than no per cent.

Had Talbot known earlier that Victor's research was thrust in the direction of actualizing advanced theoretical breakthroughs in the nature of the structure of fundamental particles, he would never have wasted his time with the pseudos and deadenders who had spent years on his problem, who had promised everything and delivered nothing but dust. But then, until Information Associates had marked the trail—a trail he had previously followed in every direction but the unexpected one that merged shadow with substance, reality with fantasy—until then, he had had no need for Victor's exotic talents.

While CEERN basked in the warmth of secure knowledge that their resident genius was keeping them in front in the Super Accelerator Sweepstakes, Victor was briefing his oldest friend on the manner in which he would gift him with the peace of death; the manner in which Lawrence Talbot would find his soul; the manner in which he would precisely and exactly go inside his own body.

"The answer to your problem is in two parts. First, we have to create a perfect simulacrum of you, a hundred thousand or a million times smaller than you, the original. Then, second, we have to *actualize* it, turn an image into something corporeal, material, something that exists. A miniature *you* with all the reality you possess, all the memories, all the knowledge."

Talbot felt very mellow. The milky liquid had smoothed out the churning waters of his memory. He smiled. "I'm glad it wasn't a difficult problem."

Victor looked rueful. "Next week I invent the steam engine. Get serious, Larry."

"It's that Lethe cocktail you fed me."

320

Victor's mouth tightened and Talbot knew he had to get hold of himself. "Go on, I'm sorry."

Victor hesitated a moment, securing his position of seriousness with a touch of free-floating guilt, then went on, "The first part of the problem is solved by using the Grasers we've developed. We'll shoot a hologram of you, using a wave generated not from the electrons of the atom, but from the nucleus . . . a wave a million times shorter, greater in resolution than that from a Laser." He walked toward the large glass plate hanging in the middle of the lab, Grasers trained on its center. "Come here."

Talbot followed him.

"Is this the holographic plate," he said, "it's just a sheet of photographic glass, isn't it?"

"Not this," Victor said, touching the ten-foot square plate, *"This!"* He put his finger on a spot in the center of the glass and Talbot leaned in to look. He saw nothing at first, then detected a faint ripple; and when he put his face as close as possible to the imperfection he perceived a light *moiré* pattern, like the surface of a fine silk scarf. He looked back at Victor.

"Microholographic plate," Victor said. "Smaller than an integrated chip. That's where we capture your spirit, white-eyes, a million times reduced. About the size of a single cell, maybe a red corpuscle."

Talbot giggled.

"Come on," Victor said wearily. "You've had too much to drink, and it's my fault. Let's get this show on the road. You'll be straight by the time we're ready . . . I just hope to God your mite isn't cockeyed."

They stood him, naked, in front of the ground photographic plate. The older of the female technicians aimed the Graser at him, there was a soft sound Talbot took to be some mechanism locking into position, and then Victor said, "All right, Larry, that's it."

He stared at them, expecting more.

"That's it?"

The technicians seemed very pleased, and amused at his reaction. "All done," said Victor. It had been that quick. He hadn't even seen the Graser wave hit and lock-in his image. "That's *it?*" he said again. Victor began to laugh. It spread through the lab. The technicians were clinging to their equipment; tears rolled down Victor's cheeks; everyone gasped for breath; and Talbot stood in front of the minute imperfection in the glass and felt like a retard.

"That's it?" he said again, helplessly.

After a long time, they dried their eyes and Victor moved him away from the huge plate of glass. "All done, Larry, and ready to go. Are you cold?"

Talbot's naked flesh was evenly polka dotted with goosebumps. One of the technicians brought him a smock to wear, then ignored him. Talbot stood and watched. Clearly, he was no longer the center of attention.

Now the alternate Graser and the holographic plate ripple in the glass were the focuses of attention. Now the mood of released tension was past and the lines of serious attention were back in the faces of the lab staff. Now Victor was wearing an intercom headset, and Talbot heard him say, "All right, Karl. Bring it up to full power."

Almost instantly the lab was filled with the sound of generators phasing up. It became painful and Talbot felt his teeth begin to ache. It went up and up, a whine that climbed till it was beyond his hearing.

Victor made a hand signal to the younger female technician at the Graser behind the glass plate. She bent to the projector's sighting mechanism once, quickly, then cut it in. Talbot saw no light beam, but there was the same locking sound he had heard earlier, and then a soft humming, and a life-size hologram of himself, standing naked as he had been a few moments before, trembled in the air where he had stood. He looked at Victor questioningly. Victor nodded, and Talbot walked to the phantasm, passed his hand through it, stood close and looked into the clear brown eyes, noted the wide pore patterns in the flesh covering his nose, studied himself more closely than he had ever been able to do in a mirror. He felt: as if someone had walked over his grave.

Victor was talking to three male technicians, and a moment later they came to examine the hologram. They moved in with light meters and sensitive instruments that apparently were capable of gauging the sophistication and clarity of the ghost image. Talbot watched, fascinated and terrified. It seemed he was about to embark on the great journey of his life; a journey with a much-desired destination: surcease.

One of the technicians signaled Victor.

"It's pure," Victor said to Talbot. Then, to the younger female technician on the second Graser projector, "All right, Jana, move it out of there." She started up an engine and the entire projector apparatus turned on heavy rubber wheels and rolled out of the way. The image of Talbot, naked and vulnerable, a little sad to Talbot as he watched it fade and vanish like morning mist, had disappeared when the technician turned off the projector.

"All right, Karl," Victor was saying, "we're moving the pedestal in now. Narrow the aperture, and wait for my signal." Then, to Talbot, "Here comes your mite, old friend."

Talbot felt a sense of resurrection.

The older female technician rolled a four foot high stainless steel pedestal to the center of the lab, positioned it so the tiny, high-polished spindle atop the pedestal touched the very bottom of the faint ripple in the glass. It looked like, and was, an actualizing stage for the real test. The full-sized hologram had been a gross test to insure the image's perfection. Now came the creation of a living entity, a Lawrence Talbot, naked and the size of a single cell, possessing a consciousness and intelligence and memories and desires identical to Talbot's own.

"Ready, Karl?" Victor was saying.

Talbot heard no reply, but Victor nodded his head as if listening. Then he said,"All right, extract the beam!"

It happened so fast, Talbot missed most of it.

The micropion beam was composed of particles a million times smaller than the proton, smaller than the quark, smaller than the muon or the pion. Victor had termed them micropions. The slit opened in the wall, the beam was diverted, passed through the holographic ripple and was cut off as the slit closed again.

It had all taken a billionth of a second.

"Done," Victor said.

"I don't see anything," Talbot said, and realized how silly he must sound to these people. Of *course* he didn't see anything. There was nothing to see . . . with the naked eye. "Is he . . . is it there?"

"You're there," Victor said. He waved to one of the male technicians standing at a wall hutch of instruments in protective bays, and the man hurried over with the slim, reflective barrel of a microscope. He clipped it onto the tiny needle-pointed stand atop the pedestal in a fashion Talbot could not quite follow. Then he stepped away, and Victor said, "Part two of your problem solved, Larry. Go look and see yourself."

Lawrence Talbot went to the microscope, adjusted the

knob till he could see the reflective surface of the spindle, and saw himself in infinitely reduced perfection

staring up at himself. He recognized himself, though all he could see was a cyclopean brown eye staring down from the smooth glass satellite that dominated his sky.

He waved. The eye blinked.

Now it begins, he thought.

Lawrence Talbot stood at the lip of the huge crater that formed Lawrence Talbot's navel. He looked down into the bottomless pit with its atrophied remnants of umbilicus forming loops and protuberances, smooth and undulant and vanishing into utter darkness. He stood poised to descend and smelled the smells of his own body. First, sweat. Then the smells that wafted up from within. The smell of penicillin like biting down on tin foil with a bad tooth. The smell of aspirin, chalky and tickling the hairs of his nose like cleaning blackboard erasers by banging them together. The smells of rotted food, digested and turning to waste. All the odors rising up out of himself like a wild symphony of dark colors.

He sat down on the rounded rim of the navel and let himself slip forward.

He slid down, rode over an outcropping, dropped a few feet and slid again, tobogganing into darkness. He fell for only a short time, then brought up against the soft and yielding, faintly springy tissue plane where the umbilicus had been ligated. The darkness at the bottom of the hole suddenly shattered as blinding light filled the navel. Shielding his eyes, Talbot looked up the shaft toward the sky. A sun glowed there, brighter than a thousand novae. Victor had moved a surgical lamp over the hole to assist him. For as long as he could.

Talbot saw the umbra of something large moving behind the light; he strained to discern what it was: it seemed important to know what it was. And for an instant, before his eyes closed against the glare, he thought he knew what it had been. Someone watching him, staring down past the surgical lamp that hung above the naked, anesthetized body of Lawrence Talbot, asleep on an operating table.

It had been the old woman, Nadja.

He stood unmoving for a long time, thinking of her.

Then he went to his knees and felt the tissue plane that formed the floor of the navel shaft.

He thought he could see something moving beneath the surface, like water flowing under a film of ice. He went down onto his stomach and cupped his hands around his eyes, putting his face against the dead flesh. It was like looking through a pane of isinglass. A trembling membrane through which he could see the collapsed lumen of the atretic umbilical vein. There was no opening. He pressed his palms against the rubbery surface and it gave, but only slightly. Before he could fine the treasure, he had to follow the route of Demeter's map—now firmly and forever consigned to memory—and before he could set foot upon that route, he had to gain access to his own body.

But he had nothing with which to force that entrance.

Excluded, standing at the portal to his own body, Lawrence Talbot felt anger rising within him. His life had been anguish and guilt and horror, had been the wasted result of events over which he had no control. Pentagrams and full moons and blood and never putting on even an ounce of fat because of a diet high in protein, blood steroids healthier than any normal adult male's, triglycerol and cholesterol levels balanced and humming. And death forever a stranger. Anger flooded through him. He heard an inarticulate little moan of pain, and fell forward, began tearing at the atrophied cord with teeth that had been used for similar activity many times before. Through a blood haze he knew he was savaging his own body, and it seemed exactly the appropriate act of self-flagellation.

An outsider; he had been an outsider all his adult life, and fury would permit him to be shut out no longer. With demonic purpose he ripped away at the clumps of flesh until the membrane gave, at last, and a gap was torn through opening him to himself . . .

And he was blinded by the explosion of light, by the rush of wind, by the passage of something that had been just beneath the surface writhing to be set free, and in the instant before he plummeted into unconsciousness he knew Castañeda's Don Juan had told the truth: a thick bundle of white cobwebby filaments, tinged with gold, fibers of light, shot free from the collapsed vein, rose up through the shaft and trembled toward the antiseptic sky.

A metaphysical, otherwise invisible beanstalk that trailed away above him, rising up and up and up as his eyes closed and he sank away into oblivion.

He was on his stomach, crawling through the collapsed lumen, the center, of the path the veins had taken back from the amniotic sac to the fetus. Propelling himself forward the way an infantry scout would through dangerous terrain, using elbows and knees, frog-crawling, he opened the flattened tunnel with his head just enough to get through. It was quite light, the interior of the world called Lawrence Talbot suffused with a golden luminescence.

The map had routed him out of this pressed tunnel through the inferior vena cava to the right atrium and thence through the right ventricle, the pulmonary arteries, through the valves, to the lungs, the pulmonary veins, crossover to the left side of the heart (left atrium, left ventricle), the aorta—bypassing the three coronary arteries above the aortic valves—and down over the arch of the aorta—bypassing the carotid and other arteries—to the celiac trunk where the arteries split in a confusing array; the gastro-duodenal to the stomach, the hepatic to the liver, the splenic to the spleen. And there, dorsal to the body of the diaphragm, he would drop down past the greater pancreatic duct to the pancreas itself. And there, among the islets of Langerhans, he would find, at the coordinates Information Associates had given him, he would find that which had been stolen from him one full-mooned night of horror so very long ago. And having found it, having assured himself of eternal sleep, not merely physical death from a silver bullet, he would stop his heart—how, he did not know, but he would—and it would all be ended for Lawrence Talbot, who had become what he had beheld. There, in the tail of the pancreas, supplied with blood by the splenic artery, lay the greatest treasure of all. More than doubloons, more than spices and silks, more than oil lamps used as djinn prisons by Solomon, lay final and sweet eternal peace, a release from monsterdom.

He pushed the final few feet of dead vein apart, and his head emerged into open space. He was hanging upside-down in a cave of deep orange rock.

Talbot wriggled his arms loose, braced them against what was clearly the ceiling of the cave, and wrenched his body out of the tunnel. He fell heavily, trying to twist at the last moment to catch the impact on his shoulders, and received a nasty blow on the side of the neck for his trouble.

He lay there for a moment, clearing his head. Then he stood and walked forward. The cave opened onto a ledge, and he walked out and stared at the landscape before him.

The skeleton of something only faintly human lay tortuously crumpled against the wall of the cliff. He was afraid to look at it very closely.

He stared off across the world of dead orange rock, folded and rippled like a topographical view across the frontal lobe of a brain removed from its cranial casing.

The sky was a light yellow, bright and pleasant.

The grand canyon of his body was a seemingly horizonless tumble of atrophied rock, dead for millennia. He sought out and found a descent from the ledge, and began the trek.

There was water, and it kept him alive. Apparently, it rained more frequently here in this parched and stunned wasteland than appearance indicated. There was no keeping track of days or months, for there was no night and no day—always the same even, wonderful golden luminescence—but Talbot felt his passage down the central spine of orange mountains had taken him almost six months. And in that time it had rained forty-eight times, or roughly twice a week. Baptismal founts of water were filled at every downpour, and he found if he kept the soles of his naked feet moist, he could walk without his energy flagging. If he ate, he did not remember how often, nor what form the food had taken.

He saw no other signs of life.

Save an occasional skeleton lying against a shadowed wall of orange rock. Often, they had no skulls.

He found a pass through the mountains, finally, and crossed. He went up through foothills into lower, gentle slopes, and then up again, into cruel and narrow passages that wound higher and higher toward the heat of the sky. When he reached the summit, he found the path down the opposite side was straight and wide and easy. He descended quickly; only a matter of days, it seemed.

Descending into the valley, he heard the song of a bird. He followed the sound. It led him to a crater of igneous rock, quite large, set low among the grassy swells of the valley. He came upon it without warning, and trudged up its short incline, to stand at the volcanic lip looking down.

The crater had become a lake. The smell rose up to assault him. Vile, and somehow terribly sad. The song of a bird continued; he could see no bird anywhere in the golden sky. The smell of the lake made him ill.

Then as he sat on the edge of the crater, staring down, he

327

realized the lake was filled with dead things, floating belly-up; purple and blue as a strangled baby, rotting white, turning slowly in the faintly rippled gray water; without features or limbs. He went down to the lowest outthrust of volcanic rock and stared at the dead things.

Something swam toward him. He moved back. It came on faster, and as it neared the wall of the crater, it surfaced, singing its bluejay song, swerved to rip a chunk of rotting flesh from the corpse of a floating dead thing, and paused only a moment as if to remind him that this was not his, Talbot's domain, but its own.

Like Talbot, the fish would not die.

Talbot sat at the lip of the crater for a long time, looking down into the bowl that held the lake, and he watched the corpses of dead dreams as they bobbed and revolved like maggoty pork in a gray soup.

After a time, he rose, walked back down from the mouth of the crater, and resumed his journey. He was crying.

When at last he reached the shore of the pancreatic sea, he found a great many things he had lost or given away when he was a child. He found a wooden machine gun on a tripod, painted olive drab, that made a rat-tat-tatting sound when a wooden handle was cranked. He found a set of toy soldiers, two companies, one Prussian and the other French, with a miniature Napoleon Bonaparte among them. He found a microscope kit with slides and petri dishes and racks of chemicals in nice little bottles, all of which bore uniform labels. He found a milk bottle filled with Indian head pennies. He found a hand puppet with the head of a monkey and the name *Roscoe* painted on the fabric glove with nail polish. He found a pedometer. He found a beautiful painting of a jungle bird that had been done with real feathers. He found a corncob pipe. He found a box of radio premiums: a cardboard detective kit with fingerprint dusting powder, invisible ink and a list of police band call codes; a ring with what seemed to be a plastic bomb attached, and when he pulled the red-finned rear section off the bomb, and cupped his hands around it in his palms, he could see little scintillae of light, deep inside the payload section; a china mug with a little girl and a dog running across one side; a decoding badge with a burning glass in the center of the red plastic dial.

But something was missing.

He could not remember what it was, but he knew it was

important. As he had known it was important to recognize the shadowy figure who had moved past the surgical lamp at the top of the navel shaft, he knew whatever item was missing from this cache . . . was very important.

He took the boat anchored beside the ¡pancreatic sea, and put all the items from the cache in the bottom of the watertight box under one of the seats. He kept out the large, cathedral-shaped radio, and put it on the bench seat in front of the oarlocks.

Then he unbeached the boat, and ran it out into the crimson water, staining his ankles and calves and thighs, and climbed aboard, and started rowing across toward the islets. Whatever was missing, was very important.

The wind died when the islets were barely in sight on the horizon. Looking out across the blood-red sea, Talbot sat becalmed at latitude 38° 54′ N, longitude 77° 00′ 13″ W.

He drank from the sea and was nauseated. He played with the toys in the watertight box. And he listened to the radio.

He listened to a program about a very fat man who solved murders, to an adaptation of *The Woman in the Window* with Edward G. Robinson and Joan Bennett, to a story that began in a great railroad station, to a mystery about a wealthy man who could make himself invisible by clouding the minds of others so they could not see him, and he enjoyed a suspense drama narrated by a man named Ernest Chapell in which a group of people descended in a bathyscaphe through the bottom of a mine shaft where, five miles down, they were attacked by pterodactyls. Then he listened to the news, broadcast by Graham MacNamee. Among the human interest items at the close of the program, Talbot heard the unforgettable MacNamee voice say:

"Datelined Columbus, Ohio; September 24th, 1973. Martha Nelson has been in an institution for the mentally retarded for 98 years. She is 102 years old and was first sent to Orient State Institute near Orient, Ohio, on June 25th, 1875. Her records were destroyed in a fire in the institution some time in 1882, and no one knows for certain why she is at the institute. At the time she was committed, it was known as the Columbus State Institute for the Feeble-Minded. 'She never had a chance,' said Dr. A. Z. Soforenko, appointed two months ago as superintendent of the institution. He said she was probably a victim of 'eugenic alarm,' which he said was common in the late 1800s. At that time some felt that be-

329

cause humans were made 'in God's image' the retarded must be evil or children of the devil, because they were not whole human beings. 'During that time,' Dr. Soforenko said, 'it was believed if you moved feeble-minded people out of a community and into an institution, the taint would never return to the community.' He went on to add, 'She was apparently trapped in that system of thought. No one can ever be sure if she actually *was* feeble-minded; it is a wasted life. She is quite coherent for her age. She has no known relatives and has had no contact with anybody but Institution staff for the last 78 or 80 years.' "

Talbot sat silently in the small boat, the sail hanging like a forlorn ornament from its single centerpole.

"I've cried more since I got inside you, Talbot, than I have in my whole life," he said, but could not stop. Thoughts of Martha Nelson, a woman of whom he had never before heard, of whom he would *never* have heard had it not been by chance by chance by chance he had heard by chance, by chance thoughts of her skirled through his mind like cold winds.

And the cold winds rose, and the sail filled, and he was no longer adrift, but was driven straight to the shore of the nearest islet. By chance.

He stood over the spot where Demeter's map had indicated he would find his soul. For a wild moment he chuckled, at the realization he had been expecting an enormous Maltese Cross or Capt. Kidd's "X" to mark the location. But it was only soft green sand, gentle as talc, blowing in dust-devils toward the blood-red pancreatic sea. The spot was midway between the low tide line and the enormous Bedlam-like structure that dominated the islet.

He looked once more, uneasily, at the fortress rising in the center of the tiny blemish of land. It was built square, seemingly carved from a single monstrous black rock . . . perhaps from a cliff that had been thrust up during some natural disaster. It had no windows, no opening he could see, though two sides of its bulk were exposed to his view. It troubled him. It was a dark god presiding over an empty kingdom. He thought of the fish that would not die, and remembered Nietzsche's contention that gods die when they lose their supplicants.

He dropped to his knees and, recalling the moment months before when he had dropped to his knees to tear at the flesh

330

of his atrophied umbilical cord, he began digging in the green and powdery sand.

The more he dug, the faster the sand ran back into the shallow bowl. As in a nightmare, it ran back ceaselessly. He stepped into the middle of the depression and began slinging dirt back between his legs with both hands, a human dog excavating for a bone.

When his fingertips encountered the edge of the box, he yelped with pain as his nails broke.

He dug around the outline of the box, and then forced his bleeding fingers down through the sand to gain purchase under the buried shape. He wrenched at it, and it came loose. Heaving with tensed muscles, he freed it.

He took it to the edge of the beach and sat down.

It was just a box. A plain old wooden box, very much like an old cigar box, but larger. He turned it over and over and was not at all surprised to find it bore no arcane hieroglyphics or occult symbols. It wasn't that kind of treasure. Then he turned it right side up and pried open the lid. His soul was inside. It was not what he had expected to find, not at all. But it *was* what had been missing from the cache.

Holding it tightly in his fist, he walked up past the fast-filling hole in the green sand, toward the bastion on the high ground.

> *We shall not cease from exploration*
> *And the end of all our exploring*
> *Will be to arrive where we started*
> *And know the place for the first time.*
> ——T. S. Eliot

Once inside the brooding darkness of the fortress—and finding the entrance had been disturbingly easier than he had expected—there was no way to go but down. The wet, black stones of the switchback stairways led inexorably downward into the bowels of the structure, clearly far beneath the level of the pancreatic sea. The stairs were steep, and each step had been worn into smooth curves by the pressure of feet that had descended this way since the dawn of memory. It was dark, but not so dark that Talbot could not see his way. There was no light, however. He did not care to think about how that could be.

When he came to the deepest part of the structure, having passed no rooms or chambers or openings along the way, he

331

saw a doorway across an enormous hall, set into the far wall. He stepped off the last of the stairs, and walked to the door. It was built of crossed iron bars, as black and moist as the stones of the bastion. Through the interstices he saw something pale and still in a far corner of what could have been a cell.

There was no lock on the door.

It swung open at his touch.

Whoever lived in this cell had never tried to open the door; or having tried, and succeeded, had decided not to leave.

He moved into deeper darkness.

A long time of silence passed, and finally he stooped to help her to her feet. It was like lifting a sack of dead flowers, brittle and surrounded by dead air incapable of holding even the memory of fragrance.

He took her in his arms and carried her.

"Close your eyes against the light, Martha," he said, and started back up the long stairway to the golden sky.

Lawrence Talbot sat up on the operating table. He opened his eyes and looked at Victor. He smiled a peculiarly gentle smile. For the first time since they had been friends, Victor saw all torment cleansed from Talbot's face.

"It went well," he said. Talbot nodded.

They grinned at each other.

"How're your cryogenic facilities?" Talbot asked.

Victor's brows drew down in bemusement. "You want me to freeze you? I thought you'd want something more permanent . . . say, in silver."

"Not necessary."

Talbot looked around. He saw her standing against the far wall by one of the Grasers. She looked back at him with open fear. He slid off the table, wrapping the sheet upon which he had rested around himself, a makeshift toga. It gave him a patrician look.

He went to her and looked down into her ancient face. "Nadja," he said softly. After a long moment she looked up at him. He smiled and for an instant she was a girl again. She averted her gaze. He took her hand, and she came with him, to the table, to Victor.

"I'd be deeply grateful for a running account, Larry," the physicist said. So Talbot told him; all of it.

"My mother, Nadja, Martha Nelson, they're all the same," Talbot said, when he came to the end, "all wasted lives."

332

"And what was in the box?" Victor said.

"How well do you do with symbolism and cosmic irony, old friend?"

"Thus far I'm doing well enough with Jung and Freud," Victor said. He could not help but smile.

Talbot held tightly to the old technician's hand as he said, "It was an old, rusted Howdy Doody button."

Victor turned around.

When he turned back, Talbot was grinning. "That's not cosmic irony, Larry . . . it's slapstick," Victor said. He was angry. It showed clearly.

Talbot said nothing, simply let him work it out.

Finally Victor said, "What the hell's *that* supposed to signify? Innocence?"

Talbot shrugged. "I suppose if I'd known, I wouldn't have lost it in the first place. That's what it was, and that's what it is. A little metal pinback about an inch and a half in diameter, with that cockeyed face on it, the orange hair, the toothy grin, the pug nose, the freckles, all of it, just the way he always was." He fell silent, then after a moment added, "It seems right."

"And now that you have it back, you don't *want* to die."

"I don't *need* to die."

"And you want me to freeze you."

"Both of us."

Victor stared at him with disbelief. "For God's sake, Larry!"

Nadja stood quietly, as if she could not hear them.

"Victor, listen: Martha Nelson is in there. A wasted life. Nadja is out here. I don't know why or how or what did it . . . but . . . a wasted life. Another wasted life. I want you to create her mite, the same way you created mine, and send her inside. He's waiting for her, and he can make it right, Victor. All right, at last. He can be with her as she regains the years that were stolen from her. He can be—*I* can be—her father when she's a baby, her playmate when she's a child, her buddy when she's maturing, her boy friend when she's a young girl, her suitor when she's a young woman, her lover, her husband, her companion as she grows old. Let her be all the women she was never permitted to be, Victor. Don't steal from her a second time. And when it's over, it will start again . . ."

"*How*, for Christ sake, how the hell *how?* Talk sense, Larry! What is all this metaphysical crap?"

"I don't *know* how; it just is! I've been there, Victor, I was there for months, maybe years, and I never changed, never went to the wolf; there's no Moon there . . . no night and no day, just golden light and warmth, and I can try to make restitution. I can give back two lives. *Please*, Victor!"

The physicist looked at him without speaking. Then he looked at the old woman. She smiled up at him, and then, with arthritic fingers, removed her clothing.

When she came through the collapsed lumen, Talbot was waiting for her. She looked very tired, and he knew she would have to rest before they attempted to cross the orange mountains. He helped her free herself from the ceiling of the cave, and laid her down on soft, pale yellow moss he had carried back from the islets of Langerhans during the long trek with Martha Nelson. Side-by-side, the two old women lay on the moss, and Nadja fell asleep almost immediately. He stood over them, looking at their faces.

They were identical.

Then he went out on the ledge and stood looking toward the spine of the orange mountains. The skeleton held no fear for him now. He felt a sudden sharp chill in the air and knew Victor had begun the cryogenic preservation.

He stood that way for a long time, the little metal button with the sly, innocent face of a mythical creature painted on its surface in four brilliant colors held tightly in his left hand.

After a while, he heard the crying of a baby, just one baby, from inside the cave, and turned to return for the start of the easiest journey he had ever made.

Somewhere, a terrible devil-fish suddenly flattened its gills, turned slowly belly-up, and sank into darkness.

Larry Niven

Remember I said in the general introduction that I don't say anything about the stories in these story introductions because I didn't select them and it was therefore inappropriate for me to make comments?

But I'm only human and I would like to make a comment on *classes* of stories. There are, after all, all kinds and varieties of science fiction (which is good, for the more kinds and varieties, the more flourishing and healthy the field). The trouble is that I don't like them all equally. Nobody does. Everyone has his preferences.

There are the funny or grisly science-fantasies, and the heroic or bloody sword-and-sorceries, and the artistic or puzzling new-waves, and the clever or satiric social-futures, and so on. All have their points; each pleases some of the readers most of the time and all of the readers some of the time.

But then there is something which is called, for want of any other title, "hard science fiction." That is the kind of science fiction that deals with science. The authors know science and use part of the story wordage to explain some interesting scientific point that manages to drive the story, set up the catastrophe, or resolve the problem.

That's the kind of stuff I like to write and that's the kind of stuff I like to read. Most of the writers who do it, like myself and Arthur Clarke and Hal Clement, are old-timers dating back to the early days of the Campbell era, and that would ordinarily make me feel as though we are part of a vanishing breed. I would be sad because all the soft science fiction in the world wouldn't compensate me (and the others who think like me, if any) for the loss of the hard.

But then I realize that there are new hard science fiction writers, too, entering the field all the time. There's Larry Niven, for instance, who had one story in Volume Two and two stories in Volume Three and who has won Hugos in the novel category as well. And when I think of that, I'm glad, and I feel that the world may survive after all.

THE HOLE MAN

One day Mars will be gone.

Andrew Lear says that it will start with violent quakes, and end hours or days later, very suddenly. He ought to know. It's all his fault.

Lear also says that it won't happen for from years to centuries. So we stay, Lear and the rest of us. We study the alien base for what it can tell us, while the center of the world we stand on is slowly eaten away. Its enough to give a man nightmares.

It was Lear who found the alien base.

We had reached Mars: fourteen of us, in the cramped bulbous life-support system of the *Percival Lowell*. We were circling in orbit, taking our time, correcting our maps and looking for anything that thirty years of Mariner probes might have missed.

We were mapping mascons, among other things. Those mass concentrations under the lunar maria were almost certainly left by good-sized asteroids, mountains of rock falling silently out of the sky until they struck with the energies of thousands of fusion bombs. Mars has been cruising through the asteroid belt for four billion years. Mars would show bigger and better mascons. They would affect our orbits.

So Andrew Lear was hard at work, watching pens twitch on graph paper as we circled Mars. A bit of machinery fell alongside the *Percival Lowell*, rotating. Within its thin shell was a weighted double lever system, deceptively simple: a Forward Mass Detector. The pens mapped its twitchings.

Over Sirbonis Palus, they began mapping strange curves.

Another man might have cursed and tried to fix it. Andrew Lear thought it out, then sent the signal that would stop the free-falling widget from rotating.

It had to be rotating to map a stationary mass.

But now it was mapping simple sine waves.

Lear went running to Captain Childrey.

Running? It was more like trapeze artistry. Lear pulled himself along by handholds, kicked off from walls, braked with a hard push of hands or feet. Moving in free fall is hard work when you're in a hurry, and Lear was a forty-year-old astrophysicist, not an athlete. He was blowing hard when he reached the control bubble.

Childrey—who *was* an athlete—waited with a patient, slightly contemptuous smile while Lear caught his breath.

He already thought Lear was crazy. Lear's words only confirmed it. "Gravity for sending signals? Dr. Lear, will you please quit bothering me with your weird ideas. I'm busy. We all are."

This was not entirely unfair. Some of Lear's enthusiasms were peculiar. Gravity generators. Black holes. He thought we should be searching for Dyson spheres: stars completely enclosed by an artificial shell. He believed that mass and inertia were two separate things: that it should be possible to suck the inertia out of a spacecraft, say, so that it could accelerate to near lightspeed in a few minutes. He was a wide-eyed dreamer, and when he was flustered he tended to wander from the point.

"You don't understand," he told Childrey. "Gravity radiation is harder to block than electromagnetic waves. Patterned gravity waves would be easy to detect. The advanced civilizations in the galaxy may all be communicating by gravity. Some of them may even be modulating pulsars—rotating neutron stars. That's where Project Ozma went wrong: they were only looking for signals in the electromagnetic spectrum."

Childrey laughed. "Sure. Your little friends are using neutron stars to send you messages. What's that got to do with us?"

"Well, look!" Lear held up the strip of flimsy, nearly weightless paper he'd torn from the machine. "I got this over Sirbonis Palus. I think we ought to land there."

"We're landing in Mare Cimmerium, as you perfectly well know. The lander is already deployed and ready to board. Dr. Lear, we've spent four days mapping this area. It's flat. It's in a green-brown area. When spring comes next month, we'll find out whether there's life there! And everybody wants it that way except you!"

Lear was still holding the graph paper before him like a shield. "Please. Take one more circuit over Sirbonis Palus."

Childrey opted for the extra orbit. Maybe the sine waves convinced him. Maybe not. He would have liked inconveniencing the rest of us in Lear's name, to show him for a fool.

But the next pass showed a tiny circular feature in Sirbonis Palus. And Lear's mass indicator was making sine waves again.

The aliens had gone. During our first few months we always expected them back any minute. The machinery in the base was running smoothly and perfectly, as if the owners had only just stepped out.

The base was an inverted pie plate two stories high, and windowless. The air inside was breathable, like Earth's air three miles up, but with a bit more oxygen. Mars's air is far thinner, and poisonous. Clearly they were not of Mars.

The walls were thick and deeply eroded. They leaned inward against the internal pressure. The roof was somewhat thinner, just heavy enough for the pressure to support it. Both walls and roof were of fused Martian dust.

The heating system still worked—and it was also the lighting system: grids in the ceiling glowing brick red. The base was always ten degrees too warm. We didn't find the off switches for almost a week; they were behind locked panels. The air system blew gusty winds through the base until we fiddled with the fans.

We could guess a lot about them from what they'd left behind. They must have come from a world smaller than Earth, circling a red dwarf star in close orbit. To be close enough to be warm enough, the planet would have to be locked in by tides, turning one face always to its star. The aliens must have evolved on the lighted side, in a permanent red day, with winds constantly howling over the border from the night side.

And they had no sense of privacy. The only doorways that had doors in them were airlocks. The second floor was a hexagonal metal gridwork. It would not block you off from your friends on the floor below. The bunk room was an impressive expanse of mercury-filled waterbed, wall to wall. The rooms were too small and cluttered, the furniture and machinery too close to the doorways, so that at first we were constantly bumping elbows and knees. The ceilings were an inch short

338

of six feet high on both floors, so that we tended to walk stooped even if we were short enough to stand upright. Habit. But Lear was just tall enough to knock his head if he stood up fast, anywhere in the base.

We thought they must have been smaller than human. But their padded benches seemed human-designed in size and shape. Maybe it was their minds that were different: they didn't need psychic elbow room.

The ship had been bad enough. Now this. Within the base was instant claustrophobia. It put all of our tempers on hair triggers.

Two of us couldn't take it.

Lear and Childrey did not belong on the same planet.

With Childrey, neatness was a compulsion. He had enough for all of us. During those long months aboard *Percival Lowell*, it was Childrey who led us in calisthenics. He flatly would not let anyone skip an exercise period. We eventually gave up trying.

Well and good. The exercise kept us alive. We weren't getting the healthy daily exercise anyone gets walking around the living room in a one-gravity field.

But after a month on Mars, Childrey was the only man who still appeared fully dressed in the heat of the alien base. Some of us took it as a reproof, and maybe it was, because Lear had been the first to doff his shirt for keeps. In the mess Childrey would inspect his silverware for water spots, then line it up perfectly parallel.

On Earth, Andrew Lear's habits would have been no more than a character trait. In a hurry, he might choose mismatched socks. He might put off using the dishwasher for a day or two if he were involved in something interesting. He would prefer a house that looked "lived in." God help the maid who tried to clean up his study. He'd never be able to find anything afterward.

He was a brilliant but one-sided man. Backpacking or skin diving might have changed his habits—in such pursuits you learn not to forget any least trivial thing—but they would never have tempted him. An expedition to Mars was something he simply could not turn down. A pity, because neatness is worth your life in space.

You don't leave your fly open in a pressure suit.

A month after the landing, Childrey caught Lear doing just that.

The "fly" on a pressure suit is a soft rubber tube over your male member. It leads to a bladder, and there's a spring clamp on it. You open the clamp to use it. Then you close the clamp and open an outside spigot to evacuate the bladder into vacuum.

Similar designs for women involve a catheter, which is hideously uncomfortable. I presume the designers will keep trying. It seems wrong to bar half the human race from our ultimate destiny.

Lear was addicted to long walks. He loved the Martian desert scene: the hard violet sky and the soft blur of whirling orange dust, the sharp close horizon, the endless emptiness. More: he needed the room. He was spending all his working time on the alien communicator, with the ceiling too close over his head and everything else too close to his bony elbows.

He was coming back from a walk, and he met Childrey coming out. Childrey noticed that the waste spigot on Lear's suit was open, the spring broken. Lear had been out for hours. If he'd had to go, he might have bled to death through flesh ruptured by vacuum.

We never learned all that Childrey said to him out there. But Lear came in very red about the ears, muttering under his breath. He wouldn't talk to anyone.

The NASA psychologists should not have put them both on that small a planet. Hindsight is wonderful, right? But Lear and Childrey were each the best choice for competence coupled to the kind of health they would need to survive the trip. There were astrophysicists as competent and as famous as Lear, but they were decades older. And Childrey had a thousand spaceflight hours to his credit. He had been one of the last men on the moon.

Individually, each of us was the best possible man. It was a damn shame.

The aliens had left the communicator going, like everything else in the base. It must have been hellishly massive, to judge by the thick support pillars slanting outward beneath it. It was a bulky tank of a thing, big enough that the roof had to bulge slightly to give it room. That gave Lear about a square meter of the only head room in the base.

Even Lear had no idea why they'd put it on the second floor. It would send through the first floor, or through the bulk of a planet. Lear learned that by trying it, once he knew enough. He beamed a dot-dash message through Mars itself to the Forward Mass Detector aboard *Lowell*.

Lear had set up a Mass Detector next to the communicator, on an extremely complex platform designed to protect it from vibration. The Detector produced waves so sharply pointed that some of us thought they could *feel* the gravity radiation coming from the communicator.

Lear was in love with the thing.

He skipped meals. When he ate he ate like a starved wolf. "There's a heavy point-mass in there," he told us, talking around a mouthful of food, two months after the landing. "The machine uses electromagnetic fields to vibrate it at high speed. Look—" He picked up a toothpaste tube of tuna spread and held it in front of him. He vibrated it rapidly. Heads turned to watch him around the zigzagged communal table in the alien mess. "I'm making gravity waves now. But they're too mushy because the tube's too big, and their amplitude is virtually zero. There's something very dense and massive in that machine, and it takes a hell of a lot of field strength to keep it there."

"What is it?" someone asked. "Neutronium? Like at the heart of a neutron star?"

Lear shook his head and took another mouthful. "That size, neutronium wouldn't be stable. I think it's a quantum black hole. I don't know how to measure its mass yet."

I said, "A *quantum* black hole?"

Lear nodded happily. "Luck for me. You know, I was against the Mars expedition. We could get a lot more for our money by exploring the asteroids. Among other things, we might have found if there are really quantum black holes out there. But this one's already captured!" He stood up, being careful of his head. He turned in his tray and went back to work.

I remember we stared at each other along the zigzag mess table. Then we drew lots . . . and I lost.

The day Lear left his waste spigot open, Childrey had put a restriction on him. Lear was not to leave the base without an escort.

Lear had treasured the aloneness of those walks. But it was worse than that. Childrey had given him a list of possible escorts: half a dozen men Childrey could trust to see to it that Lear did nothing dangerous to himself or others. Inevitably they were the men most thoroughly trained in space survival routines, most addicted to Childrey's own compulsive neatness, least likely to sympathize with Lear's way of living. Lear was as likely to ask Childrey himself to go walking with him.

He almost never went out any more. I knew exactly where to find him.

I stood beneath him, looking up through the gridwork floor.

He'd almost finished dismantling the protective panels around the gravity communicator. What showed inside looked like parts of a computer in one spot, electromagnetic coils in most places, and a square array of pushbuttons that might have been the aliens' idea of a typewriter. Lear was using a magnetic induction sensor to try to trace wiring without actually tearing off the insulation.

I called, "How you making out?"

"No good," he said. "The insulation seems to be one hundred per cent perfect. Now I'm afraid to open it up. No telling how much power is running through there, if it needs shielding that good." He smiled down at me. "Let me show you something."

"What?"

He flipped a toggle above a dull gray circular plate. "This thing is a microphone. It took me a while to find it. I am Andrew Lear, speaking to whoever may be listening." He switched it off, then ripped paper from the Mass Indicator and showed me squiggles interrupting smooth sine waves. "There. The sound of my voice in gravity radiation. It won't disappear until it's reached the edges of the universe."

"Lear, you mentioned quantum black holes there. What's a quantum black hole?"

"Um. You know what a black hole is."

"I ought to." Lear had educated us on the subject, at length, during the months aboard *Lowell*.

When a not too massive star has used up its nuclear fuel, it collapses into a white dwarf. A heavier star—say, 1.44 times the mass of the sun and larger—can burn out its fuel, then collapse into itself until it is ten kilometers across and composed solely of neutrons packed edge to edge: the densest matter in this universe.

But a big star goes further than that. When a really massive star runs its course . . . when the radiation pressure within is no longer strong enough to hold the outer layers against the star's own ferocious gravity . . . then it can fall into itself entirely, until gravity is stronger than any other force, until it is compressed past the Swartzchild radius and effectively leaves the universe. What happens to it then is problematical. The Swartzchild radius is the boundary beyond which nothing can climb out of the gravity well, not even light.

The star is gone then, but the mass remains: a lightless hole in space, perhaps a hole into another universe.

"A collapsing star can leave a black hole," said Lear. "There may be bigger black holes, whole galaxies that have fallen into themselves. But there's no other way a black hole can form, *now*."

"So?"

"There was a time when black holes of all sizes could form. That was during the Big Bang, the explosion that started the expanding universe. The forces in the blast could have compressed little local vortices of matter past the Swartzchild radius. What that left behind—the smallest ones, anyway—we call quantum black holes."

I heard a distinctive laugh behind me as Captain Childrey walked into view. The bulk of the communicator would have hidden him from Lear, and I hadn't heard him come up. He called, "Just how big a thing are you talking about? Could I pick one up and throw it at you?"

"You'd disappear into one that size," Lear said seriously. "A black hole the mass of the Earth would only be a centimeter across. No, I'm talking about things from ten-to-the-minus-fifth grams on up. There could be one at the center of the sun—"

"Eek!"

Lear was trying. He didn't like being kidded, but he didn't know how to stop it. Keeping it serious wasn't the way, but he didn't know that either. "Say, ten-to-the-seventeenth grams in mass and ten-to-the-minus-eleven centimeters across. It would be swallowing a few atoms a day."

"Well, at least you know where to find it," said Childrey. "Now all you have to do is go after it."

Lear nodded, still serious. "There could be quantum black holes in asteroids. A small asteroid could capture a quantum black hole easily enough, especially if it was charged; a black hole can hold a charge, you know—"

"Ri-ight."

"All we'd have to do is check out a small asteroid with the

343

Mass Detector. If it masses more than it should, we push it aside and see if it leaves a black hole behind."

"You'd need little teeny eyes to see something that small. Anyway, what would you do with it?"

"You put a charge on it, if it hasn't got one already, and electromagnetic fields. You can vibrate it to make gravity; then you manipulate it with radiation. I think I've got one in here," he said, patting the alien communicator.

"Ri-ight," said Childrey, and he went away laughing.

Within a week the whole base was referring to Lear as the Hole Man, the man with the black hole between his ears.

It hadn't sounded funny when Lear was telling me about it. The rich variety of the universe . . . But when Childrey talked about the black hole in Lear's Anything Box, it sounded hilarious.

Please note: Childrey did not misunderstand anything Lear had said. Childrey wasn't stupid. He merely thought Lear was crazy. He could not have gotten away with making fun of Lear, not among educated men, without knowing exactly what he was doing.

Meanwhile the work went on.

There were pools of Marsdust, fascinating stuff, fine enough to behave like viscous oil, and knee-deep. Wading through it wasn't dangerous, but it was very hard work, and we avoided it. One day Brace waded out into the nearest of the pools and started feeling around under the dust. Hunch, he said. He came up with some eroded plastic-like containers. The aliens had used the pool as a garbage dump.

We were having little luck with chemical analysis of the base materials. They were virtually indestructible. We learned more about the chemistry of the alien visitors themselves. They had left traces of themselves on the benches and on the communal waterbed. The traces had most of the chemical components of protoplasm, but Arsvey found no sign of DNA. Not surprising, he said. There must be other giant organic molecules suitable for gene coding.

The aliens had left volumes of notes behind. The script was a mystery, of course, but we studied the photographs and diagrams. A lot of them were notes on anthropology!

The aliens had been studying Earth during the first Ice Age.

None of us were anthropologists, and that was a damn shame. We never learned if we'd found anything new. All we could do was photograph the stuff and beam it up to *Lowell*. One thing was sure: the aliens had left very long ago, and they had left the lighting and air systems running and the communicator sending a carrier wave.

For us? Who else?

The alternative was that the base had been switched off for some six hundred thousand years, then come back on when something detected *Lowell* approaching Mars. Lear didn't believe it. "If the power had been off in the communicator," he said, "the mass wouldn't be in there any more. The fields have to be going to hold it in place. It's smaller than an atom; it'd fall through anything solid."

So the base power system had been running for all that time. What the hell could it be? And where? We traced some cables and found that it was under the base, under several yards of Marsdust fused to lava. We didn't try to dig through that.

The source was probably geophysical: a hole deep into the core of the planet. The aliens might have wanted to dig such a hole to take core samples. Afterward they would have set up a generator to use the temperature difference between the core and the surface.

Meanwhile, Lear spent some time tracing down the power sources in the communicator. He found a way to shut off the carrier wave. Now the mass, if there was a mass, was at rest in there. It was strange to see the Forward Mass Detector pouring out straight lines instead of drastically peaked sine waves.

We were ill-equipped to take advantage of these riches. We had been fitted out to explore Mars; not a bit of civilization from another star. Lear was the exception. He was in his element, with but one thing to mar his happiness.

I don't know what the final argument was about. I was engaged on another project.

The Mars lander still had fuel in it. NASA had given us plenty of fuel to hover while we looked for a landing spot. After some heated discussion, we had agreed to take the vehicle up and hover it next to the nearby dust pool on low thrust.

It worked fine. The dust rose up in a great soft cloud and went away toward the horizon, leaving the pond bottom covered with otherworldly junk. And more! Arsvey started screaming at Brace to back off. Fortunately Brace kept his

345

head. He tilted us over to one side and took us away on a gentle curve. The backblast never touched the skeletons.

We worked out there for hours, being very finicky indeed. Here was another skill none of us would own to, but we'd read about how careful an archaeologist has to be, and we did our best. Traces of water had had time to turn some of the dust to natural cement, so that some of the skeletons were fixed to the rock. But we got a couple free. We put them on stretchers and brought them back. One crumbled the instant the air came hissing into the lock. We left the other outside.

The aliens had not had the habit of taking baths. We'd set up a bathtub with very tall sides, in a room the aliens had reserved for some incomprehensible ritual. I had stripped off my pressure suit and was heading for the bathtub, very tired, hoping that nobody would be in it.

I heard the voices before I saw them.

Lear was shouting.

Childrey wasn't, but his voice was a carrying one. It carried mockery. He was standing between the supporting pillars. His hands were on his hips, his teeth gleamed white, his head was thrown back to look up at Lear.

He finished talking. For a time neither of them moved. Then Lear made a sound of disgust. He turned away and pushed one of the buttons on what might have been an alien typewriter keyboard.

Childrey looked startled. He slapped at his right thigh and brought the hand away bloody. He stared at it, then looked up at Lear. He started to ask a question.

He crumpled slowly in the low gravity. I got to him before he hit the ground. I cut his pants open and tied a handkerchief over the blood spot. It was a small puncture, but the flesh was puckered above it on a line with his groin.

Childrey tried to speak. His eyes were wide. He coughed, and there was blood in his mouth.

I guess I froze. How could I help if I couldn't tell what had happened? I saw a blood spot on his right shoulder, and I tore the shirt open and found another tiny puncture wound.

The doctor arrived.

It took Childrey an hour to die, but the doctor had given up much earlier. Between the wound in his shoulder and the wound in his thigh, Childrey's flesh had been ruptured in a narrow line that ran through one lung and his stomach and part of his intestinal tract. The autopsy showed a tiny, very neat hole drilled through the hipbones.

346

We looked for, and found, a hole in the floor beneath the communicator. It was the size of a pencil lead, and packed with dust.

"I made a mistake," Lear told the rest of us at the inquest. "I should never have touched that particular button. It must have switched off the fields that held the mass in place. It just dropped. Captain Childrey was underneath."

And it had gone straight through him, eating the mass of him as it went.

"No, not quite," said Lear. "I'd guessed it massed about ten-to-the-fourteenth grams. That only makes it ten-to-the-minus-sixth Angstrom across, much smaller than an atom. It wouldn't have absorbed much. The damage was done to Childrey by tidal effects as it passed through him. You saw how it pulverized the material of the floor."

Not surprisingly, the subject of murder did come up.

Lear shrugged it off. "Murder with what? Childrey didn't believe there was a black hole in there at all. Neither did many of you." He smiled suddenly. "Can you imagine what the trial would be like? Imagine the prosecuting attorney trying to tell a jury what he thinks happened. First he's got to tell them what a black hole is. Then a quantum black hole. Then he's got to explain why he doesn't have the murder weapon, and where he left it, freely falling through Mars! And if he gets that far without being laughed out of court, he's still got to explain how a thing smaller than an atom could hurt anyone!"

But didn't Dr. Lear know the thing was dangerous? Could he not have guessed its enormous mass from the way it behaved?

Lear spread his hands. "Gentlemen, we're dealing with more variables than just mass. Field strength, for instance. I might have guessed its mass from the force it took to keep it there, but did any of us expect the aliens to calibrate their dials in the metric system?"

Surely there must have been safeties to keep the fields from being shut off accidentally. Lear must have bypassed them.

"Yes, I probably did, accidentally. I did quite a lot of fiddling to find out how things worked."

It got dropped there. Obviously there would be no trial. No ordinary judge or jury could be expected to understand what the attorneys would be talking about. A couple of things never did get mentioned.

For instance: Childrey's last words. I might or might not

have repeated them if I'd been asked to. They were: "All right, show me! Show it to me or admit it isn't there!"

As the court was breaking up I spoke to Lear with my voice lowered. "That was probably the most unique murder weapon in history."

He whispered, "If you said that in company I could sue for slander."

"Yeah? Really? Are *you* going to explain to a jury what you think I implied happened?"

"No, I'll let you get away with it this time."

"Hell, you didn't get away scot-free yourself. What are you going to study now? The only known black hole in the universe, and you let it drop through your fingers."

Lear frowned. "You're right. Partly right, anyway. But I knew as much about it as I was going to, the way I was going. Now . . . I stopped it vibrating in there, then took the mass of the entire setup with the Forward Mass Sensor. Now the black hole isn't in there any more. I can get the mass of the black hole by taking the mass of the communicator alone."

"Oh."

"And I can't cut the machine open, see what's inside. How they controlled it. Damn it, I wish I were six years old."

"What? Why?"

"Well . . . I don't have the times straightened out. The math is chancy. Either a few years from now, or a few centuries, there's going to be a black hole between Earth and Jupiter. It'll be big enough to study. I think about forty years."

When I realized what he was implying, I didn't know whether to laugh or scream. "Lear, you can't think that something that small could absorb Mars!"

"Well, remember that it absorbs everything it comes near. A nucleus here, an electron there . . . and it's not just waiting for atoms to fall into it. Its gravity is ferocious, and it's falling back and forth through the center of the planet, sweeping up matter. The more it eats, the bigger it gets, with its volume going up as the cube of the mass. Sooner or later, yes, it'll absorb Mars. By then it'll be just less than a millimeter across—big enough to see."

"Could it happen within thirteen months?"

"Before we leave? Hmm." Lear's eyes took on a faraway look. "I don't think so. I'll have to work it out. The math is chancy . . ."

348

I started these volumes by making a fuss over the fact I had never won a Hugo. Winning three since then leaves me unsatisfied.

No, I'm not greedy. I'm logical. As I explained, one of the Hugos was for a non-fiction science column, one for a novel series, one for an individual novel.

Not one of them was for any of the shorter categories—novellas, novelettes, or short stories—which are included in the various volumes of the Hugo winners. So though twenty-five different authors have been included in the three volumes so far, with anywhere from one to five stories apiece, I myself am not represented.

Well, in 1976, I published a novelette which *may* finally make it. If it is nominated, it will come up for a vote in the thirty-fifth convention, to be held in Miami, Florida, in 1977. That's a little far for me, but I'm thinking of taking a train or something and going there.

After all, if I win, taking the train will be worth it.

If I don't win, of course, I will just give the train back.

The Hugo Awards

1953–1961 inclusive—*See Volume One*
1962–1970 inclusive—*See Volume Two*
1971–1972 inclusive—*See Volume Three, Book One*

1973: 31st Convention—Toronto

NOVEL—THE GODS THEMSELVES by Isaac Asimov
NOVELLA—"The Word for World Is Forest" by Ursula K. Le Guin
NOVELETTE—"Goat Song" by Poul Anderson
SHORT STORY—"The Meeting" by Frederik Pohl & C. M. Kornbluth
        "Eurema's Dam" by R. A. Lafferty
PROFESSIONAL EDITOR—Ben Bova
PROFESSIONAL ARTIST—Frank Kelly Freas
DRAMATIC PRESENTATION—"Slaughterhouse Five"
FAN MAGAZINE—*Energumen*, Michael & Susan Glicksohn, eds.
FAN ARTIST—Tim Kirk
FAN ARTIST—Terry Carr

1974: 32nd Convention—Washington

NOVEL—RENDEZVOUS WITH RAMA by Arthur C. Clarke
NOVELLA—"The Girl Who Was Plugged In" by James Tiptree, Jr.
NOVELETTE—"The Deathbird" by Harlan Ellison
SHORT STORY—"The Ones Who Walk Away from Omelas" by Ursula K. Le Guin
PROFESSIONAL EDITOR—Ben Bova
DRAMATIC PRESENTATION—"Sleeper"
PROFESSIONAL ARTIST—Frank Kelly Freas
FAN MAGAZINE—*Algol*, Andy Porter, ed.
        The Alien Critic by Richard E. Geis, ed.

Fan Artist—Tim Kirk
Fan Writer—Susan Wood
Special Hugo Award—Chesley Bonestell

1975: 33rd Convention—Melbourne

Novel—THE DISPOSSESSED by Ursula K. Le Guin
Novella—"A Song for Lya" by George R. R. Martin
Novelette—"Adrift Just Off the Islets of Langerhans:
        Latitude 38° 54′ N, Longitude 77° 00′
        13″ W" by Harlan Ellison
Short Story—"The Hole Man" by Larry Niven
Dramatic Presentation—"Young Frankenstein"
Professional Editor—Ben Bova
Professional Artist—Frank Kelly Freas
Fan Magazine—*The Alien Critic* by Richard Geis, ed.
Fan Writer—Richard Geis
Fan Artist—Bill Rotsler
Special Hugo Awards—Donald A. Wollheim
                  Walt Lee